It was the quietest explosion in television history.

SATAN'S SISTERS

An irresistible novel about ruthless ambition, guarded secrets, scandalous drama, and true sisterhood from veteran TV insider

STAR JONES

Praise for Star Jones's books

Satan's Sisters is also available as an eBook

STAR JONES

~

SATAN'S SISTERS

A NOVEL WORK OF FICTION

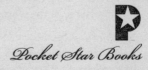

Pocket Star Books

NEW YORK LONDON TORONTO SYDNEY NEW DELHI

Pocket Star Books
A Division of Simon & Schuster, Inc.
1230 Avenue of the Americas
New York, NY 10020

This book is a work of fiction. Names, characters, places, and incidents either are products of the author's imagination or are used fictitiously. Any resemblance to actual events or locales or persons, living or dead, is entirely coincidental.

First Pocket Star Books paperback edition December 2011

POCKET STAR and colophon are trademarks of Simon & Schuster, Inc.

For information about special discounts for bulk purchases, please contact Simon & Schuster Special Sales at 1-866-506-1949 or business@simonandschuster.com.

The Simon & Schuster Speakers Bureau can bring authors to your live event. For more information or to book an event contact the Simon & Schuster Speakers Bureau at 1-866-248-3049 or visit our website at www.simonspeakers.com.

Cover design by Faceout Studio, Tim Green

Manufactured in the United States of America

10 9 8 7 6 5 4 3 2 1

ISBN 978-1-4391-9301-3
ISBN 978-1-4391-9303-7 (ebook)

"The human race is faced with a cruel choice:
work or daytime television."

—UNKNOWN

This book is gratefully dedicated to those
who sometimes choose the latter.

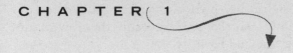

CHAPTER 1

It was the quietest explosion in television history.

Heather Hope took a quick glance to her left and then her right, satisfied with the stricken looks she saw on the five faces around her. She sat back on the famous red couch wearing a tiny hint of a smirk. This was exactly the reaction she had been hoping for, from the moment she decided to make a glorious return to *The Lunch Club*, the talk show that had catapulted her to a level of superstardom that seemed to have no limits. She knew that once she dropped her tidbit, the uproar would be instantaneous. It was said that only the Pope could command more headlines at the snap of a finger than Heather Hope—yet the glamorous Heather easily beat the pontiff in sex appeal.

Heather's grenade was doubly effective because it was so unexpected, so casual. One minute she was sitting on the couch with the five current cohosts of *The Lunch Club*, chatting about upcoming guests on her own ultrasuccessful syndicated talk show, *Heather's Hope*—and then, without warning, she had let it fly.

"As you all know, another sweeps month starts in four short weeks, and of course, I plan to wow you all month long with surprises galore, but I'm busting at the seams with the way we're kicking it off. I'm so thrilled that this woman has agreed to come on *Heather's Hope* about a month from now for an exclusive interview! My special guest will be none other than Missy Adams! Surely you all remember her, right?"

Oh yes, they knew Missy. Melissa "Missy" Adams had been a cohost on *The Lunch Club* for five years, the first few of which overlapped with Heather's time on the show. A self-described "Southern belle," Missy liked to project the image of a sweet, peaches-and-cream Georgia gal, but in fact she was a tough, unrelenting former prosecutor who had been added to *The Lunch Club*— reportedly at the strong urging of NBN president Riley Dufrane—to break up the "Northern liberal bloc" that tended to dominate the daytime talk-fest. Thanks to her Southern charm and conservative politics, Missy had quickly become the most popular cohost on the show. But she left abruptly several years back under a cloud of suspicion and innuendo. No one had ever revealed the true reasons for her departure.

"Yes, Missy Adams is back, ladies, and she has secretly written a juicy tell-all book that promises to explain all the details of her leaving *The Lunch Club*." Heather paused, still smiling sweetly. "Also, she said the book contains a ton of other good stuff; some of it may interest a few of you ladies sitting right here on the couch! I know *I* can't wait to hear what little Miss Missy has to say! Even the book's title sounds juicy—but she made me promise not to reveal it until she's ready!"

After Heather's announcement, there was utter silence around the curved couch. Crickets-chirping silence. It was the strangest thing that anyone on the crew had ever seen: the cohosts had all been rendered mute at the exact same time. The studio audience was also stunned into silence. From the fringes of the set, Lizette Bradley, the show's publicist, watched in disbelief. She even looked down at her Cartier wristwatch—a thirtieth-birthday gift from her mother—and timed the deafening silence.

Four seconds. Five seconds.

"Somebody say something!" Karen Siegel, the show's longtime director, screamed into their tiny hidden earpieces, her voice edged with panic. There were audible gasps in the control room.

Six seconds. Seven seconds.

While most viewers might expect the commanding and always professional Maxine Robinson to be the one who would come to her show's rescue, perhaps with a well-placed but slightly dismissive rejoinder to Heather Hope's bombshell, it was no surprise to the ladies on the couch that Shelly Carter raced in to fill the dead air. Shelly Carter and dead air got along about as well as Michael Vick and pit bulls.

"Well, Heather, only you could take a little summer drizzle and turn it into a category-five hurricane!" Shelly said finally, flashing her brightest smile.

Nine seconds of silence. Lizette looked up from her watch, her eyes wide. She already knew that she would have to be the one to fix this, to mend the ruptures from this disaster. In television land, nine seconds might as well be an hour. Television careers could implode in nine seconds of silence.

For just an instant, Heather shot Shelly the look that she reserved for dog shit, divorce lawyers, and her ex-husband. But Shelly pretended not to notice. Heather had left *The Lunch Club* before Shelly Carter joined the cast, but she had heard stories about the diva-in-training's unbridled ambition. The joke inside the NBN network was that Shelly Carter is what you'd get if you mated Maxine Robinson with a Rolodex.

Speaking of Maxine, the queen bee of *The Lunch Club* looked like she had been slammed in the head several times with a two-by-four. In the control room, Karen, on the verge of hyperventilating, shrieked out loud when camera 4, *Maxine's camera*, caught a close-up of her with her mouth hanging open like a bass flopping on a hook. Karen knew she could say good-bye to her career if she let that image beam out over television land. Karen had never seen her boss, the epitome of grace under fire, look so shocked. What did Missy Adams know about the ladies of *The Lunch Club* that would make them piss their collective Spanx?

"Well, don't shoot the messenger, darling," Heather said coolly in Shelly's direction. The studio audience, already giddy over getting a two-for-one Heather Hope and *The Lunch Club* daytime TV bonanza, exploded in laughter and applause upon hearing Heather's most famous expression. She had used it on her show many times to maximum effect, confronting irate corporate swindlers, cheating celebrity husbands, crooked insurance company execs. The expression had wormed its way into the American popular lexicon, usually employed as a quick and easy way to shut down somebody who disagreed with you.

Karen caught Shelly's large, smoky eyes flash in anger. She saw Whitney Harlington toss her Nice 'N Easy no. 87 blond locks back so hard that Karen was surprised not to hear a whipping sound. Whitney was the closest thing the show had to a traditional journalist. She had won many awards over the years for her courageous reporting, and at times, Whitney didn't seem entirely comfortable on the red couch, particularly when the ladies occasionally dropped the syrupy pretenses of their fake friendships and really went after each other. Whitney said the ladies were worse than her four children arguing at the dinner table over the last piece of chicken. Karen could see Whitney's face turning a rich shade of red, even through the thick layer of TV makeup designed to hide those encroaching crow's-feet.

There was movement on the far end of the couch, the side opposite from where Maxine Robinson sat, still frozen, her smooth, nearly unlined brown face a disturbing mask of distress. The movement came from Molly McCarthy Stein, shifting her hefty bulk. This is what she usually did when she was about to drop one of her comic bombs and send the room into a laughing fit. Karen prayed fervently that Molly could come through right now with one of her "Stein Stingers." The ladies were slowly dying out there.

"Okay, okay, we can't shoot the messenger— but maybe we could drag her out back and beat the crap out of her?!"

The crowd exploded again, this time in peals of laughter that sounded like music to Karen's ears. She scanned the couch and saw her ladies start to loosen up a bit. If she wasn't mistaken, that might actually be a smile showing at the corners of Maxine's mouth. Heather didn't look all too pleased at the Stein Stinger, but at this point that really didn't matter. Molly, who was also Karen's neighbor on Manhattan's Upper West Side, had come through for her again. And it was time for a commercial break. Thank God! She decided to let Dara Cruz bring them to the break. The young, beautiful Dara was the newest member of *The Lunch Club* and the one least likely of the "fabulous five" to be affected by what Heather had just told them. In fact, as she watched Dara adjust her blouse and focus on the camera, Karen wondered if Dara even knew what fresh chapter of hell was swirling around her.

⊰ ⊱

IN THE CONTROL ROOM, a frantic Lizette rewound the tape to the show's opening. She wanted to absorb the entire scene once more, to see if there was any further meaning to be extracted from Heather's words. As the ladies stormed off the set earlier, an intimidating cacophony of clicking Louboutins and Jimmy Choos, Maxine had headed straight for Lizette.

"Lizette!" she said through clenched teeth, trying to keep her emotions under control. "I need for you to find out what's in that damn book. *Before* she's on Heather's show!"

Though Maxine hadn't raised her voice, the order was overheard by most of the crew because she still had her microphone clipped to her lapel. Lizette couldn't be sure, but she thought she saw Shelly and Whitney glance in her direction after Maxine had spoken. *Great, even more pressure!* She had caught the slightly crazed look in Maxine's eyes and shuddered at the notion of what Maxine would do to her if she failed to find out what Missy was up to.

Lizette watched the show's opening again, leaning in close to the monitor to see the cheerfully smiling cohosts looking into the camera and delivering the well-known opening, "We always wanted to do a show where we could sit around and talk like we were sisters. This is that show; welcome to *The Lunch Club*." Then Whitney took the lead: "Today is extra special because we are joined by probably our most famous alumna, the fabulous Heather Hope. We're going to catch up with one of our best girlfriends and see what she has coming up on her always top-rated show, *Heather's Hope*."

Despite the stress, Lizette chuckled to herself. It was one of the television industry's worst-kept secrets that Maxine despised Heather. Lizette had never understood why. After more than forty years in the business, Maxine was practically a television institution herself. You'd need several sheets to list all of her "firsts": first African-American woman to become a network news anchor, the first to be a solo anchor (Barbara Walters had been the first woman, but she was only a co-anchor), first African-American to be inducted into the Museum of Media Hall of Fame, first African-American woman to own her own production company, and so on. She had been the go-to girl for every celebrity, politician, and newsmaker for the last three decades. Even though Heather Hope's rise had been fast and mind-boggling, Lizette didn't think Maxine had any reason to be jealous of her. But perhaps there was more to it than mere jealousy. Because the hate was so intense on Maxine's part. Maxine always referred to Heather, behind her back, of course, as "the Saint . . . with the rather unfortunate face." Once the entire cast of *The Lunch Club* was struck dumb when Maxine picked up a magazine with Heather on it and announced to the room that "airbrushing is obviously *that* poor woman's best friend." Clearly, something else had transpired between the two powerful women.

Lizette closely watched the reaction of each of the ladies as Heather Hope made her way onto the set and sat down on the iconic red couch between Whitney and Dara. Perhaps Heather thought that was the safest spot for her, between the two women least likely to make things uncomfortable for her. Dara appeared to be genuinely pleased to see Heather, almost worshipful in fact. She couldn't hide the glee on her perfect, diamond-shaped face. Whitney, who Lizette had heard was still actually a fairly close friend of Heather's, also wore a genuine smile. But the faces of the other ladies told a different story. Lizette could recognize phony smiles in an instant, particularly on the ladies of *The Lunch Club*—ladies that she was paid handsomely to be able to read like the pages of a book.

Heather's appearance was expected to be a ratings blockbuster. Thanks to Lizette's hard work over the previous two weeks, the whole country likely had tuned in to watch—or record it on their DVRs and TiVos. What the country saw was the show blow up right in front of their faces. Lizette wondered just how obvious the explosion had been to the viewing audience. She would have to call her mother, who never missed a show, and get a read on how it all looked to the outside world. Lizette glanced down at her phone. She was holding the "outside world" in her hand. The text messages and e-mails were piling up like the designer shoes in Lizette's overstuffed closet. She saw that the TV and gossip reporters, plus the bloggers, were going nuts. Everyone wanted some behind-the-scenes dirt. It dawned on Lizette that if she worked things right, she might be able to spin this disaster into more ratings gold. But first she had to find out what was in that damn book!

Lizette had always been a big fan of Heather Hope's, much like the rest of the civilized world, but she was astounded to see up close how manipulative and spiteful the woman could be. Of course she suspected that a woman couldn't rise as far and as fast as Heather had without squeezing off a couple of rounds of machine-gun fire on occasion, but now that the gunfire was directed at her show and the ladies she was paid to protect, Lizette was stunned at its carefully planned precision and destructive intent.

She watched Heather's performance several more times, growing more certain that Heather Hope was a woman she'd be wise not to turn into an enemy. But that just might be necessary if she was going to protect *The Lunch Club*. Lizette might be forced to jump out in front of some of that machine-gun fire herself.

Lizette checked her watch. It was time to call the websites and bloggers first, then she might respond to the TV and newspaper reporters—once she came up with something clever but noncommittal, something that would make them think they got just a little taste of dirt.

⊰ ⊱

AS SHE CLOSED HER office door behind her, Maxine almost sprinted to her desk. Although she had given Lizette the assignment of finding out what was in Missy's book, Maxine was far too much of a control freak to leave it in someone else's hands. No, she would have to employ all of her industry horses to get out ahead of this one. She settled in behind her exquisite dark burnished mahogany partners desk, a gift from her second husband, Chad Ross, an extravagantly wealthy banker who had lavished Maxine with the finest things money could buy. Her office was the epitome of understated elegance. Even after the marriage ended, Chad stayed with her in spirit because her expensive tastes had been set.

Maxine took a deep breath, trying to settle her nerves. She couldn't imagine how painful it would be if she had a starring role in Missy's book. A shudder ran down her spine. With hard work, she had built herself into an industry legend. It was upsetting to imagine her legacy could really be in jeopardy. She swept her gaze across the office walls, which were covered with dozens of framed photos of Maxine with presidents, prime ministers, Hollywood royalty, and captains of industry. Practically every important person of the last four decades. Maxine's walls virtually screamed "It's all about me." Though she had recently celebrated her sixty-fifth birthday, Maxine looked remarkably similar in every picture, as if she had managed to freeze the aging process at forty-two. She was still beautiful, some might even call her sexy, bearing a striking resemblance to the actress Diahann Carroll, whom she had been mistaken for so many times over the years that she and Diahann used to joke they could trade places and their husbands probably wouldn't even know the difference.

Maxine knew who her first call would be. She pulled out her BlackBerry and searched for the phone number of Lance Overton, the flaming gay (but still in the closet) New York gossip columnist. Though Lance was probably two decades past the peak of his powers as the gossip king of the *New York Courier*, Maxine knew that Lance still managed to keep his fingers in many a juicy pot around the city. You never knew where he might pop up with his translucent skin, black wide-frame glasses, and oodles of old-school charm. Maxine loved to introduce Lance as her "dearest friend"—more as a warning to all comers than as a term of endearment—but in fact she mostly giggled behind the old queen's back, calling him "my sad and lonely friend Lance."

"Lance, how have you been, *darling*?" Maxine said into the cell phone. She knew that Lance would want to spend at least ten minutes on mindless chatter, so she got right to the point without even waiting for Lance to respond. Maxine hated mindless chatter. "I have something I need to talk to you about. We had an interesting guest on the show today."

"Oh yes, I saw—" Lance tried to get a word in, but like many celebrities, Maxine never considered that somebody like Lance might actually contribute something to the conversation that she'd be interested in hearing.

"Yes, Heather Hope was on, talking about upcoming guests on her show. Apparently our former cohost, Melissa Adams—you remember her, right?—has written some kind of book, supposedly a tell-all, about her time on the show. Now, I don't think we have anything to worry about. I think Missy is just trying to make a quick buck. But if you have some time, I was just wondering if you might make a few calls and see if you can find out what's in that book."

Now Maxine paused, waiting for Lance to answer. Maxine knew that Lance didn't really have much access to the good dirt anymore. Even if his old crowd of aging Broadway and Hollywood stars and media moguls who used to hold court at the 21 Club tried to do something juicy and scandalous, these days no one would care. Now it was all about the kids. The single-name celebs had gone from Cher and Madonna to Lindsay and Rihanna and Zac, with a few rappers, the Kardashians, and Hollywood bad boys thrown in for good measure.

But it couldn't hurt having Lance Overton feel like he had been given an assignment by Maxine Robinson. It had been a while since Maxine had initiated the contact, but the two of them had worked as a team for years. Maxine would invite Lance to her parties, where Lance would inevitably scrape together enough material for at least a week's worth of columns. In return, Lance would trash whoever crossed Maxine.

When it came to Missy and the book, Maxine didn't have high hopes. But if Lance made enough calls, they both might get lucky.

"Sure, Maxine. I'll shake the trees and see what falls out," he said, using one of his favorite expressions for gossip gathering.

Maxine thanked him and rushed him off the phone before Lance tried to change the subject. Maxine scrolled through some more numbers on her BlackBerry. After years of stubborn resistance, she had finally given in to the pleas of her staff and friends and allowed someone to hand her a Black-Berry. At first she found the endless array of keys and commands to be hopelessly confusing and pointless. But now that she had gotten the hang of it, she couldn't live without it. What she enjoyed most was the privacy that it provided. No longer did she have to rely on assistants and secretaries to retrieve names and numbers—meaning that it was harder for those around her to keep tabs on what she was doing. Privacy was one of Maxine's most prized possessions, more than all of the ridiculously expensive items she had acquired over the years. She guarded it with the same intensity that she brought to everything she did.

Maxine made two more desperate calls around town, casting her net to see what she could pull in. She could feel her chest start to tighten. She tried to shake it off. She liked to think of herself as a cool customer—she didn't appreciate that this book had her so frazzled. She looked up at one of her favorite pictures, a shot of her standing on the steps of the White House before one of her presidential interviews, looking like she owned the place. Behind that portrait was a safe.

Inside the safe was "the book"—her own secret.

Every year for thirty-five years, Maxine's loyal butler, William Clark, had been presenting her with the annual Christmas gift of a diary. Specifically, a Smythson of Bond Street diary, the lovely little leather handbooks from London. This year's version was cased in yellow goatskin leather with a natural horn clasp, and just four months into the year Maxine had filled half its pages. The color of the diary rotated every year, but its purpose never changed. Maxine kept all her secrets and private thoughts in this little book, then stashed the volume in a safe at her Park Avenue home every New Year's Day. She would start each book with a page listing her "Goals for the Year"; on the last page, sometime before the clock hit midnight on New

Year's Eve, she would look back and record how many goals had been successfully accomplished. As Maxine got older, she became even more meticulous, preparing for her own big tell-all memoir. Her few close friends called the books her "dirty diaries," knowing they probably contained enough dirt to bury a whole roomful of celebrities. Every year, she postponed starting the memoir, thinking she wasn't quite old enough yet. But though she loved her books, they had caused her a great deal of anguish. The Missy Adams mess almost made her want to throw the little yellow book across the room.

A few years earlier, during a lunch with Paul McCartney, whom the tabloids suggested she was "doing" at the time—*as if*—Maxine got so frazzled by the horde of paparazzi hovering outside the restaurant that she left her purse in the ladies' room at the Carlyle. It was just her luck that Missy Adams was the one to go in the stall after her. Maxine almost had a breakdown when she discovered the purse containing her private diary was missing. She actually did have a small breakdown when that little bitch Missy sweetly returned it the next day— the day that coincidentally was to be Missy's last on *The Lunch Club*. Dammit. One slip and now she had to worry about what Missy saw in that book, even though Missy swore she didn't read one word. *Lying tramp! I should have beat that bitch with a bat when I had the chance,* Maxine thought.

As she riffled through the current diary, trying

to get some ideas, her intercom buzzed. It was her secretary, Eileen.

"Miss Robinson, it's Riley Dufrane for you on line two."

Maxine scooped up the desk phone. To reach out this quickly, Riley must have been watching the show.

"How can I help you, Riley?" she said, hoping she sounded calm.

"Uh, well, how have you been, Maxine?"

Maxine rolled her eyes. Again with the dumb small talk. She wished he would get to the point, which she knew was to ask her what the hell had happened out there on the set. But Riley always acted a little goofy around her. He was one of the most powerful men in the television industry, and she knew he had a reputation for quick and decisive action, but whenever he was around Maxine, he seemed a bit tentative, maybe even intimidated. Riley was gorgeous, in a square-jawed, patrician sort of way. If you were trying to cast a network president, Riley's portrait would be the first one the casting director would send over. He was more than a decade younger than she was, but his awkwardness around her didn't seem to be about age. Maxine wasn't sure what it was that shook him so, but the idea amused her—though it was an effect she had grown accustomed to having on both men and women. In Riley's case, she pushed her advantage as much as possible, which usually made him even more uncomfortable.

As a result, he just tried to stay out of her way.

"I've been fine, Riley. How is the family? I hope Virginia is well."

"Yes, Ginny is well. As are the kids. We are all great."

"Sooo . . . how can I help you, Riley?"

"Yes, well, there are a few things I'd like to discuss with you. I'm wondering if you might be available tomorrow for lunch?"

He wanted to waste an entire, uncomfortable lunch hour just to talk about Heather Hope's appearance? Maxine thought that was a bit over-the-top. She decided to just get it over with now.

"Is this about the show we just did with Heather Hope?" she asked, trying hard to soften her tone.

"Uh, no, not really. Although I was curious about what happened out there. But I wanted to talk about something else."

"Okkaaaaay," Maxine said, pointedly reacting to Riley's mysteriousness. "I'm sure I can make myself free if you need to talk."

"Great. One o'clock at the Four Seasons . . . the restaurant, not the hotel."

No shit, Sherlock, Maxine thought. What a moron. Like she'd ever mistake the two.

"Sounds fine," Maxine said.

"Oh, and about today's show, that looked a bit, uh, painful out there. I couldn't imagine a situation that would have all five of you ladies with nothing to say." He had meant it as a joke of sorts, but Maxine thought she detected a hint of sexism and condescension in his comment. So she just let it sit there.

Riley realized his error right away. He hurried on, sounding even more flustered. Maxine guessed that his lovely, perfect face was probably turning a nice shade of crimson about now.

"Anyway, uh, have you been able to find out any information about Melissa's book?"

Instantly, Maxine understood. Riley had plenty of his own secrets that he needed to keep hidden, things that could jeopardize not only his reputation but also his marriage and possibly even his career. A little smile formed at the corners of Maxine's perfectly shaded lips.

"No, I haven't, Riley. But I'm working on it. Perhaps I'll know something by tomorrow. Goodbye."

⊰⊱

FOR THE THIRD TIME since she entered her office, Molly made sure her door was locked. She did not need any intruders right now. She had become overly neurotic about intruders because one of the set assistants had walked in on her a few months back while she was struggling to get out of an itchy wool dress after the show. When she had finished pulling the dress over her head, there he was, standing with his hand still on the doorknob and his eyes wide in shock and terror. Her breasts, spilling out of her bra, heaved in panic. The situation cried out for a joke, something to bring down the tension, but all Molly wanted to do was scream. She was standing, nearly naked, in front of a twentysomething kid barely out of college. She had hoped the joke wasn't on her. Every time she saw him for the next six months, she felt her face turning red. She was relieved when he got a job on another show.

After the bombshell Heather had dropped, Molly felt like she was about to lose it. What if Missy told the world about the little bottle that she kept in her bag? She kept telling herself to calm down, to breathe easy, to relax, but it wasn't working. She needed some help, some assistance in settling her nerves. What she needed was in her bag, locked in her desk drawer. She needed her pills. From day to day, hour to hour, Molly had been fighting with herself for at least the past two years, trying to stop herself from downing another pill every time she felt the slightest anxiety. But it was a battle that she had been losing. Badly. She tried to think of something that would take her mind off the Xanax. All at once, she loved and loathed the pills, thanked and cursed the day that she first met the little bastards. She looked around the office, pushing away the panic. Did Missy know about her, um, problem? If word got out that Molly was a drug addict, she knew Maxine would kick her under the nearest oncoming bus with about as much thought as Maxine put into applying deodorant in the morning. You could be a pill-popping, pot-smoking, blond-wig-wearing tranny with a rubber fetish on your own time, but if you made Maxine look bad or caused her to be cast in a light other than rose-colored, you were toast. God, just the thought of that heartless bitch gave Molly the shakes!

As she held her hand to her chest, Molly was comforted by the massive collection of pig-themed doodads that engulfed her office. The collection included magnets, stuffed dolls, napkin holders, and even a gold-plated piggy bank. Over the last decade or so friends and colleagues had tripled the size of her collection. She saw a wine opener with a pig's-tail corkscrew from Sonoma Valley and remembered all the wonderful restaurants she had hit in the region. And of course the thought of restaurants brought her to food. She always made her way back to food.

Molly unlocked the desk and reached behind a stack of anonymous files, where she hid her food stash. Drakes Apple Pie. Her latest food obsession. Food had been Molly's archenemy for as long as she could remember. Even when she was in elementary school, she would hide stashes around the house, insurance for her mother's arbitrary food restrictions. One week potato chips were off-limits, the next week she'd let Molly stuff her face with a family-size bag of Lay's in one sitting. In fact, it was food that led to the "problem" with the Xanax. Molly had made the monstrous error of signing on to become a celebrity spokeswoman for a national weight-loss company. The popular company was started by a former television actress named Karen

Collins and Molly was all over the television air-waves and magazine covers because of her pledge to take the "Collins Challenge" and try to lose fifty pounds in six months. The money was good, but it was so not worth it. What was it her ex-agent used to say? "Scared money never wins"—and he ain't never lied. That paycheck almost sent her to the nuthouse. The campaign, so public and in-your-face, turned Molly into a nervous wreck. Suddenly her weight and eating habits were the subject of watercooler discussions and late-night comedians—all of whom were her buddies, all of whom were having a field day. Her doctor prescribed anti-anxiety pills to calm Molly down, and to her amazement, they also killed her appetite. She was thrilled at the twofer she got—lessen anxiety and lose weight at the same time! She wondered why she hadn't stumbled across this magic formula decades earlier. With the help of her darling little pink pills, she actually lost the weight. It was a huge story. Molly even posed on the cover of *People* in a bikini. She looked fabulous! But after a short while, the pills lost their appetite-suppressing properties and she found that she was craving food again. She began to steadily gain the weight back—causing her even more anxiety. The heavier she got, the more she pounded the pills. To top off the story, Karen Collins fired her from the campaign, giving the comics and the tabloids weeks' worth of mate-rial. One of the late-night hosts, Jimmy Kimmel, that fat fuck, even came up with a name for her:

the Unsinkable Molly McCarthy—because she was the size of an aircraft carrier. As she had blinked through the tears watching Kimmel's show, Molly vowed never to speak to him again.

Molly could tell that the other ladies on the couch suspected that something was wrong with her. They didn't talk about it, but she had seen the many strange looks from them. Before the pills, she was a big, fun, hyper ball of energy. Now she needed to summon all the grit she could muster to display even half the energy she used to have. And she was doing weird stuff, like talking to herself very loudly in her office, or accusing the secretaries around the office of laughing at her. But Molly figured she was okay as long as her "problem" didn't become public knowledge and embarrass the show. She knew this view wasn't shared by the rest of the hosts, especially Whitney and Dara. But even if she were to admit that she needed help, which she wasn't quite sure she was ready to do—she still thought the problem was the food, not the pills— how could she ever get it without the whole world finding out about it, thus ending her career? No, Molly knew she was better off staying under the radar, out of the limelight.

She just prayed that Missy wasn't about to mess it all up.

CHAPTER 2

For the third time in an hour, Callie Sherman loitered outside of the office of Josh Howe, the executive producer of *The Lunch Club*. Josh's secretary eyed Callie but didn't say anything. Callie hated to look like a stalker, but she couldn't help herself. Something about Josh's ways brought it out of her. Callie was a production executive for the NBN network, assigned to *The Lunch Club,* and it was her job to make sure that NBN knew every bit of minutiae about the program on and off the set. Especially anything that might cost the network money or ratings. Callie and Josh had been carrying on a torrid affair for years, almost since the moment she began working with the show. The steamy relationship had its ups and downs, ebbs and flows, sometimes introducing more than its share of drama to the set. After the Heather Hope appearance, Callie was desperate to talk to Josh, to see how much damage he thought Missy's book could do to the show—and more specifically, to the two of them. Josh was married with three kids, so he certainly would have no interest in having their affair outed in a tell-all book. Callie had an even deeper secret, one that was considerably more explosive than her affair with Josh. Up until that morning, Callie was sure that she would be able to take her secret with her to her grave if she wished, she was so certain that it would never get out. But Heather Hope's statements on the couch had frightened Callie to her core. She just *had* to talk to Josh.

"Is he still in there with Shelly?"

The secretary looked at her and nodded curtly. Callie knew the woman was probably cursing her under her breath. It was important not to annoy a man's secretary if you wanted any kind of access to him, but Callie was much too far down the road to panic to be thinking logically. Why was he spending so much time with Shelly? Could there possibly be something going on between them? With Josh, she knew anything was possible. She turned abruptly and made her way back to her office, which was a floor below Josh's. As she scurried down the stairs, her long, shapely legs moving so fast that the heels of her René Caovilla stilettos clacking on the hard concrete sounded like machine-gun fire, she thought back to that first time with Josh, when all of this madness officially began.

Almost from the first day that she began working with *The Lunch Club*, Josh had been all over her. She was accustomed to male attention, something she had gotten from the moment puberty bloomed at age thirteen. Callie somehow managed to be long and lean but very curvaceous at the same time, like the women you'd see walking the streets of Paris and Rome. In fact, with her long, dark hair and easy, beautiful smile, Callie was sometimes mistaken for a European. Callie was disappointed to learn that Josh was married to boring-ass Barbara, his high school sweetheart, and they had three kids and a big house in Bridgeport, Connecticut. But he also had an apartment in the city and a reputation as a walking hardon. Josh had tried to bed every attractive woman remotely connected to *The Lunch Club*, and in many cases succeeded. Although Callie found him attractive in a clean-cut, Connecticut-preppie sort of way (which was ironic, since Josh was originally a country boy from Nebraska), allowing him into her panties was the last thing she thought she'd do. But he wore down her resistance with his quick wit and inviting smile. She found herself looking forward to the time she had to spend with him talking about the show. Soon they started finding excuses to have even more frequent meetings, then lunches outside of the office. After several months, during a lunch filled with longing, fuck-me stares from both of them, she accepted his invitation to go back to his apartment. He might have started out as a country boy from Nebraska, but somewhere along the way Josh Howe had learned how to make a woman bay at the moon. Callie couldn't believe the way her body responded to his touch, to his tongue, to him inside her. It was like he turned into a totally different person in the bedroom, a sexy, sensitive version of Arnold Schwarzenegger's Terminator cyborg—he wouldn't stop until she had had at least five orgasms and felt like she might pass out. After that, Callie was hooked, "turned out." She couldn't get enough of him and his magical penis. She didn't even care that he went back up to his idyllic existence in Connecticut most nights and on weekends. As long as she got a healthy dose of Josh a few times a week, she was good.

At least that's how she felt the first few months. Until she started catching feelings. Until she found herself tossing in her bed at night, trying to use her hand or any toy she could find to simulate the way he made her feel. Until she found that she couldn't stop thinking about him every waking hour. So then she became what she had always despised, what she had always vowed never to be: the jealous mistress praying that her man would leave his wife for her. She became irrational and unstable, and the combination led her to make a fateful decision. She stopped taking her birth control pills so that Josh could get her pregnant. Though she was forty-two, apparently she was still quite fertile because her gambit worked right away. Within two months, Callie was knocked up, carrying Josh's baby. But she knew that her having Josh's baby would not be a good career move at all. So she made up a story about going to a sperm bank for an anonymous donor. It was done in the city all the time by scores of hardworking single women; everyone at *The Lunch Club* was totally supportive of her decision. Even Josh. He told her that perhaps they should take a few steps back and give each other some "space." Callie was not happy, but she felt like she was trapped—she had lied to him, so now she was stuck with the lie.

The pregnancy was brutal for Callie—her emotions were already in shambles, so the added doses of hormones flooding her system turned her into a neurotic, unpredictable mess, the pregnant woman everyone tried to avoid. When the ladies of *The Lunch Club* saw Callie coming, everyone quickly came up with reasons why they had to flee. Maxine ordered everyone on the staff never to leave her alone with Callie because, as Maxine said, "I'd probably go to jail for a long time if I choked the shit out of that crazy bitch."

After Megan came—wonderful, delightful, entertaining little Megan—and Callie's Coke-bottle curves returned, Josh forgot about all the "space" he was supposed to be giving her. Soon she was back in his bed and they were right back to their passionate ways, now with the added complications of single momhood—no more sleepovers at Josh's apartment, no more all-night sex sessions. Callie had always planned that the sperm donor cover story would suffice for the public, but she desperately wanted to tell Josh the truth. After three years, the truth was eating her up. One night she floated a "fantasy"—wouldn't it be wonderful if Megan were really his?—during one of their lovemaking sessions and he went totally ballistic. He told her he didn't want any more kids, that his family was complete. It was a painful statement for Callie to hear.

So now Callie was biding her time, keeping up the sperm donor lie and holding out hope that Josh would come around, that the idyllic Connecticut life would one day be hers and he would dump that plain, ordinary little woman from Nebraska. That would have been enough stress for Callie to endure, but she now had a new worry, one that scared her to death. During one of her crazy spells while she was pregnant, she made the fatal error of telling the whole story to Missy Adams, who was her best friend at the time. Missy had listened, commiserated, and never judged . . . she was the consummate good friend, and Missy was the only other person in the world who knew that little Megan, supposedly fathered by the anonymous sperm donor, was really Josh's daughter and that Callie had been lying to Josh and everyone else about Megan's parentage. And to make matters worse, why did Callie so thoroughly dis Missy when she left the show? She never returned her calls and even cosigned statements the show made to the press that unfairly denigrated Missy's work and contribution to the show. Of all the people in the world to write a tell-all about *The Lunch Club*, it had to be Missy

Adams?! Callie was still partially in shock. She needed to know what Josh was thinking, what he planned to do about Missy's book. Callie needed him. Missy could ruin her—and deep down Callie knew she deserved everything that was coming her way.

She circled back upstairs, to Josh's office. The door was still closed; he was still inside with Shelly. Callie thought she heard a sound coming from behind the door. She looked over at his secretary to see if she'd also noticed, but the secretary was pretending not to be aware of Callie's stalker-like presence. She heard the noise again. Was that a moan?

⋈ ⋈

IN FACT, THAT *WAS* a moan coming from inside Josh's office. But what Josh was doing with Shelly was not what Callie would ever have imagined. Josh and Shelly were watching an episode of the old sitcom *Three's Company*, getting many good laughs from the antics of the hilarious John Ritter. This had become a ritual between them in recent months, a way that Shelly had cleverly deployed to do some bonding with Josh.

"My God, that guy is so damn funny!" Josh said. "I can't believe you found this episode. It was like, I think, my favorite when I was a little kid." He paused and his voice got a little softer. "I think this might have been the episode that made me want to work in television."

Shelly glanced over at him, momentarily touched. Once again, she was surprised by how much she actually liked Josh. He had turned out to be a very different person than she originally thought he'd be.

"When was it that *you* knew you wanted to work in television?" he asked her.

Shelly thought for a second. Should she give him the real answer or the magazine-interview answer? Her actual feelings or the quote she would pass along to Lizette to go in her bio? She saw that he was watching her, waiting. For some reason, Shelly felt less guarded with Josh, like she could be real with him.

"Well, when I was younger, my goal was to be the first black female CEO of a Fortune 500 company," she said. "That was still my goal when I was at Harvard Business School. But right after I got my MBA, while I was doing the whole bond-trader thing down on Wall Street, as you know, I got 'discovered.'" She used her fingers to make air quotes and laughed. "So all of a sudden, and it really did feel like it happened overnight, I was walking the runways of Paris and Milan and draped in diamonds and Versace on the pages of *Vogue* and *Elle*. It was crazy and—I ain't gonna lie—it was a whole lot of fun. At one point, I was living in Paris, sleeping with some of the sexiest guys I've ever seen, hitting every party within a twenty-mile radius. Like a modern fairy tale. It was not at all what I had planned for my life, you know? But I learned to just roll with it. I think after Harvard, so many crazy things started flying at me. TV was just one of them. It seemed like fun, like a chance to make some serious dough by just talking shit with a bunch of fun, crazy women. What's not to like about that? But once I got here, and got the TV bug, now I can't imagine doing anything else."

Josh nodded. He could tell that what she gave him was the truth, not some varnished bull meant to impress him. They both looked back at the screen in time to see Suzanne Somers do something silly in a ridiculously low-cut tank top.

"Damn, Chrissy was all about the boobs, huh?" Shelly said, laughing. She reached down with both hands and lifted her own impressive (and surgically enhanced) pair. "I'm not mad at her!"

Josh laughed at Shelly's antics. He was especially enjoying his time with her because he knew that the other ladies on the show, particularly Maxine, were probably in such a state right now from Heather Hope's appearance that their heads were about to explode. That was precisely why he was spending this time with Shelly, to escape the craziness, to give himself some breathing room. He wanted to be as far from that stew of estrogen-fueled lunacy as possible. While he was a bit concerned about Missy's book and what effect it might have on his show, he didn't think he had anything to worry about. He didn't think his little liaisons with women on the staff were worthy fodder for anybody's tell-all memoir. He had never had any blowups with Missy Adams and, he could thank the Lord, had never tried to get in her pants, mainly scared off by her whole sweet, conservative, Southern-gal persona. Though he knew Shelly was filled with unbridled ambition, he thought she was probably the sanest member of the cast, with the possible exception of Dara. He hadn't really gotten to know Dara that well—probably because he knew she preferred the females. No point in wasting his time there. Shelly was smart and funny as hell. And while he was attracted to her in the same way that he was attracted to anything with a pretty smile and a vagina, Josh found that he was actually comfortable around Shelly. She put him at ease and made him laugh. As opposed to practically every other person in the building, Shelly actually relieved his stress, rather than added to it. For him, it was a welcome and lovely surprise.

As for Shelly, she could manage to be a bit more relaxed about Missy's book than the rest of them because, frankly, she didn't think she had anything to hide. After she replaced Heather Hope on the couch, she had overlapped for a couple of years with Missy, who was replaced by Dara. While Shelly never appreciated Missy's ultraconservative politics and suspected that there was something fake about her whole Georgia peach act, she and Missy had never had any personal clashes off the set. They usually went head-to-head on matters of politics and social issues, but once the cameras stopped rolling it was all smiles and air kisses between them. Besides, Shelly's modeling years had been so out of control and legendary that there was really nothing that Missy could write about her that would be shocking to anybody. She had been such a well-known wild girl that she was virtually scandal-proof. *So bring it, Miss Missy*, Shelly thought. *It'll only enhance my rep and bring me more Benjamins*.

Shelly smelled opportunity in the air with the Missy tell-all. If that book came along and shook things up on the couch, it might be a great chance for her to step out in front. Shelly didn't believe in stepping *on* people to get ahead . . . but as her mother would say, she "sure as hell would step *over* them" if they were in her way.

Josh and Shelly didn't exactly stumble upon their relationship by accident, but things had turned out differently than Shelly expected. Besides Maxine, Josh was the person who had the most power to raise her stock on the show. But instead of using her looks to lure Josh, which she concluded was too obvious and shortsighted, she had decided to become his friend. She invited his secretary, a pretty young black woman, out to a couple of "girlfriend" lunches at a fancy midtown restaurant, instantly pretending to be her best friend. Shelly had cleverly pulled as many usable facts as she could from the secretary. One of the most usable was Josh's obsession with seventies sitcoms, like *Three's Company*, *Happy Days*, and *Mork & Mindy*. Shelly was too young to have watched them herself, but armed with this info she set out on a mission. She scoured the shelves of video stores around her Upper West Side neighborhood and she visited sites all over the Internet, trying to find episodes of the old sitcoms for her and Josh to watch together. She managed to put together quite a stockpile. At first Josh was understandably suspicious and confused, wondering how easily Shelly thought he might be influenced. She would pop into his office after a show, bearing a few discs. They'd put in a DVD and crack themselves up. While they watched, they talked about their families, their childhoods, their ambitions. Shelly found that she was actually starting to enjoy the time she spent with Josh, and Josh let down his guard around her. But despite the new relationship, Shelly hadn't lost sight of her original purpose in befriending him. When she had him where she wanted him, heavily dependent on their friendship, she would start leaning on him to have her officially announced as the main host of *The Lunch Club*, the one who carried the show during Maxine's frequent absences to interview God knows who God knows where. That was her next goal. After that, she had her sights set on becoming the next Heather Hope.

⊰ ⊱

AS SHE SAT HUNCHED over her desk, Lizette still had Maxine's words ringing in her ear. *"I need for you to find out what's in that damn book."* It might as well be above her desk now in flashing neon. And she could still picture that crazed look in Maxine's eyes, the look that warned Lizette that her future in television would be imperiled if she failed to produce Missy's book. She had a feeling that this day would haunt her for a long time. She had been calling sources all over the city for hours and had come up empty. *Nada.* Mostly, people were asking her all the questions, trying to get info on the behind-the-scenes fallout. Their questions were not helping her at all with her task. The failure was causing an acidic pit to form in her belly, spreading dread through her limbs.

Just in time, a bit of good news came by way of Lizette's cell phone. It was a call from Channing. Her gorgeous, darling Channing, always a bright spot in her life.

"What the hell is going on over there?" Channing said. "There are stories all over the Internet about the show today. How are you holding up?"

"Channing! All hell has broken loose over here! Heather Hope came on the show to say that Missy Adams has written this juicy tell-all, and now Maxine has put me in charge of finding out what's in the book before its publication. It almost sounded like a threat, like my job could be in jeopardy if I come up empty!"

"Damn, that's horrible, Lizette. How does she expect you to work *that* miracle? That book is probably better guarded than the president right now. I'm really sorry she's putting you through this."

"Thanks. I just don't know what to do right now."

"Well, I'll start making some calls too. I have a few publishing-industry sources that I can try leaning on. But babe, if the book is as explosive as you seem to think, it's going to be wrapped up in non-disclosure agreements so tightly . . . a gnat's ass couldn't get through it."

"Channing, I've already found that out, but whatever you can do would be great! Thank you!" Channing Cary was one of the top freelance writers in the country, so Lizette was pleased that she would have his skills on her team. With all the magazine profiles he had done on Hollywood and music superstars over the years, he was bound to come across information that could prove useful to her.

"No problem. Anything for you, sweetheart." He paused for an instant. "I also have something else that might cheer you up a bit."

"Oh, really? And what would that be?" Lizette felt her heart skip a few beats.

"Well, I've made reservations for us at the Union Square Cafe for Friday night. I have something important I want to share with you."

Now Lizette's heartbeat did triple time. The Union Square Cafe wasn't cheap. Not the kind of fare that a freelancer's salary usually brought, even one as successful as Channing. This must be something serious. Lizette didn't even want to let her mind go there, but she couldn't help it. Perhaps this was when Channing was going to propose to her. She tried to remember his exact words. Did he say "something important to ask you" or "something important to share with you"? She wished that the conversation had a rewind button like her DVR box.

"You can't give me any hints what this is about, huh?" she asked playfully.

"Sorry, darling. You're gonna have to wait!"

At that precise moment, the Missy Adams book was suddenly far from her mind. At thirty, Lizette wasn't getting any younger. She was tired of everybody she knew asking her if she thought Channing would ever propose. She had started telling them all that they needed to direct their inquiries to Channing, not her. But perhaps her boyfriend was now about to make her a fiancée. No more premarital sex! That made Lizette smile. An aunt of hers had asked her last Christmas if she and her "fella" were having premarital sex. Lizette had been tempted to answer "as often as possible," but she had held her tongue. Aunt Ruth didn't deserve any rudeness from her niece—"the only niece who's still not married," she liked to remind Lizette. Wow, this might turn out to be the best week of her life. But just that thought, of the joy that this week might bring, brought her back to Missy and Maxine with a thud.

"How are the rest of the women on the staff reacting?" Channing asked.

"Huh?" Lizette wasn't sure if she heard him correctly.

"I said how are the rest of the ladies on the show, the other cohosts besides Maxine Robinson, reacting to that book?"

Lizette thought the question was a little odd. Channing had never expressed any interest in the ladies of *The Lunch Club*. But maybe this was his awkward way of making her feel like he was interested in her work. She had once complained to him, when he was immersed in some mammoth profile for the *New Yorker* on Martin Scorsese, that he didn't care enough about *her* job. Apparently that complaint had hit its mark.

"Oh, well, I think they're a bit flustered. I haven't really had a chance to speak to any of them because once the show is over they usually all run out of here like the building is on fire. But from the way they reacted on the couch and the looks on their faces, I don't think they were happy. Missy was on the show for a long time. I'm sure she knows a lot of dirt. And the way Maxine treated her at the end was kinda brutal."

Channing didn't answer right away. "Max is pretty ruthless, huh?" he said.

Lizette laughed. "Well, if you actually did ever call her 'Max' to her face, then you'd find out exactly how ruthless she is. She *hates* that name! I once saw an intern call her that and I think the boy is probably still in therapy. She said, 'Do I *look* like a *Max* to you, young man? I'm going to need for you to stay as far away from me as possible until you learn my name!'" Lizette had tightened her throat and tried to do her best Maxine Robinson impersonation. The key was to put a little bass in your voice and pretend you were a principal talking to a misbehaving second grader.

Channing cracked up at her dead-on impression. "Wow, that was damn good!"

Lizette laughed. "Yeah, I've been working on it for a few years now. Maybe if I get fired, I can try out for *Saturday Night Live*."

"Aw, baby, you're not going anywhere," Channing said. "But I'll let you get back to your work. And I'll call you right away if I find out anything."

After she hung up, Lizette sat still for several minutes, imagining for about the thousandth time what designer she would pick for her wedding dress. She had been coming across some fabulous dresses by Amsale, the talented Ethiopian designer. She wondered how much an Amsale cost.

Just then, her cell phone rang. She looked down. It was Clare, one of her best friends from Yale. While Clare, an art history professor at NYU, was about as far as you could get from a publishing-industry insider, Lizette had called her earlier just to vent.

"Hey, I just thought of something," Clare said without a hello. "Have you tried Tim Stratton?"

"What do you mean?" Tim Stratton was one of Lizette's old college boyfriends. She hadn't thought about him in years.

"Well, I ran into him a few months back. I forgot to tell you. Actually, I didn't forget to tell you.

I decided not to tell you. He looked gorgeous and he's still single and for a split second I wondered how you would feel if I went out with him. After I came to my senses, I decided to keep all of this to myself. After all, even though you went out with him like a million years ago, there really was no need for you to know all of this. And anyway, you're so happy with Channing. I mean, who wouldn't be happy with Prince Channing? He's so, like . . . perfect!" Not for the first time, Lizette wondered how Clare managed to give a college lecture without wandering off on a thousand tangents. She had a hard time conjuring a mental image of Clare commanding a big lecture hall, all waving hands and giggles and big-eyed wonderment. On second thought, the students would probably love it.

"Clare!" Lizette barked into the phone.

"Yes?" she said, somewhat meekly. "Too much?"

"Yes, too much. Why did you ask if I had tried Tim?"

"Oh, right! I guess you didn't know that Tim Stratton is an attorney for one of the big publishers, huh? So I'm thinking that he may know someone over at Patterson and White. At least it's worth a shot, right?"

It took Lizette only about five minutes to get Tim Stratton on the phone.

"Wow, Lizette Bradley!" he said right away. "It's been way too long. How have *you* been?"

As soon as she heard his deep, sexy voice, a flood of memories came rushing back. Very good memories.

⊰ ⊱

AS SHE CLIMBED INTO the second taxi, Whitney Harlington felt as silly as she usually did when she was trying to pretend she was James Bond. But she was certain the destination at the end of her journey would be worth every cloak-and-dagger detail. It always was. He claimed that the secrecy was necessary, crucial. And Whitney had to admit that the secrecy and danger of their assignations were sometimes just as thrilling as the meetings themselves.

When the taxi pulled up in front of the building, Whitney could feel the commotion in her stomach. These meetings still managed to get her so excited that they gave her an upset stomach, like the gripping nervousness she'd feel in the early days of her career in the moments just before she went on the air. But she knew that the minute she stepped into the room, the nerves would disappear, replaced by more intense passion than her body had ever known. She was almost starting to feel like she was addicted to the passion, that she couldn't stay away even if she tried. After all, the revelation that Heather Hope had just made on *The Lunch Club* couch, that Missy Adams was publishing a tell-all memoir that would possibly include scandalous dirt on all the *Lunch Club* ladies, should have given her reason to reconsider these liaisons. If Missy outed their affair, it could be disastrous for Whitney *and* for him. But knowing all this, Whitney still ran headlong into his strong arms, almost as if she were racing toward her own self-destruction. If she were ordered to sit down on a therapist's couch and explain her actions, Whitney would be speechless. How could she justify this? She knew it was wrong and she knew it was dangerous, but she also knew that she couldn't stay away. She needed him—seemingly now more than ever.

It didn't hurt that the setting for her "dangerous liaisons" was sexy as hell and straight out of a romance novel. Everything about the Inn at Minetta Lane was intended to signify class and privacy. It was located a few blocks from Washington Square Park in a brownstone originally constructed in 1834 that had been restored, so you truly felt like you were stepping into the nineteenth century when you crossed its ornate threshold. The place had only twelve guest rooms, each more elaborate and detailed than the last, from the four-poster beds and Frette linens to the marble fireplaces and plush upholstered sofas. Whitney loved its charm and also its furtiveness. She raced up the narrow carpeted staircase to their usual room. She was already starting to feel flush and warm inside. She couldn't get to the room fast enough. She was out of breath when she reached the top, but that didn't slow her down. She lunged toward the door and knocked five times, their signal. The door opened and Whitney was greeted by the wide smile of her lover, Riley Dufrane. The president of NBN.

"Welcome to Fantasy Island," Riley said, doing his best Ricardo Montalban impersonation.

Whitney laughed and practically jumped into Riley's arms. They brought their mouths together in a frantic kiss, as if they were trying to devour each other. They shed their clothes in seconds as they laughed and giggled their way to the bed. At age fifty-four, Whitney still couldn't believe how horny she got when she was with Riley. After so many years of marriage to Eric, the last several of which had become nearly sexless, she had been thrilled to discover that this intensely passionate side of her still existed. And she didn't want to give it up. Riley was seven years younger than she was and had the trim, buff body of a man at least fifteen years his junior. Whitney had grown accustomed to her lovemaking sessions lasting about ten minutes at the most, so she was still amazed at how long he could go. The first time they were together several years back, after months of panting indecision about whether they should cross the adultery line, Riley had stayed hard inside of her for more than an hour, moving and alternating the speed and tempo of his thrusts in a long, powerful dance that was almost agonizing. Whitney had lost count of how many orgasms she'd had, probably more than the total she'd had in the previous five years with Eric. Because of his staying power, she had jokingly started calling Riley

"Sting" in honor of the tantric-sex-practicing rock musician.

"My God, I can't get enough of you, my darling," Riley said as they fell on the bed. As she tugged at her skirt, Whitney was pleased to see that Riley had remembered to turn down the comforter. They might be ridiculously expensive and beautiful Frette linens, but Whitney knew that the amount of bodily juices spilled on them over the years probably could impregnate an entire college campus. When they were both naked, Riley flipped her around so that they could feast on each other at the same time. It was one of their favorite positions—one that she and Eric hadn't even bothered to try since W's first term in the White House. With his head and mouth squirming between her legs and spasms of intense pleasure flowing up and down her torso, Whitney had to summon reserves of concentration to give the proper attention to Riley's manhood, which stood at full attention. This was another thing that had been transformed with Riley, her new love of giving. She had to admit that up to this point, she primarily had been a receiver in bed. Especially when a man knew what he was doing. Her first husband knew what he was doing. Eric, not so much. Riley most definitely knew what he was doing. His lips and tongue and teeth in and around the folds of her most intimate areas could actually make her scream in pleasure. Whitney had never been a screamer. She now even got regular Brazilian bikini waxes to give Riley better access. Eric didn't even seem to notice the "landing strip" she now sported down there. But her time with Riley had slowly turned Whitney into a lover who took pride in being a giver. Ever the journalist, she had even done some investigating on it. She had bought a book and accompanying DVD called *The Art of Giving* and, in the privacy of her bedroom, when Eric was away on one of his trips and the twins were at one of their many sleepovers, she had watched the DVD with rapt intensity, replaying the good parts over and over until she had it all down. That weekend she had wanted to rush to the Inn as soon as possible to try out her new skills, but Riley had been away with his wife. The next time they were together, as she took him more deeply inside her mouth than ever before, Riley's eyes grew wide. He couldn't stop complimenting her on her newly acquired skills. She was now good enough to make a DVD herself.

After several minutes of Whitney and Riley pleasuring each other, Riley actually had to reach down and move her head away.

"Damn, you're good!" he said. "I don't want to come yet."

"So much for Sting!" Whitney said with a teasing laugh.

With that said, Whitney swung her body around and quickly sat down on top of him, impaling herself on him so hard that their thighs met with a loud smack. Whitney bounced up and down on top of Riley with pleasure, with vigor, like it could save her life. Riley gazed up at her with a wide smile. Whitney moaned loudly, probably too loudly. But she knew there was no chance that management would come knocking on the door. Several months back, to ensure the cooperation of everyone employed at the Inn, Riley had handed over a very large stack of cash to the Inn's manager, a very nice gay man named Reinhardt. Every day, Reinhardt would hold this room for them until three o'clock. If he had not heard from Riley, only then would he give the room to another guest. Whitney had promptly bestowed the room with a name, one that they now both used. They called it Voluptas, which was the name of the Roman goddess of sensual pleasure, who also happened to be the daughter of Cupid. Whitney adored these little gestures of intimacy. They made her feel incredibly close to her lover, like they inhabited their own secluded world. It was a world that made her feel young and desirable and alive. Whenever they wanted to signal to each other their availability for a rendezvous, they would send a simple text that said "Voluptas" with a time, like "Voluptas 1 pm." The other would either respond "Yes" or "No" or suggest an alternate time. In this way, they usually got together at least three times a week, which was remarkable considering how busy they both were, especially the network president.

Riley flipped Whitney around and took her from behind. He grasped her hips and pulled her onto him, hard, again and again. A big smile crossed his face as he looked down and watched her cheeks bounce and jiggle every time they met his thighs. Riley reached up and grabbed a handful of Whitney's hair. He knew she liked this, when he got a little rough. Whitney moaned loudly as he tugged. She started making her high-pitched mewling sounds, indicating that she was about to have another orgasm. Riley decided that he would join her.

"Okay, I'm going to come with you, baby!" he said. "I'm coming with you!"

Riley felt the rush of the orgasm start at his toes and race up his legs. He held nothing back as he let go inside of her. When the spasms were over, he leaned forward and rested his head on her smooth, naked back while still inside of her. He wrapped his arms around her from behind and they fell sideways onto the bed. He felt himself slowly shrinking inside of her. They both wore contented smiles as they lay in the post-sex glow, their thoughts focused on the pleasure they found in each other. Fuck Missy Adams, fuck Heather and her bombshell. In the back of her mind, Whitney knew she wasn't going anywhere.

CHAPTER 3

Dara had spent most of the day doing her own fretting about what was in Missy's book and what it might do to her career, so she was relieved when her lover, Rain Sommers, finally got home and they could begin one of their favorite activities, cooking together. Dara purposely avoided telling Rain about Missy and the book because she knew what Rain would say—she'd say the possibility of Missy outing her in a book was all the more reason why Dara needed to come out of the closet. Dara did not want to go down that road on this night, so she welcomed Rain with open arms and led her by the hand into the kitchen so they could start the cooking ritual.

They both had their own separate reasons for enjoying the cooking process as much as they did. For Dara, who was convinced that her lover was easily the funniest woman in the country, their time together in the kitchen became like an impromptu Rain Sommers stand-up routine. She would take

Dara through her day, mocking everyone who had crossed her path, trying out new routines, changing old ones, all with the purpose of thrilling her most important audience of one, Dara Cruz. And Rain got her own thrills from the process. She loved to watch Dara every minute of every day, still dismayed that this unbelievably beautiful creature was the love of her life. Dara knew that their time in the kitchen had become like a show of sorts for Rain, so she played it up to the hilt. She preferred tight jeans or clingy sweatpants, but sometimes, if she was in an especially generous mood, she would wear just an apron over some frilly bra and panties, her fleshy round Latin ass protruding from the rear of the apron like a back porch. Rain would tell her that her ass was like a work of art, like a gorgeous Modigliani taken down from the museum walls and brought out into the world for the regular folks to admire.

In fact, it was Dara's ass that had brought them together. They were both at a party celebrating the release of one of Molly McCarthy Stein's albums, but they had never met. As two of the most successful and best-known female entertainers in the country, Molly and Rain had been best friends for almost twenty years, since their days struggling together on the circuit. They had even roomed together for a time. Rain was a well-known lesbian, though her sexual partners hadn't drawn as much attention as those of Ellen DeGeneres, her main rival in the comedy world, probably because Rain tried to stay away from anything having to do with a Hollywood actress. The women Rain preferred to bring into her bed were a bit more normal, lawyers and accountants and bartenders. At the time of Molly's party, Dara had only recently been added to *The Lunch Club* couch, so she was still a bit starstruck at these gatherings, trying hard to keep her jaw from dropping as she was introduced to major stars left and right. Dara had gone back to a coffee table to retrieve the white wine and crackers she had left there a few minutes earlier. Wearing skintight jeans that hugged her curves like a Ferrari, Dara wasn't paying much attention to what was behind her as she bent over.

"Okay, while this has to be the most perfect ass I have ever seen, I suggest you remove it from my face if you don't want it to come back with bite marks," said a female voice behind her. Still bent over, Dara swiveled her head and realized that her ass was almost smacking Rain Sommers in the face. She stood up abruptly and tried to hide her embarrassment, though she knew that her face had probably turned purple.

"Oh my God, excuse me!" Dara said. "That was so incredibly rude of me. I can't believe I did that."

Rain smiled and stuck out her hand. Dara thought her smile was much warmer and prettier than it looked on television.

"I'm Rain Sommers. And I know who you are. You are the brilliant new cohost on *The Lunch Club*. Molly has told me all about you. I've seen you in action a few times and, I must admit, you're a damn smart bitch. You used some words that I couldn't spell even if I swallowed a dictionary." Rain smiled even more broadly and leaned in closer to Dara. "And one more thing. You are even more beautiful in person than you are on television."

Dara blushed. "I have to say the same thing about you," Dara said. "You're much prettier in person than you are on television."

"See! I knew you were brilliant!" Rain said. Then she stood up. They were exactly the same height, but Dara's heels were a lot higher than Rain's. Rain was a bit stocky, fleshy around the middle. Dara had always preferred to have something to hold on to, in her men and in her women. Dara looked deeply into Rain's eyes and felt a slight tug somewhere down around her midsection. Already she could tell that something was happening between them. There had been a lot more men than women in Dara's sexual history, but most of her recent lovers had been women and she had started to come to the realization that perhaps she wasn't bisexual, as she had previously believed, but actually a full-fledged lesbian.

Rain made some room for Dara on the couch. Dara snuggled in next to her, aware that her thigh was pressed against Rain's and her breasts were just inches from Rain's right shoulder. The two of them began talking and completely forgot about everybody else in the room. By the time Molly made her way over to them an hour later, both Dara and Rain knew that something special was occurring. Within two weeks, they both had professed their love for each other. Within a month, Dara had moved into Rain's gorgeous Jamie Drake–designed condo loft with the sixteen-foot ceilings down in Tribeca.

Dara absolutely treasured their life together. Rain was an incredibly tender lover, and they had become increasingly adventurous in bed. And of course Rain made her laugh so hard that sometimes Dara would tell her to stop because her stomach hurt. Dara found that she didn't mind at all Rain's obsessive focus on her looks and her body. It felt different with her than with the men she had been with, more natural, like an appreciation of one of God's masterworks rather than a sexualized lusting and coveting. And she knew Rain loved her mind because Rain told her all the time and told everyone who would listen about all of Dara's degrees and her impressive Ivy League background. One magazine profile, noting Dara's medical *and* law degrees from Columbia, said she was "Sonia Sotomayor trapped in J.Lo's body." Rain had cut out that line from the magazine and she carried it around in her purse, much to Dara's embarrassment. Theirs was like a match made in heaven. The only problem they had was the closet.

Rain had grown frustrated and angry with Dara's fears about going public with their relationship. It was becoming a frequent source of conflict between them. Dara wasn't ashamed at all to be gay. She now considered it an elemental part of what she was, like being Latin or being Christian. But Dara had two primary fears—her parents and her career. Dara's parents were about as traditional as Puerto Rican Catholics could get. Mass at least twice a week, baptism, confirmation, and holy communion for the kids, big *quinceañera* bash for the girls, weekly servings of *cuchifritos* and arroz con pollo. The father ran the household—or at least was led to believe he did—and boys only married girls and girls only married boys. Any other combination was unthinkable. Dara couldn't remember her parents ever stating a position against homosexuality—it was so out of the question on the streets of Spanish Harlem when she was growing up that the subject never came up. Dara wasn't sure what they would do if she ever came out to them. She shuddered at the thought. And her fears about coming out publicly were tied to her desire not to embarrass her parents and her uncertainties about what it would mean to her image to be known as a lesbian. Would she become a tabloid caricature, the Puerto Rican "carpet muncher"? She couldn't stomach the idea of her father standing in the checkout line at the supermarket, picking up a celebrity-obsessed tabloid and possibly reading something like that. Dara had enough challenges in trying to fight Latina stereotypes; now she would be expected to pick up the lesbian mantle too?

"Did you see that poll on gay marriage?" Rain asked as they sat down at the dining room table and began eating. She picked up an asparagus spear with her fingers and popped it in her mouth.

Dara shook her head. She really didn't want to talk about this. "No, I didn't," she said, sliding a piece of the broiled salmon in her mouth. "What did it say?"

"It said that for the first time in this country, more people say they support gay marriage than oppose it," Rain said. "It's almost like a twenty percent jump in the number of people who support it from just like five years ago."

Dara nodded. She wanted to be as political as Rain on this issue, but it was still too personal and scary for her right now to even think about the politics. However, she knew that Rain would get mad if she didn't show enough enthusiasm. She tried to add a smile, but it was too late.

"You know, when the state is knocking at our door, telling us we don't have the right to be together, then you think maybe you might want to care about this issue?" Rain said, her green eyes flashing. "I mean, you all sit there on that fuckin' show and argue all day about every damn bit of stupid minutiae that parades as news, but you don't have an opinion on this, something that affects you so directly?"

Dara sighed. This was exactly why she hadn't brought up Missy's book. Rain was such a gay-rights militant that you could never win going down this road with her. She was a half step from picking up an automatic weapon and taking out the state legislature. Until Dara was willing to march down on city hall or the capitol building in Albany next to Rain, holding up a picket sign—"Would you fear me if I were your daughter?!" was Rain's favorite—as they tongue kissed before the cameras, she knew she would continue to disappoint Rain.

"Rain, you know that's not fair," she said. "Of course I care deeply about this issue. I just don't want to talk about it right now, okay?"

"But you never want to talk about it!" Rain said. "That's the fuckin' problem. If I was an insecure person, I might think it was me. Like you were afraid to tell the world I was your lover."

"Oh my God, Rain, you're going there again?" Dara bolted up from the table. She started into the kitchen, to retrieve the dessert. "You know I love you, baby," she said over her shoulder. "And you know I'm incredibly proud of you. Just give me a little more time, okay?"

She came back to the table carrying one of her specialties, *budín de pan*, Puerto Rican bread pudding. Her mother had taught her to make it before she went away to college and Dara had perfected it over the years to the point where she thought hers might be better than her mother's, though she'd never dare say that anywhere in the vicinity of East 123rd Street.

"Would I have made you this *budín*, your favorite dessert, with my own loving hands, if I didn't think you were the most special person in the whole world?" Dara said. She set the dish on the table and ran her right hand softly across Rain's cheek. She saw Rain soften instantly at her touch. Dara chuckled to herself. It worked every time.

"That's not fighting fair!" Rain said, grinning and grabbing a spoon. "You know I'm a weak, greedy bitch!"

"Who said anything about a fight?" Dara said, scooping up a big juicy chunk and putting it on a plate for Rain. "Fighting's not in my plans at all. As a matter of fact, when we're done here, I'm going to open up a bottle of that Santa Margherita pinot that you swear by, get you good and drunk, then take advantage of your body."

Rain reached out and pulled Dara to her. Dara sat down on her lap. As their lips met in a deep kiss, Rain reached down with her left hand and slipped it inside Dara's sweatpants, pleased to discover that Dara wasn't wearing any panties.

"Fuck that," Rain said, her voice growing heavy. "I don't need no stinkin' wine to take advantage of your body." They got up from the table and headed over to the couch, the *budín* all but forgotten.

-♯ ♭-

ERIC HARLINGTON PACED FROM the living room to the kitchen and back to the living room, checking his watch every fifteen seconds. Where the hell was Whitney? It was well past dinnertime and his wife was nowhere to be found. She also wasn't answering her cell phone. This last was no surprise—Whitney rarely answered her cell, particularly when he was desperate to find her. Though they still lived in the same house, Eric and Whitney behaved more like barely cordial roommates than like husband and wife. Eric wasn't exactly sure what had happened between them, but he was far too distracted by other concerns to try to figure it out. At this point, Whitney's disinterest in his affairs just made things easier for him. But right now he needed her to come home so that he could leave their Upper West Side town house and go to their summer home in Nantucket. He had important matters to attend to in Nantucket, things that he needed to do to prepare for his European trip the following week.

"Dad, where's Mom?"

It was his daughter Ashley, the twin most likely to pry into everyone else's business. She was the family drama queen and social butterfly, always in search of a party or ready to plan her own. Her sister, Bailey, was more of a loner, content to stay in her room for hours with the door locked. Eric used to wonder what she did in there all that time, but he had given up worrying about that.

"Why do you care where Mom is?" Bailey said, smirking at her sister from the other side of the kitchen table. "You haven't even spoken to her in like two weeks."

"I think you need to mind your business," Ashley said, slurping a big forkful of pasta into her mouth. "Go back to your little cave and let the humans talk."

"Daddy! Did you hear what she said to me!" Bailey said, looking at Eric as if she expected him to step into their spat. She turned back to her sister. "Anyway, that's why I heard that Peter Richmond called you a hogwart."

"What?! Who told you that? Did he really say that?" Ashley's brow furrowed in worry. "What does that even mean, anyway? What's a hogwart?"

"It's from Harry Potter, stupid!"

"I know it's from Harry Potter, Bailey! It's the name of their stupid school. But what is it; what's a hogwart?"

Bailey shrugged. "I don't know, Ashley. But I can tell you this—I don't think it's a compliment."

With that, Bailey burst into laughter. She could see her sister getting increasingly upset, but she didn't care.

Ashley pursed her lips, which is what she did when she was mad. Suddenly her face brightened. "Well, Bailey, I wasn't even going to tell you about this. But if you insist. You'll never guess what Jeb Friedman called you!"

Bailey watched her sister, her face full of distrust. "What?" she asked warily.

"He said we all should start calling you Dotty!" As soon as she said it, Ashley burst into laughter of her own.

Bailey frowned. "I don't get it. Dotty?"

Ashley smirked at her sister. Then she raised her right index finger and slowly started pointing to imaginary spots on her smooth, clear face. "Get it? Dotty."

Bailey's face instantly flushed and her hands instinctively lifted to finger the profoundly bad acne on her cheeks and forehead. Both girls were strikingly pretty, but Ashley's completely smooth face unfortunately dramatized the many bumps on Bailey's, as if the teenage gods had decided that instead of spreading out the acne evenly between the two of them, Bailey would get all of the bumps and Ashley none of them.

Eric looked up and saw one of his daughters crying while the other one was trying to stop herself from laughing. What in the world was going on? For about the thousandth time, Eric wondered why he couldn't have been blessed with the kind of twins who read each other's thoughts and finished each other's sentences. Instead, what he got in his house was a daily reenactment of a World Wrestling Entertainment battle-to-the-death steel cage match. Their constant bickering—no, bickering was too mild; their constant warring—could quickly drive him crazy. Ironically, his twins got along better with Whitney's sons, their half brothers, than they did with each other. The older boy, Todd, was a senior at Tufts in Massachusetts. Eric used to check in on him sometimes when he went up to Nantucket, but he rarely bothered anymore. The younger son, Ron, was a sophomore at Lafayette College in Pennsylvania. Over the past two years, Whitney and the twins had frequently made the short drive through New Jersey to Easton, Pennsylvania, to spend time with Ron, particularly during football season. Eric had joined them in November to visit the campus for the annual Lafayette-Lehigh game. It was cold, but they all had a ball. It was the last time he could remember them having fun as a family. Even he and Whitney enjoyed their time together that day.

Where the hell *was* Whitney? Eric checked his watch again. What he wanted to do was leave the twins in the house by themselves while he took off for Nantucket. But Whitney, much to his chagrin, didn't think the girls were old enough at fourteen to be left at home by themselves. "Maybe sixteen, but definitely not fourteen," she'd said. It didn't matter that he disagreed with her; he couldn't act on his disagreement without drawing her considerable wrath. He saw no benefit in antagonizing his wife to that degree. It was better for him if he didn't draw that type of attention from her. So he just waited, pacing the floor of their well-appointed town house, praying that he would soon hear the key in the lock, trying his best to ignore his daughters' fighting. He couldn't even remember what excuse Whitney had given him for her absence. She was out of the house so much these days that he didn't even try to keep track of her schedule. Though she had pretty much left journalism behind for *The Lunch Club*, she seemed to be much busier as a talking head on a couch than she had ever been when she was doing major investigations for the network news. But Eric couldn't complain because he had been spending more time out of the house too. They were a long way from their loving days when they first got married sixteen years earlier. Whitney conceived when she was forty because she was so desperate to have a child with Eric, whom she called the love of her life. He wasn't even sure what had happened. Well, that wasn't exactly true. About five years earlier, after their tenth wedding anniversary, Eric began to lose interest in Whitney sexually. His sexual predilections had moved in another direction, one that he couldn't control.

Just then they heard the front door opening and the *click-clack* of Whitney's heels on the hardwood floor. Whitney walked into the kitchen to see one of her daughters in tears and the other one looking guilty but pleased with herself. Apparently, things were normal in her house. She looked over at her husband and could see the frustration and impatience on his face. As usual, Eric was in a hurry to get out of the house. Whitney scowled to herself. Even though she had been doing naughty things with Riley and had stayed out far longer than she intended, Eric could still manage to incite her wifely outrage when he acted as if his affairs were more important than hers. Okay, well, maybe "affairs" was a poor word choice.

She didn't want to get into a verbal tussle with

him, so she ignored the look on his face that made her skin crawl. When had he become such a bastard?

⚓ ⚓

"**BUT I DON'T WANT** to go to bed yet, Mommy!"

Josh could hear Megan pleading with Callie for more time. Callie's daughter was a cute, charming little pixie and Josh did enjoy playing with her, but he hadn't come over to Callie's for playtime with a three-year-old. He could have gone back home to Connecticut if he wanted to play with kids. His own. No, he had only one thing on his mind: Callie's luscious body. In other words, this was a booty call, not a rendezvous to watch *Barney*. But, truth be told, he could see the effect it had on Callie when he played with Megan. She would watch them with a look on her face of pure glee. Josh knew that if he put in enough time with the little tyke, Callie would practically jump him after Megan went to bed. So playtime in this instance almost served as foreplay. But by the fourth game of Candy Land he thought he might take a flying leap from the apartment's fourth-floor window if he couldn't stop soon. But he didn't want to let Callie know that, so he bravely soldiered on. When Megan ducked into her room and came back lugging the Barrel of Monkeys game, Josh silently moaned. But Callie came to his rescue.

"No, Megan, that's enough," she said. She looked at Josh and gave him a sexy wink. That was his signal. It was on. As she dragged a braying

Megan out of the living room, he popped up from the floor and went into the kitchen to look for a couple of white-wineglasses.

Ten minutes later, after it was explained to her that her protests weren't going to work, Megan was back, in her pajamas, hiding shyly behind her mother's leg.

"Say good-bye to Josh," Callie said.

Megan peeked out from behind Callie. "Bye-bye," she said.

"Come give me a good night kiss," Josh said, holding out his arms. Megan ran to him, wrapping her little arms around his neck and giving him a squeeze. He buried his face in her neck and hair, smelling the sweet goodness of a three-year-old. He glanced at Callie; she looked like she was on the verge of melting. *Ahh*, Josh thought. The sex was going to be good tonight. In fact, Callie was noting once again how much Megan looked like Josh—and wondering why Josh had never noticed this himself. Josh smiled at Callie. He calculated that he would have her naked in no more than thirty minutes. As she led Megan by the hand to her bedroom to tuck her in, Josh poured himself a glass of the Chateau Ste. Michelle Eroica Riesling. No harm in getting a head start. Savoring the wine, Josh chuckled to himself, remembering how he'd discovered the Eroica by accident. He'd seen it on the shelf and misread the label, thinking it said "erotica," and, of course, that reminded him of Callie, which of course gave him an erection. Now it was all they drank.

He caught a glimpse of Callie through the open bedroom door at the beginning of the hall. She was bending over Megan's bed, tucking in the covers. He could see her breasts swinging under the loose-fitting blouse. He had noticed earlier that she had taken off her bra. Josh was a real big fan of Callie's breasts. They were round, firm, and juicy before she had gotten pregnant with Megan, but her breasts after Megan were spectacular. Josh had been astounded by the improvement. They were much bigger now, fuller, with that glorious, slightly upturned tilt as they curved down to the nipples. He could sit and stare at them all day. In his experience with his wife, Barbara, pregnancy did horrible, unsightly things to a woman's breasts. After their first pregnancy, his wife's had gone from below average—a little saggy without much shape—to downright unpleasant, with stretch marks and inverted nipples. Josh was an inveterate breast man, a damn connoisseur, and he had almost wept when he got a good look at them after she had stopped breast-feeding their daughter, Caitlyn. After she had Brian they got worse. And then came little Keith, who was now eight. That last time Josh had almost been afraid to see how the breasts would emerge from breast-feeding. It wasn't pretty. He was almost tempted to ask her to keep her bra on when they made love now every Friday. Like clockwork, they met in their bed every Friday night, usually between the first ten minutes of the evening news—that was the only part worth watching, Josh would say every week—and Letterman twenty-five minutes later. Josh still loved Barbara and didn't want to disappoint her, so he made sure she still had at least one orgasm. But he had given up on bringing his A game into bed with her. It's not that she wouldn't appreciate it; he had just grown bored. They had gotten married much too soon, the year after they had graduated together from the University of Nebraska. Josh had been bored now for at least a decade. Sometimes when he walked the streets of New York, he almost couldn't control himself with all the startling varieties of incredibly sexy, beautiful women whizzing by him every moment. Once he had gained some power and found that many of these beautiful women were willing to give him access to their bodies in exchange for the possibility that they would get something in return, he went crazy with it. Over the years, he had been given little reason to stop. And Barbara didn't say a word. He sometimes got the impression that as long as he paid the bills, didn't blanch at the credit card statements, and kept her country club membership current so she could play tennis three times a week, she didn't really care too much what he was up to when he stayed in the city.

As Callie swept back into the living room, Josh handed her a glass of wine. She took a sip and snuggled next to him on the couch. These were Callie's favorite moments with Josh, when he held her close, when she felt familiar and intimate with him, like they were a loving, married couple. It was at these times when her ache was the strongest. She desperately wanted to tell Josh the truth—that he, not some anonymous sperm donor, was Megan's father. But she was too scared to do it, knowing how spooked Josh would be by the admission. She thought there was too much of a risk that she'd lose him altogether. But with this Missy Adams book looming on the horizon, there was a chance that it would all come out anyway, except in the worst way imaginable. Callie needed to find out what was in that book, to know whether she had to tell Josh about Megan before Missy told the world.

"Josh, what do you think about Missy's book?" she said carefully.

Josh had moved his hand down to her left nipple, which he was now softly stroking outside of her blouse. He took a deep breath. Missy's book was the last thing he wanted to talk about right now.

"What do I think?" He shrugged. "I don't know. I know Maxine and the ladies are pretty shaken up about it. So it could be bad for them if Missy has some real juice in there." He stopped, then added, "But, to be honest, that might not be too bad for the show's ratings."

As an executive at NBN, Callie knew that the ratings also should be the most important concern in her world; without decent ratings, they'd have no show. It was their lifeblood, the essence that flowed through the veins of the network. But she just couldn't get past her selfish worries.

"You think she might have anything in there about us?" Callie asked.

"Us? What do you mean—the two of us together?" Josh said, suddenly sounding alarmed. "Does she know anything about us? Did you tell her about us?" Josh took her by the shoulders and turned her around so that they were face-to-face.

"Callie, did you tell Missy about us?"

Callie could hear his breathing. She looked in his eyes. Was that fear? What was that? She hadn't expected this reaction at all. She assumed Josh knew that virtually every woman on the entire staff knew about them, from the short, fat ladies who swept the floors and emptied the garbage cans to Maxine Robinson herself. Did he really think they had been discreet? Callie in recent years had had some of her most embarrassing moments because of their affair, slamming office doors, breaking down in tears, screaming at Josh behind very thin walls. Now he was asking about things she had told Missy? This was dangerous territory for her.

Callie shook her head. "No, Josh, of course not," she lied. "But I'm sure that she found out about us from other people on the staff. We haven't exactly been discreet, Josh."

"How do you know other people on the staff know?" he asked.

She studied his face. He was serious. Callie was astounded. *My God, what planet is this guy on?* Maybe Josh didn't even realize that every woman within a twenty-mile radius of *The Lunch Club* knew that he had a reputation as a man-whore. She almost felt sorry for him all of a sudden. Such cluelessness was a bit sad.

Callie shrugged. "Josh, women pick up on things, particularly when the same women are around one another for long periods of time. You hear things, see things. People make little smart-ass, snide comments. Believe me, dear, the ladies of *The Lunch Club* know that we're fucking."

Josh was a bit stung by her words, her use of "fucking." He wasn't even sure why it hurt his feelings. He wasn't in love with Callie or anything, but he liked carrying around the idea that she thought they had something special. To hear her call it "fucking" was a little disconcerting.

Josh blinked a few times. Callie could see that she had shaken him up a little. At the moment, she was glad about that. Josh needed to wake the hell up. But she knew he would be of no use to her in figuring out what to do about Missy. She wished that she had a partner, someone who could help her figure out how to handle this. For instance, she was considering just picking up a phone and calling Missy straight up. Was that a good idea? Maybe it wasn't. But who could she confide in who would tell her that?

Josh let go of her shoulders and slumped back down on the couch. He was starting to feel sorry that he had chosen to spend the night with Callie. He had gotten a call just before five from Arianna, one of his new fuck buddies, a delightful blonde with an incredible rack whom he had met at the gym a couple of months back. Arianna was so easy, so laid-back and open, that they were in his bed only ninety minutes into their first date. But he had already begun to set up the evening with Callie, so he told Arianna he wanted a rain check. What had done it was the sight he caught of Callie, bent over a file cabinet in a short, tight skirt. The skirt had been riding up her lovely round ass, showing that long, wonderful expanse of flesh that she called legs, stretching into infinity. He imagined her long legs wrapped around him and decided instantly that they would spend the night together, even if it meant an evening of toddler playtime.

Callie rested her head on his chest. There was an uneasy silence between them, both of them lost in their thoughts. Josh wondered if he should perhaps split—maybe it wasn't too late to give Arianna a call. Callie wondered if this lugheaded man on her couch would ever come to his senses, ever get a clue about what was swirling around him. Ever realize that the precious little girl in the other room was his. She decided that she would have to accept him for what he was, at least at the moment. She'd have to go elsewhere to get some intel about Missy. Maybe a good, intense sex session with Josh was exactly what she needed to take the stress off.

Callie stretched her neck and planted a hard kiss on Josh's lips. She moved up so that she was lying directly on top of him. She opened her lips and their tongues met. He moved his hands down and slipped them inside of her slacks, cupping her smooth ass cheeks with both hands. She shivered at his touch and pressed her crotch against his, feeling the bulge in his pants pushing into her. They explored each other's mouth and tongue for several minutes. Callie began moaning loudly as they kissed. Their eyes were both closed so tight that neither of them saw Megan come into the living room.

"Why are your hands inside Mommy's pants?" Megan said. She was standing right next to the couch, so close that her voice sounded like it had been amplified by speakers. Josh bolted upright so quickly that Callie was suddenly pitched over onto the floor. She hit the carpet with a thud, right at Megan's feet. Megan giggled as she looked down at her flustered mommy, whose face had turned a deep shade of red.

"Megan!" Callie said, scrambling to her feet. "What are you doing out here?"

"I need a drink of water," Megan said.

Callie grabbed her daughter's hand and yanked her toward the kitchen, pulling a bit harder than she intended. Josh wanted to be upset, but in fact was amused by the scene—it was like something that would have happened on one of those hilarious seventies sitcoms like *Laverne & Shirley*. He rolled his eyes and slammed his head back down onto the couch pillows. *Boy, Megan knows how to kill a mood.* He thought back to his teenage years, to his grandmother in Nebraska, constantly interrupting him and Barbara as they tried to sneak kisses and gropes while they watched a movie in the family room. Josh smiled at the memory.

"What are you smiling at?" Callie said, as she stood in the kitchen next to Megan, who was downing a cup of water, half of it running down her pajama top.

"Just thinking back to something from my childhood," he said. He pointed at Megan. "Looks like she's taking a little bath."

Callie looked down. "Megan! You're getting it all over you!"

She grabbed a paper towel and patted the girl's chest, then pulled her back toward her bedroom.

"Josh, maybe you should meet me in the other room," she said over her shoulder.

Josh knew that the "other room" was Callie's bedroom. He jumped up from the couch. He collected their glasses and the wine bottle and rushed toward Callie's bedroom, which thankfully was on the opposite side of the apartment from Megan's. Five minutes later, Callie joined him in the bedroom. She turned the latch on the doorknob, locking Megan out just in case. Callie turned around and smiled at Josh, who was already naked under the sheets. She slipped off her blouse and slacks, leaving on her panties. She stood at the side of the bed for a moment, as if she was posing. In fact, that's exactly what she was doing. Callie loved the look on Josh's face when he saw her naked. Whenever her confidence was lagging, a night spent with

Josh was precisely what the doctor ordered to get her strut back. She had always been pretty, so her attractiveness was something she had long taken for granted—until she got pregnant and gained forty-eight pounds. When she looked in the mirror during those months, she was devastated by what she saw. She had worked hard to drop the pounds after Megan was born, but she knew never again would she take her looks for granted.

"My God, you're so perfect," Josh said. And he meant it.

Callie beamed. She bent over and slowly slid her panties off. She pulled back the covers and joined Josh in the bed. She was glad that she had just changed the sheets that morning. They met in the middle of the bed in a long, impassioned embrace, both enjoying the feel of the other's naked flesh. Josh buried his face in Callie's neck. He loved her smell, fresh and sweet, like a meadow of new flowers in springtime. Josh left her neck and began nibbling her shoulders. He moved the nibbles and kisses down to her breasts, those glorious breasts. He could spend the rest of the night savoring and worshipping her breasts. But Callie had other ideas. She pushed Josh back on the bed and then made her own way south. She grabbed his shaft tenderly, lovingly, like it was an old friend. When she moved her head and took him inside of her mouth, she couldn't help but smile to herself as he unleashed a deep, guttural groan.

CHAPTER 4

Lizette arrived at the Starbucks before Tim, so she sat over her cup of Mocha Light Frappuccino and waited for his arrival. She was a little apprehensive about seeing him after all these years. For about two years, she had worshipped the ground that Tim Stratton walked on. She remembered the first time she saw him strutting across the Yale campus, walking toward her while he chatted with a few buddies. All she could see was blond hair, dimples, and incredibly broad shoulders. She thought he was one of the most gorgeous boys she had ever laid eyes on. She wanted to just reach out and touch him to make sure that he was real. Lizette was by no means the boy-hungry type, so she was surprised by her visceral reaction to him. She was afraid that she might never see him again, that he might continue walking past her and be gone from her life forever, like a mirage. She desperately wanted to say something, do something to get his attention. But she was tongue-tied and paralyzed.

Tim, who was about six-five, glanced down at her as he walked by. Lizette gave him the broadest, most embarrassing smile she had ever mustered. And it worked. Tim slowed down. After he had passed her, he turned and told his buddies he would catch up to them. He strolled over to Lizette and began a conversation that didn't end for two years.

The door to the midtown Starbucks swung open and Tim walked in. He spotted Lizette right away and gave her a bright smile. He was still as gorgeous as ever. In fact, more so. The last ten years had treated him well. He sauntered over wearing his usual khakis and a blue blazer with a crisp baby blue shirt, his gait still as relaxed and unhurried as ever. He approached her with his arms wide, as if he expected a big hug. Lizette popped up from her chair and gave him the hug. He held her close and tight, for a little too long. Lizette had wondered what his mind-set would be. She was already getting a clue.

"My God, you look fantastic!" he said, as he gripped her shoulders and held her away so that he could get a good look at her. Lizette didn't want to blush at the compliment, but she couldn't help it.

"Thank you, Tim. You look pretty great yourself."

They sat down together, Tim studying her like there would be an exam later. Lizette looked in his direction, but she couldn't match the intensity of his gaze. She didn't want to.

"So, let's get the important stuff out of the way,"

he said. "I know you're not married because Clare told me you weren't when I ran into her a while back." He smiled. "That is, unless you've gone and gotten married since I saw her." He looked at her quizzically, waiting for an answer.

Lizette shook her head. "No, I'm not married."

"Engaged?" he said.

Lizette hesitated for just a second, thinking about her upcoming dinner with Channing later that night. She might be engaged in about twelve hours, she wanted to tell him. But she wasn't yet. So she had to shake her head, though it pained her to do so.

"But I have a serious boyfriend," she said, just to make sure Tim didn't get any ideas.

He nodded. "I'm sure you do. You look incredible. I would have been surprised if some guy hadn't snatched you up by now. In fact, I'm a little surprised you aren't married yet. As I recall, you wanted to have three kids by the time you were thirty-two. So you're a bit behind schedule, aren't you?"

Lizette had forgotten about her silly college schedules for her life. Things don't always work out according to the college schedule. She was a bit touched that Tim had remembered. She shrugged.

"Well, life has a funny way of coming along and messing up our college plans, doesn't it?" she said. "Why aren't *you* married?"

"Well, as you might recall, I told you that I had no intention of getting married. Remember, that was one of the things that led to our breakup? You weren't pleased at all to hear that. So since I was graduating and going to law school, we thought it best if it just ended. This doesn't ring a bell?"

It was all starting to come rushing back now, a flood of memories, those last painful days with Tim, the arguments, the crying, the accusations. She was supposed to stay on campus with him until graduation—in fact, they had plans to spend that entire week leading up to graduation in bed, with no worries, no classes to interrupt their love-making—but she had fled back home to New Jersey several days before graduation. His exiting back as he left her room after the fight was the last thing she saw of Tim Stratton, up until the moment when he walked into the Starbucks ten years later. Tim had gone on to law school at Columbia and she'd lost track of what happened to him after that. She had graduated from Yale a year later and gotten a job at NBN in the publicity department, starting a steady rise.

"Yes, it does ring a bell, Tim. I guess things didn't exactly end on a smooth note with us, huh?"

He shook his head. "No, they didn't." He leaned forward, his big, piercing blue eyes searing a hole in her face. "But that doesn't mean we can't, uh, be nice to each other now."

Lizette could tell that he wanted to say something else, but he hesitated and changed his mind at the last minute. He had been flirtatious over the phone, but she didn't expect him to be this—what was the word?—aggressive. But she had come here for a purpose, to persuade Tim to help her get her hands on Missy's manuscript. She wasn't above using her feminine wiles to get what she wanted, even if it meant exploiting a previous relationship. These were not the kinds of lessons she learned in the classrooms of the Ivy League; no, these lessons had come later, after she left Yale behind and got her instruction from life in the big city.

"How's your family, Tim?" Lizette said, trying to change the subject. "Your sisters, your parents?"

Tim sat back in his chair. His relationship with his parents had always been complicated. It was the typical blue-blood WASP story—the hard-driving, incredibly successful father pushes his son too hard and earns his undying hatred and resentment while the mother sits back and watches in anguish as her son flees the homestead.

"Ah, my parents are fine. My mom is trying to convince my dad to retire. But after the hits Wall Street took in the last few years, my dad doesn't want to leave the firm he started when it's in the most vulnerable state that it's been in in decades. So he's probably working almost as hard now as he did when he first started the firm like forty years ago. I try to get up to Connecticut to see them as much as I can. Mom's health hasn't been that great. My sisters are both married and living in the suburbs, one in Greenwich and one in Scarsdale. One of their husbands works for Dad's firm, the other is at Goldman. It's all terribly predictable, isn't it?"

Lizette smiled. It *was* terribly predictable, but she would never have volunteered that herself. "How about your family?" he asked. "How's your mom and your brother?"

"Mom's doing great," Lizette said. "She's still principal of the same high school since our days at Yale. She loves it so much, I think they're going to have to wheel her out with her toes pointed up. My brother is okay. He went into the military and did two tours in Iraq. He got a construction job when he got out. I think he's been promoted to a foreman. He's still living back in Bergen County. He just got engaged to a girl he used to date in high school."

Lizette wondered if Tim would pick up on that last statement. He didn't disappoint.

"Ah, he's marrying the old high school sweetheart, huh? Isn't that nice. So you mean it *is* possible to restart an old flame? That's good to hear!"

Lizette didn't even want to engage Tim. He was pushing much too hard. She was willing to play along, but only up to a certain point. She already had a serious boyfriend and Tim needed to respect that.

"Sooo," Lizette said. "About this manuscript. Do you think you might be able to help me?"

Tim gave her a quick smirk, as if to say, *Okay, I'll back off.* He leaned forward and gave her a detailed plan for how she might go about digging up Missy's book. It just so happened that one of his current drinking buddies, Martin, was an attorney for Patterson & White and likely had actually done some of the legal work on Missy's book. But Tim warned her that the young lawyer was a "horn dog" who would be taken by Lizette's beauty and would probably try to get something in return for helping her out, if she caught his drift. So he said if she could stomach this Martin guy, it might be in her best interest to talk to him. As he spoke, he leaned forward and rested his hand lightly on Lizette's knee under the table. The irony wasn't lost on Lizette that as he warned her about the "horn dog," he was trying to see what he might get for helping her.

"Don't you think about us sometimes, Lizette?" he asked, his hand feeling a bit heavier on her knee. She moved her knee to the side with a quick jerk so that his hand fell off. Enough was enough.

She shook her head. "No, not really," she said. She was telling the truth. She hadn't given Tim a second thought in years.

"Not even a little? Remember that week we spent together during spring break? At our place in Martha's Vineyard? I will never forget that week, even if you don't remember it."

He smiled at her, his dimples still deep and affecting. The mention of Martha's Vineyard brought the memories all rushing back. For five straight days, they had barely left his family's gorgeous Chilmark oceanfront estate. They had had sex in every room of the house, including the two-story great room and the screened-in porch. That week, they had used each other's body as an erotic lab of sorts, exploring the sexual frontier as only college students can. Tim was a member of Yale's heavyweight crew team and, in addition to being in great shape, was incredibly strong. She could remember that feeling of weightlessness as they had sex while he carried her around the house, settling in front of the palatial stone fireplace, both of them laughing and moaning at the same time as her legs hooked over his arms and he managed to stay inside of her while he walked. Yes, now that he mentioned it, that *was* an unbelievable week. She recalled how jealous Clare had been when she got back to campus and gave her friends a blow-by-blow, day-by-day account of the week and all the places around the house—oh, and a couple of times on the rocky beaches as the sun was setting!—where they had done it. Lizette gazed across the table at Tim's still amazing shoulders and thought about how it had felt that week to be lifted and held up by his biceps as she impaled herself on him. The memory brought a tingling sensation down below. Lizette knew she had to snap out of it.

"Okay, I have to get going now," she said, pushing back her chair and gathering up her new red Prada handbag (like all New York fashionistas on a budget, Lizette acquired her stash from discount designer websites like gilt.com and ruelala.com). She hoped her face didn't look as flushed as it now felt. Tim rose along with her.

"Okay, Lizette, it was great seeing you. I hope

we can get together soon. It doesn't have to be another ten years. I'll give Martin a call and see if he might be willing to help you. But remember, if you're going to work your magic on Martin, you *have* to see him in person."

Lizette nodded. *God, what kind of raging erection is this horn-dog Martin fellow?* Tim's description of him frightened her a bit, like she needed a bodyguard or something just to occupy the same space as him. But if she ever got cold feet, all she needed was a quick image of Maxine Robinson's angry face to find some courage.

⊰ ⊱

INSIDE THE HAIR AND makeup room, the ladies were laughing at Lilly the hairdresser's minute-by-minute account of her date the previous week with a guy she had met online—turns out that the "six-two and athletic" man she was expecting to meet turned out to be the spitting image of Jason Alexander, formerly of *Seinfeld*.

"Now, I got nothing against Jason Alexander," Lilly said. "I think the man is hilarious. I might even go out with Jason Alexander. So I'm not superficial! But if you tell me you're six-two and athletic, at least be, like, five-ten, and in reasonably good shape, you know?"

Maxine, who was listening in a corner of the room, interrupted the laughter to start the topic prep for the day's show. "Ladies," she said, peering out from under her turban, "I have a question."

Maxine wore a turban before almost every show. It was how she preferred to cover her head before she put on her "hair" for the show.

Shelly, Molly, and Dara turned their eyes to her. Whitney uncharacteristically hadn't arrived yet.

Satisfied that she had everyone's attention, Maxine continued. "Are we going to ask Carla Reynolds about those gay rumors?"

All eyes shifted from Maxine to Dara, whose face began to turn a shade of crimson. Their big guest this morning, the day after Heather Hope, was Carla Reynolds, the Hollywood actress/diva who had a new romantic comedy coming out the following Friday. Though she had been an American darling in the 1990s and early 2000s, her last two movies had been big flops, and the only time she had made news in recent months was when stories had surfaced about her carrying on a relationship with a woman.

No one wanted to answer Maxine's question. "Oh, come on, ladies," Maxine said. "Don't be such pollyannas! If it's in the news, aren't we being irresponsible if we don't ask her about it?"

Typical of Maxine, starting shit just to be starting shit. "But she's here to promote her movie, not talk about this bullshit in the gossip rags," Molly said. "When she's ready to come out of the closet, then we can ask her about whether her lovers have a dick or a va-j-j. We can even ask her who gives better head, a man or a woman. I'm sure America is dying to know! Until then, it's none of our damn business." Molly sat back in her chair, enjoying the snickers around the room, but she gave Dara a quick glance.

"Oh, Molly, you do enjoy the value of the shock, don't you?" Maxine said dismissively. "And it would be so nice if that were our only concern, deciding what is and isn't our 'business.' But we don't do this show just for us and our friends on the two coasts. We do this show for the little chubby lady in Kansas with four children and six teeth, who lives in a double-wide trailer and reads the *National Enquirer* like it's the goddamn *New York Times*. And if she wants to know if a guest likes to do it with a snake, then we bloody well better find out." Maxine was on a roll. It was time to let these privileged bitches know how their croissants got buttered every friggin' morning, she thought to herself. "You all may not be concerned, but there is something else we *have* to be concerned about. It's called ratings. I don't know if you care, Molly, but ours haven't been so great lately."

More silence. No one wanted to argue with Maxine about ratings. That was not a debate worth having.

"Oh, so what you're saying is you're willing to invade the woman's privacy and try to embarrass her in front of millions of people for the sake of ratings?" Dara said, fighting through her own embarrassment.

"I said no such thing, Dara," Maxine answered. "I merely posed a question. But maybe you need to recuse yourself from this discussion anyway, since it might be hard for you to be objective here. You seem a bit emotionally connected to this particular subject."

"Damn, Maxine!" Molly said. "That's fucked-up."

"Is it, Molly? If we can't be frank and honest with one another here in this room, then how can we be frank and honest on the set?" Maxine said.

More silence. The ladies knew that statement was bullshit—they had never had any interest in being frank and honest with one another. And nobody was less frank and honest than Maxine. Dara couldn't believe Maxine was purposefully trying to force her to out herself . . . under the guise of being frank and honest. When that sneaky bitch had more secrets than anyone in the room. And God forbid someone bring them up even peripherally in a discussion on air. No one would dare bring up her son's suicide, her multiple marriages or her multiple face-lifts. *Frank and honest my ass*, Dara thought. She wouldn't know frank and honest if it walked in here and pissed on the floor.

There were more glances in Dara's direction. Dara finally had had enough. She pushed herself out of the chair and snatched the makeup cape from around her neck. She stormed out of the room without saying another word.

"Well, looks to me like one of our ladies would not be comfortable with that area of discussion, Maxine," Shelly said. "So I vote that we let the woman promote her stupid movie and keep it moving."

"Yeah, that would be my vote too," Molly said.

Just then Whitney breezed into the room. "What the hell is wrong with Dara?" she said as she put her handbag in a corner. "She almost knocked me over storming out of here."

Everyone glanced in Maxine's direction. Maxine, satisfied that she had caused enough havoc for a morning, had had enough herself. "Oh, for heaven's sake!" she said. She got up from the chair. "See you on set," she said, to no one and everyone. She shot a look at Ricardo, her longtime hairdresser. Ricardo was the only person allowed to touch Maxine's hair. Before every show, they retired to her office suite, where Ricardo removed her turban and carefully placed a wig on her head. No one on the cast or crew had ever seen her without a wig or a turban. Ricardo stood and darted out of the room, hot on Maxine's heels.

"I'll tell you later," Molly said in Whitney's direction as she pushed herself up from the chair and headed out of the room. Molly had something she needed to get from her office before the show, something in a little bottle.

When the show started and Carla Reynolds joined them on the couch, Dara Cruz's hands shook with trepidation. But the ladies treated their guest with respect and discretion. The famous actress was funny and engaging, talking about the movie-making process and even joking about how badly her last two movies had flopped. She never knew how close she had come to discussing the sexual equipment of her bedmates on the set of *The Lunch Club* in front of millions of viewers.

After the show, Maxine looked around for Lizette and was not pleased at all that her publicist was nowhere to be found. How could that girl have missed the show after a day like yesterday? Maxine marched into her office and slammed the door behind her. She was meeting Riley Dufrane at the Four Seasons for lunch and she wanted to have an update on the Missy Adams book to report to the network president. But apparently that wasn't going to happen, since Lizette was nowhere around. God forbid Lizette be where she was actually *needed.* Little Lizette had better deliver that damned manuscript, Maxine thought, or she might find herself *not* needed in the very near future.

Maxine sat down behind her desk and shook her head, angry at herself for getting flustered. She knew she needed to calm down. After all, it was just Riley. He was about as intimidating to her as a fluffy poodle.

⊰ ⊱

THERE WERE LOTS OF restaurants in the city where patrons flocked to taste some of the most inventive, interesting food around, and then there was the Four Seasons restaurant. This legendary New York institution was all about the spectacle, the place to see and be seen, where the city's power brokers lunched like peacocks strutting through the zoo with their grand plumes on display. The food *was* delicious, but the reason that people like Maxine and Riley Dufrane had been flocking to this shrine of power for the past fifty years was to cement their "juice," to make sure everyone in the city knew they still had it and how much they had. The latter was determined by where the proprietors, Julian Niccolini and Alex Von Bidder, decided to seat you when you arrived. First of all, if you were coming for lunch, once you walked up the massive staircase and were greeted by Julian and Alex, you might as well slit your throat if the maître d' made you turn left to bring you to your table. The left meant you were being taken to the Pool Room. While it's an incredibly lovely space with lighted trees (that change with the seasons) surrounding the square marble pool, it was the desired spot for dinner, not lunch. The Grill Room was the only spot to be for lunch. Only nobodies and tourists were brought to the Pool Room for lunch—people who wouldn't even know how thoroughly they had just been dissed.

Maxine was a bit out of sorts as she approached Julian and Alex at the top of the staircase because Friday was not her day. Maxine had a well-established Four Seasons schedule: she usually arrived promptly on the first Monday of every month at twelve thirty, and after Julian and Alex had sufficiently fawned over her, she would be escorted to her table against the back wall, the same table where she had been sitting for the past twenty years. The back wall, known to regulars as the banquettes, was the prime Grill Room real estate for the power elite. If someone else got those tables ahead of you, it meant that Julian and Alex had seen your reservation and decided you weren't important enough for the banquettes. The Four Seasons was such a fixture in Maxine's life that she couldn't even remember a major deal that she had ever signed during her career that hadn't been first negotiated or broached there. But instead of walking into her beloved restaurant on her schedule, on her reservation, she was coming in this time as a guest of Riley Dufrane. Riley was a Friday regular.

"Ms. Robinson!" Alex cried out when he saw her. "You look marvelous! How have you been, my dear? We are so glad to see you on a Friday. Mr. Dufrane is waiting for you. Please, come this way."

Maxine was curious to see who got a better table at the Four Seasons, she or Riley. Yes, he *was* the president of NBN. But she was Maxine Robinson. As she glided behind Alex toward the back of the room, she saw Barbara Walters at a table in deep conversation with Vernon Jordan. Although she'd never acknowledge it to anyone in the business, Maxine had great respect for the octogenerian broadcaster, who was for years *the* woman in television, after all. Maxine also spotted Diane Sawyer chatting with another woman Maxine didn't recognize.

"Maxine!" Diane said, rising to greet her.

"Hello, Diane," Maxine said. "You look fabulous, darling." In fact, Maxine was thinking that Diane was starting to look her age, though she still was a very attractive woman. "Burning the midnight oil, I see," Maxine said, as she touched the corners of her eyes as if to suggest Diane's eyes were sagging. Of course, that was bullshit. Maxine had had more "work" done than a New York City street after a water main explosion and Diane was gorgeous, but God forbid Maxine pay another woman a compliment. Especially someone she perceived as a competitor. Her own ego was far too fragile to admit that someone else could be talented, smart, beautiful, and younger than she. So naturally she took a subtle dig every chance she could. Diane chuckled to herself at the obvious crack, but of course was as gracious as ever because she knew the deal and actually felt sorry for the aging grande dame. The two women exchanged air kisses; Maxine kept it moving and Diane went back to her conversation.

Maxine spotted Riley sitting against the wall—at Maxine's usual table! So apparently their juice was about equal. She was annoyed to see that he was sitting with his back to the wall, the spot Maxine usually sat in.

"Hey, Maxine!" She turned toward the cheerful voice, which she recognized before she even saw the face. Katie Couric. Maxine despised Katie even more than she did Diane because Katie had what

Maxine envied most . . . youth and time. Smart and likable can be manufactured, but no Park Avenue doctor with his fancy creams, gels, laser treatments, or injections—and she had tried them all—could give back to Maxine the years Katie and Diane had on her.

"How are you, Katie? When are you going to come back on the show?" Maxine said, though she had no intention of inviting her back anytime soon.

"Whenever you invite me back, I'll be there, Maxine," Katie said. Maxine knew that was Katie's way of throwing in her face the fact that Katie hadn't been on *The Lunch Club* since she became an anchor. But Maxine had no interest in having Katie sit on her couch, telling them how grand it was to be a network anchor, the first female anchor in CBS history, how humbled she was to follow in the footsteps of Walter Cronkite and Dan Rather. No, Maxine had no interest in hearing all that from Miss Cute, Young, and Perky. Besides, she had been there, done that—and bought the T-shirt. After their air kisses, Maxine gave Katie a wave and kept moving.

Riley rose as Maxine approached the table. But she saw someone else nearby she had to greet. Oprah Winfrey and her best friend Gayle. Riley would have to wait.

"Maxine!" she said. The two exchanged a hearty hug; there was nothing fake about it. "I haven't heard back from you about possible show opportunities at my new network. I've loved everything you've done and want to brainstorm."

Maxine smiled at the compliment. "I know, I know. Things got so busy. Let's set up a lunch."

BW, Katie, Diane, Oprah, and Maxine at the same restaurant for lunch on the same day. If a terrorist wanted to deal a death blow to female broadcasters, today would be the day to pop by the Four Seasons. TV would never be the same.

Maxine finally faced Riley, who was still standing awkwardly, waiting for her to finish. "I'm sorry, Riley," she said. "Please have a seat."

They sat down together. While Maxine enjoyed the idea that Riley was intimidated by her, she hoped this lunch wouldn't be too painful. She ordered a glass of white wine and a salad to start. She had the same thing every time she came to the Four Seasons, the Caesar salad and the Dover sole with the delicious lemon-caper sauce. For the next fifteen minutes, they crunched on crudités and engaged in a bit of small talk about the network, the news, and politics, three favorite topics for these two news junkies. Maxine wondered how long it would take Riley to get to the point of the lunch. She knew he likely wasn't here to give her a raise, so she needed to know how bad it was going to be.

"Maxine, let's talk a bit about *The Lunch Club*," Riley said finally. "I'm sure you've noticed the ratings drop. In some markets you've been losing regularly to shows that you used to trounce.

I think the show is starting to feel a bit stale. We need to do something to shake things up."

Maxine held her breath. She prayed that this wasn't his way of forcing her to put his wife, Virginia, on the show. He had been dropping hints now for at least a year and Maxine had ignored all of them.

"I'm thinking that we need to make some changes to the couch," Riley continued. "I have some thoughts as to who I might like to see replaced, but I'd like to hear your thoughts."

"Well," Maxine said with a sigh, "this is coming as a bit of a surprise, Riley. I think I need to give it some thought before I tell you what I think." Maxine was really thinking, *What crap! Shows always tried shaking things up for ratings and inevitably there is fallout.* "Riley, we've been together for quite a few years now and I feel like we've got a nice rhythm going. But of course I've noticed the ratings and I recognize that something probably needs to be done. Let me think about it over the weekend. I'll get back to you early next week."

Riley nodded. He relaxed noticeably, relieved to have gotten that bad news over with.

"Do you have any thoughts as to whom you might like to add to the show?" Maxine asked him. She smiled to herself, waiting for him to mention his wife's name.

"Well, I have a few thoughts, but I'm still pondering," he said. "Of course, as I told you before, Ginny has been driving me crazy about it. But with all due respect to my wife, I don't think she's what the show needs right now. Not by a long shot." Maxine saw a hint of a smile at the corners of his mouth. She sensed that he was laughing at the ridiculousness of his wife. Maxine was glad to see that she wasn't the only one laughing at Ginny.

"On another topic, have you, uh, heard anything else about the, uh, Missy Adams book?" Riley said. He looked uncomfortable. Of course Maxine knew about his affair with Whitney—she'd gotten a tip from a waiter at the Inn at Minetta Lane a couple of years back when she had gone there for tea at the adorable and famous little tea salon attached to the Inn. *Yep, buddy,* she thought, *I know you're doing the do with Whitney the WASP and I'll bet our favorite little Southern belle knows too.* Even though Maxine was nervous about what Missy had on her, she couldn't help but think that it served Riley right for putting that fake bitch on *her* show. If Missy included anything in the book about Riley's affair with Whitney, things could get incredibly uncomfortable for Mr. Network President. His job could even be in jeopardy—not to mention his long-time marriage to Virginia Roberts-Dufrane, a marriage that had as much to do with his rise to the network presidency as did his talent and square-jawed good looks. Ginny's grandfather, Burl Roberts, had been a high-ranking executive at CBS for many years and had acted as a rabbi of sorts for Riley as he rose through the network TV ranks, making phone calls, patting backs, and greasing Riley's path whenever necessary. When Burl died a few years earlier at the ripe age of eighty-five, Maxine had gone to the funeral, along with practically everyone else in the industry over fifty. She could never forget the image of Ginny clutching Riley's arm much too hard as he led her to the front of the church. Ginny's father, a red-faced alcoholic who looked almost as old as *his* father, Burl, was there too, clearly in desperate need of a drink.

While she didn't have any info yet—Just what the hell was Lizette up to, anyway?—Maxine did have some intel that Riley might find interesting. She had stumbled across it the previous night while looking through her diaries at home. It was some information she had heard about three years earlier, from one of her Saudi friends. He had told her some very disturbing information about Eric Harlington, Whitney's husband. It was so disturbing that Maxine had tried to block it out. But she knew that if it was true and it ever bubbled to the surface, or God forbid Missy knew about it and put it in her book, there was no way that Whitney Harlington could remain on her show. Maybe it was time to go back to the diaries, time to put that information to use. She looked across the table at Riley as she picked over her Dover sole. The fish was divine as usual, but Maxine's mind was racing.

CHAPTER 5

Heather Hope hung up the phone and sat back in her chair with a big smile on her face. One of the production assistants at *The Lunch Club* had told her everything she wanted to hear: Maxine Robinson was in a tizzy over the bombshell that Heather had dropped on the show the day before. That was the whole point in going over there and saying the things she said—to make life miserable for that evil so-and-so who ran *The Lunch Club* like her own personal fiefdom. Of course, Heather had established her own fiefdom at *Heather's Hope*, but she liked to believe that her show was used to improve people's lives, not to allow her to continue to stay relevant and accumulate more power, the way Maxine used *The Lunch Club*. It wasn't like Heather walked around every day nursing a grudge against Maxine—she didn't believe in grudges, because the only person they really hurt was the holder of the grudge, not the target. But given the chance to shove Maxine off her high horse, if just for a minute, Heather would take it every time.

Heather shifted in her seat behind an enormous hand-carved desk, which had been a gift to her from Steven Spielberg, so that she could see the shelf that displayed her Oscar. It wasn't the real thing—she had gotten a replica made of her Academy Award to display in her office; the real one held a prominent perch in her living room at home. When she sat in her expansive office after doing another great show, Heather sometimes liked to gaze upon her Oscar, all polished and gleaming and inspiring. Walking up there on that stage in front of every luminary in Hollywood, hell, in front of the whole world, was undoubtedly the proudest moment of her life. The Academy Award was where it all began for Heather, when her career really took off into the stratosphere. It was also what led to her departure from *The Lunch Club*.

Heather had been one of the original cohosts of *The Lunch Club*, hired by Maxine Robinson to add a touch of sweetness and warmth to the panel—attributes that Maxine wisely recognized she herself utterly lacked. Maxine and Heather first met when Maxine was the nightly news anchor at NBN and Heather hosted a local public affairs program in New York whose set was in the same building as the *World News* set. The two women struck up a conversation in the hall one day and became friends. Maxine started to watch Heather's little show and was impressed by the class and humor she brought to the no-win task of interviewing local politicians and business owners, each one more boring and humorless than the last. Maxine knew right away that this funny, attractive woman with the winning smile was destined for greater things. Whenever she got the chance, Maxine would seek Heather out and compliment her on a job well done, and pass along helpful tips. Heather was floored by Maxine's compliments and interest in her career. She even came to the wrongheaded conclusion that Maxine was a sweet, warm person and would argue with any one of her friends or colleagues who tried to claim otherwise. When Maxine was booted from the nightly news because of low ratings and an inability to connect with the audience, Heather sent her an enormous bouquet of flowers—a move that earned Maxine's appreciation at a moment in her career when most everybody else she knew was quietly cheering her failure. Two years later, when Maxine got the green light for *The Lunch Club,* one of the first phone calls she made was to Heather. Heather was incredibly honored and grateful to be rescued from the dregs of local television.

It didn't take long for Heather to see the real Maxine, the one who wouldn't hesitate to cut off a U.S. senator's balls if she thought he had crossed her. (Heather knew Maxine's third husband had been a U.S. senator, so perhaps Maxine felt comfortable handling a senator's balls!) Heather was both appalled and fascinated by Maxine's take-no-prisoners, relentless approach to everything she did.

Hell, the woman was even competitive about the length of the shag in her office carpeting—Heather had overheard her on the phone once reaming out a network executive because Diane Sawyer had nicer carpet in her office! Heather vowed about a thousand times that if she ever got half as big as Maxine, she would bring a measure of humility and civility to her interactions with fellow humans. In other words, Maxine served as her constant model of what not to do, how not to be when you become a star.

These days, because she knew how competitive Maxine was, Heather really enjoyed it when she bested her in competing for a big interview or covering a big issue. For instance, Maxine probably didn't even know yet that Heather had just gotten a commitment from Troy Randolph, the bad-boy tennis superstar, that he would make *Heather's Hope* his first television appearance after getting out of rehab for sex addiction. Troy had told Heather personally that Maxine had been calling his people almost every day to get the interview, but he thought he'd get fairer treatment with Heather than with "those mean old ladies" on *The Lunch Club*. Heather had laughed at that one. Mean old ladies. Clearly he was talking about Maxine and only Maxine. She wondered if Troy even knew that Heather had once been one of those "mean old ladies."

On the wall above Heather's Oscar was a large framed picture of her on Oscar night, resplendent in her yellow haute couture, hand-plucked- and hand-dyed-ostrich-feather gown, gently attached to a light apricot-textured chiffon base, designed by Balenciaga. Yes, the gown had been a risk, but the designer had assured her that it would be wildly applauded by the fashion press and she would be called "fierce and fearless" in the 1965 vintage dress. Heather was called a lot of names by the fashion and gossip press, but "fierce" and "fearless" were not among them. Perez Hilton said she looked like "Big Bird in drag." The idea had been to make the yellow a nod to her little independent film, *The Yellow Rose of Texas*, in which Heather played the tough, wise older sister of a poor struggling welfare mom in a hardscrabble town in the middle of Texas. The title of the movie actually referred to the young mom's biracial daughter, whose African-American father had been shipped off to fight in Iraq. At the end of the film, the little girl froze to death during a harsh winter because the family's heat had been shut off, with her wailing mother clutching her tightly in her arms and screaming, "Rose! Rose!" No one in America walked out of the theater with dry eyes. Critics gushed over the movie for "giving a vivid, painful face to white poverty in America" and over Heather for "bringing a rare humanity to a people who have been long ignored and forgotten." Heather "went Charlize Theron," as she told the viewers on *The Lunch Club*, gaining twenty pounds for the role and wearing prosthetic teeth and a ratty blond wig.

Despite its modest budget and humble beginnings, the movie did huge numbers at the box office and earned Academy Awards for the screenwriter and the director, in addition to Heather. Heather remembered how much things changed between her and Maxine when she returned to the show the day after she won the Oscar. "Grandma" (as Maxine was called behind her back by the crew of *The Lunch Club*) was so jealous that the envy was practically leaking a viscous green from her ears.

So what did Maxine do? She brought on a surprise guest to talk about Oscar fashion—none other than Perez Hilton! He hadn't been on the grid—the listings the cohosts get about upcoming guests—and none of the ladies knew about it. When he walked out onto the set as Maxine introduced the segment on Oscar fashions, Heather literally almost fainted. Even Perez looked a little uncomfortable, throwing a glance at Heather and making sure he sat as far from her as he could on the couch. For the next ten minutes, Heather was speechless, in disbelief that another human being could be so cruel and heartless. The other cohosts were in shock too. As they flashed pictures of actresses up on the screen and Perez was asked to give his opinion, everyone waited for the shot of Heather. To Heather it felt like nobody on the couch was breathing, including herself. Those minutes sitting there, waiting for her picture to come up, were easily the most painful, embarrassing, nerve-racking moments of her life.

But Heather's picture never came up. The whole segment was one big taunt to Heather, engineered by Maxine, seemingly to keep Heather in her place, to knock her back down to size. The gossip columns were abuzz the next day with the curiosity of Perez Hilton coming on *The Lunch Club* but neglecting to discuss Heather's dress, which was probably the most talked-about dress of the night. One television writer likened Maxine bringing Perez Hilton on the show to a Third World dictator beheading his closest rival. As soon as they walked off the set that day, Heather was on the phone with her agent, begging him to find her another job. The events of the next four weeks were a blur: in a state of outrage—a place Heather doesn't visit very often—Heather gave an interview to *People* and called Maxine a "loon"; on the set, Maxine pretended she didn't exist; there were rumors coming from NBN executives that Heather's contract would be torched; and within a month she had been offered her own show on another network. While her anger at Maxine had subsided over the years, particularly as her own career took off so spectacularly, Heather had never forgotten how she felt, sitting there on the couch with Perez Hilton. And she had the picture above her Oscar to serve as a daily reminder if ever she needed it.

Heather thought about her appearance the previous day on *The Lunch Club*, which was only the second time she had been back in the seven years since she had left the show. She wondered if Maxine ever was apprehensive about bringing her on. That look on Maxine's face was priceless after she told the world about Missy's book.

It was time to check in with Missy. Heather's old friend was still a bit fearful and apprehensive about all the dirt she was shoveling in her book, still unsure about whether publishing it was doing the right thing. Heather had had to give her numerous pep talks over the past months, to keep her eyes on the prize, which was Maxine's head on a platter. Missy didn't mind the stuff she was revealing about Maxine; she said she didn't want to take down the other ladies on the show at the same time. But her editors at Patterson & White had encouraged her to be as sensational as possible—especially if they were going to justify the seven-figure advance they had paid her. Missy couldn't give the money back, so she had to soldier on.

There was no answer when Heather called. As she listened to Missy's sweet Southern drawl on the outgoing voice-mail message, Heather started to panic, just a little. It was the first time Missy had failed to answer Heather's call on the first or second ring. Usually it felt like Missy was sitting there clutching the phone and waiting for Heather to call her. Heather told herself now was not the time to panic. The woman was probably in the shower or something. But she couldn't help but think about the utter embarrassment if the big Missy book reveal fell through. After all the ruckus she had raised. But Heather was basically an optimistic person, with more than enough self-confidence to convince herself that things would always fall her way. Heather knew that if Missy was wavering, she could figure out a way to stiffen her friend's spine. She was absolutely sure of it.

⊰ ⊱

MOLLY WONDERED IF PEOPLE who were about to die could tell that the end was near, because she surely felt like she was about to punch her card. She didn't even know how she had gotten through the show that morning. The last twenty-four hours all seemed like a hazy dream. Since Heather's news about Missy's book, Molly had dived off the deep end, pushed by her panic about Missy's revelations. If Missy told the world about her pills, she just knew it would be over for her. She couldn't remember how she got up that morning, how she made it to the set, how she got back home. She was now stretched out on the couch in her living room, trying to stave off the desire to eat or take the pills. In her confused, misguided effort to beat back the food cravings, Molly had been living on Xanax alone for the past day. Her body was literally crying out for food, protein, *something*, but in her dazed state Molly was misreading the signs as the food cravings that tortured her daily—rather than a starving body screaming for sustenance. She had once told a friend that food addictions were the hardest thing in the world to overcome because, while a crack addict doesn't need crack to stay alive, a food addict still has to eat. Molly wondered if Maxine could tell that morning in how bad a state Molly was. If she could, she didn't say a word about it. She also wondered again just how much Missy knew about what she was going through. After all, Missy still had many friends on the set. Molly tried to push herself up from the couch. She was ready to give in to the food craving and find something to eat in the kitchen. But she started to feel a heavy dullness settle over her. She recognized it as sleep, so she gave in to it. She let go, even though she was crouching next to the couch. She collapsed next to it, stretching out in the middle of her living room floor.

Molly remained out cold on the floor for more than an hour. Luckily, her cleaning lady, Susanna, came in every Friday afternoon to give the place a deep clean—and Susanna had her own key. As soon as she saw Molly stretched out, she let out a scream and rushed over to her.

"Miss Stein!"

Molly heard muffled noises but assumed it was part of a dream, so she didn't wake up. In a panic, Susanna grabbed the phone and dialed 911. Slowly, Molly finally opened her eyes, to find the round, pudgy face of her cleaning woman staring down at her, a terrified look on her face.

"Miss Stein! Are you okay?"

Molly sat up. She noticed that the cleaning woman, whose name she suddenly couldn't remember, was holding a phone to her ear.

"Who are you calling?" Molly said, her voice starting to rise in panic.

"I call 911," Susanna said in her heavy Portuguese accent.

Molly bolted upright. "You called 911?! Oh my God!"

Molly snatched the phone from the woman and pressed the Off button as she heard a voice calling out on the other end. No, she couldn't have an ambulance rushing to her house, attracting all kinds of attention! Something like that could make its way into the newspapers. Maxine could find out and decide Molly needed to be taken off the show. It all could spell total disaster. Molly pushed herself up from the floor. She glared at Susanna, whose face was a mask of confusion.

"You shouldn't have done that!" Molly yelled. "What am I going to do now?! They're still gonna come! You can't stop them from coming, once you call. Oh God!"

She put her hands to her head, trying to think. "We have to get out of here," she said. In a rush, suddenly moving quickly, she started pushing Susanna toward the door. Susanna pulled back her shoulder in a gesture of annoyance, trying to keep this crazy woman from putting her hands on her. Molly slammed the door shut behind Susanna, then looked around the room, deciding what she needed to bring with her. But she had a hard time thinking clearly. Where could she go? She picked up her purse and scurried toward the door. She gave her place one more look, then she ran down the hall, already out of breath by the time she got to the elevator. There were only three other apartments on Molly's floor; she hoped none of her neighbors emerged now to see her in such a state, disheveled, confused, panicked, looking a bit psychotic.

When Molly got down on the street, she could hear the wail of ambulance sirens approaching. Or maybe it was the police. She still felt light-headed and out of sorts. Her nap on the floor hadn't helped much. Molly remembered that she had a show in Atlantic City the next night and she needed to save her voice so she could hit the high notes. Maybe she could go down there a day early, get some rest. Maybe Rain, who was headlining, could go with her. Molly fished her cell out of her big handbag and called Rain's number. Dara answered.

"Dara, this is Molly. I was looking for Rain. I want to go down to AC tonight, maybe do something to rest. I feel *real* tired."

Right away, Dara knew something was wrong. Molly sounded almost unintelligible, like she was talking with a mouth full of cotton in a wind tunnel. Dara knew about Molly's pills and all of her various problems. Something had happened to her. Maybe something bad.

"Molly, where are you right now?" Dara said, trying to keep the panic out of her voice.

"Where am I? I don't know, somewhere on the

street. I had to get out of there. You know what that fat bitch did, she called the fuckin' ambulance on me! She called 911. I couldn't stay there."

Now Dara was panicked. "Molly, honey, can you get in a cab and come over here, you think?"

"You want me to come all the way down there to Tribeca?"

Perhaps that was a bad idea, Dara thought. Maybe she should go and get her. "Where are you right now, Molly?"

"I feel like I need to sleep. I think that's my problem." Her voice started to trail off.

"Molly!" Dara practically shouted into the phone. "Molly! You can't go to sleep right now because you have to come here!" Dara wondered if perhaps Molly had OD'd on the anti-anxiety pills. How serious was a Xanax overdose?

"Okay, Dara. I'll see you soon." And with that, Molly was gone.

"Molly!" Dara shouted into the phone. She heard nothing but the coldness of cell phone silence. Her heart pounding, Dara punched in Rain's number.

"Rain! I think something is wrong with Molly, like maybe she overdosed or something."

"Huh? Where is she?" Rain said.

"I think she's on her way here!"

"You *think*? What does that mean? How could she be on her way there if she overdosed?!" Now Rain was yelling.

"Rain, why are you arguing with me?" Dara said. "Just get down here as soon as you can!"

⊱ ⊰

AS SHE WALKED OUT of the Four Seasons, her discussion with Riley still bouncing around in her head, Maxine called Karen Siegel and told her they needed to meet right away. Karen fretted for the next forty-five minutes, wondering what was about to go down. When Maxine finally breezed into the office, she gestured at Karen to follow her.

Maxine didn't waste any time. As soon as she hung up her coat, Maxine turned to Karen and said, "Riley Dufrane wants us to shake things up. Somebody has to go."

Karen almost gasped out loud. It had been several years since Dara replaced Missy, the last change that had been made to the couch. The trauma surrounding Missy's dismissal had taken months to die down. It took a while, but eventually everyone had grown comfortable with the current cast of characters. Now they were going to have to endure another traumatic upheaval? Karen sighed. Never a dull moment.

"Let's discuss our options here," Maxine said as she sat behind her desk and leaned back in the oversized leather chair. "Who do we think is the least effective cast member right now?"

Karen took the seat opposite Maxine, a bit flattered that Maxine still valued her opinion. But she wasn't willing to start the discussion. She'd let Maxine go first.

"My first thought is Whitney," Maxine said.

"I'm starting to think that she's getting increasingly distracted of late. I don't really see her contributing a lot to most of the discussions. She's usually not prepared, either."

Karen cleared her throat. "Um, well, I'm not sure I agree with that." Out of the corner of her eye, she saw Maxine's right eyebrow rise. But she didn't let that scare her. "She's not always willing to discuss some of the gossip items at length, but I think that's because she finds it distasteful, not because she's unprepared. I feel like Whitney's certainly more prepared than, say, Molly."

"You think I enjoy tossing around all that ridiculous crap about who's sticking it to whom this week?" Maxine said, a bit offended by Karen's insinuation. But Maxine caught herself before she pushed further. She wanted to encourage Karen to speak freely, not to scare her away. "Anyway, back to Whitney; how much of a fan base does she have? Do you get the impression that people would care one way or the other if she were replaced?"

Karen was cautious about answering that question. Whatever Whitney's fan base was, Karen thought it odd that Maxine would start with her. Did she really think that Riley would go along with slashing his lover, his mistress of at least the past two years? Was Maxine really aiming to get rid of Whitney, or was something else going on here? But it wasn't her job to second-guess the all-powerful Maxine Robinson.

"I think she lends us significant credibility,"

Karen said. "With her background and, of course, *your* background combined, we're able to talk about any major issue of the day, including politics and the economy."

Maxine nodded. "Yes, that's true." She was silent for a moment. "What about Molly? Can we afford to get rid of her?"

Karen shook her head. "In my opinion, she's kind of indispensable. Her wit is invaluable." Karen thought back to the previous day's show, when Molly was able to take Heather down a few notches at exactly the right moment and defuse an incredibly tense situation. She was like a one-woman bomb squad.

"*Nobody* is indispensable," Maxine said. She might have added, "except me," but didn't really consider that necessary. Karen didn't consider it necessary either. Karen wondered if Riley Dufrane considered Maxine indispensable. Would he be willing to pull Maxine off her own show, a television groundbreaker that she had created from her own imagination and that had sprouted imitators all over the dial?

Karen wasn't sure how to respond to Maxine, so she nodded and remained silent. "How about Shelly?" Maxine asked. "What are your feelings on her?"

Karen shrugged. "Well, I think she represents an important demographic, both she and Dara. I think Shelly adds some spice to the show. And Dara adds a great deal of class. I can't really see letting either of them go. We'd take a serious hit if we did."

Maxine scowled. She didn't like the idea of anybody attacking her commitment to blacks and Latinos. She had opened doors for so many black and Latin women in television, she deserved her own museum somewhere. So if she wanted to axe a black woman or a Latina from her damn show, anybody who wanted to challenge her on it could kiss her big, round, light brown, sixty-five-year-old ass. But then again, she knew Karen was right. They *would* take a serious hit.

"So damn, where does that leave us?" Maxine said, mainly to herself. "I think that brings us back to Whitney."

Again, Karen wondered if Maxine knew something about Whitney she didn't know. Maybe something was coming down the pike, headed straight at Whitney's head.

"Okay, well, we'll revisit this," Maxine said. She pivoted around in her chair and turned on her computer. That was Karen's cue to get the hell out.

⊰⊱

LIZETTE WAS HEADED BACK to her office when her cell phone rang. The phone played the ominous opening notes of Beethoven's Fifth. That was the ringtone Lizette used for Maxine.

"Lizette, where *are* you, dear?"

Lizette didn't like the strained, unhappy sound of Maxine's voice. This definitely was not a social call.

"Um, I'm on my way back to the office. I met

with a publishing contact this morning. I think I might be close to getting my hands on that manuscript." Lizette figured that she would throw everything she had at Maxine right away, to lessen the sting of what was about to come.

There were a few seconds of hesitation on the other end, as if Maxine were recalibrating her tone to account for the new information. "Hmm, that's good, Lizette. Very good. But in the meantime, have you seen this new gossip site on the Internet, this chattercrazy.com?"

Lizette had never heard of chattercrazy.com. She had a sinking feeling in her stomach. A new gossip website that could get Maxine's attention was something a publicist was supposed to know about.

"Um, no, Maxine, I haven't seen it."

"Well, darling, there is an interesting little story on this chattercrazy today. Actually it's the lead story. It's about me, and it says that I was *apoplectic* yesterday after Heather Hope's appearance, and that I directed my publicist to get her hands on Missy's book."

Lizette stopped walking, right in the middle of a New York City sidewalk, causing two people behind her to bump into each other, like a pileup on the expressway. Lizette was floored. She felt a sudden hurricane brewing in her stomach.

"Wow, that's crazy, Maxine! Where the hell did they get that from?"

"Well, that was exactly the question I had for

you, Lizette. How many people could have known what I said to my publicist?"

Damn, was Maxine actually accusing her of leaking something like that? What exactly would Lizette have to gain by giving such information to a gossip site?

"Well, Maxine, quite a few people heard you yesterday when you came off the set and gave me those instructions," Lizette said. She tried to keep her voice steady, to not reveal any anger over Maxine's crazy accusation.

"So what you're saying is that we have a *rat* on our staff?" Maxine's voice was rising, meaning she was getting angrier by the minute. Lizette's job at this moment was to calm her boss, not to get her more riled up.

"No, that's not really what I'm saying, Maxine." Lizette started walking again. She was just minutes from the office, but now she wasn't so sure she wanted to see Maxine in person. Maybe it was better to let this cool down over the weekend. "Let's just think about this for a second," she continued. "Really, that story could have gotten to them in a million different ways. Usually the way these things spread is not through a direct source, but through a secondary source. Or maybe even more than secondary. Somebody on the crew like a cameraman or something could have gone home and told his wife after dinner about his day, and he mentioned what happened on the set. His wife could have gotten on the phone and told her girlfriend. The girlfriend then calls up somebody she knows at some random website that nobody's ever heard of, and next thing you know it's all over the place."

Maxine was silent for a moment, considering what Lizette said. "Well, okay, I can see something like that happening. But maybe I should give a speech to the crew about the need for them to show some discretion."

"Yeah, you could do that. But maybe we should just let it go for now and be more careful in the future about discussing things we wouldn't want to see in a gossip column," Lizette said. She could imagine the behind-her-back eye-rolling that would accompany a Maxine speech to the crew. She was just trying to save Maxine from herself.

More silence from Maxine. "Well, I tell you, Lizette, I really don't want to read any more on the Internet about what I tell my publicist."

That sounded to Lizette like a threat. But she let it go—after all, what else could she say? She could, however, turn back around and make sure Maxine didn't have a chance to get in her face about it. Besides, she had an important dinner to attend that night with Mr. Channing Cary. If she headed uptown to Saks, she had time to get something utterly fabulous that would make Channing beg her to marry him.

Lizette turned around and dashed toward the curb, waving frantically for a taxicab. After she had settled into the cab, she got out her cell phone and typed chattercrazy.com into the browser. When she read the item, she could feel the sweat forming in her palms. The item was eerily accurate and longer than Lizette expected, describing in detail how the crew reacted when none of the cohosts said anything for all those seconds after Heather's bombshell. It almost sounded like it could have come directly from Lizette's mouth. Where did this chattercrazy.com get this information from? Maybe Maxine was right—maybe there *was* a rat on the crew.

CHAPTER 6

Eric Harlington was happy. He was far away from civilization's prying eyes, locked down in the basement of his Nantucket home, where he was free to indulge his obsession. In his earlier years he tried to deny it, to ignore it, to close himself off from it. That was easiest. But only in the last five years or so had Eric allowed himself to engage the thirst, to take steps to feed it. Eric Harlington liked having sex with young girls. Before giving in, Eric had tried other ways to deal with his obsession. He tended toward thin women who weren't overly endowed—though that certainly didn't describe the woman he ended up marrying, Whitney, whose large breasts and round hips were Eric's lame attempt to force his desires in a different direction.

In his basement in Nantucket, Eric accumulated a stash of photographs of his conquests over the years, little girls he had had the pleasure of possessing, of worshipping. He resisted the many urges to look for additional pictures on the Internet, knowing that such searches would easily attract attention and leave him open for discovery. Eric was a clever pedophile; he had seen all the *Primeline* specials and read reports of FBI stings, so he was always wary about leaving a trail. His primary method of selecting victims was to do most of his dirty work overseas, far from the meddling eyes of U.S. authorities. Over the last four years, Eric had taken a half dozen trips to Southeast Asia. He used his position as an international correspondent for the Affiliated Press to feed his addiction. When he heard about a new country or city that was a haven for child prostitution, Eric would find a story there that he could cover.

He was a top-notch reporter with the unbeatable combination of an unerring nose for scandal and a smooth, accessible writing style. In the early 1990s, when Eric was an investigative reporter at the *Philadelphia Ledger*, he and a colleague won a Pulitzer Prize for a series of stories uncovering a vast scheme of kickbacks on Philadelphia city contracts that had led to eight indictments, including the deputy mayor. When Eric was hired away, he was told that he could go anywhere in the world he wanted and write about whatever he wanted. It was a reporter's dream job. He could probably go five or six months without producing copy and still not raise any eyebrows, but Eric had never gone that long—primarily because he couldn't go that long without tasting some young girls somewhere in the world.

The overseas days would be spent working as a news reporter exposing every ill imaginable; at night he would dive with glee into his own world of fantasy, where men can love little girls and no one will judge them. In the ultimate irony, Eric had developed a reputation in journalistic circles as something of an expert on Southeast Asia and he had even been a finalist for another Pulitzer for a story he had done three years earlier about sweatshops in Kuala Lumpur—oh, the joys Eric found while working on that story in Malaysia, where the sweatshops were sometimes just around the corner from endless dens of young girls willing to fulfill his aching need.

A ritual developed when Eric was alone in Nantucket. He would go to the store and get enough groceries to last him several days. He would bolt the doors and close all the blinds, then he would descend into the basement. Eric had purposely left the basement unfinished and resisted all entreaties by Whitney and the kids to have it completed. The more unattractive and scary the basement was, the less chance that his wife or his kids would snoop around down there. Eric would remove all of his clothes, get a bottle of baby oil, and pleasure himself for hours at a time while his lurid slideshow played on the laptop, the more explicit the better. Eric liked them about thirteen or fourteen, when their bodies were still in the process of growing into womanhood. The pictures were all stored on memory cards that Eric kept stashed away in a lockbox that he buried underneath boxes of discarded children's clothing, holiday decorations, and unused china in a basement crawl space.

Never once did he see his actions as perverse or exploitive. He rationalized that in many cultures, at that age the girls were already married and having children of their own. He made himself believe they were old enough to know what sex was and even to like it, so he could tell himself that they were enjoying themselves as much as he was. He would take many shots of the girls, some half clothed, some completely nude, their shy eyes sometimes fearful, sometimes empty. Then, using a tripod and a timer, Eric would join them on the bed and he would take pictures of the two of them engaged in sexual positions that he had dreamed up while excited and alone in the Nantucket basement.

Eric's predilections had come up against an unwelcome development when his twins, Ashley and Bailey, grew into young womanhood. How could he justify the things he did to these other girls when his own daughters were the same age, when he actually recognized some of his daughters' mannerisms and facial expressions in these adolescent girls halfway across the globe? Somewhere deep inside, Eric knew his attraction to young girls was a time bomb waiting to explode, so he put as much distance as possible between him and his own growing girls. He slowly began withdrawing a bit from his daughters when they hit middle school—a change noticed by Whitney, who didn't understand it, and which led to further rifts in her relationship with her husband. But the twins had become intent on spending as much time as possible away from their parents anyway, so they appreciated having a dad who no longer pried in their business.

Eric recently found a new spot on the global map of child exploitation, Prague in the Czech Republic. This time he stepped up his plans to memorialize the trip—he had purchased a small, high-definition video camera. Eric was giddy about the possibility of taking actual video footage of his pleasures that he could relive over and over again in his basement. He was scheduled to leave the following Tuesday, under the guise of a big feature on the rise and prevalence of plastic surgery in Eastern Europe. The trip was all that he could think about for the past week. He had a few more phone calls to make to his new contact in Prague, and he had to wire some money across the Atlantic. This trip was going to cost Eric much more than his excursions to Southeast Asia. White European girls were a lot more expensive than Asian ones—or maybe the dealers (pimps) who procured the girls in Europe were a lot greedier than the ones in Asia. Eric was still working on the story he would give Whitney about why their bank account suddenly had a twenty-five-thousand-dollar hole. But he would worry about that when he got back. He just knew that whatever the cost, it would be worth every penny.

⇥ ⇤

WHEN THE BUZZER SOUNDED and they heard Molly's voice through the intercom, Dara and Rain were so happy that they almost started dancing around their apartment. But when Molly appeared at the door and nearly collapsed inside, their joy turned to horror. Molly looked frightening. Her face was so pale that she could have starred in a vampire movie; her eyes were deadened, almost as if the life had been drained from them. Molly could see from the expressions on her friends' faces that she must have looked as bad as she felt.

"Damn, girl, what the fuck have you done to yourself?" Rain said, as she put her arm around Molly and escorted her over to the living room couch. "Is it those pills, Molly? How many did you take?"

"No, it's not the pills," Molly said, annoyed at Rain's insinuation that she was a drug addict or some crazed suicidal woman. "I think I just need to eat. It's been a long time since I had something to eat."

Dara and Rain exchanged skeptical looks. In all her years of knowing Molly, Rain hadn't ever known Molly to miss many meals, except for when she went through that Collins Challenge craziness, which most of her friends, especially Rain, had told her was a major mistake. That was a big reason why Molly had never told Rain about her recent struggles with food—and the pills.

"Oookay, Molly, if you insist. We got food here. We can get you something to eat." Rain threw a sidelong glance at Dara, who hurried into the kitchen and peered into the refrigerator. As Dara stood in front of the fridge, she went into doctor mode and cursed herself for not insisting more forcefully that they get Molly into rehab for the Xanax addiction. She had even discussed it with her friend Brad Lamm, who was an addiction specialist and had promised Dara that he would be able to get Molly well again and do it with discretion. But Rain had said Molly would never go along— though Dara suspected that Rain was thinking too much about the negative publicity and not enough about the best thing for Molly. In recent months Dara could see it beginning to affect Molly's work. Her sharp mind and biting wit sometimes seemed to elude her of late. Dara would glance over at Molly on the couch and she'd seem to be somewhere else, not engaged in the conversation at all. But she still got off her trademark Stein Stingers on a regular enough basis for others not to notice.

Dara now eyed the leftover *budín*, which she and Rain had barely touched after they feasted on each other the previous night on the couch where Molly was now sitting. Dara chuckled to herself at the jokes Molly would throw at them if she knew what they had done to each other on that couch twenty-four hours earlier. Instead of dessert, Dara prepared a healthful plate of cheese, crackers, carrots, and apple slices and brought them to Molly, who was busy chiding Rain for her continued insistence that the pills were to blame for her current state.

"What do I look like, a friggin' rabbit?" Molly said as she looked down at the plate. But she devoured the food, nevertheless, leaving the plate empty in about two minutes flat. They could already see some color returning to her face when she was done. Perhaps she was telling the truth—maybe she had just starved herself. But that begged the question: why hadn't Molly eaten in more than twenty-four hours?

"Explain this to me like I'm an idiot," Rain said. "Why again would you go more than twenty-four hours without eating food?"

"Explain it like you're an idiot? Jesus, Rain, since when do you give me setup lines like that? I don't even need to come up with a joke."

"No, seriously, Molly, I want to understand," Rain said, not smiling.

"All you two nosy carpet-munching bitches need to understand is that I was hungry, that's all," Molly said. "Stop trying to get all Sigmund Freud on me, okay? Dara, I know you're a doctor, but you practiced medicine about as long as it takes me to douche in the morning, so leave it alone. And Rain, you got some nerve, going on about these pills. You used to do enough drugs to make Pablo Escobar nervous about running low. I've seen you so coked out of your mind that you once even sucked a real dick, remember that? Of course, after I found you with the guy's thing down your throat, you claimed that you thought it was a dildo—yeah, a dildo with a gorgeous 220-pound black man attached to it! So ladies, back the fuck off with the pills. As I said, I was just hungry. As a matter of fact, I'm still hungry. You think you can steal some more food out of the rabbit's cage?"

Dara laughed, even though she didn't want to. She just couldn't help it; Molly was too damn funny. Rain shot her an angry glare. They had talked many times about how comedians often used humor to avoid difficult situations, or to escape the need for some introspection. That's exactly what Molly was doing right now. She could tell all the jokes she wanted, while singing those wacky, satirical songs to an always enthusiastic audience, but they both knew if she didn't confront her sickness and get some help, it would come to a tragic ending.

"Okay, Molly, we'll let this go for right now. But we're going to talk about it again and again and again until you listen to us," Rain said. "You can stay here tonight and then we can all leave for AC in the morning. I'll call my assistant and send her to your place to get you some clothes."

"I don't want one of your little peons going through my shit!" Molly protested.

Rain sighed. "Okay, I'll go myself."

"No, you two can stay here, rest, get ready for your show. I'll go back to Molly's," Dara said.

Rain smiled. "See, Molly, that's why I love this girl," she said. Then she reached out and smacked Dara on her butt, loud enough for it to make a big noise. "That, and this perfect, heart-shaped ass!"

"Ow!" Dara said, pretending to scowl. Then a smile spread across her face and she stuck her butt out, pointing it at Rain. "Do it again."

⊰ ⊱

JOSH HAD BEEN LUSTING after the secretary for weeks and on Friday afternoon he finally met with some success. He promised her that if she came back to his place, he would promote her from her lowly position in the accounting pool to work as one of his secretaries—as soon as he could. He was careful to add that last part. They were standing in a remote corridor, away from the foot traffic. Most of the staff and crew of *The Lunch Club* had already gone home—on Fridays, the place usually looked like a ghost town by five o'clock. When Josh had seen Kara walking by, her bountiful breasts posing a constant threat to the buttons on her preppy yellow oxford shirt, he sprung into action. With one hand on her hip and the other softly stroking her forearm, after about ten minutes of sweet cooing in the girl's ear, Josh had come up with his quid pro quo. Blushing shyly, her perfect dimples setting his heart racing, Kara agreed.

So when Callie came over to Josh's office at about six, a time when he usually could be found preparing for Monday's show, he was gone. Callie was upset. She was going to try to convince Josh to stay in New York for the weekend, maybe to go to the Central Park Zoo with her and Megan on Saturday morning. She knew it was a long shot—Josh had told her a thousand times that he *had* to devote his weekends to his kids, otherwise they would forget his name—but at least once every few months Josh would surprise her. Callie wondered whether he had already left for Connecticut without telling her. She scowled and headed back to her office.

While Callie was standing outside of Josh's darkened office, Josh's face was buried between Kara's legs. They were both naked on the bed in his midtown apartment. Amazingly, Kara's body turned out to be even more fantastic naked than clothed. Josh found that that was often the case with well-endowed women—God's work was infinitely more impressive than some gay designer's vision of the female form covering their bodies. Kara was a dizzying collection of curves, hills, and valleys, all natural, the female form in its perfect state. My God, he thought as he ran his hands over her astoundingly smooth skin, this girl would make a killing in the strip clubs! Her breasts were particularly unbelievable to him, two illustrations of the conquest of youth over gravity. With their size and heft, Josh couldn't fathom how they managed to jut out so far without even an inch of sag. Was this girl even in her twenties yet?

"How old are you?" he asked, lifting his mouth from her tangy center long enough to get out the four words.

Through her moans, Kara managed to shout out, "Twenty-one!"

Josh smiled inside. He hadn't gone this young in years.

Two hours later, Josh wondered whether he would ever be able to stay away from this girl. He hated to think it, but Kara made Callie look like a geriatric by comparison. Somehow, at twenty-one, she had learned how to perform oral sex better than women twice her age. Better than Callie, that's for sure. *Where are these young girls learning this stuff?* Josh asked himself. Kara was a firecracker, so sensitive and responsive that she had had four orgasms in the first thirty minutes they were together. Josh had already had two, and she was begging him to bring his "magic stick" back over to the bed.

"Magic stick?" he said, laughing.

"Yeah, like the Fifty song!" she said, giggling prettily.

"Fifty song?" he repeated, frowning. *What the hell was she talking about?*

Kara rolled her eyes. "Fifty Cent, silly! Oh forget it. Just get back in the bed." Kara rolled over onto her stomach and jiggled her naked ass, trying to entice Josh. He groaned and crawled toward her. How could he say no to an ass like that? For the first time in his life, he wondered if he could get his hands on some Viagra. He was getting too old to expect more than two orgasms in a two-hour period, no matter how sexy the girl or mind-blowing the sex. As he climbed on top of her and slid back inside, two hours' worth of female moistness giving him easy entry even though he wasn't yet fully hard, Josh prayed that his wife wouldn't be horny when he got home later that night. Friday-night sex had become a ritual of sorts for them, no matter how late he got home. He knew she would not understand if he turned her away, not when she had waited the whole week for his return. Friday night was the minimum work he was required to put in at home. But he felt a little sore even now, sawing in and out of Kara. If he was going to fuck Barbara, he would have to do it with somebody else's dick.

❧ ❦

AFTER LIZETTE AND CHANNING were seated at the Union Square Cafe and ordered drinks, Lizette was pleased to see that Channing appeared to be nervous. He was normally a picture of cool confidence, but as he fussed with the napkin in his lap and fidgeted in his chair, he was anything but. Lizette also noticed that Channing wasn't looking her in the eye. She thought that was a bit odd, but maybe he felt that his proposal would go off more smoothly if there wasn't a deep connection between them first.

To get the conversation going, Lizette started talking about the latest news at *The Lunch Club*.

She told Channing about the disagreement over whether they would ask Carla Reynolds about her sexual orientation during the show that morning. It was reported to Lizette by Lilly the hairdresser, who was Lizette's spy in the hair/makeup room. Lizette thought it was important for her to have a spy in makeup, so that she would get no surprises from the ladies and their personal lives. In fact, it was Lilly who told Lizette that Dara was a lesbian.

"So, what happened on the show?" Channing asked. He was looking at her face now. "Did they say anything about her sexual preference?"

Lizette shook her head. "No, they didn't. I think Maxine decided to actually show some respect for somebody else's privacy, believe it or not. But I'm sure Maxine would have been all up in Carla's business if Dara and the other ladies hadn't spoken up in the makeup room."

Channing grew silent, deep in thought. This was originally supposed to be a celebratory occasion. The idea was to take Lizette out to a fancy dinner and, with much fanfare, tell her about his new job. Several weeks ago, Channing had been approached by a major media company to start up a new website. The site was to focus on celebrity news and gossip and to be edgy and hard-hitting. Channing was initially tepid about the idea of doing a celebrity news and gossip site—after all, he was a real journalist, one of the finest feature writers in the country. But then they threw a number at him: they agreed to pay him a million dollars a year to run the site, with even more bonus money thrown in if he was able to hit their page-view goals during the first year. With the state of the economy, freelance writing assignments had started to shrink, even for somebody like Channing. Especially for somebody like Channing, who commanded as much as five dollars a word, far more than most of the writers he was competing with for assignments. Channing jumped at the opportunity. They even allowed him to come up with the name for the site. He chose chattercrazy. com, in honor of his deceased mother, who always used to call Channing a "chatterbox" when he was a little boy because he talked so much.

This dinner was Channing's opportunity to tell Lizette about his new job and especially his new salary. With money like that, they'd be able to buy a beautiful apartment downtown, where Lizette had always told him she wanted to buy some property when she "struck it rich." Now Channing *had* struck it rich and he planned on making Lizette his wife so they could enjoy the riches together.

But Channing now had a dilemma.

When he had used some of the behind-the-scenes stuff Lizette had told him about *The Lunch Club*, the freshman site got more than a hundred thousand page views within a few hours—already blasting the goal they had set for his first month. And Lizette had just given him even more juicy information about Carla Reynolds that no one else would have. If he waited awhile longer before telling Lizette about his job, Channing knew that he would get tons more dirt for his site. His page views would go through the roof—and untold riches would flow their way. In the end, he'd be able to get Lizette to understand. So even though the purpose of the fancy dinner had been to tell Lizette about the job, Channing made a fateful decision as he sat there listening to his girlfriend talk about her show: he stayed quiet. He took mental notes of everything that she said, then ran to the bathroom and regurgitated her comments into his little voice recorder so that he would get them right.

Before he went back to the table, Channing stared at himself in the mirror. He knew what he was doing was wrong, but once he showed Lizette how much money was at stake, how could she hold it against him? After all, how often did people in their professions get a chance to make this kind of cash? He was doing it all for Lizette. He prayed that she would understand that. In the end, wasn't that more important than some publicist job? With his projected salary, Lizette wouldn't even need to work.

As Channing returned to the table, Lizette admired the confidence in his stride, as she often did. That was one of the first things that she had noticed about him, the way he entered a room as if he owned it. Lizette had always been attracted to supremely confident men. The two of them had first met at a book party for a mutual friend. When he joined the party, she noticed him right away.

It was as if all the music and conversation ceased and he moved toward her in slow motion, like the first-meeting scene in a Hollywood romantic comedy. At first she figured, *This guy must be pretty arrogant, walking in here like that.* But instead of dismissing Mr. Arrogance, Lizette found herself drawn so powerfully to him that she practically followed him around the rest of the night until he asked her out. As he caught her watching him appreciatively now, he smiled, his dimples so deep that they looked like cavernous valleys in the middle of his face. Lizette *loved* Channing's dimples. At that moment, her feelings for Channing were as strong as they had ever been. She couldn't wait to say yes.

But then the suspenseful minutes turned into an hour, the entrées turned into coffee and dessert, and still Channing hadn't popped the question. *What in the world is he waiting for?* she wondered. She watched his hands, which kept touching something in his left-side suit pocket. Surely that must be the box holding the engagement ring, right? For a while, she thought he was going to present the ring in the dessert, like on top of the chocolate cake, or hidden inside the banana tart. So she asked Channing what she should order for dessert. He looked at her with a surprised and slightly confused expression.

"Uh, I don't know, Lizette," he said. "Since when do you ask me what you should order?"

Lizette frowned. Damn, no dessert surprise,

huh? And why did Channing have to be so snarky about it? She had to be honest with herself—he didn't have the glowing demeanor of a guy who was about to propose marriage. He seemed distracted and worried—but now she considered the possibility that maybe it was about something else. Maybe Channing had no intention of asking her to marry him, now or ever. Once Lizette came to that conclusion, the dinner went downhill in a hurry. She was mortally embarrassed by her presumptions, by her flattering thoughts about her boyfriend. Hell, she had even told Clare and a few other girlfriends that she thought Channing was going to propose tonight. They all had their cell phones on high alert, waiting for a text from her the second he popped the question. Now she would have to go back to each of them and report that nothing had happened. How disappointing. How infuriating.

"I don't even want this," Lizette said quickly, staring down at the famous Union Square Cafe Flourless Chocolate Cake with Salted Caramel Sauce and pushing it away. "I want to go home."

Channing looked up, surprised. What had happened? And from her tone, he knew she wasn't inviting him back to her little apartment for some torrid sex.

"Okay," he said. "Let me get the check."

"Yeah, you do that," she said. She rose from the table. "I don't feel well. I'm going to catch a cab back home and go to sleep." She picked up her pocketbook and her jacket and started toward the door.

"Lizette!" Channing said. Should he follow behind her? But she didn't even turn around as she walked past the bar, pushed open the door, and left the restaurant. Just like that, she was gone. Channing stood next to the table, his thoughts in a jumble. What the hell had just happened?

The waiter appeared at his side like magic. "Is everything okay, sir?" he asked. Channing stared blankly at the waiter for several seconds. Maybe he should have chased after her; maybe that's what she expected him to do. But she didn't act like that's what she expected at all.

"Sir?" the waiter repeated. Channing really noticed him for the first time. He sat back in his chair, realizing now that all the diners around him were staring.

"I'll just take the check, please," he said softly, absentmindedly patting the little voice recorder in his suit pocket.

CHAPTER 7

Though Atlantic City liked to see itself as the Las Vegas of the Northeast, anyone who had spent more than five minutes in Las Vegas knew that this was far from the truth. Atlantic City's shabby boardwalk was to the Vegas strip as a McDonald's fish sandwich was to lobster. Nevertheless, performers and comedians based in New York appreciated the presence of Atlantic City as a local venue and cash cow that didn't require a day-long plane ride to reach. Zip down in a limo, do a show, grab the cash, maybe lay your head in a nice room, get up the next morning, and be back in the city in time for brunch.

Rain, Dara, and Molly climbed into a limo early Saturday morning for the car ride along the Jersey shore with snacks, alcohol, and an abundance of good energy. Molly had awakened in a much better state than when she had gone to bed. They planned a day of spa treatments, great food, and a little blackjack in the casinos. Rain and Molly were in rare form in the car, doing abbreviated versions of their routines, making Dara laugh so hard that one time the mimosa she was drinking actually came out of her nose. When Molly poured her first drink, Dara put on her doctor hat for a second and looked on disapprovingly, worried about the interaction of the alcohol and the pills. But Rain was watching her and knew what she was thinking. She frowned at Dara and stage-whispered the words "Lighten up!" Dara shrugged and decided to let it go.

And let it go she did. At one point, after all three were sufficiently buzzed, they started rolling down the windows of the limo and flashing their tits at cars passing by with solitary male drivers.

"I can't believe I'm doing this!" Dara said, falling back on the seat and giggling like a little girl. "I haven't done anything like this since my college days!"

"And when exactly were your college days, Dara, like six months ago?!" Molly said as she crammed her own twin DDs back in their bra. "Why are you two flashing men, anyway? Shouldn't you be flashing broads?"

They heard the earsplitting honk of a tractor trailer and peered out through the darkened glass. They could see a truck driver grinning down and waving at them from the right-hand lane.

"Dara, show him your ass!" Rain said.

Dara looked over at her lover, who had that familiar wicked gleam in her eye. "My ass?" Dara repeated.

"Yeah, your ass! That'll get him so excited he might drive off the road!" Rain said. She looked toward Molly for confirmation. Molly nodded eagerly.

"Yeah, show him your lovely ass, darling! Why not?" Molly said. "Don't worry—I don't think his dick would be long enough to reach you from the right lane."

Dara hesitated. For some reason, flashing tits seemed to be a lot more casual than flashing her ass. But then again, ass flashing was how this all started. That's what a "moon" was, after all. As she sat up and started fidgeting with the buckle on her belt, cheered on by the whooping of Molly and Rain, Dara said, "Oh my God, if my parents could see me now! I think they would conclude that I was spending too much time around you *gentuza blanca*!"

Dara pulled her jeans down to her knees. She put her fingers inside her panties, prepared to pull them down too. She looked at Rain. "Panties on or off?"

Rain hesitated for just a second. "Panties off, bitch!" she yelled.

Molly and Rain looked through the window and saw that the truck driver was still peering down at them.

"Looks like he's ready and waiting for you, Dara!" Molly said.

"Okay, let's do it!" Rain said. Dara pulled her panties down to her knees, kneeling on the seat with her ass poised.

"My God, Dara, you do have a great ass!" Molly said.

Rain pressed the button to again roll the window down. When it reached halfway, Dara moved backward and stuck her large, round ass through the opening. She even wiggled it to make it jiggle a little. Molly and Rain looked out at the trucker, whose face creased with a grin so big it looked like he had just won the lottery. He gave them a thumbs-up, then honked his horn five times in appreciation of Dara's prodigious posterior. Up in front, even the limo driver could see Dara's ass protruding from the window in his sideview mirror. He also wanted to honk his appreciation.

After about ten seconds of the most glorious moon the New Jersey Turnpike had ever seen, Dara fell back in the car, laughing so hard she could hardly breathe. She tried to pull her panties back up but was having a hard time of it through the giggles. Molly and Rain, giggling uncontrollably themselves, both reached down and helped her pull up her panties and her jeans. When Dara sat up, the three of them all looked at one another, then started laughing again.

"By the way, Dara, what did you call us?" Molly said. "*Gentuza blanca*? What does that mean?"

Dara grinned. "It's the perfect name for the two of you," she said. "It means white trash!"

The ladies finally calmed down as the limo approached Atlantic City, the skyline of ornate casinos rising up in the distance, beckoning all to come dump their hard-earned cash. Dara and Rain were very pleased about Molly's emotional state, but they weren't taking anything for granted. They made a pact that one of them would be with her at all times over the weekend—they weren't to let Molly out of their collective sight until she closed her eyes that night to go to sleep.

Molly and Rain each took the stage at Caesars and killed. They had the crowd eating out of their hands. It was an impressive performance by each of them. Their styles were different enough that a Rain Sommers–Molly Stein double bill was a great one-two punch of woman-centered, snarky, insightful comedy, the kind that made you laugh so hard that you feared you might vomit but also had you still thinking about their observations, and Molly's snarky songs, days and weeks later.

When the show was over, Molly and Rain were on such a high that they insisted the three of them try their hand at blackjack. But an hour later, their pocketbooks about a thousand dollars lighter, but their spirits still floating, they moved on to Dusk, the nightclub at Caesars, one of those strobe-lit, flashing, pounding joints that try to bludgeon the clubgoers into believing they are having fun. The three of them hit the dance floor together, shaking their booties and screaming wildly to the infectious house music spun by the DJ, a skinny white kid with way too many tattoos. Though everybody on the floor pretended to be busy dropping it like it was very hot, Molly,

Dara, and Rain still managed to attract a lot of sideways stares. Most of the clubgoers tended to be tourists—much more so than at a club in New York City—so these three well-known stars moving wildly on the dance floor were bound to draw some notice.

"Ladies!" The three of them looked up at the same time to see a very tall, heavyset white guy approaching with a huge grin on his face. Dara thought he looked familiar—a thought that was confirmed when Rain shrieked happily and vaulted herself into his big arms.

"Roger!" Rain screamed. He picked her up and swung her around on the dance floor, narrowly avoiding taking out several dancers in the process. He finally put her down and she came back to Dara and Molly with a big grin on her face.

"Ladies, I want to introduce you to the *third*-best comedian in the country, Roger Mason! Me and Roger go waaay back. This is my girlfriend, Dara. I told you all about her. I'm glad you're finally getting a chance to meet her!"

Roger took Dara's hand and bent over to give it a delicate kiss. She wasn't sure whether the gesture was real or was meant to be amusing.

"I've seen a couple of your specials on HBO," Dara said. "You're a funny guy. You were at Bally's tonight, right?"

Roger nodded. "I must tell you, you look even more beautiful in person than you do on that television show," he said. Then he turned to Molly.

"And of course I know who this is. I've been admiring this lady forever, and I can't believe that this is the first time we're meeting."

He took Molly's hand and planted a kiss on it. Molly found herself drawn to him. Though she usually seemed to wind up with men smaller than she was, she had always wondered what it would be like to be with a very large man who could make her feel small in comparison. Roger was enormous—easily six-six and well over three hundred pounds. His size was a big part of his act. He called himself Jolly Roger and Roger the Giant.

"You better watch it—you start kissing my hand and I might not let you stop!" Molly said.

"I start kissing your hand and I might not be able to stop," Roger said, grinning pleasantly at Molly.

Rain and Dara shot each other a look, each wondering what was going on so quickly between these two. They were not accustomed to Molly showing any kind of attraction to men—in effect, she was the perfect third wheel for a lesbian couple. So they both were taken aback—and extremely pleased— by her bold flirtations with Roger Mason.

"You ladies mind if I join you on this here dance floor?" Roger said.

"We weren't going to let you sit down, even if you wanted to," Molly answered.

Dara looked over at Rain again. Was Molly drunk?

All three of them watched Roger as he started

feeling the music. For such an enormous guy, Roger was very light on his feet. He snapped his fingers and smoothly moved his legs and feet to the beat, even throwing in some impressive hip shaking. Molly grinned, delighted at the way he moved.

Rain moved in closer to Dara, wearing her devilish smile, the one she gave the audience before an especially naughty joke. "Hey," she said, putting her mouth near Dara's ear, "maybe we could get Molly laid tonight!"

Dara wanted to laugh and tell Rain that was ridiculous, but when she looked over at the new pair, suddenly it didn't seem so far-fetched. They were smiling in each other's faces and had the body language of a couple who wanted to get much more familiar with each other.

Dara nodded. "That would be awesome!" she said, grinning at Rain.

A half hour later, Dara and Rain had moved to a table near the dance floor, where they could giggle and watch Molly and Roger send out major fuck-me signals to each other. "Shit, I can't believe this!" Rain said. "If I would have known she'd be into him, I would have set this up years ago! I didn't think Molly cared whether she ever saw another dick again!"

"She's not *that* old," Dara said. "I'm sure she gets urges. She must have decided to just keep them squelched. But that's not healthy at all."

Rain shook her head and squeezed Dara. "Ever the doctor, right? So I guess that means the doctor is prescribing a big, fat penis for Miss Stein? Take two hot beef injections and call me in the morning!"

Out on the dance floor, Roger had moved in close behind Molly. He had his arms around her and her ample behind was pressed up against his crotch—well, maybe about eight inches south of his crotch, since Molly was about five-five. But it was still close enough to his crotch for Molly to feel a bulge start poking her in the back. The sensation unnerved her slightly, but she didn't pull away. She was enjoying the feel of his big arms too much.

"You know, I think I'm too old for you," Molly said, tilting her head up toward him so that he could hear her over the pounding music.

Roger snorted. "Nice try, lady, but I know exactly how old you are—forty-five. I'm forty-three, darling. Two years sounds to me like a match made in heaven."

"Hmm, what else do you know about me?" Molly asked.

"I know that you are single. I know that you are the funniest woman I've ever seen. I know that you are also quite intelligent, though you try to hide it sometimes with the jokes. I also know that you are the sexiest forty-five-year-old comedian I've ever seen."

Molly felt herself blush. She wasn't used to all this gushing male attention. She also wasn't used to feeling a big erection bulging into her back. She couldn't help but let her mind wander to Roger's size. It was probably real big, maybe too thick for her to get her whole hand around. Molly blushed some more, embarrassed that she had let her mind go there. But she couldn't deny the tingle that she was starting to feel in her lower belly.

"Well, certainly I'm too big for you," she said. She was eager to hear his response to that one.

Roger snorted his amusement again. "Lady, apparently you didn't get a good look at me. I'm not exactly Mick Jagger over here. I'm kind of a big guy. Speaking from experience, I'd be a little afraid for a small woman with me. Not only would I be afraid I'd squash the little thing, but I also might split her in half!"

Molly thought that last line was an unmistakable reference to his penis size, wasn't it? He seemed to be confirming in his funny Roger Mason way what she suspected, that his tool was proportional to the rest of his enormous body. Molly felt flushed, like an oven door had just been opened in front of her. She couldn't be sure if that was arousal or a premenopausal flash, what one of her friends called her "personal flame."

"Well," she continued, "just because you're big doesn't mean that you necessarily like big women. I know some big guys who prefer little, itty-bitty women."

"Yes, true," he said. He moved in closer to her, so close that she could feel his breath pass over the nerve endings in her ear, sending a tingling sensation racing down her spine. "But that definitely doesn't apply to me. I like having something to hold on to. A lot of something."

With that, Roger gave Molly a squeeze. She emitted a little girlish squeal—and was a bit embarrassed that such a noise came from her mouth. She pressed up against him even harder. Molly was still in a state of disbelief that this was happening to her. It had been so sudden. Just twenty-four hours earlier, she thought she was about to die. Now she was in the big, sexy arms of a man who was acting like he wanted to devour her.

When Molly felt like she was about to faint from arousal, she pulled away from him and turned around. She had to be careful here—there could be paparazzi lurking somewhere with a camera. Or some wannabe paparazzi looking for a big score. They weren't exactly in the VIP section of some secluded Manhattan club. This was Atlantic City, the spiritual home of all sorts of drifters and losers from up and down the East Coast.

"I think I need to sit down," Molly said. She walked toward the table where Dara and Rain were sitting and watching. Molly got the sense that Roger was watching her ass as she moved. She was glad that Rain and Dara had talked her into wearing the dress, even though it was more clingy than she was comfortable with. She had to squeeze her butt into a pair of large Spanx in order to make the dress look right. She put a little extra sauce in her step, giving Roger a good look at her butt in action.

"Wow, girl, you were doing your thing out

there!" Dara said as Molly sat down. Roger took the seat next to her.

"Roger, I forgot how good a dancer you were!" Rain said. "The two of you looked like you've been dancing together for years."

Again Molly felt herself blushing. She enjoyed the way Roger's arms felt wrapped around her. She wondered where this evening was headed. And, more important, was she ready for it?

"Listen, Dara and I are going to go back up to our room now," Rain said. "We'll leave you two down here to burn a hole through the dance floor—or wherever else you might find yourselves tonight!" She grinned at Molly, then leaned over and gave Roger a kiss on the cheek.

"Looks like it's just us chickens," Roger said with a chuckle. He turned to Molly and stretched his arm around the back of her chair. "Hey, I wish I could have caught your show tonight. I haven't seen you in about four or five years. The first time I saw you was one night at Dangerfield's. It was maybe like fifteen years ago. Let me tell you, you killed that night. I was blown away. Seriously. Not only were you fuckin' hilarious, but I thought you were sexy as hell. I've been following your career ever since."

Molly was terribly flattered. Sometimes she forgot that she actually had a strong base of fans out there in the world.

"That's so nice of you to say," Molly said, blushing for about the tenth time in the past hour. "I'm surprised I didn't see you in the crowd. It's probably hard for you to blend in, I'm guessing."

Roger laughed. "Yeah, I do stand out. Like a one-legged man in an ass-kicking contest!"

"I always loved that joke!" Molly said.

"Yeah, me too!" Roger said. They grinned at each other. Roger saw an opportunity. He leaned in closer. "Do you want to get out of here, maybe go somewhere a little more quiet and have a drink?"

Molly nodded. She took a deep breath. "I know just the place," she said. "My room. I got alcohol and I got quiet."

Roger grinned. "That sounds like a fabulous idea," he said, rising from his chair and holding out his hand to her. Molly took it. They remained holding hands as Roger led her through the dance floor and out of the club. Molly felt her heart fluttering.

⊰ ⊱

ONCE THEY WERE IN Molly's room, she was unsure of her next move. It had been so long since she had been in such a situation that all her skills in the art of romance were laden with rust, weighed down from disuse. Should she just wait for Roger to do everything? Should she have gone to his room instead of bringing him to hers? But then again, hadn't she heard that it was better to be on your home turf? And besides, Roger's room was all the way over at Bally's and the last thing she wanted to do was get short of breath before they even did the deed.

There was no need for Molly to fret; Roger was a take-charge kind of guy. And his romance skills certainly weren't weighed down from disuse. A well-known comedian like Roger Mason who spent the majority of the year on the road got more than his share of ass thrown his way. He moved over to her in-room Bose speaker and found an appropriate radio station. It was playing smooth jazz. Molly would have preferred some Frank Sinatra or Tony Bennett, but this was certainly better than heavy metal or hip-hop to set a mood. Molly sat down on the edge of the bed and watched Roger remove his jacket. He was immense. Much of it was pudge, but she could tell that he was probably an impressive specimen at one time.

"Did you play football or something when you were younger?" Molly asked. She realized that she actually knew very little about Mr. Roger Mason.

He nodded and flexed his biceps, chuckling the whole time. Molly really liked his chuckle. It was like rolling thunder, with a low, slow vibrato that made her bones rattle.

"Two-year starting defensive end for the University of Michigan Wolverines," he said. "My job used to be to kill as many people as I could every Saturday."

"Wow," Molly said. "I bet you were pretty good, huh?"

Roger nodded. "As a matter of fact, I was. I was even invited to a few NFL training camps. But I had already gotten the comedy bug in college, so I knew what I wanted to do with my life. And it didn't include becoming a piece of human chattel in the NFL, the property of some asshole billionaire."

"Well, would you mind being my property for a little while?" Molly said. She reached up to Roger and he sat down next to her on the bed, taking her in his arms and holding tight. Molly ran her hands over his arms and shoulders, loving the feel of strength and energy. Roger pulled back and looked into Molly's eyes. They moved forward at the same time, their lips meeting in soft, tender kisses that gradually built up in intensity. After several minutes, their mouths were wide open and they were engaged in the most passionate kissing that Molly had done in a long time. They fell back together on the bed, their hands roaming while their mouths explored. Molly heard a loud sound in her ears and was tempted to stop until she realized that it was her own moaning. She felt like her body was about to explode, she was so hot and horny. Roger's hand went to the back of her neck and she heard the sound of her dress zipper being lowered. He was trying to take off her dress now? But they hadn't even turned off the lights!

When the zipper was down, Roger smoothly went to her shoulders to pull down her dress. Molly felt a severe panic start to set in. It had occurred to her in a vague way that she would have to disrobe at some point, but now that the moment was at hand she felt like she couldn't go through with it. She didn't know him well enough; she wasn't sure if she could trust him. What if he was disgusted by what he saw? He said he liked his women big, but what about flabby and old? The rapid weight loss and subsequent weight gain had not been kind to her skin; it was much too loose and droopy. She *hated* the way she looked in the mirror. She was certain that a man would hate it too—particularly a popular comedian who probably had access to some very high-quality ass. He surely was used to bedding starlets and starstruck twenty-five-year-olds. How was he going to react to a decidedly low-quality forty-five-year-old with a big, fat ass and very large, sagging tits? Molly felt a painful sensation in her chest, like she was short of breath. She started to gasp for air. She pushed Roger off of her, held the top of the dress against her heaving breasts, and ran toward the bathroom.

"What the fuck?!" Roger said as he watched her run away, her retreating ass jiggling as if it too were trembling in fear. For him, her reaction seemed to come out of nowhere, as if her body had suddenly been taken over by an alien force. He shook his head, alarmed by the look of terror he saw on her face. He had thought he was about to have the night of his life, a chance to become intimate with one of his idols, but she had run from him like he was wielding a butcher knife. He did not want to believe that his beloved Molly McCarthy Stein was schizo.

Inside the bathroom, Molly was just on the verge of a meltdown. There was only one thing that could bring her back, perhaps return her to a semblance of calm. Her pills. But they were in her pocketbook, which was sitting in the chair right next to where Roger was waiting on the bed. Well, actually she wasn't sure where Roger was right now. That poor man. His head must be spinning.

"Molly?"

She heard his voice from the other room, sounding tentative, maybe even a little afraid. Molly stood over the sink, staring at her face in the mirror. She saw the bags under her eyes, the vertical lines starting to form above her lips, like prison stripes. She looked at the flab under her chin, which was more like two chins. Her jowls were heavy and just starting to sag. In other words, what man in his right mind would want to be with her? She was a fat, ugly, aging woman who probably would go the rest of her life without having sex. But then again, there was a great guy in the other room, on the bed, eager to have sex with her. Apparently she wasn't as fat and unattractive as she thought if he was willing to get naked with her and partake in her body, right? Molly was confused and scared. She knew that this was a pivotal moment for her. If she couldn't beat back this panic and allow herself to enjoy a night with this man, she didn't know if she could ever let herself get to this point again. How could she trust that she wouldn't freak out the next time a man showed some romantic interest in her? If only she could get a pill in her system. Then she might be prepared to face whatever was waiting for her out there.

She started hatching a plan. Maybe she could run out there, grab her purse, then rush back into the bathroom and take the pill. All she had to do was tell Roger that she would be right back, she just needed something from her purse. He'd understand.

Molly took about ten deep breaths, trying to calm her shaking hands. She opened the door and saw Roger sitting on the edge of the bed with a look of utter consternation. She felt sorry for him at that moment, getting mixed up with a wacky broad like her.

"Are you okay?" he asked. But Molly wasn't ready to talk yet. As she came out of the bathroom, her focus on that pocketbook containing those pills, Roger mistakenly thought Molly was walking back to him. When she was near, he reached out and swooped her back down onto the bed. He was laughing at the time, thinking that she would be laughing too. He moved down and started kissing her ears and her neck, thinking to himself that she smelled really nice and that the rest of her would smell just as good. But what he didn't expect was a loud, crazy-as-a-loon scream. He looked up and saw Molly's mouth wide open, her eyes terrorized, her hands and arms pushing against his chest, trying to get him off of her.

"Molly, what's wrong—"

"Aaaahhhh!" She kept screaming at him. It was all too much for her. And Roger too had had enough.

"Would you please shut the fuck up?" he said

as he pushed himself up from the bed. He reached over and grabbed his jacket, all the while looking at Molly, who had stopped screaming, as if she had two heads.

"Whatever the hell is wrong with you, Molly, I hope you get some help real soon!" he said as he moved toward the door. "I really liked you. I was really excited about getting to know you better. I thought that maybe this could be something. But I've had enough crazy fuckin' broads in my life. I certainly don't need another one."

The door slammed shut behind him, leaving stunned silence in his wake. Slowly, unsteadily, Molly reached out and grabbed her pocketbook. She saw a tear fall down and stain the beige leather. It was followed by many others. As she drew the pill from the bottle, Molly couldn't stop the torrent of tears. She fell back on the bed, sobbing, feeling sorry for herself, feeling as low as she had felt in a long time.

CHAPTER 8

For Maxine, the weekend was by far her least favorite time of the week. It was when all the work halted, her friends and colleagues busied themselves with family and loved-one obligations, often traveling out of the city to do so, and Maxine was left alone to rattle around her massive Park Avenue apartment and think about all the people who had left her, all the family members who avoided her. The weekends forced her to come to grips with some of the unfortunate turns her life had taken, the bad marriages, the ugly state of her relationship with Jared, one of her twin sons. The weekends made her think about her other son, Darren. Darren had taken his own life about seven years earlier. He had mentioned his mother in the suicide note, saying that he knew this final act would be his greatest disappointment in her eyes, but he didn't know anymore whether he was capable of pleasing her. She had managed to keep the note out of the press, but she still felt his words like a bitter slap. How could her own child hate her so much that he would leave such haunting words to torture her in perpetuity?

After the suicide, Jared kept his distance. It had been several years since Maxine last spoke to him. He moved to Washington state, about as far from New York City and Maxine as he could get in the United States, and now she heard he was running a food co-op outside of Seattle. Maxine didn't even have his phone number. What kind of mother didn't even have her son's phone number? Maxine knew that Jared did keep in touch with his father, Chad Ross, Maxine's second husband. This was especially galling to Maxine because she knew that Chad's family had been part of the reason Chad left her. In the end, they couldn't stomach the idea that the family estate could one day wind up in the hands of a poor black woman from Texas. No matter how famous and accomplished she eventually became in her own right, no matter how much Chad loved her and told her over and over that he didn't care about her race, in his family's eyes she was still the daughter of a sharecropper. Chad's parents were long gone now, but in her most bitter moments Maxine sometimes considered telling Jared the real reason why his father and mother divorced.

Maxine opened a bottle of wine and wallowed in her self-pity. The weekend, usually Saturday night, when she was sipping on some of the vintage selections from her wine room, was the only time that Maxine ever allowed self-pity to do a slow creep through her soul. By the time Monday morning rolled around, it was all but erased. Maxine curled up her feet on her burgundy silk couch and poured another glass of the delicious Château Pavie Bordeaux. At over three-hundred dollars a bottle, it was probably best saved for a special occasion—but at the moment, keeping her sanity seemed special enough. She gazed around her at the glory of her home, but she could get no satisfaction from its beauty. Maxine's apartment was the envy of the city. On Park Avenue, the apartment was an interior design geek's wet dream, overflowing with exquisite drapes, Oriental rugs, and heavy damask silks with gorgeous fringes framing enormous windows that allowed the sun's rays to wash over rooms full of judiciously chosen pieces of furniture and artwork. Because she had owned the twelve-room, two-story space for so long, Maxine brought in new teams of designers every three years to create a totally new home—one that had been featured in *Architectural Digest* not once but twice. She wasn't even sure how much the place would fetch on the open market these days—probably some obscene number with lots of zeros—but it didn't matter because she wasn't going anywhere.

Maxine was halfway through the bottle of Bordeaux when the front door opened and her longtime butler, William Clark, walked in, carrying a bag of groceries. He smiled at her. "Maxine, I thought we'd have some roasted chicken for dinner tonight and watch a movie."

"Yes, William, that sounds lovely," Maxine said, smiling back at him. She knew that William could help her shake off the loneliness. Dear William would make it better. He always did.

Everybody in Maxine's world knew of her butler, but there was something about him that none of them knew: William was also her lover. Her relationship with William managed to be remarkably simple yet complicated at the same time. Over the years, in between and during her marriages, William had become her "maintenance man," a warm body and reassuring presence who was there when she needed some private bolstering. William was also a skilled lover who had become adept at satisfying Maxine's needs. Most of Maxine's friends and colleagues assumed that she no longer had sexual needs, that she found them too inconvenient and had long ago banished them. She knew that the cast and crew of *The Lunch Club* called her "Grandma" behind her back. But Maxine was a different person when she was around William, looser, more relaxed, happier . . . and certainly not anyone's grandma.

There was just one problem: Maxine wanted to keep their relationship closeted. She was a bit embarrassed about anyone knowing she had established a real relationship with her butler. What would people think about the distinguished Maxine Robinson consorting with the help? Of course she never expressed these sentiments to William—though he sensed them anyway. She told William she would let him know when she was ready to go public. It had been a source of tension between them for the past few years. After much discussion—with Maxine doing most of the talking—they had agreed to keep their real relationship private. But William wasn't totally content with their arrangement, and every once in a while he would let Maxine know it.

Their relationship really started way back in the 1980s, during Maxine's marriage to Chad. Chad was one of the most successful arbitrage kings of the eighties, exploiting imbalances in the stock market for maximum, breathtaking financial profit and, like the better known Ivan Boesky and Michael Milken, often destroying venerable companies in the process. Chad was usually gone for days, sometimes weeks, at a time. Maxine was busy too, with a fast-rising television career. But Maxine also had two little boys at home, trying to raise them while tending to an increasingly demanding career. Chad did the one thing he knew how to do best. he threw money at the problem, hiring a nanny, a butler, and a housekeeper to ease the burden on Maxine—and reduce the anger she was aiming at him with growing frequency. Maxine wasn't even forty—still fairly young, beautiful, and sexually unsatisfied. William was kind and he was gorgeous, tall and graceful with a blinding smile and a body that looked like it had been carved by Michelangelo out of burnished mahogany.

Maxine was amused by her husband's clueless cockiness, to hire a sweet and beautiful black man to look after his needy and lonely black wife. It was just asking for trouble. Maxine and William danced around each other for two years, exchanging lingering stares and not-so-accidental physical contact in the many rooms of the new Park Avenue home. Maxine's longing for William was reaching a point of desperation, but William refused to make a move. Maxine would even do things like walk around the house wearing see-through lingerie or leave her bedroom door ajar when she was getting dressed. But William would not cross that line. Finally, one night, when it was storming outside and Chad was on a weeklong trip to Europe, Maxine took matters into her own hands. Literally. She got out of her bed in the middle of the night and she went to William's room. She stood over him for several long minutes, gazing appreciatively at his strong, square jaw and long, fluttering eyelashes as he slept. At last Maxine crossed the line. She removed her silk chemise and slipped into his bed, completely naked. She climbed on top of him, pleased to discover that William also was naked. When his eyes opened slowly, he found himself staring deep into Maxine's eyes. Their lips met in a deep kiss and Maxine's hands went south, taking hold of William's thickening penis, delighting as it grew in her hand. They proceeded to explore each other's bodies for the rest of the night. Maxine had three orgasms that first night, the most she had ever had in one session. She was hooked on William; he became her drug. During the day she honed her image as the tough-as-nails, unforgiving television reporter and interviewer, but at night she was disappointed when Chad was around. On a few occasions she was so desperate for William's touch that she slipped out of the bed she shared with Chad and ran through the apartment in the middle of the night to William's bed. Once she even forgot to go back to Chad after their lovemaking was done; they both awakened to the smell of Olivia, the cook, frying bacon in the kitchen. Her heart racing, Maxine rushed back to her bedroom, only to find the bed empty. Chad had already left for work. But he was so arrogant that he never would have suspected his wife was spending her nights with the help. While he had interviewed and hired William—leaving it to Maxine to hire the nanny and the cook—Chad proceeded to ignore him after that, going weeks at a time without exchanging more than two words with William. William hated Chad and the way he ignored Maxine's needs. Once they had crossed that line, William was all too glad to have his way with Chad's wife.

While Chad found Maxine's brown skin to be exotic and sexy, she liked being married to a powerful man. It worked for them. That is until they started building a family. It was one thing for this scion of New York to dally with a little brown sugar, but when children were added to the mix, it became clear that his parents thought Maxine and her children were in the family for the long haul. Chad's father had a sit-down with him and threatened to shred his inheritance if he didn't cut his losses and divorce that woman. So he started to distance himself from their marriage and their family, and right about the time that Maxine was tapped to be the first African-American anchor of a nightly news broadcast, Chad left her. He was kind in the divorce settlement, giving her the Park Avenue apartment, several expensive cars, their Sag Harbor home, millions of dollars in cash, and extremely generous monthly child support payments for their boys, Darren and Jared. In a few years, the boys would be shipped off to boarding school anyway at Phillips Academy in Andover, Massachusetts, so her time as a single parent would be very short. Years later, Maxine would regret the decision to send them away—she knew, and they were all too willing to confirm, that it was the wrong move for them, two shy, sheltered boys who still needed to be mothered. The distance was never closed. Once they were at Andover, emotionally disconnected from their parents, consorting with the children of presidents and senators (one of whom became their stepfather for about twenty minutes), they were effectively lost to her forever. Soon they both began to express their anger at their absentee mother by acting out—stealing from their classmates, sleeping with every townie tramp they could find, and taking every drug imaginable. Yes, Maxine tried rehab for both . . . but she had lost them long before Darren took his own life. Jared just walked away. He said it was because of self-preservation that he didn't want to see her. Maxine knew it was unadulterated hate.

Maxine went into her formal bedroom—the fancy one that she used for photo shoots, not the more comfortable one that she slept in—and removed a piece of art from the wall. *Blue Shade*, an original Romare Bearden, was a piece that she had bought for herself during her first marriage, before she had more money than she knew what to do with. The Bearden collage remained special to her because it started her art collection, which by now had grown to more than two dozen major pieces, and it was something she had bought with her own money when she got her first big network raise more than thirty years earlier, when Bearden was still alive.

Behind the Bearden piece was Maxine's safe, the home of the diaries. Maxine had been itching to go back a few years, to see exactly what she had written down about Whitney's husband, Eric, the disgusting details she had tried to block out. She opened the safe and pulled out a stack of the last few years. She thought it was two years ago that she had gotten the tidbit. It came at a birthday party she had attended for Mick Jagger, a wild affair that seemed to go on for at least two days. She got friendly with an obscenely wealthy Saudi prince who was quite taken with Maxine and her fame. He told her he knew some bad things about one of the women on her show. Maxine was interested right away. But then he took it in a direction she hadn't at all expected, about information he had come across concerning Eric and little girls. Reading it again made Maxine's skin crawl. Maxine knew there was no way Whitney was aware of this stuff—and Whitney was too busy rolling around the Inn with Riley to be keeping tabs on her pervert husband anyway. Ugh, what a mess! Maxine had to figure out how she could use this information, maybe get rid of Whitney and her pompous WASP ass once and for all.

"Maxine. Dinner's ready, darling," William called to her from the kitchen. She hurriedly put the diaries back into the safe before William came looking for her. He hated when she let the food get cold. She went into the kitchen and sat down at the table, which William had artfully decorated with candles and a beautiful centerpiece he got from the dining room table, which Maxine rarely used. He put a plate of roasted chicken, garlic mashed potatoes, and a colorful salad in front of her, simple but delicious.

William sat down to join her at the table. This he had only started doing in the last year. Even after she was no longer married to Chad, William stubbornly ate in the small kitchen in his own living quarters. He said if he was only going to be her lover in private, then he should stay in his place and let her eat in private too.

"You were in there looking at the diaries, weren't you?" William said. Maxine could hear the scold in his tone and she instantly got annoyed. She had long since grown tired of William's efforts to "reform" her, to make her into a "better" person. As she had told him a thousand times, she liked herself plenty just the way she was.

"Why do you give them to me as gifts if you don't want me to use them?" Maxine said.

"I thought you were going to use them to write your memoirs, not for all your vendettas," he said, shaking his head like a disappointed dad. "Every time you go to the diaries, somebody's head's gonna roll."

Maxine frowned. Okay, maybe there was just a little bit of vendetta involved, enough so that she really couldn't deny his accusation. William was just about the only person on the planet who could get away with scolding Maxine—but that didn't mean she liked it.

"It's all about self-protection, William. I told you what Missy is trying to do to me."

"Maxine, when are you going to stop caring about what all these ridiculous people think?" he said. "You are one of the most famous journalists in the world, one of the richest, one of the most accomplished. At this point, no one can ever take any of that away from you. So just calm down and enjoy what you have accomplished. Why can't you do that?"

Maxine shook her head. William would never understand this side of her, the drive that kept her pushing 24/7. She was a sharecropper's daughter from Texas and she always would be. No matter how much she accomplished in her life, she knew she would never be able to erase that basic fact of her being. It would always be the dependent clause in the first sentence of her obit: "Maxine Robinson, the daughter of a sharecropper from Texas . . ." Even if she found one day that she wanted to stop, or let up on the accelerator, she didn't think she'd ever be able to. Her drive was such an elemental part of her personality now that she didn't think she could ever turn it off.

They ate the rest of their dinner in silence, both of them lost deep in their thoughts. Maxine helped William wash the dishes and they retired together to her entertainment room, where she had a mammoth television and several extremely comfortable sofas lined up like pews. William asked her to choose between two movies, a new one starring Denzel Washington in a rare romantic comedy and a political thriller starring Tom Hanks. Though she preferred to snuggle with William and watch Denzel be romantic, Maxine chose the Hanks thriller—after all, he was due to be a guest on the show in a couple of weeks.

⊱ ⊰

AS SHE SAT ACROSS from Martin Peters on Monday morning at the same Starbucks where she had met Tim Stratton, Lizette chuckled to herself that Martin was just as advertised. The guy was as obvious as the clock on the wall. Or the breasts that were staring him in the face. Lizette had labored for about an hour over what she should wear. She had consulted with two different girlfriends. The dilemma was whether she should go for the cleavage-baring temptress and risk offending him with her obviousness, or go for a slinkier dress that was form-fitting but a bit more subtle. Lizette had gone for the obvious and as she watched Martin fidget, his eyes drawn to her breasts like a fly to sugar, Lizette instantly knew she had made the right decision. Subtlety would have been wasted on Martin Peters. But she also felt an inkling of embarrassment. It was one thing to play dress-up and imagine herself as the vampy seductress, as if wearing one of those slutty Halloween costumes, but it was another thing to actually play out the scene and watch the guy salivate over her breasts. A real, live guy with real, live saliva. His reaction was making her a bit squeamish, a bit ashamed that she was becoming, if just for an hour, one of those women she had always despised—the ones who used sex to get ahead.

"Wow, you're as gorgeous as Tim said you were," Martin said, trying real hard to keep his gaze from sliding down to her chest. "It's really nice to meet you."

Lizette almost wanted to laugh at his struggle to look her in the face. She had to fight against the urge to get cocky, thinking this had the potential to be as easy as taking candy from a baby. If there were even a distant possibility of coochie staring him in the face, how much would Martin be willing to give up? That was the only real question here.

While he wasn't as achingly good-looking as Tim, Lizette was sure Martin Peters was sufficiently good-looking to score enough success in the desperate New York singles market to keep up his "horn dog" reputation. He had a mop of sandy blond hair and a genial expression, reminding her a bit of the actor Owen Wilson. Lizette had to remind herself not to take Martin too lightly. After all, he apparently was bright enough for a major publishing house to hire him as a lawyer. But the guy looked like silly Owen Wilson, with the same innocent expression and goofy smile—how seriously could she take him?

"So," Martin said. He was smiling at her, his baby blues sparkling in the morning sunlight. "You said you were interested in talking about a particular book."

"Yes, I am. As I told you, I'm the publicist for a television show."

"You didn't tell me which show," he said.

"It's *The Lunch Club.*"

"Oh, the Maxine Robinson show! Well then, I know which book you're interested in. That's all you had to tell me. You want to know about *Satan's Sisters.*"

Lizette almost choked on her coffee when she heard the title. Did he really say *Satan's Sisters*? That was the name of Missy's book? Oh God, Maxine's head was going to spin like in *The Exorcist* when she heard that. Lizette tried to play off her shock, to pretend she already knew the book's title.

"Yeah, that's the one," Lizette said, aiming for breezy nonchalance.

Martin laughed. "Yeah, that book is pretty outrageous. But I know we have high hopes for that title. The preorders have been through the roof. I think we're supposed to be shipping like two hundred thousand to Barnes and Noble alone. That means it's sure to debut on the *New York Times* list in the first week. It's going to be explosive when it hits."

With every word he said, Lizette's heart felt like it inched higher up her throat. Words like "explosive" and "*New York Times* list" were exactly what she didn't want to hear. She *had* to know what was in it; what did Martin consider explosive? Perhaps now was the time to dangle the sex card in front of him a little, let him know what was at stake.

"I've always thought it must be an exciting job, to be a lawyer at a publishing house," she said, smiling warmly at him and sticking out her chest just a wee bit, enough to quickly draw his eyes downward. But again, his immediate reaction chastened her. Slowly, without drawing his attention, she pulled her chest back in. Why was she tripping? She was starting to get annoyed with herself. This was no time to pick a fight in her own head over sexual politics. *If you're going to play the damn vamp*, she thought, *then go ahead and do it right*.

Martin matched her warm smile. He leaned

in over the table, close enough that Lizette could smell his breath. He must have downed a whole pack of breath mints before he walked into the Starbucks. He had really nice teeth.

"Last year I worked on the book of that ex-CIA bigwig," he said, his voice dropping conspiratorially. "There was some crazy shit in the original version. Like Tom Clancy shit that would make you want to pick up and move to another country."

Lizette actually was interested in the political gossip. And she knew if she could get him talking about the stuff he wanted to impress her with, then moving over to *Satan's Sisters* would be a cinch. "Oh yeah?" she said. "What was he like to work with?"

"He was very businesslike," Martin said. "He wasn't a monster or anything." Then he leaned forward again. "But you could easily tell he could turn into Darth Vader if he wanted to. I think all the lawyers were a little scared to piss him off. One time we had to make him get rid of a particular passage about the lead-up to the war. We drew straws to see which of us would call him about it."

"Who got the short straw?" Lizette said. "Was it you?"

Martin drew his hand across his face, like he was wiping his brow. "No, thank God it wasn't me," he said, grinning. "We were joking that if one of us got him pissed, he would order a drone to strike our parents' house or something, or like have the CIA take out our grandma."

Lizette laughed. "That's hilarious," she said. She reached out and let her hand casually linger on top of his. Martin noticed right away, but she could see him trying not to react. She fluttered her fingers a bit—it wasn't exactly a stroke, but pretty close to one.

"You're so interesting," she said. She had meant to say "Your job is so interesting," but at the last minute she changed it. God, how stupid was she sounding right now? She hoped it wasn't too over-the-top silly. She was being about as transparent as cellophane. *A guy would have to be an idiot to not see right through this, right?*

Martin grinned. "So are you," he said. The word "idiot" might as well have been printed on his forehead. "Interesting and beautiful," he continued. "I mean, Tim told me you were hot, but he didn't say you were this gorgeous." Martin paused for a second. "So you and Tim used to go out, huh?"

Lizette wondered how much Tim had told the old horn dog about their relationship. It had been a long time; she wasn't sure how protective Tim was of their old relationship these days—or of her.

"Yeah, it was pretty hot and heavy for a while," she said. "You know those college days. Spending like all day in bed, devouring each other." She looked up at Martin with a smile. But Martin wasn't smiling. It looked like Martin was imagining.

Lizette continued, pushing it a little more, throwing her previous hesitation out the window.

"I remember there were a couple of days there where we decided we wouldn't even go to class because we didn't want to get out of bed. The only time we even put clothes on was to go get some food in the dining hall. And the only reason we ate was so we could keep up our energy."

Lizette almost wanted to laugh at the expression on Martin's face. That's probably what he looked like when he watched porn. Martin was in full fantasy mode now. Lizette knew it was a bit cruel, but now she was having fun.

"I think I learned so much about sex from my days with Tim," she continued. "I learned what I liked, what I didn't like." She leaned forward with a giggle. "Although there wasn't much that I *didn't* like," she said. "Tim was such a great lover. God, he turned me on so much."

Lizette looked away, as if she were lost in memory. But she could still see Martin out of the corner of her eye. He looked like he was about to explode.

"You have any girlfriends like that in college?" she said, looking at him again with a sweet smile. She didn't think she'd be able to tell any of her girlfriends about this encounter, especially Tricia, who was the dean of women at Brown University. They would all demand that she return her feminist card.

"Huh?" Martin said, realizing she had just asked him a question.

Lizette laughed. "Martin! What are you thinking about right now?" she said, smacking his hand.

Martin's eyes were heavy now, like Lizette had

just reached down and taken his dick out of his pants. She knew at that moment she could probably get him to walk across Broadway buck-naked if she wanted. Once again, she was shocked by how easy this was. No wonder women like Maxine and Shelly were so skilled at manipulating men—so many of these guys were about as perceptive as Rex the German shepherd that her family used to own when she was a little girl. Actually, that might be an insult to Rex.

"Damn!" he said, shaking his head. "I would give my left arm right now to turn back the clock ten years and put myself on the Yale campus so I could replace Tim."

Lizette giggled. "Well, Martin, too bad no one has invented a time machine! It might be fun to go back to those Yale days."

She wasn't exactly telling him she would willingly spend days with him in bed, but she wasn't denying it either. Martin was wide open, ready for Lizette to pounce. She rested her hand on top of his again. She saw him fidget in his seat. She wondered if he was fidgeting because he was hard. She leaned forward, knowing that her tits were probably sitting up on the table like an entrée. *If Shelly Carter could see me now,* she thought.

"Martin, you think you could help me? My job depends on it," she said. That might have been the truth.

"What do you need?" he said, his voice a bit hoarse-sounding.

"I need to find out what's in Missy Adams's book," she said. She stroked his hand now, being obvious about it. She wondered what her "Power of the Feminist" professor from Yale, Claudia Reiss, would think if she saw Lizette now. Professor Reiss had been a favorite, back in Lizette's more radical days. But that was a long time ago.

"Well, I think I might be able to help you with that," Martin said, his voice still hoarse.

Maybe, Lizette thought, she should call up Professor Reiss and suggest that she change the title of the course to "Power of the Pussy."

Lizette gave Martin her sexiest, most suggestive smile. "That would be wonderful, Martin!" she said. "I would seriously owe you one!"

Lizette wondered if she would ever allow herself to spend a night with the horn dog. He *was* kinda cute. But after a performance like this one, she felt like she'd need Oscar-caliber acting skills to keep a straight face with this guy.

Martin turned over his hand so that he could hold hers. "I'll see what I can do," he said. "Maybe we can have dinner in a week or so and I can give you a report on what I've come up with."

Lizette nodded vigorously. "I'd like that very much!" she said. *My God*, she thought, *the things I do for this job.*

⇥ ⇤

HEATHER HAD BEEN CALLING Missy all weekend without any success. She was in full panic mode by the time Missy actually answered her cell phone on Monday.

"Missy! Is everything okay?" Heather said. She heard a deep sigh on the other end.

"Girl, these damn attorneys are driving me crazy!" Missy said in her heavy Southern drawl. Her drawl got heavier when she was tired or stressed. Maxine used to claim that it got heavier as soon as that red light came on, that Missy used the heavy accent to appeal to her conservative base.

"What attorneys?"

"These attorneys from Patterson and White," Missy said. "They've had me in meetings for three days straight. I didn't want to call you back when one of them was around and could overhear me, and then when I got home I was too tired to talk. I feel like I been talking for a week without stopping."

"Well, what's the problem, darling?" Heather said. "Are they trying to get you to change things in the book?"

"Change things, delete things, justify things, prove things! You name it," Missy said. "I think all of a sudden everybody in the company is getting cold feet. They told me that with the state of the economy and the publishing industry, they can't afford to have any legal troubles with this book or, heaven forbid, have to pull it from the shelves. Everybody's pushing to make this a bestseller."

"Well, that's good news, isn't it?"

"Yeah, I guess. But I'm starting to get kinda

nervous. What if Maxine comes after me? Maybe I should just give P and W the money back and go back to my honey. Forget about all this stuff."

Heather sighed. Missy had been in desperate need of pep talks from Heather at various points during the writing of the manuscript and even after the book was done. Now was not the time to back down. Heather could hear the trepidation in Missy's voice. It wasn't something that Missy let many people see, a vulnerable side. Certainly no one saw it when she was the ultrasuccessful assistant U.S. attorney down in Atlanta, specializing in child pornography and sex trafficking, at one point racking up thirty convictions in a row. She got her big break when she won the conviction of a former NFL star accused of running a prostitution ring out of his multimillion-dollar mansion in Buckhead, Atlanta's wealthiest neighborhood. Missy began popping up all over the television dial, offering commentary and wooing fans with her golden-girl good looks, facile legal mind, and ease in front of the camera. Her conservative politics didn't hurt either. After Riley Dufrane tapped her to join the couch, Missy became a bona fide star when she made a startling confession on *The Lunch Club* during a show on sexual violence: that she had been raped by a black man when she was a teenager and had gotten pregnant, but because of her staunch opposition to abortion had birthed and raised her biracial child by herself. Not only did glowing profiles spring up on the pages of conservative magazines, but Missy became a regular in pop-culture bibles like *People* magazine. She now was an honest-to-goodness celebrity. The religious right loved her antiabortion politics; she not only talked a good game but lived it too—actually mothering a black child in the process! The less strident right-wingers loved her prosecutor background—the woman sent perverts and child molesters to prison, for heaven's sake!

As she became more and more famous—in some Republican circles, her name was even mentioned as a possible senatorial or even vice-presidential candidate—she drew more and more ire from the doyenne of *The Lunch Club*. Maxine couldn't stand the acclaim that was directed Missy's way. She didn't trust it, thought Missy was somehow too good to be true. When she got her chance to do something about it, Maxine pounced.

"Missy. You have to stay focused, girl!" Heather said, a bit of nervousness evident in her voice. "Think about how you felt, what Maxine did to you."

Heather brought Missy back to her final days on *The Lunch Club*, the way Maxine brutally forced her to walk the plank. Through her sources, Maxine had heard that the Innocence Project, a New York–based nonprofit that fought on behalf of convicted felons that many people believed to be innocent of their crimes, was trying to reopen the case that sent Missy's rapist to prison. They had reason to believe the rapist may have been wrongly convicted. The Innocence Project was having a hard time finding a judge who would order a DNA test of a child and reopen the case based merely on new advances in DNA testing since the man had been sent to prison sixteen years earlier. But Maxine Robinson could go places the Innocence Project couldn't. She was still friendly with a couple of the longtime aides on the U.S. Senate Judiciary Committee, where her former husband was now one of the most senior senators. One day, Maxine snuck into Missy's office and found a baseball cap that belonged to Corey, Missy's adorable teenage son. A few phone calls and several weeks later, Maxine had in her possession a piece of paper that spelled Missy's disgrace. She had compared Corey's DNA with that of the man convicted of raping Missy. According to the test results, they were not a match; the man in prison had not been Missy's rapist.

"That woman went into your office and stole your son's DNA!" Heather reminded Missy. "She took something that belonged to your baby so she could get rid of you. Then she didn't even give you time to have a smooth exit. There was no reason for her to make you leave the next week! It made you look like some kind of criminal or something!"

Heather had been watching from afar, having left the show several years earlier to start *Heather's Hope*. She couldn't believe the things that Maxine put Missy through in those last days, releasing a vague, accusatory statement to the press that made it look like Missy had done something horrible. And to Missy's shock, no one on the show came to her defense. They all gave statements to the press that made it look like they thought she deserved her fate.

"Remember the way Whitney just dismissed you on the show, saying that the show wouldn't suffer at all when you were gone, that we all have to take responsibility for our actions, some kind of bullshit like that?" Heather said, getting riled up all over again. "When she had been running off to hotel rooms with the fucking president of the network? And Molly, with her pill addiction, making all those jokes at your expense? And Callie Sherman, making it look like the network might have had something to do with your dismissal? Callie was supposed to be your friend, Missy! How would all the people at the network feel if they knew that Callie had given birth to the executive producer's child and was covering it up with some bullshit story about a sperm donor? Imagine the sexual harassment suits and countersuits!"

"Yeah, you're right," Missy said, her voice sounding a bit stronger now. "They *do* need to pay for what they did."

Heather exhaled a long, cleansing breath. Had she been holding her breath that whole time? She hadn't even realized her body had been so tense. She was spooked by even the remote chance that Missy would run scared. Heather couldn't have that. Not when they were all *so* close to a once-in-a-lifetime opportunity to disgrace the queen bee herself. Heather strongly believed that people reaped what they sowed. Maxine had been destroying people for so long, with seemingly no remorse, that Heather was starting to see it as her duty to make sure some of that karma started coming back to Maxine. That was one of the driving forces on her show, to make sure that justice was served. Here was a chance to bring some justice to Mrs. Robinson. As she let Missy hang up, Heather could hear the Simon & Garfunkel song "Mrs. Robinson" playing in her head.

"So here's to you . . ."

CHAPTER 9

When Lizette reached the West Side studios of *The Lunch Club*, she raced upstairs to find Maxine. The ladies were in the postshow debriefing with the producers, in a small lounge next to the makeup room. Lizette peeked inside the doorway and saw bored expressions around the room—except for Maxine, who looked annoyed. When Lizette and Maxine made eye contact, Lizette saw a darkness descend over Maxine's face. Something told Lizette that she might be the one responsible for Maxine's pissed-off expression. Well, whatever it was, Lizette knew she would get a quick parole when she presented Maxine with her tidbit, the title of Missy's book.

Lizette waited outside the lounge for the meeting to end. She waved at Callie, the NBN executive, who slipped out of the meeting early. Lizette watched Callie disappear down the hallway. Lizette had never felt totally comfortable around Callie. Lizette considered herself a romantic, one who respected the sanctity of marriage. When she heard that Callie was having an affair with the very married Josh Howe, the show's executive producer, she lost a great deal of respect for Callie. Lizette had always thought Callie was beautiful and classy, but she had felt the need to reevaluate that second adjective. Of course Josh was a big boy and shouldered much of the responsibility for cheating on his wife, but Lizette didn't understand how Callie could look at herself in the mirror every morning. Lizette and her friends had a word for women like Callie: skeezer. It was a combination of skank, sleaze, and whore.

"And where have you been?"

It was Maxine, emerging from the meeting in front of the bunch, and it was directed at Lizette.

"Had an interesting meeting uptown," Lizette said. She stepped closer to Maxine, drawing looks from Shelly, Molly, and Whitney as they walked by. "I have a bit of news about Missy's book."

She saw Maxine's eyebrows rise. "Okay, let's duck in here for a minute," Maxine said, heading for an unoccupied office that belonged to one of the producers. They went inside and Maxine shut the door behind them—oblivious to the fact that the producer was just about to follow them into her own office. The producer was going to say something, to object to the door being slammed in her face. But instead she turned around and decided to go get another cup of coffee.

"Well, what is it, Lizette?" Maxine said. Maxine was trying to be cool about it. She didn't want to look so eager in front of a subordinate because she thought eagerness in this situation translated into fear.

"I had a meeting with a lawyer from Patterson and White. He's one of the lawyers actually working on Missy's book."

Maxine pursed her lips together. She looked impressed, but she didn't say anything.

"He said he would work on getting me a copy of the manuscript. But he did have one piece of information for us. He told me the title of the book. It's called *Satan's Sisters.*"

Maxine's eyes widened so much that Lizette could see white all around her pupils. Lizette thought she could even see redness rushing to Maxine's heavily rouged cheeks, which were still wearing the TV pancake makeup.

"My God, is that really the title?" Maxine said. She couldn't even veil her shock and nerves. She looked down and sat in the nearest chair she could find. Lizette had expected Maxine's head to spin around and pea soup to spout from her mouth, but for a split second she was worried that Maxine might actually pass out.

"That damn Chris Rock!" Maxine said, her face now a scowl.

The "Satan's sisters" line had actually come from the great comedian's only appearance on *The Lunch Club,* quite a few years back. He had sat on the couch between them and explained why he had always thought it would be the scariest, most unpleasant thing in the world to be sitting on the couch between them. He said, "I know Maxine says this show is like sitting down and having a conversation with your sisters—well, I don't have sisters . . . but trust me . . . this is not like sitting with your sisters. It's more like sitting with Satan's sisters." The audience howled with laughter, and the media loved the analogy, but Maxine did not appreciate the joke any more than she appreciated all those years of parodies of her slightly sleepy eye. Lord knows she had spent enough money over the years tightening it to the point where it was barely noticeable now . . . but when she first started out in the business it was very pronounced and the bane of her existence. This fresh new hell Rock unleashed with his comment was as if her eye had gone back to sleep.

"Okay, so we know just by the title that Missy is trying to get all the attention that she can," Maxine said. "Is this lawyer a reliable source? What's his name? Perhaps I should talk to him."

The idea of putting Martin Peters and Maxine in the same room kind of scared Lizette to death. She wasn't a journalist, but her instincts told her she needed to protect her source on this one.

"Yes, he's very reliable," Lizette said, now a little worried that she just attached the adjective "reliable" to Martin Peters—an attorney who was about to break all kinds of ethics laws for the possibility of a piece of ass. Lizette purposely didn't answer Maxine's second question, hoping Maxine would just keep it moving.

"Well, the second you get your hand on that manuscript, you let me know," Maxine said.

Lizette nodded.

Maxine got up and headed for the door, indicating that the meeting was over. But before she walked out, she turned around and said to Lizette, "Oh, and great work, by the way." Then she smiled. Lizette was stunned. It didn't happen very often, Maxine smiling at her. She wished she could have taken out her cell phone and snapped a picture, something to show her grandkids one day.

⊰ ⊱

WHITNEY HAD GOTTEN A text from Riley on Sunday night, just before she went to bed, telling her that they could meet at the Inn right after Monday's show. Because Eric was either in Nantucket or already on his way to Europe for some big exposé on plastic surgery, Whitney had all night and morning to think about her rendezvous. She had gone out over the weekend to Kiki de Montparnasse, the French lingerie shop in SoHo, and picked up a couple of extremely risqué items—things that Whitney wouldn't have dared purchase a few years ago. As a matter of fact, before she started her affair with Riley, Whitney would never have even gone into such a place. She would have thought it was a store for high-priced escorts or something.

As Whitney made her way back to her office

after the post-show debriefing, she couldn't believe how different decadent underwear made her feel. It had been a long time since she had purchased sexy panties and bras for herself. Actually, thinking about it a little more, she realized this had been a first—all the other occasions had been gifts from men, or tacky bridal shower presents. Skimpy lingerie from the famous Greene Street store wasn't exactly at the top of the must-buy list for a mother of four who had been married for sixteen years. But Whitney, who discovered Kiki in Paris when she covered France's fashion week several years ago, was thrilled by how sexy and confident the lingerie made her feel. She even felt sharper and wittier on the show that morning, like crotchless drawers had some kind of superpowers. When she slipped them on, she turned into Super Slut! The thought made her laugh to herself.

When she reached her office, she got a call on her cell phone. She saw from the caller ID that it was from Dalton, the fancy Manhattan private school that the twins, Ashley and Bailey, had attended since they were in kindergarten. It could only mean something was wrong. Whitney snatched up the phone and answered while her stomach suddenly went into a spin cycle.

"Mrs. Harlington?" the voice on the other end said. "Sorry to bother you, but your daughter Ashley is here in the office and seems to be sick. We were wondering if perhaps you could come pick her up?"

Whitney flashed on an image of Ashley, the drama queen, conning the school nurse so that she could get out of school early. Whitney was incredibly annoyed. She was just about to catch a cab to the Inn. She *really* didn't want to call Riley and cancel. She had been dreaming all weekend about his head between her legs and the things he would soon do to her. No, she *had* to see him.

"Um, okay," Whitney said, trying to think. Where the hell was Eric when she needed him? The man was always working on some damn "big" story. As if Whitney spent her days watching soap operas. He was utterly useless to her and to the family. Whenever something came up, it always landed on her, hard. Well, this time she was going to push back. The fact that she was a mother didn't mean she wasn't entitled to a life. If she wanted to meet her lover for some spicy afternoon delight, her daughter was going to have to come second for once. And besides, it was Ashley. Whitney could never totally believe Ashley when the end result would be Ashley getting something that she wanted. Now, if Ashley had been begging Whitney to *let* her go to school, then she'd be believable.

"Mrs. Harlington?" the school nurse said, probably wondering why this was taking Whitney so long.

"Can you put Ashley on the phone, please?"

Well, the girl certainly tried to sound sick when she got on the phone. Her voice sounded like somebody had just slammed the child in the head with a baseball bat. But Whitney wasn't going to be swayed. Ashley had Meryl Streep–like skills when it came to acting and manipulation. Fighting every maternal instinct in her being, Whitney told Ashley to catch a cab home.

"Catch a cab?!" Ashley said, stunned. Her voice suddenly sounded a lot stronger. "Mom, you *can't* be serious?!"

Whitney felt bad, but dammit, the girl was fourteen. There were kids two years younger than Ashley taking the subway to school every day. Even kids at Dalton. One cab ride wouldn't hurt her.

"Oh, come on, Ash, it's really not that big a deal," Whitney said. "If you don't have any cash, you can pay the cabbie with your debit card."

"But Mom, I'm sick!" Ashley said.

"Yes, I'm aware of the fact that you said you don't feel well. But unless I'm mistaken, I didn't hear that something was wrong with your legs?"

A long pause on the other end. "Wow, okay, Mom. I hope I make it home."

Whitney almost wanted to laugh. Any other time, this girl would lie, cheat, and steal for some independence. Now she was acting as if a cab ride by herself would lead her into a life of white slavery.

"I'm sure you'll make it, dear," Whitney said. "I have a meeting I can't miss. I'll see you very soon."

Whitney was already daydreaming about lying in Riley's arms. As far as she was concerned, Ashley was over, resolved. The thought of Riley naked and waiting at the Inn was inspiring enough to overcome any remnant of Whitney's maternal guilt.

⊰ ⊱

MOLLY WALKED BACK INTO her apartment and collapsed on the couch. She was having a hard time purging the image of Roger Mason fleeing her room at Caesars. That stunned look on his face was going to haunt her. She saw his shock and she saw a little fear, but she also thought she saw something else in Roger's face: disappointment. The man actually liked her and he was looking forward to being intimate with her. This was a man who fucked women who looked like Dara Cruz every weekend. The fact that he might have been disappointed that she went psycho on him spoke volumes. Molly could feel the loneliness in her belly, like a stomachache. That was her big shot at finding some companionship and she had screwed it up. Roger wasn't the best-looking guy in the world, but she did like the way she felt in his massive arms. And who was she kidding—she was so lonely she'd do Freddy Krueger if he threw a glance in her direction. The fact of the matter was that Molly was still gun-shy when it came to men. She still hadn't fully recovered from her marriage that had ended so dramatically several years back.

Douglas Stein was a smart, handsome, brilliant doctor who swept Molly off her feet at a time when she had resigned herself to the possibility that marriage and children might never be a part of her life.

Doug was a dermatologist whom Molly had met at a dinner party thrown by a mutual friend. He was so popular among the wealthy ladies who lunch that you had to wait three months for an appointment, even if you were married to the mayor. Doug had invented some newfangled dermabrasion treatment that his devotees claimed could take ten years off your face. Of course, anything in youth-obsessed Manhattan that had the makings of a fountain of youth would be pursued with the zeal of gold prospectors in 1840s California. Molly thought he was terribly cute at the party, but she had long ago ceased to have romantic thoughts about men as good-looking as Doug Stein. She was a fat girl in Manhattan; that meant she had to adopt certain survival instincts, one being to divorce yourself from the brutal singles market.

But something strange happened at the dinner party: Doug behaved as if he thought Molly was the most beautiful woman he had ever seen. He flirted shamelessly and followed her around the party, even when she had decided that the guy must be some sort of psycho killer who wanted to take her home and turn her into hamburger meat. She asked him what his deal was and, in a line she would never forget, he leaned into her ear and said, "You ever hear of Rubens? Well, like him, I think big women are beautiful and unbelievably sexy. If you had been born a few hundred years earlier, you would have been on a Rubens canvas."

With that line, Doug had won her heart—or at

least the chance to make a bid for her heart. It took months of hard work on his part for Molly to believe that this gorgeous man actually desired her. Within a year, they had become husband and wife. Raised as a devout Irish Catholic, Molly even converted to Judaism because it was important to Doug that their future children be raised Jewish. For about nine months, everything was perfect, like a fat-girl fairy tale. Molly even stopped taking birth control pills, hoping that she might still be able to conceive at forty-one. But little by little Molly noticed that they weren't having sex as much. They'd go a week without doing it, then two weeks, then three. Doug, after being ravenous for her body in the beginning, started coming up with a million excuses why he couldn't make love to her. For a woman as insecure as Molly about her body and desirability, this was the worst thing that could happen in her marriage.

Actually, it wasn't the worst thing—that came one night when Molly returned early from a gig. Doug didn't expect her back until the next morning, but Molly had decided to surprise him by coming right home after the show instead of spending the night in the Poconos, which was only about ninety minutes from the city. When she came into the apartment, she heard Doug in the bedroom, talking loudly to someone on the phone. Just as she was about to burst in the room and surprise him, she heard him say her name. So she lingered outside the door to listen a little longer. What she heard on the other side horrified her so profoundly that she still hadn't recovered years later.

"But I just don't know if I can do it anymore, man," she heard Doug say, apparently to one of his male friends. "I mean, at first I thought, well, I can kind of hold my breath and stick my dick in there if it's going to mean I get a flood of new patients. The broad knows everybody, in Hollywood *and* in New York. Already I've seen like dozens of new patients through her. She's like a big, fat gold mine. But now it's really starting to make me nauseous, the idea of having to fuck that cow. And I think she's even getting fatter, believe it or not. I've been trying to avoid her, but I don't know how much longer I can do it. I don't think she can even get my dick hard anymore."

Molly fell apart after that. Well, after she kicked his scheming ass out. Realizing that your husband pimped you for access can cause some serious trauma. In Molly's case, she started doing heavy-duty eating. Double Quarter Pounders with Cheese, heavy ketchup, and heavy mayo were her drug of choice. Soon, before she knew it, she was morbidly obese, tipping the scales at 250 pounds. In the midst of her depressed binge, Molly was contacted by actress-turned-fitness-guru Karen Collins and offered the chance to take the Collins Challenge—lose fifty pounds in six months and make a ton of money in the process. For a short period, the challenge was good because it gave her something else to concentrate on besides her depression. In fact, the stinging words of her evil soon-to-be ex-husband became a motivating tool for her on those days when she desperately craved a Quarter Pounder. When she dropped all the weight and graced the cover of *People* in a swimsuit, Doug even had the gall to call her and claim that he wanted them to try to "work it out." Molly barely let him get the sentence out before she hung up the phone.

But soon the pressures of trying to keep off the weight caught up to her. She began eating again— in one infamous tabloid shot, a paparazzo snagged a picture of her sitting in a McDonald's, wolfing down a cheeseburger. By the time Karen Collins fired her, Molly's stomach was protruding again and she was well into her pill addiction.

With all that drama, Molly hadn't had sex since her marriage to Doug. She had used food and pills to purge those urges, to become virtually asexual. That three-hundred-dollar-an-hour therapist helped for a while, but she stopped going several months back. When she started getting intimate with Roger, the urges had come roaring back with a vengeance—as did her anxiety about her body and about sex. Perhaps she stopped going to the therapist too soon.

Molly decided she needed a distraction, something to take her mind off her disastrous weekend. So she called Garrett, who was her closest male friend. In actuality, Garrett was her own personal "gay." All the fat girls in Manhattan had one; it was sort of a rite of passage. You know you're not going to get a real man to fuck you, so you find a queen to hang out with so at least you look like you're having a good time—even if you're slowly dying inside.

"Garrett! I don't care what you're doing tonight, dear. I need for you to take me somewhere fabulous!" Molly said loudly into the phone.

"Molly! You crazy whore! I just saw you on *TMZ*, flashing your tits! I was just about to call you!" Garrett was practically yelling at her.

Molly was sure she hadn't heard him correctly—did he say he saw her on television flashing her tits?

"Excuse me, what did you say?" Molly asked.

"I was watching *TMZ*, and they did a story about someone who they said appeared to possibly be Molly McCarthy Stein, flashing her breasts to drivers on the New Jersey Turnpike from the back window of a black limo!" Garrett said breathlessly, sounding about as excited as Molly had ever heard him.

Molly felt a jolt of nerves and embarrassment. "Wow, really?" she said softly. "Could you, uh, see my face?"

"No, not really," Garrett said. "It looked like somebody took the video with a camera phone. It wouldn't work in a court of law or anything. But that was really you?! What the hell were you thinking?"

Molly sighed. "I was thinking with my little alcoholic brain, as opposed to my full-sized regular brain," she said. "Wow, I can't believe somebody recorded that."

"They sure as hell did, girl! And who were you with? There was another woman flashing her tits too. I figured that it was probably Rain. At least they looked like I would imagine Rain's tits look—not that I've ever seen them. And there was another woman. She actually showed her naked ass! Like a real moon. They had the images kinda like blurred out, but you could tell that she had a pretty nice ass. It looked very round!"

Molly was mortified. So much for living on the wild side. In this age of video phones and TMZ, a celebrity had to be vigilant every minute of the day. No room for stupid pranks. Thank God they could only guess it was she. "It was Rain and Dara with me."

"Dara! I should have figured, with that perfect round Latin ass of hers! Look at y'all, acting like some silly-ass teenagers! But it looked like fun! I wish I was there. I would have flashed my skinny little white ass."

Molly grimaced at the image. "I don't want to talk about this anymore, Garrett," she said. "I just want you to take me out."

"But it's a Monday, darling," Garrett said. "Nothing fabulous happens on Monday." It sounded like he might have been yawning now. Garrett was all about the radical mood swings. "But then again, we could go to the Box and hang with the trannies," he added.

"The trannies are some funny motherfuckers!" Molly said. "I always get some material from them."

But as she hung up the phone and headed toward her bedroom to figure out what to wear to a tranny club, Molly felt embarrassed and more than a bit gloomy. This was what her life had been reduced to—telling jokes, taking pills, and trolling for trannies. And flashing strangers on the turnpike for kicks.

"Good God, no wonder I'm trying to kill myself," she said.

CHAPTER 10

Maxine had an idea. It came to her like a thunderbolt—she needed to have a dinner party. Instead of playing these games with Lizette and her slow-ass minions, it was time for her to put the Maxine Robinson name into action. Her plan was to invite a mind-boggling lineup of media, Hollywood, and publishing movers and shakers, the kind of folks who could greenlight a picture, a book, or a new show with a nod of their heads. Of course, the big fish here was Bill Murphy, the president of Patterson and White. Ideally she'd like to get him alone, at a private dinner at her place, but naturally he'd see right through that and turn it down. He'd be much more likely to come if he knew he was going to be in a room with people whose stories in print could potentially make him a lot of money. She also knew that, even though Murph was publishing a book that might make Maxine look bad, he'd have no particular allegiance in a pissing match between Missy and

Maxine. All he cared about was moving copies. He might even want to follow up Missy's book with a Maxine Robinson memoir. Keep the pissing match going. She'd have to be sure to dangle that possibility in front of him—even as she tried to lure information out of him about whether the contents of Missy's book should cause her worry. Maxine was confident in her powers of persuasion; she had been using them for forty years to get her way. She saw no reason why that would end now.

Maxine picked up the phone and made a few quick calls. Within minutes, she was surrounded in her office by her two assistants and by Lizette, her publicist.

"Okay, I need your help," she said, looking around the room. "I'm going to hold a dinner party at my house. All the bigwigs from media, publishing, and Hollywood, from Kissinger to Koppel, Seinfeld to De Niro. I have to have enough moguls there to make it enticing to my main target, Bill Murphy from Patterson and White. I will personally make the phone calls to our guests, but I need the three of you to do the rest of the planning— food, alcohol, servers, bartenders, decor. But we don't have much time—I want to hold the party on Saturday."

"*This* Saturday?" Lizette said, her voice rising in shock. She didn't mean for it to come out so loud and so challenging. Actually, maybe she did.

Maxine stared at her without speaking. Lizette didn't stare back; she averted her eyes.

"Do you have something to say, Lizette?" Maxine asked her.

"Uh, no. I was just surprised when you said Saturday. I thought you were going to say like a month from now, that's all. Saturday doesn't give us much time."

"No, it doesn't," Maxine said. "So ticktock . . . don't you think?"

Lizette and the two assistants, both recently graduated twentysomethings who were still suffering from Maxine awe, exchanged worried looks. They all knew that the next five days for them would be living hell—not only did they have to plan a major dinner party, they had to do it with the notoriously hard-to-please Maxine breathing down their necks the whole time.

After she dismissed them, Maxine sat down with a pen and pad and started making a guest list. A dinner party guest list was a delicate science—it had to be balanced, mixed with people who were interesting, people who were powerful, people who were smart, people who were beautiful, people who were single, people who were married. If your balance was off, you either had a party full of guests looking to flee immediately after dessert because of extreme boredom, or you had two drunken drama queens coming to blows in the midst of some passionate debate about religion or politics. Maxine had seen both scenarios—and everything in between—so after four decades she considered herself an expert on the science of guest lists. But she couldn't finalize the list until she got home and consulted her diaries. She might need to call in some favors—or, more accurately, make some threats.

⚞ ⚟

"¿DARA? *ES TU MADRE*. *Necesito hablar contigo, niña.*"

Dara took a deep breath. Her mother was on the phone, saying she needed to speak with her. This couldn't be good.

"Hello, Mommy," Dara said. "Why are you calling so late? Is something wrong?"

"No, it's not late, Dara. It's only nine thirty," her mother answered. But Dara knew her parents well—they didn't want to have anything to do with the telephone after eight o'clock. All of their friends and family knew that too, and respected it. So for Magdalena Cruz to pick up a phone at nine thirty, it must be a matter of national security.

"Tell her I said hi too, Lena!" Dara could hear her father in the background. Her father never answered or dialed the phone himself, but he was always hovering in the background, trying to give directions.

"Tell Daddy I said hi. So what's wrong, Mommy?"

"Why does something have to be wrong for me to call my daughter?" her mother said, trying but failing to sound insulted.

"Nothing has to be wrong, Mommy. But I talked

to you earlier this afternoon, so I know you're not just calling to talk."

She heard her mother suck her teeth. "My daughter the doctor and the lawyer is so smart, she just knows everything."

The words were sarcastic, but Dara could hear the joy in her mother's voice, right below the surface, as if Magdalena truly did believe that Dara knew everything. Manuel and Magdalena were so aggressive in promoting Dara that they should be on *The Lunch Club* payroll, getting some of Lizette's publicist salary. It was one of the reasons Dara sometimes dreaded going up to Spanish Harlem to see them. She could never trust where the trip would end up—Magdalena might decide that she just *had* to have her daughter accompany her to the grocery store, where she would proceed to practically get on the store intercom to announce that the famous Dara Cruz was in the store. Her father was just as bad—he once even dragged Dara into the neighborhood bar, where she was forced to endure the painful entreaties of about a dozen old, drunk Puerto Rican men, who would make their clumsy moves whenever Manuel turned his back. It was sometimes uncomfortable, but it still made Dara proud to see the pleasure her success brought to her parents' lives.

"Are you busy on Wednesday night?" Magdalena asked. "We're having a little get-together and we want you to be here."

Dara was immediately suspicious. First of all,

her parents never did anything on Wednesday night because her mother never missed Wednesday services at Church of the Holy Rosary—the same church whose grammar school Dara and her sister Lisa attended from kindergarten to eighth grade. Second of all, a get-together? Magdalena and Manuel didn't do get-togethers—primarily because there were only a handful of people that her father would trust to have up in his home.

"What kind of get-together, Mommy?" Dara somehow managed through the phone line to convey her air quotes around "get-together."

"Nothing fancy, *niña*. Just a few people here for dinner, that's all."

"What people? Who else is coming?"

She heard her mother's pause, about as pregnant and suspicious as a pause could get. She heard her whisper something to her father.

"I don't think you know them, Dara. We just thought it might be nice for our daughters to spend some time with us," her mother said.

"Lisa's gonna be there?" Dara asked.

"Yes, I'm going to invite her. But I haven't called her yet. I called you first. So don't you go calling your sister and starting trouble, trying to make her jealous."

"Mommy! You know I don't do that! I don't have to do anything to make Lisa jealous. That's just the way she is, whether I say anything to her or not."

She heard her mother suck her teeth again.

The feuding between Dara and Lisa was a constant source of heartache for Magdalena and Manuel. Lisa was a schoolteacher with a husband and two great kids who tried to use her familial bliss as a defense shield whenever she got too sick of everyone cooing over her ultrasuccessful younger sister. The result was that whenever the two girls happened to be in their parents' home at the same time, usually during holidays and birthdays, at some point a nasty argument wound ensue—usually over something silly.

Dara sighed. "Okay, Mommy, I'll be there. What time?"

"That's great, baby! I think seven thirty would be good. Maybe you could bring a bottle of good wine? You know better than us which one to pick."

Even before Dara hung up the phone, her stomach felt unsettled, like there was something going on, something right in front of her face, that she was failing to see.

"Your parents inviting you to some kind of party?"

It was Rain, who was lounging next to her on the bed, clearly hanging on every word. They had been halfway through an episode of *Law and Order: SVU*, their favorite show. They were always at least four or five episodes behind, so every couple of weeks they would have a marathon and knock them off the DVR, one by one.

"Yeah, they say they're having a 'get-together,'" Dara said, using the air quotes again. "But they're acting all suspicious. I think they have something up their sleeve, like a blind date or something."

"Maybe this might be a good time to introduce them to me," Rain said.

Her statement just sat there for several seconds. Dara didn't expect it, but now that it was out there she had no idea what to do about it. She didn't want to get into a tiff with Rain over this issue yet again, but she knew that she couldn't keep avoiding it.

"You're not going to say anything? Like 'Great idea,' or 'Shut up, bitch'? Nothing, huh?" Rain said.

Dara turned to her. "What if this *is* some kind of blind date? Do you think that would be the best time to introduce you to my family?"

Rain shrugged. "Listen, Dara, no time is going to be easy. Believe me, I know. I put off telling my parents for like three years, and then they happened to stumble across one of my stand-up routines where I'm talking about being a lesbian. It was horrible. So I'm just trying to help you here. It's going to hit the papers any minute, girl, and you know it. And now you got this crazy bitch, Missy Adams, and her fuckin' book to worry about. Let's just go up there and get it all out in the open. I promise, I'll charm their fuckin' socks off!"

Dara shook her head in frustration. She knew this issue wasn't going anywhere; it was only going to get worse. She wished there was someone she could call, a wise mentor or something, who could tell her what to do.

"Listen," Rain said. Dara turned to look at her.

Rain's expression was as serious as Dara had ever seen it. She might play the joker most of the time, but this was not the joker in front of her. This was a subject that Rain took *very* seriously. "You *have* to get out in front of this, baby. You *have* to," Rain continued. "Too many celebrities get trapped in this little box that you're in, hiding, denying, scared to death that somebody, somewhere, is going to out them. It's a horrible way to live. I love you too much, and you are too important to me, to let you close yourself in the box."

Dara could see the tears starting to form in Rain's eyes. She felt herself growing more tender in her feelings for this woman. She knew her own tears would be coming in a matter of seconds. *How could something as powerful as this, feelings as strong as these, be considered wrong by* anybody?

"You have to be the author of the only dictionary that defines you. You can't allow anyone else to write that definition because when it changes— and believe me it always does—you won't know who you are. If we tell your parents now, it would be the first big step in you taking control of this issue. Doing it *your* way," Rain said, then added, more softly, "*Our* way."

Maybe Rain was right—maybe it was time to get it over with. She looked up and smiled at Rain. The passionate closing argument had won over the jury. "Okay, if I agree to do this, can you at least promise me that you won't use the word 'fuck'?"

Rain broke into a grin. "Oh shit, is that a yes?"

"And you can't use the word 'shit' either!" Dara said, giggling and pointing a finger in Rain's face.

"Fuck! Shit! You are basically rendering me mute then," Rain said.

Dara pointed her finger again. "Promise me, Rain."

Rain put her hand on her chest. "I promise, I promise." Rain shook her head. "Is this really going to happen? I'm in shock. Dara, this is wonderful!"

Dara lifted her hands and covered her eyes, shaking her head at the same time. She was pleased that Rain was so happy, but Dara was scared to death.

⊰ ⊱

"WOULD YOU LOOK AT the hair on that one over there, the one in the green dress!" Garrett pointed to a woman on the edge of the dance floor. "That bitch looks like she got into a fight with a pair of hedge clippers! And it's clear that she didn't win!"

Molly giggled and smacked Garrett on his arm. "You asshole! How come you always make fun of the women and not the men? I swear, you queens are more sexist than the Irish men I grew up with!"

"Can I help it if these sluts are such a mess?" Garrett said, sweeping his hand across the width of the club. After ditching the almost-empty club, the Box, they were snuggled in a corner of Excess, a hot new club downtown in the Meatpacking District, a fabulously decadent space created out of the guts of an old decrepit warehouse. Like snipers, they moved their gaze across the dance floor, aiming their brutal wit at one poor clueless target after another. It was their favorite pastime, something that Molly thoroughly enjoyed because it kept her comic sensibilities sharp—and the bitchy Garrett was one of the funniest men she knew. As she told him on a weekly basis, he could make a killing on the stand-up circuit. But he was a hairdresser—he'd told her he had looked around for the most stereotypically gay profession he could find, but all the interior decorator jobs were taken—and made a ton of money at his Upper East Side salon attending to the locks and the fragile psyches of Manhattan's wealthy ladies who lunch.

Molly's night with Garrett was doing just the trick, taking her mind off her disastrous weekend with Roger. She had studiously avoided Dara before and after the show that morning, even though Dara was obviously desperate to pull her aside. Molly had hired her own limo and fled Atlantic City at the crack of dawn. She had called Rain and left a message on her cell, letting them know she was still alive but was eager to get back home—Molly knew Rain turned off her phone when she went to sleep. She and Garrett had downed a large, decadent portion of Gnudi with Brown Butter & Sage at the Spotted Pig, their favorite restaurant in the West Village. Sometimes she'd meet Garrett there in the middle of the night—the Spotted Pig stayed open until two a.m.—and she'd try some new adventurous delight. Garrett loved the place because they sometimes had special dishes with names like Gentleman's Relish with Boiled Egg Salad, and Pork Belly Faggot with Risotto, which Garrett would order even if it wasn't on the menu, giggling the whole time.

"Okay, look at that guy over there," Molly said, pointing to a tall, skinny guy in leather pants on the dance floor whose shirt was unbuttoned all the way down to his navel. "Isn't he the worst dancer you've ever seen?"

"My God, he looks like he's in the middle of an epileptic seizure!" Garrett said.

"That's an insult to epileptics. Even one in the middle of a seizure has more rhythm than that," Molly said.

"I swear, like I always say, they ought to require that white people get a license or something before they allow us on a dance floor!" Garrett said. "That would save a lot of people from injury."

"And from cmbarrassment!" Molly added.

Garrett shook his head. "I don't understand how that guy cannot see how pathetic he is. He probably can't fuck to save his life."

"In your exhaustive research, have you determined that there is in fact a correlation between dancing ability and skill in bed?" Molly said. "So what would that be saying, only like ten percent of the white population knows how to fuck?"

"First of all, why you gotta call me a ho, talking about my *exhaustive* research?" Garrett said. "Just because, unlike you, I've actually encountered a dick in the new millennium, doesn't make me a ho. I think my eighty-four-year-old grandmother probably gets more dick than you! And second of all, I *know* that guys who *can* dance are usually great in bed. But that's not saying the opposite is true, that if you're a lousy dancer then you're lousy in bed."

Molly was silent for a moment. The line about Garrett's grandmother struck a nerve, especially considering what had just happened to her in Atlantic City. For a second, she considered telling Garrett the whole story, about how she had been so close to actually having sex—but in the end went all psycho on the guy. No, it was too embarrassing a revelation. Maybe she could tell Garrett about it one day, but it would be a while before that sore healed over. And with the TMZ clip, she had already had enough embarrassment for one day.

"Oh my God!" Garrett said. "Isn't that one of the Real Housewives of New York over there, walking in like she owns the place? What the hell is *she* doing down here? Hilarious. And I always thought you needed to own a home and actually *be* a wife to be a real housewife. Oh well."

"Oooh, look at that slut over there!" Molly said, pointing to the edge of the dance floor.

Garrett turned to see what Molly was pointing at. Truly, there was a woman on the dance floor wearing a miniskirt so transparent that they were looking straight at her ass in a thong. And she wasn't shy about displaying it, either, sticking out her ass while she bent over at the waist. Apparently, she was supposed to be dancing.

"My God, what is that woman thinking?" Molly said. "I can't even make a joke. I just want to bring her home and make her go to her room."

"You sound like somebody's mother, Molly," Garrett said, suddenly sounding angry. "You can't come down here to the Meatpacking District carrying some bullshit morality with you. Yeah, it's clear that she's a dumb skanky trick, but if you want to be passing judgment, you need to take that back uptown. Especially after you were just flashing your tits on the turnpike. You're a hypocrite."

Molly looked closely at Garrett, to see if he was serious with the tongue-lashing. But he had his head turned away, acting like he was sulking.

"Garrett! Are you serious?"

He turned to her with a naughty giggle. "Of course I'm not serious, you crazy broad!"

Molly laughed along with him, but she realized that maybe Garrett was right—she probably did belong back uptown. Under no circumstances was she ever going to be able to see a young woman wearing a thong and see-through skirt in public and think that it was okay, no matter how many times she came to these clubs with Garrett. But though she started to feel like maybe she should call it a night—after all, she did have a show to do in the morning—she was happy that she had made Garrett take her out. It had been three days since she had downed one of her pills. She wasn't going to lie—at times she had desperately craved them, but she had shown more strength than she realized she had. Maybe this was the start of something. Maybe she would be able to beat this pill problem on her own, without the need for any further intervention.

"Garrett, I think it's time for me to call it a night," she said.

❦

"**WHEN WAS THE LAST** time *this* happened?" Whitney said, holding aloft a copy of the *New York Post*. "When was the last time we had two of us in the gossip pages on the same day? And I thought we were some old corny broads!"

Everybody except Molly and Shelly was in makeup, discussing the items in the newspaper. They were especially enjoying the story on Shelly. Apparently, Miss Carter was with a group of rowdies at another downtown club and they ran into some sort of conflict with other folks there. A fight ensued. One guy wound up in the hospital and two guys were led away in handcuffs. While the *Post* took pains to point out that Shelly was not involved in the fight, according to the eyewitnesses, she was definitely a member of the rowdier group.

"Shelly's little rapper friends are gonna get her in trouble," Dara said. "She's not some crazy supermodel diva anymore."

"What I want to know is, doesn't anybody here have a job anymore?" Whitney said. "Since when are we hitting the clubs on a Monday night? Is that like the new hot club night and I missed the memo?"

"Whitney, if it was a memo about hot clubs, I think you got crossed off the list about twenty-five years ago," Maxine said from the corner of the room. The ladies all responded with enthusiastic laughter, even joined by Whitney herself, who couldn't disagree with Maxine.

"But what about this picture of Molly and her friend Garrett?" Maxine asked. "It says here that Molly McCarthy Stein was seen at Excess with her *boyfriend*, Garrett Carson. When did her 'walker' become her boyfriend?" Maxine was snickering, but everyone in the room knew that Maxine had more than a few "walkers" of her own. "Garrett is so flaming, he's like a burning bush," Maxine said. "And speaking of Molly, what the hell was she thinking, flashing drivers on the New Jersey Turnpike? I heard she was maybe on that god-awful show, *TMZ*, and they had video of somebody who they claimed looked like Molly, flashing her tits through the window of a limo. The face was kind of obscured. I don't believe that was really her, though. Not even Molly would be *that* stupid."

"They had video of that?" Dara said. To anyone paying attention, Dara's voice would have sounded suspiciously high and uncomfortable. But no one was paying attention.

Just then, Shelly breezed into the room, looking as refreshed and chipper as if she had just had a spa treatment. "Oh, I see we're getting a little giggle from the gossip columns," Shelly said, observing the reading material around the room. But Shelly didn't appear to be very upset. Anytime she was written up in the gossip columns, it just confirmed her status as an object of fascination. When she was ripping the runways, Shelly used to celebrate when she saw her name in boldface. Now she was used to it, but she still got a thrill out of it, even when it was something stupid like a fistfight.

"That was so dumb, I can't believe it even made the papers," she said. "Some drunk asshole spilled some of his drink on my girl LaDashah. The guy she was with told the drunk that he needed to apologize, the drunk's friend stuck his nose in it and said something to LaDashah's friend, then some other guy said something back to him, next thing I know these guys are actually swinging at each other. Me and LaDashah actually left before the police came. I didn't even realize somebody got arrested. I think the police actually arrested the guy who started it all, the drunk who spilled the drink. But it was all kinda stupid."

"LaDashah? Is that the one with the crazy spelling to her name?" Maxine asked.

Shelly rolled her eyes. Maxine knew the answer to that question. She had met LaDashah on several occasions and knew exactly who she was. The purpose of the question was to try to humiliate Shelly by calling attention to her ghetto friends.

"Yes, Maxine, that would be her," Shelly said.

"Wait, how does she spell her name?" Whitney asked.

Dara was the one who answered, saving Shelly the trouble.

"It's spelled, L-A, and then a dash, and then A-H," Dara said. "So you pronounce the middle part like D-A-S-H, but those letters aren't actually spelled out in the name. Instead, you just use a dash."

"Wait, let me get this straight," Whitney said, stifling a laugh. "Instead of letters, this woman uses punctuation? Is that legal?"

The ladies around the room all tried to stifle their snickers, but they weren't successful. Shelly had heard all the jokes about her friend's name. Yes, it was unbelievably ghetto, nonsensical, and ridiculous. But La—ah was her friend, and she wasn't going to tolerate people making fun of her girl. Besides, the name was extremely memorable.

"LaDashah is one of the most levelheaded, logical women I know," Shelly said. "If I were ever in some kind of trouble, I'd want LaDashah to have my back every time. She may not have gone to Harvard or Columbia"—Shelly shot a glance in the direction of Dara, who had gone to Columbia Law School and medical school—"but the chick is smart as hell. And I'll tell you something else: once you hear her name, you never forget it."

"Well, that's for sure," Maxine said, already bored with the conversation about some ghetto bunny with a tacky name. The thought that someone would name his or her child La—ah on purpose was foreign to Maxine. *No wonder some black people would never get ahead,* she thought, *just a bunch of "postslavery syndrome" suffering fools.*

At that moment, Molly appeared at the doorway. Her hair was disheveled, her eyes were sporting heavy bags underneath, and she looked like she was in some sort of daze. The ladies all were inclined to laugh at her, but they were not sure laughter was appropriate. Molly had had some rough days of late.

"I know I look like shit," Molly said, trudging toward an empty chair and collapsing. "You can go ahead and laugh."

The ladies did exactly that, filling the room with laughter. Molly even laughed at herself. She then proceeded to give the ladies a blow-by-blow recounting of her evening, including Garrett's efforts to ensure that their picture was taken by the paparazzi and how he made sure the photographer spelled his name right.

"Was it Garrett's idea to describe himself as your boyfriend?" Maxine asked.

"Ew, is that what it says?" Molly said. "Garrett called me this morning, so excited that we had made the paper. He didn't tell me the *Post* had turned him straight and me into an official fag hag!"

❧ ❦

DURING THE POSTSHOW BRIEFING, word flew around the room that Maxine was throwing a huge bash at her place on Saturday night.

"Maxine, I didn't get my invitation yet," Shelly said.

Maxine was expecting to be confronted by Shelly about the party. Shelly could sniff out another step on her career ladder like an NBA star locating a blond hoochie.

"But it's a couples night, Shelly," Maxine said, in a bald-faced lie. "Who would you bring, for heaven's sakes—Fifty Cent?" The thought of one of Shelly's tacky homeboys in her home made Maxine shudder. If she was going to hang in that world, the least she could do was pick someone like Russell Simmons. Now, he had money, status, and entrée to everything. *Hmmm, I gotta put that one in the yellow book when I get a chance,* Maxine thought.

Around the room, people—particularly the producers, including Josh Howe, who decided to sit in on this meeting—started staring at their watches or cell phones, pretending they weren't hearing this wicked exchange.

"She could bring me. We could go together," said Whitney. Whitney had discovered that Riley had been invited to the party. Eric was still out of town, so Whitney was a free agent. She enjoyed private visions of slipping off into a closet or spare bedroom and getting nasty with Riley while his wife sat by herself, bored and not happy about it.

She was surprised that the element of danger was so thrilling. When she had begun the affair with Riley, the idea of getting caught mortified her. Now it kind of turned her on. Who knew she was such a freak?

But Maxine would have none of it. "Don't be ridiculous," she said. "What do you think this is, a GLAAD party?"

Shelly, Molly, and Whitney turned to look at Dara, as did a few of the producers who were more in the loop. Dara turned crimson, but she didn't say anything. It occurred to Maxine that perhaps she should apologize, but she had no patience for that. So she threw up her hands and said, "Oh, for heaven's sakes!" She got up from the chair and left the room in a huff, as if she were the one who had been insulted. Meeting over.

⊰ ⊱

"WHAT THE HELL IS this!"

Maxine sat at her fancy desk in her office and stared at the screen. A friend of hers had sent her a link to a story on that gossip site, chattercrazy .com. Headlined "Maxine's Having a Party!" the story discussed the dinner party that Maxine was having on Saturday night. There was no byline, nor any contact info anywhere on the site. The story mentioned a few of the guests who were invited and talked about how Maxine was such a media big shot that when she scheduled a party, every mogul on both coasts came running. But then the next line made the hairs stand on the back of Maxine's neck.

> **Rumor has it that Maxine's main target is Patterson & White president Bill "Murph" Murphy, whose company is publishing the highly anticipated tell-all memoir by Melissa "Missy" Adams, former cohost on *The Lunch Club* and darling of pro-life, pro-gun archconservatives across the land. If Maxine can get Murph to her dinner party, the thinking is perhaps she can somehow influence the publication of Missy's book. The public never got a real accounting of why Missy was removed from *The Lunch Club*. The rumors were that she was taken down by Maxine Robinson because of her political views. Now the real story will come out in the book, scheduled to be released next month—unless Maxine can work her magic and stop it.**

Her face aflame, Maxine snatched up the phone and called Lizette. "Lizette, I need for you to come in here right now!"

Thirty seconds later, Maxine stood aside with her arms folded while Lizette sat down at Maxine's computer and read what was on the screen, her face turning redder with each word. When she was done, Lizette slowly backed away from the screen and looked at Maxine with a confused, sheepish expression.

"I swear, Maxine, I had nothing to do with this," Lizette said. She felt her stomach churning; her thoughts were a jumble. Maybe one of the invitees had called the website? But they couldn't know about Bill Murphy and Maxine's motives behind the party. The only people who could know that were in this building, somewhere on the staff or cast of *The Lunch Club*. Maybe one of the couchmates did it? Like Shelly or Whitney, who Lizette had heard were angling for an invite. But how would it help their chances by pissing off Maxine? Maybe it was one of the twentysomething assistants? Not bloody likely—those girls worshipped and feared Maxine, like she was some sort of Greek goddess. No, Lizette could see how Maxine would suspect her. Anybody in Maxine's situation would suspect her.

"That's what you keep saying," Maxine said "But then this keeps happening. I'm having a real hard time understanding what's going on here, Lizette. Imagine how I feel, suspecting that we need to protect our show from our own damn publicist!"

Lizette could feel her hands starting to shake. She was having a hard time even thinking clearly. Was Maxine about to fire her?

"I, I, uh, it's easy to, uh, understand how you could think I, uh, had something to do with this," Lizette said. She was trying, unsuccessfully, to take the whine out of her voice. But she was scared, so she had no real control over how her voice sounded. "But I swear to you, Maxine, that I was not the source of these stories. I swear!"

Maxine shook her head. "You think it would be wrong of me to fire you right now?"

Lizette's head dropped. Here it was; her beheading was about to come. All these years of fighting, sacrificing, living with nasty crazy women because she couldn't afford her own place on a junior publicist salary; was it about to become a wasted decade? This was how it was going to end for her, doomed by some website she had never even heard of two weeks earlier?

"All I can say, Maxine, is that it wasn't me," Lizette said softly. She had tears in her eyes; she refused to look up at Maxine's face.

Maxine saw the tears running down Lizette's cheeks. She wanted to be hard and decisive at that moment and throw the woman out on her ass, but she needed more evidence before she could take such a drastic action. Everyone deserved a fair trial.

"I'm not going to fire you right now, Lizette. Not until I have proof that this stuff came from you. But what I *will* do is have someone find out more information about this damn chattercrazy."

Lizette wanted to scream her relief, but she kept her head bowed. She thought maybe it would be good form for her to volunteer for the chattercrazy assignment.

"You want me to do the digging about chatter-crazy?" she asked, looking up at Maxine.

Maxine shook her head. "That would be like appointing the defendant as the special prosecutor, don't you think? And besides, I think you should have enough to do this week." She began walking across her office and picked up a file from a far table. It had "Dinner Party" written on the front. "Here are some things I've put together to help with the menu." She handed the file to Lizette. Then she waited. Lizette realized it was time for her to go.

"Oh, okay, Maxine." Lizette got up and hurried from the office, feeling like she had just gotten a last-minute stay of execution.

CHAPTER 11

Eric Harlington raced through the streets of beautiful, historic Prague, conducting interviews and trying to keep busy so that he wouldn't be distracted by the thought of the wonders that awaited him. Friday was the big day, when he would get to delve into the sweet Eastern European delights that he had been promised. After exchanging several e-mails with his contact, he got some news that thrilled him. Since he said he was interested in two girls, his contact told him that if he desired, he could spend some time with two sisters at once, ages thirteen and fourteen. Eric had been blown away by the opportunity. He responded with an emphatic "yes." The sisters added another thousand to the fee, but at this point he didn't even care about the money anymore. He was much too far down the path to temptation to even find pause in the price tag. The contact gave him detailed instructions. He would enter the designated apartment and place his money on the living room table. Naturally, only cash was accepted. Then he would proceed to a small room to the right and wait on the bed for the girls to enter. The contact said he could bring his recording equipment and do as much filming as he liked, though he was prohibited from selling or distributing images.

Eric had sent a couple of e-mails to Whitney to let her know he was all right and "incredibly busy." She had responded with terse, one-sentence replies. He knew that his marriage had entered a state of damage so severe that repair would be about as much fun as disabling a bomb. He also knew that the longer this cold war went on, the more pain it would cost him later on to reach a state of détente. But he wasn't yet willing to confront that reality. It was much easier for him to remain in fantasy land.

Eric had been to Prague once before, about a decade earlier, and he was pleased to see that the city hadn't much changed. For Americans, Asians, and other well-to-do travelers from around the world, Prague was a hugely popular stop on the European tourism tour, which meant it had its good and its bad. Bad overpriced restaurants, busy streets, and overcrowded museums went hand in hand with fabulous food, breathtaking architecture, and moving, legendary works of art. The Gothic spires that loomed across the expansive skyline, the bridges that spanned the Vltava River like guitar strings, the cafés that gave the place a jaunty bohemian feel, all made Eric conclude that Prague was a city that he could like. He found the temperature to be much colder than he anticipated; he hadn't brought along a warm enough coat for April, so whenever he was outside, particularly after dark, he couldn't shake the sensation of a heavy chill that settled into his bones. It was almost an ominous feeling, like a foreboding that something bad was about to come his way. But he easily shook off the feeling every time he thought about the sisters. He didn't know how he was going to be able to last until Friday. He thought about trying to find an actual woman to spend time with, like one of the incredibly beautiful adult escorts he saw advertised in a few of the underground newspapers. But he knew he was kidding himself—he had no interest in the charms of a grown woman.

※ ※

CALLIE SHERMAN WAS ONCE again in a tizzy. And once again the cause was her "boyfriend," Josh Howe. He had promised her that after Wednesday's show, they would have lunch together at some fancy place he had heard about, then they would go back to his place for some midafternoon "snuggling." That was a new inside joke between them after Megan had caught them on the couch together. The little girl had peppered Callie with questions for days after she had come out of her room to find them together, with Josh's hand down Callie's pants. Finally, Callie had come up with the word "snuggling" to describe to her three-year-old what they were doing. Josh loved it. It had become a euphemism for sex that he tried to use as often as possible; it became a way that he could ask Callie if she was interested in screwing without sounding too boorish. With snuggling, he had a handy, kid-approved replacement.

Callie was anxious all morning, but she had back-to-back meetings all day, so she couldn't see Josh until after the show. But when Callie went looking for him, he was nowhere to be found. She stood outside his office, staring through the glass at the darkened interior. Where the hell was he? She had gone shopping after work the day before, just to find a sexy little outfit for their hot date. Now he had disappeared? She asked his secretary about his whereabouts, but the young black woman just shrugged. Callie thought his secretary didn't like her at all. She wondered what it was—did it have anything to do with race? But she failed to think back on all the desperate, irate exchanges she had had with the woman over the past couple of years. She also failed to recall all the crying fits, slammed doors, and awkward moments she had put the entire staff through over the years with her Josh obsession. Callie tended to do that often—she had difficulty seeing the big picture.

Maybe something had happened to Josh. Maybe he had even gotten sick and had gone home early. Last week he had been suffering from a cold, prompting Callie to bring an assortment of cold medicines to work with her to take care of her man. Maybe he wasn't over the cold yet and he had gone home early. The more she thought about it, the more plausible that scenario became. She would go buy him some chicken noodle soup and then surprise him with it at his home. She wouldn't even call him first, so that he would be really surprised. Like a rookie detective with her eyes fixated on the probable culprit, Callie never even considered any other alternatives once she had grabbed on to the cold scenario. She rushed back to her office and grabbed her jacket and purse. If her baby wasn't feeling well, Callie wanted to be his hero and make him well.

About forty-five minutes later, Callie stood outside of Josh's apartment door, balancing the hot deli soup in her hand while she fished through her purse for her keys. She hadn't used them in nearly a year, but once again she was grateful that she had cajoled Josh into getting her a key to his apartment. She tried to be quiet so that she wouldn't wake Josh if he happened to be asleep. Slowly, gently, she slipped the key in the lock and turned the doorknob. Once she opened the door and quietly stepped inside . . . Callie got the shock of her life. She saw a familiar face on the couch, a woman that she recognized from *The Lunch Club* offices, sitting astride Josh, naked above the waist, while Josh licked and sucked on the woman's large, round breasts like a baby hungry for milk. Callie wasn't sure, but she thought the woman's name was Kara and that she was a secretary somewhere in *The Lunch Club* bureaucracy. The woman's eyes were closed and a big, satisfied smile was spread across her face, as if she had been transported to a private place. Josh made loud slurping noises, like the sound effects from some forgettable porn flick.

Callie screamed and at the same time lost her grip on the cup of hot soup. Just as Josh's head popped up from the left breast, his eyes widening and his mouth falling open, the soup made an explosive noise as it hit the carpet and splashed around the room in a circular pattern. Kara opened her eyes and immediately looked terrified. Callie couldn't hear, but she thought she could make out the words "Oh fuck!" formed by Kara's lips. As a secretary in the accounting pool, the woman was well aware of who Callie was—one of the most important executives in the entire galaxy of bigwigs at *The Lunch Club*. Callie was largely responsible for the size of her checks. She knew that getting caught half naked in Josh's apartment was not the best thing for her job security.

"Oh God, I'm sorry!" Kara yelled out as she jumped off Josh's lap. She scrambled to find her bra and blouse.

For his part, Josh was frozen, paralyzed by indecision. Despite all of his whoring, he had never been caught so stupidly, so ugly, so unequivocally. Amusingly, even in this position, Josh's basic nature rose to the surface—he thought to himself how yummy Callie looked today in her sexy outfit. But with a slowly dawning regret, he knew his hands would never grip Callie's wonderful hips again.

"My God, Josh!" Callie screamed. Her face was red and her eyes were ablaze, almost frightening in their fury. She was so disgusted and outraged that she didn't know what to do with herself. What gesture at this point would be grand enough to respond to this monumental betrayal? She felt her key chain in her hand. It was substantial enough to do some damage. She drew her right arm back like her father had taught her so long ago and she let go with a fastball right at Josh's head. Callie's intent was to hurt him. She missed, but she could see by Josh's reaction that the throw had shaken him even more.

"I hope you get run over by a cab!" she screamed.

It didn't take Josh long to understand that he had crossed some kind of line this time. On a day when he had promised to lavish attention on Callie, she had found him on his couch sucking on some other woman's tits. Could it get any worse? Yes, it could—he saw Kara in a panic closing the last button on her blouse and literally running toward the door. Apparently, the secretary with the porn-star body wasn't even going to stick around. What was the point in leaving now? he wanted to say to her. The damage had already been done. But with Callie, he knew that he might have done his career, and possibly even his show, some long-term harm.

"Let me explain, Callie," he said weakly. But he knew there was no real explanation available to him. What could he possibly say to make it better? Callie turned on her heels and walked toward the door. She was forgetting her keys. Josh took a deep breath and reached for them.

"Callie?" he said. "Your keys."

She turned around wearing the nastiest scowl he had ever seen. He didn't think it was possible to turn that lovely face of hers into something ugly, but she had managed. Callie was on fire and Josh didn't know it, but pure venom was about to spew forth. "Josh, you are the lowest, most fucked-up pond scum I have ever met," she said. "You were fucked-up when I met you, you were fucked-up when we were fucking . . . and you're still fucked-up." She stalked over to him and snatched the keys away. Callie had one parting shot left. "Although I wouldn't walk across the street to piss on you if you were on fire, remember that I owe you, motherfucker—and I always pay my debts."

For just a split second Josh was tempted to ask for his apartment key back—how could he have forgotten she had it!—but then the cold chill that went through his body made him think better of it.

⇥ ⇤

AS THE BLACK TOWN car cruised swiftly up Madison Avenue on its way up to Spanish Harlem, Dara couldn't stop her hands from trembling as she sat in the backseat next to Rain. Rain tried to hug her a few times to comfort her, but there was really no comfort to be gained from her lover. For Dara, making her parents happy and proud had been the basis for so many of her actions for so many years that she couldn't even fathom purposefully doing something that would make them unhappy with her. But she felt that this was exactly what she was about to do. And not only was she coming out to them, she had let Rain convince her to do it with her lover sitting right there next to her. She was having all kinds of second thoughts now. How would Rain ever have a strong, positive relationship with her parents when her introduction to them came with this *Showtime at the Apollo* drama?

"Maybe it wasn't such a bad idea to take the limo service after all," Rain said as she stretched out in the backseat. "Sure as hell beats a cab."

Dara nodded. The limo had been her idea. Rain thought it was a ridiculous waste of money to take a limo anywhere in Manhattan, but Rain didn't know anything about Harlem. Dara just imagined how hard it would be to find a cab at midnight when they emerged from her parents' apartment on Madison and 123rd Street.

"You know, I've been to Harlem before," Rain said.

Dara nodded. "Yes, yes, I know, Rain. You used to go to the Schomburg library all the time when you were a student at NYU. You told me that a whole bunch of times. I never said you didn't know anything about Harlem."

"Yeah, but you sure act like I don't, like you

need to protect the poor, naive little white girl
from harm in the big bad hood," Rain said with a
smirk. "Like I'm Little fuckin' Red Riding Hood or
something."

Dara sighed. She certainly didn't need an argument with Rain right now, as the car cruised past
120th Street and the start of Mount Morris Park—
or Marcus Garvey Park, as the tourist maps now
called it. This was scary enough already, without stepping into her parents' place with tension
between the two of them. They needed to be as
united a front as they could ever muster. The car
pulled up in front of her parents' building, an ele-
gant renovated brownstone that faced the park.
The building was actually on Madison Avenue,
a few buildings from the corner of 123rd. Dara
had purchased the condo inside the brownstone
for her parents several years earlier. The develop-
ers had converted the four-story brownstone into
three separate apartments. The Cruzes occupied
the only one that took up two floors, the ground
floor—which gave them access to the backyard—
and the second floor. Though most of their living
was done on the ground floor, where their main
bedroom was located in the back and a sitting
room was in the front, Dara's mom liked for her
guests to enter the building through the second
floor, so they would have to walk up the graceful front steps and enter the rather opulent marble
and mahogany foyer. Rain leaned in and told the
driver to pick them up in three hours and then

they ascended the stairs, each step bringing Dara closer to her Waterloo.

"This is a gorgeous block," Rain said, peering at the row of lovely brownstones facing the park, which was looking quite spiffy these days, Dara had to admit.

"Yeah, the old block is looking pretty nice these days," Dara said with more than a little pride. "Of course when I was growing up it didn't look so great."

"So how far away from here did you live when you were growing up?" Rain asked.

Dara pointed in the direction of 123rd Street. "About a block or so that way," she said. "We lived in a big apartment building. My sister Lisa and I used to play at this park like every day."

Rain nodded. Together, they stepped to the doorbell. Dara reached out and pushed it. They stood, waiting. Dara felt like she was living the final moments of her life. In the next fifteen minutes, everything could change. They heard footsteps approach. It was her father, Manuel. He had a huge grin on his face as he opened the door.

"*Hola, Dara!*" he said, reaching out both hands and taking her face in his. He leaned forward and kissed her tenderly on the forehead. He was just a little taller than she was, so with her heels she was looking him in the eye. He stepped back and beamed at her some more. He still hadn't acknowledged Rain.

"Daddy, I want you to meet a very good friend of

mine, Rain Sommers," Dara said, stepping back and pointing toward Rain. Rain held out her hand, but Manuel had no interest in a handshake; he grabbed her hand and pulled her toward him, enveloping her in a big bear hug. Dara saw a grin spread across Rain's face. Her father, still handsome and spry, could be quite the charmer when he wanted to be.

"I know who you are," he said after he let go of Rain. "I've seen you on television a bunch of times! Come on inside."

As they made their way into the building, Manuel called out, "Lena! Look who Dara brought with her!"

Magdalena popped her head into the hallway. She had an apron around her waist; Dara could see the fancy blouse and skirt underneath. Mom was dressed to the hilt. Magdalena smiled prettily. She was getting a bit thick around the middle and her long hair was now about half gray—she refused to dye it—but Magdalena Cruz was still a beautiful woman. At a glance, you could see where Dara's stunning looks came from. Dara's sister, Lisa, looked much more like their father than their mother. This meant that, while she was still an attractive woman, she had never had her sister's traffic-stopping looks—thus another source of tension between them.

"Hello, Mrs. Cruz," Rain said as she rushed forward to shake Magdalena's hand. Dara's mom had never been as affectionate as her dad. She was not a hugger; she shook Rain's hand.

"It's so nice to meet you," Magdalena said. She came over to plant a kiss on Dara's cheek, then she led them all into the dining room. As Dara suspected, there was just one lone guest at this "get-together," a good-looking Puerto Rican man with a thick mustache, slicked-back hair, and a well-tailored blue suit. He looked vaguely familiar to Dara but she couldn't quite place him. Clearly he was the blind date.

"Dara, you remember Orlando Vasquez?" Manuel said.

Orlando rose from the table and, wearing a giddy smile, came toward Dara for a hug. Orlando Vasquez. Of course. He was a boy from the neighborhood she had "dated" for a few months early in high school. With the mustache and all the Elvis hair, she hadn't really recognized him. She had to admit that Orlando looked good; he looked prosperous, happy, unlike most of the kids from the neighborhood she ran into these days. Dara stiffened as he approached, but she willed herself to loosen up and let the man hug her.

"Hello, Orlando," Dara said. "You look like you're doing well." She remembered that she used to call him "Londy" when they were together.

"He is!" Magdalena chimed in. "Orlando has his own trucking company. He is very successful. How many people you got working for you now, Orlando?"

"Um, about thirty-five, last time I checked," Orlando said proudly. "I'm doing okay." But then he shook his head and pointed at Dara. "But nothing like this one here! My God, you're doing your thing, girl! You like the most famous person from Spanish Harlem in the country. Pretty soon we gonna have to come up with a nickname for you like J.Lo. But she from the Bronx. I been working on one for you. How about D.Cru?"

Dara laughed and waved her hand dismissively. "You're crazy, Londy!"

"Ah, Londy. You remembered, huh?" Orlando said. He smiled, quite pleased that his childhood nickname had stayed with Dara.

Manuel, ever the perceptive host, noticed Rain standing off to the side, looking more than a little uncomfortable. For just a second, Dara was annoyed at the pained expression on Rain's face. Damn, she had told her what this was all about, that clearly her parents wanted her to meet some new man they had found. It shouldn't have been a surprise to Rain.

"Everybody, you guys know Rain Sommers, right? She's the famous comedian. You make movies too, right?" Manuel said, looking toward Rain for confirmation.

Rain nodded shyly. Dara had never seen Rain do anything shyly. Apparently the circumstances of this meeting had her a bit intimidated too. Dara was glad to see that she wasn't the only one who felt uncomfortable here.

"I didn't know you were bringing a guest, Dara," Lena said, scolding. "But luckily I made enough food."

"Well, Mommy, you said it was a get-together, remember?" Dara said, taking the opportunity to do some scolding of her own. "I didn't know that meant I was getting together with just one person."

Lena scowled, a bit embarrassed at her daughter's impertinence in front of Orlando. She had told the man that Dara was aware that he was coming and was fine with it. Orlando watched the looks exchanged by the two women and realized that he had been thrown in Dara's face. The knowledge stole away just a bit of his businessman swagger.

"Dara, did you bring the wine?" Magdalena asked.

Dara, terrified at what awaited her, had left it in the town car. She grimaced.

"Damn, I'm sorry, Mommy! I left it in the limo!"

"Watch your language, girl!" Magdalena said.

"You came here in a limo? To Spanish Harlem?" Orlando asked. He looked like he wasn't sure whether he should be impressed or amused.

"Not really a limo, a town car," Rain said, hoping to clarify things. But she just made them worse.

"Oh, excuuuse me, a *town car*," Orlando said mockingly. He saw several pairs of eyes on him and none of them were amused. He turned away and moved toward an empty chair in the living room. Young, good-looking, and successful, Orlando Vasquez was a star in his world. He had a long list of beautiful uptown Latinas and black girls vying for his affection. At first blush, he had no reason to believe that Dara would be a reach for him. But by now he realized he was far out of his league. As he lowered himself into the chair, his stature in his own eyes had been lowered as well.

For the next twenty minutes, a thick tension swirled around the second floor of the brownstone. Each person present had his or her own agenda and none could be too certain that it was shared by anyone else. While Manuel and Magdalena were trying to figure out how to get Orlando to resume his charming ways with Dara, they also were confused by the presence of Rain. It was nice that Dara wanted them to meet her important friends, but why did she bring this white girl to a dinner party in Spanish Harlem? Rain was using every mental trick she could think of to will Dara into making the announcement that would change everything. And Dara wanted to be anywhere else but in her parents' home. For once, she wished her big sister were around to lure her into an argument. At least that would be a respite from this.

"We don't have no wine, but I got beer," Manuel said with a smile, forcing some cheer on the group. "Anybody?"

Orlando nodded. "I'll take one of those, Mr. Cruz," he said. At least that would give him something to do with his hands.

"Well, there's no use standing around," Magdalena said. "The food is ready. Everybody should just sit down."

Everyone headed for the dinner table, which

was covered with Magdalena's best china. Dara was pleased to see that her mother had not tried to get too fancy and had gone with some traditional Puerto Rican staples, like *frijoles negros* (black bean soup), *asopao* (gumbo), *pastelón de carne* (meat pies), and *arroz con habichuelas* (rice and beans). Rain had located a table filled with framed pictures of Dara and her big sister; she chuckled quietly to herself as she scanned the many pictures of the girls in their white and frilly Catholic church finery.

"She was a cute little girl, wasn't she?" Manuel said as he watched Rain.

Rain nodded enthusiastically. "She was adorable!" she said.

Dara gestured for Rain to sit down at the table next to her. Manuel took the seat at the head of the table. Orlando sat down in the seat opposite Dara. Magdalena brought dishes in from the kitchen and placed them in the middle of the table, then sat next to Orlando, which was opposite Rain. Manuel smoothly blessed the food, saying grace in Spanish. For several minutes, the only sound in the room was the clinking of knives and forks on china and the smattering of thank-yous as the food got passed around. Dara could feel the tension inside of her chest steadily building, like the gathering of black clouds before a severe storm. When was the perfect time to do this? Would there ever *be* a perfect time? She glanced over at Rain, who was watching her closely, waiting. Dara took a long, deep breath.

"Mommy. Daddy. I have something I want to talk about with you," she said. She glanced over at Rain and added, "Actually, we both do."

Manuel and Magdalena exchanged curious looks but said nothing. Dara reached out toward Rain with her left hand. Rain slowly enclosed Dara's hand inside of hers and they rested them together on the table, almost like an offering to the rest of the room.

"Rain and I are lovers," Dara said. "We live together downtown. We love each other very much. I've known for a while now that I was attracted to women, but I was . . . I was . . . afraid. To tell both of you. I thought you would be . . . like . . . upset with me. Disappointed. But now, there it is. The truth. I'm a lesbian."

Dara waited for a gasp from Magdalena, a curse from Manuel. But she got neither. Instead, she got Orlando.

"Daaaamn," Orlando said softly, more to himself than anyone else. He nodded and looked back and forth between the two women, almost as if he were consoling himself with this new information.

Manuel reached out with his own left hand and took hold of Dara's right hand. The three of them now had a prayer chain going. "Dara, baby. You don't ever have to be afraid to tell me something," he said. "I love you, *niña*. I will always love you, no matter if you like men *or* women."

Manuel glanced over at Magdalena, who gave him a slight nod of encouragement and perhaps agreement. "Yes, you know we are Catholic and our church is kind of stupid about stuff like this," Manuel continued. "*Pero, es poco loco* because we know our church has a whole bunch of men and women who are, you know, gay—shoot, even some of the priests and probably the nuns too!"

"Manny!" Magdalena said.

"No, you know it's true, Lena! So we should leave the church out of it. But you are our baby girl, Dara. We just want you to be happy." His eyes started to tear up. He glanced again at Magdalena, who now had tears running down her face.

"Now, I don't know that much about Rain, except what I see on TV. I know she's *una mujer divertida*—one funny woman! *Pero*, if you have given your heart to this woman, she must be a very special person. *Claro*, if you love her, *niña*, then me and Lena want to love her too."

Now the tears roamed freely down Manuel's face. Dara felt a sob catch in her throat, then she let it go. She was surprised by the torrent of pent-up emotion that came pouring out of her. She let out a full, strong wail, bolted from her chair, and wrapped her arms around her father's head, holding him against her and gripping him with all her might. Magdalena groped for her napkin on the table and tried to dry her freshly flowing tears as she watched her daughter and her husband share a long, tight embrace. She looked across the table at Rain, whose face was slick from her own tears. Magdalena held out her arms to Rain, who smiled sweetly and walked over to step into Magdalena's embrace. Rain wept into this woman's blouse, this woman who was a stranger to her sixty minutes ago. Rain was floored by the reaction of this family, these special people. She thought back on her own coming-out to her parents and her older brother—the accusations, angry words, bitter curses, nasty threats. It was as fresh in her mind as if it had happened yesterday. Very few words had been exchanged since that day. An ugly cold war. That was the scene Rain expected in Spanish Harlem. Not this blubbering love fest. *My God, are these the most wonderful people I have ever met?* she thought.

The fifth member of the dinner party, the odd man out, Orlando, sat and watched the whole scene in disbelief. Damn, this was some serious shit, he thought. He reached up with the back of his hand to wipe away his own tears. Some serious shit.

CHAPTER 12

Heather Hope struggled through the final moments of her show, a special on foreign adoptions. It was the kind of mushy topic that she would normally dive into with an abundance of energy, making sure she got some tears from the guests and the audience members. But on this day, she was distracted by what was waiting for her on the desk in her office: the bound galleys for *Satan's Sisters*, Missy's book. Heather had been begging Missy for a peek at the manuscript for months, but Missy always came up with excuses why she couldn't hand it over to Heather. But this morning, just before Heather was about to walk down to the studio to begin the show, one of her assistants appeared at her door with a small padded envelope that had come by messenger. The word "Confidential" was stamped across the front of the envelope about a dozen times. Heather looked down and saw that it was from Melissa Adams. She tore into the package breathlessly and exclaimed so loudly when she held the advance galley in her hand that her assistant looked at her curiously.

"It's here!" Heather said, holding it aloft for the assistant to see. "Missy's book!"

The young girl smiled, but she clearly had no idea what her boss was talking about. Heather disappeared back into her office and shut the door behind her. She looked at the words on the back of the jacket—"explosive," "courageous," "damning," "scintillating," "shocking" were all adjectives used to describe the content. Heather gently placed it on her desk. They were doing a taping today instead of a live show. As soon as it was over, Heather planned to race back home and spend the rest of the day reading. She couldn't wait to dive in.

She was held up by a few meetings and a conference call with two of her agents, who were trying to convince her to do another movie, this time as the star. Heather had become a powerful Hollywood producer in the wake of her Academy Award. She had been involved behind the scenes as an investor and consultant on a half dozen major movies over the past few years. But she had been reluctant to get in front of the camera again. She just didn't see any value in it—why subject herself to the scrutiny and the certain attacks that would follow when she didn't have to? She didn't understand why her agents couldn't see that. She rushed them off the phone as quickly as she could with the promise to "look at" scripts if they could find some that were worth pursuing.

By the time Heather actually settled down in the buttery-soft living room couch with a glass of red wine and *Satan's Sisters*, it was already five o'clock, meaning she would have to stop at some point to eat dinner. Her driver had gotten caught up in a nasty traffic snarl on the way out to her mammoth estate in Alpine, New Jersey. Her cook was on vacation this week, so there would be no delicious meal waiting for her. But once Heather became engrossed in Missy's story, she forgot all about her stomach. She forgot about everything except the words on the page.

Heather was shocked by the raw honesty of Missy's tale. It was painful to read about the lie that she lived for all those years when she had become the darling of the conservative world. Missy recounted how she had fallen in love with a beautiful, brilliant young black man named Rayford Williams when they were both in high school in Alabama. They attended school on opposite sides of the town, which was about an hour outside of Birmingham. His school was predominantly black; hers was predominantly white. He was a star of his school's football team; Missy was a cheerleader. When their schools met during her junior year, Missy struck up a conversation with Rayford after the game. She was intoxicated by him—he was tall and muscular, with big, doelike eyes, long eyelashes, perfect white teeth, and a gorgeous smile that had her heart fluttering just minutes into their conversation. He was a year older than she, a senior. She could see a few of her friends from the cheerleading squad eyeing her suspiciously, wondering why she was talking so long to the black kid from the other side of town. Missy memorized his phone number and promised to call him. But she got the numbers mixed up and kept dialing the wrong number. She tried dozens of combinations. No luck. She was devastated, thinking she would never see him again.

But her phone rang two days later—he had somehow gotten his hands on her number! She never even found out how he had done it, but she was thrilled. They started sneaking to a secluded park on the outskirts of town to see each other. They both would creep out of the house when their parents were asleep and spend hours basking in the glow of their young love. Within a few months, they slept together for the first time. He was Missy's first lover and, while it hurt like hell the first few times, eventually she was stunned by how good it felt to have him inside of her. It got to the point where all she could think about was Rayford's body, his touch, his mouth, his penis. Her grades started slipping; her parents thought she was sick or something. No one recognized the symptoms of young love. As the school year progressed and winter turned to spring, Missy knew that Rayford would be going away soon. When she found out he was going into the military, she was mortified. He was due in basic training just a week after his graduation. On their last night together,

Missy persuaded him to make love to her without a condom because she wanted to feel him inside of her completely, totally, at least once before he was maybe gone from her life forever. They were in their usual spot, in an alcove of trees in the park, on a blanket underneath the stars on a balmy Alabama night. In the book, Missy said she felt uninhibited that night, totally free to let her passion run wild. It was probably the most intensely pleasurable experience of her life.

Heather was so blown away by what she had read that she had to put the book down. She knew exactly where this was heading and she couldn't believe it—the black father of Missy's child was her lover, not her rapist? Heather shook her head, confused and stunned by the revelation. How could Missy have let this whole thing spin so out of control? She let a man go to prison to cover up her story? Heather was furious at Missy . . . how could she be so dismissive of another human being? She had to make herself calm down so that she could continue.

After Rayford went away, everything changed for young Missy. Within six weeks, she realized she was pregnant. She was traumatized, apoplectic, dazed. She refused to eat or even get out of bed for two straight days. Her parents considered bringing her to a psychiatrist to find out what had overcome their child. After another week, while lying in bed with the television on, Missy came upon an old movie, *To Kill a Mockingbird*. She was desperate for an answer to her dilemma, and she was so afraid of what her parents and friends would say about Rayford and that they would call her a slut for getting pregnant. So she came up with the fateful idea that would trap her for the next fifteen years of her life. She told her parents that she had been raped by a black man while she was out riding her bike a few weeks earlier.

Heather put the book down again. She was breathless, disbelieving that her good friend could commit such a dastardly deed. And that she had gotten away with it for so long! And what had become of Rayford? Heather took a deep breath and went back to the pages.

Missy's parents, eager for an explanation for her bizarre behavior, never doubted her story. Though the medical examination could find no sign of rape, it did reveal that Missy was pregnant. Finding her rapist became a top priority of the town police department. When they found a young man who fit the vague description Missy had provided, she was so caught up in her tale that after a while she almost felt like it had really happened. This allowed her to feel no remorse when she testified at the trial and saw an all-white jury convict the young man. Though it was the 1990s, this area of Alabama still hadn't shaken the remnants of the segregated South. Her parents helped her raise her biracial child, Corey, while she graduated from the University of Alabama and then Vanderbilt Law School in Tennessee. When she moved to Atlanta to take a job with the U.S. attorney's office, she brought Corey with her. Her startling success in the courtroom was followed by a startling rise on television, eventually leading to *The Lunch Club* couch. Missy was taken aback by her popularity among the nation's Republican right; at first she was just speaking her mind, not really advocating any political causes. But her antiabortion views and her cover-girl looks were an irresistible combination.

It was past one a.m. when Heather came upon the Maxine section of the book. She was giddy when she saw that Missy had pulled no punches in providing a blow-by-blow accounting of how Maxine had blackmailed her into leaving the show and then forced everyone around her on the cast and crew to cosign her move—people whom Missy had grown to love and consider her closest friends. It was a brutal accounting of a heartless, egomaniacal despot at work. Heather loved every word of it.

"Yes!" Heather cried out to the beige-colored walls and ceilings of her large living room. "She got her!"

Heather was stunned by what she read next. After Missy left *The Lunch Club*, she received a phone call one day that changed her life again. It was Rayford, her old boyfriend. His military career was over, his marriage had ended, and he was curious about what his first love was up to. Missy was shocked to discover that Rayford had missed all the coverage of her rape and had no idea that she had even had a child. While stationed in Asia, he happened to stumble upon *The Lunch Club* one day and recognized his old girlfriend. On a whim, he decided to see if he could track her down again. He said it took him a year to get a phone number for her. They had no mutual friends, but there was a guy he had befriended in the navy who was from the same hometown and went to high school with Missy. That guy eventually gave him enough contacts that he was able to find one who could provide him with Missy's number. Rayford was living in Washington, D.C., so Missy said she'd be willing to meet him if he came to New York. Within thirty minutes, they realized that their old feelings were still strong and vibrant. They started dating and soon were professing their love for each other again. All the old passions came rushing back. They were both giddy that they had been able to do something everyone thinks about but no one is ever able to pull off: to go back to high school and recapture your first true love. But as the relationship got deeper and Rayford pressured Missy into introducing him to her son, Missy realized she would have to tell him everything. Frankly, she was surprised that Rayford hadn't googled her by now and read the many magazine accounts of her life story.

With her heart pounding in her chest, one day she sat Rayford down and told him the story of her life after he went into the navy. Rayford at first didn't even want to believe it. How could the woman he loved do something so cruel, so despicable? And he was devastated when she told him that the man was still in prison. How could she even begin to try to have him freed at this late date without being publicly revealed as a fraud? But it was the last part of the story that stopped Rayford in midsentence.

"You know I had a child," she told him. "Well, I told everyone that it was the rapist's baby, but it was yours."

"So wait, your son is actually my child?!" Rayford asked, wild-eyed.

Rayford broke down in tears when Missy nodded her head. He was childless and, now in his late thirties, had been wondering if it would ever happen for him. To discover now that he had a son who was nearly a grown man was almost more than he could bear. Missy managed over the next few months to show Rayford how deeply sorry she was about everything that had transpired. And when Rayford met Corey, he fully forgave her. Despite the incredible facts of their story, the unlikeliness of it, Missy, Rayford, and Corey had somehow become a happy family. Missy and Rayford had been married now for a year and were still passionately in love. In the end, Missy said she was ashamed of many of the things she had done and said in her past, including many of her more intolerant political stances, but that she was now going to devote the rest of her life to fighting injustice and making sure that her story could never be repeated in America.

When Heather finally put the book down on

the coffee table at 3:30 a.m., she had cried so much over the past two hours that she didn't think she would ever be able to shed another tear. She was spent, twisted into an emotional pretzel by her friend's mind-blowing, illogical, unacceptable, unbelievable, but ultimately moving and redemptive tale. As she got up to head for her bedroom, she knew that Missy had a sure bestseller on her hands. And she was glad she had gotten behind the book. But Maxine and the rest of the Lunch Club would be devastated. Missy had told many behind-the-scenes stories of shenanigans off the set of the popular show. Many feelings would be hurt. Secrets would be revealed. Some marriages were sure to end. A few heads would certainly roll.

⊰ ⊱

AS LIZETTE MADE HER way back to her office after the Thursday morning show, she couldn't help but notice that Karen looked distracted. She had noticed the same thing the day before, but she dismissed it. Everybody had bad days now and then. But it was unusual for Karen to look so disturbed for a second day in a row. Lizette felt she was close enough to Karen to ask her what was wrong.

"What's going on? Is everything all right? You are looking very, uh, distracted these days."

Karen stared at Lizette as if she were looking right through her.

"Karen!" Lizette said. The volume got Karen's attention.

"I'm sorry, Lizette," Karen said. She smiled sheepishly. "I guess I was off somewhere else. What did you say?"

"I asked if anything was wrong with you, that you seem very distracted lately," Lizette said.

"Wow, it's that noticeable?"

Lizette nodded. Karen let out a slow, heavy, resigned sigh. She looked up and down the hall nervously and gestured for Lizette to follow her. Lizette frowned at Karen's odd behavior, wondering for a brief second if perhaps the director was having some kind of emotional problems. They made a few turns and wound up at Karen's office. She motioned Lizette inside and shut the door behind them.

"Karen, what in the world is going on?" Lizette said as she sat down.

Karen shook her head. "I had a meeting a couple of days ago with Maxine. Believe it or not, Riley Dufrane told her that we need to make a change on the couch. Our ratings are slipping and he wants to do something to gin up some excitement."

Lizette's heart skipped several beats. This was horrible news.

"Wow, really?" Lizette said. "It's definite? Is Maxine gonna go along with that?"

Karen shrugged. "It's definitely happening. Maxine wasn't acting like she was going to try to fight it. I mean, he's the network president. How are you going to tell him no—even if you're Maxine Robinson?"

Lizette sat back in the chair, trying to come to

grips with this development. While the women in the cast weren't her best friends in the world, it was painful for her to consider that one of them would be tossed out onto the street because of ratings. None of them deserved that. Wow, television was such a harsh business. That's why they called it "show business"—it wasn't about friends. It always came down to business. She was quickly realizing that in this business they will fuck you over three minutes after they're fawning over you. And as for how it would affect her personally, her world would be turned upside down for months if they were bringing in someone new. True, it would be great for publicity and ultimately for ratings, but it would be hell to manage it all.

"Wow," Lizette said again. Then her mind drifted to the real question: who would go?

"So, what is the thinking about who would go?" Lizette asked.

Karen shrugged again. "Maxine actually asked for my help in trying to determine that. I guess that's why I've been so distracted. This is a pressure I do not need. I can't really tell which way Maxine is leaning. For each woman, I can come up with a thousand different reasons why she can't be fired. So I really don't know how to make this decision. But that's not doing my job. So I know I have to come up with something. I just hope that Maxine isn't setting me up to be the bad guy."

"You think Maxine has a problem with being the bad guy?" Lizette said with a slight smirk.

Karen looked up, to make sure her colleague was joking, then she laughed. "Yeah, I guess you're right. She's never had a problem with that in the past, has she?"

They both chuckled, enjoying their private joke at Maxine's expense. If there was one experience that everyone shared on the set and in the offices of *The Lunch Club*, it was the occasional wrath of Maxine Robinson. No, being the bad guy seemed to come quite naturally to her.

⊰ ⊱

LATER THAT NIGHT, LIZETTE snuggled under the covers with her boyfriend, giggling as he pressed his nose against her neck. Lizette had forgiven Channing the next day after their fateful "pre-engagement" dinner, partially because she loved him madly . . . but mainly because she loved his dick more. Slipping between the sheets with Channing was a quick and easy way to get her mind off the imminent changes on *The Lunch Club*. Lizette was extremely ticklish and couldn't stop laughing whenever Channing made any moves in her neck area. He said he loved the way she smelled, so he was always poking his nose around her. But she stopped giggling when his nose moved from her neck down to her naked breast. He opened his mouth and took her nipple inside, twirling his tongue around the tip and sending tremors straight down to her groin. She moaned softly, encouraging him to keep doing what he was doing. Lizette's entire breast region was very sensitive, one big erogenous zone, but her nipples were so responsive that she had even orgasmed a couple of times just from having them nibbled and sucked. This used to be a source of some embarrassment for her, but Channing had put an end to that. He said her orgasmic breasts were God's gift to the two of them—he loved her beautiful breasts and couldn't get enough of them, and she loved it when he worked his magic on them. "It's the perfect arrangement," he said.

Channing steadily increased the intensity of his licking and sucking, making Lizette start squirming and moaning even more loudly from the vibrations rumbling down her body. She wanted him to move his head farther south, to bury his face and tongue between her thighs and make her scream at the ceiling—but then again, she didn't want him to leave her breasts. Like ever.

After a few more minutes, she couldn't take it anymore. She had to feel him down below. "Channing, I want you to eat me," she said softly, sexily. She knew that he loved it when she talked nasty to him. She heard him emit a low, guttural groan as he obeyed her instructions and moved down between her legs. She heard the fairly loud sound of Channing moving his tongue amid her wetness down there. She also used to be embarrassed by how wet she got when she was turned on. A former boyfriend had once called her "Niagara Falls." He had quickly become an ex after that remark. But Channing said it made him proud to know that he could turn her on so much that she was literally "gushing." Lizette loved being with a writer, who was always quick to come up with fun and interesting new ways to describe these things that had always been a part of her. "Gushing" was a good example. Within five minutes, Lizette felt a quake starting to build from her toes, working its way slowly up her legs, picking up steam at her thighs, branching out to her midsection and arms, tingling down through her back, and finally releasing throughout her entire body in an explosion of pleasure.

"Oooh God!" Lizette screamed. She reached down and grabbed Channing's thick head of hair and pushed down as hard as she could, not even caring whether he could breathe. She let the waves run through her, wash over her. Finally, when they had run their course, she slowly let go of Channing's hair and felt her toes uncurl, easing her way back down to earth.

"Wow!" she said breathlessly. "That was unbelievable!"

She exhaled. "Mr. Cary, you got skills."

Channing's head popped up, wearing a big grin. "Why thank you, Miss Bradley."

"Let me catch my breath, then it's going to be your turn," she said. "Then I want to feel you inside of me."

Channing slid up the bed until his head was next to Lizette's. She put an arm around him and moved her body closer. She suddenly felt a chill, so she pulled the covers up around her neck. They lay in silence for several minutes, Lizette basking in the after-orgasm glow, Channing proudly enjoying his work. As she stared at the ceiling, Lizette slowly felt the latest drama from *The Lunch Club* creep back into her consciousness. The beheading soon to come.

"I just found out today that somebody from the show is about to get fired," Lizette said.

She felt Channing stir alongside her. "Really?" he asked. "What's that all about?"

"Well, I think they're concerned about the ratings. We've been slipping over the past year, losing ground to *Regis and Kelly* in some markets, even to *Who Wants to Be a Millionaire?* in some places. And even *The View* is now gaining on us. Riley Dufrane, the president of NBN, told Maxine a few days ago that we had to do something to shake things up, to bring some new energy to the show."

"Wow," Channing said. He tried to sound nonchalant, but his mind was racing as he listened to Lizette. He wished that he had a recorder with him so that he wouldn't lose a word.

"I don't think they've decided yet who's gonna go," Lizette said, anticipating his next question. "Or maybe they have and Karen just didn't want to tell me. I'm a little surprised that she told me as much as she did. I think Maxine has kind of put her in charge of making the decision, or at least helping Maxine decide, and it seems to be kind of stressing Karen out."

"Well, who do you think they might get rid of?"

Channing said. He was trying to breathe evenly, but he knew that this story on his site could drive traffic into the stratosphere. This might be good enough to get him to his next big bonus.

"I don't know," Lizette said. "I've been thinking about it constantly for like the last five hours. I think Whitney is maybe the most vulnerable, since she's been on the show the longest. But she brings the show a certain amount of credibility. I mean, besides Maxine, Whitney is the only real journalist we have."

She heard Channing snort. She knew he didn't have any respect for television journalists. "Yeah, yeah, I know you don't think she's much of a journalist. After all, how could she be a *real* journalist if she works for TV, right? Anyway, for that reason, I can't imagine how they could get rid of Whitney. And then there's Molly. She's so damn funny, she's like too important to the show to lose. But I guess they could always bring in another comedian. They could also bring in another real journalist to replace Whitney, but how exciting would that be? I mean, a journalist would just be too boring!"

Channing reached down and started tickling Lizette. "Oh yeah? Boring, huh?"

"Stop . . . Stop . . . Channing!" Lizette yelled.

Channing obeyed. Besides, he wasn't done yet. He wanted to scrape up every bit of dirt that Lizette had, even if they *had* moved beyond news to speculation. He could still use some of that. Chattercrazy.com was a gossip site, after all, not the *New York Times*.

"How about Dara and Shelly?" Channing asked.

"Nah, they're not going anywhere," Lizette said. "You can't get rid of Shelly. She's too fabulous. I think she brings in a younger, hipper audience. And she's black. Can't get rid of the black woman—even though I guess Maxine is black too. Anyway, I don't think Shelly's going anywhere. And Dara isn't going anywhere either. She's Latina, she's beautiful, she's brilliant, and she's the new kid on the block. I think she's probably the safest of all. So if I had to guess, I'd say maybe Molly. And she's seemed kind of distracted lately anyway. I don't think she's been as funny. Sometimes I think she may not be feeling well or something. I don't know. Maybe it could actually be Whitney. Who knows? This is all just speculation anyway."

Channing remembered that he had his laptop with him. He was desperate to get this all down while it was still fresh in his mind.

"Excuse me," he said, rising from the bed. "I forgot to send out an e-mail earlier. I'll be back in like ten minutes."

"An e-mail! But we're not done yet, remember?" Lizette said, her face in a frown.

"I swear, ten minutes," he said as he hurried out of the small bedroom. From the living room, he called out to her, "And don't fall asleep!"

⊰ ⊱

THOUGH SHELLY WAS HALF done with her thirties, just five short years from her forties—though she'd be more likely to describe it as just five years away from her twenties—she still liked to party like she was in her twenties. This meant that when she was ready for a night out, she was likely to show up with a crowd quite a bit younger than she. Sometimes, this meant that Shelly was going to be close by when something stupid transpired, as was the case on Monday when she got caught up in foolishness that wound up in the newspaper. But Shelly wasn't ever going to let some foolishness spoil her good time. Shelly was a pro at creating good times. She had learned from the best—the European fashion models who ran the streets of Milan, Paris, London, Barcelona, and the French Riviera like they were playgrounds specifically created for their amusement. You haven't really partied until you've snorted coke from the bare nipples of your best friend after giving a blow job to a hot stranger in the VIP section of Les Bains Douches before having an orgy in the back of a limo traveling along the Seine at 130 kilometers per hour after going three straight days without sleep and having to show up for an eight a.m. cover shoot. Shelly had done all that and much, much more. So when she came back to New York, she was much freer with her sexuality, her lifestyle, her boundaries, than probably any other Harvard Business School graduate within a thousand-mile radius. For these reasons and more, Shelly started gravitating toward the hip-hop crowd when she was looking for a good time. The rappers, musicians, and their hangers-on weren't into a hard-core drug scene—their happy juice tended to begin and end with weed—but they liked to enjoy themselves and they liked to spend money, two traits that Shelly had honed to perfection.

Some of Shelly's friends assumed that she was going to tone down the rapper forays after she joined *The Lunch Club*, but that hadn't happened at all. Particularly after she hired La—ah (LaDashah) as her assistant. La—ah's cousin, Ronny Ron, was a successful, well-connected hip-hop producer, so La—ah was apprised of every gathering of more than two hip-hop luminaries in any after-hours spot in the city, almost as soon as the first bottle of Patron had been purchased. This hip-hop grapevine perfectly suited Shelly's needs and was one of the main reasons she kept La—ah around. It certainly wasn't because of the woman's organizational abilities—sometimes Shelly had to wonder which one of them was the boss and which one was the assistant. But if Shelly were going to have an assistant, it somehow felt right that she would be almost as fabulous as Shelly.

And so it was that Shelly found herself cuddled up in the corner of Spry, the new hot West Side club, on Thursday with a gorgeous, well-known rapper named Big Sly who had decided he was going to attempt to swim in deeper waters for the night and try his luck with the fabulous Shelly Carter. Jay-Z had Beyoncé, Russell *used* to have Kimora . . . hell, it was time for Miss Shelly to step up her street cred, so Big Sly's affections had been enthusiastically reciprocated. Shelly found him to be exceedingly cute, with a bright, pretty smile and sculpted muscles that bulged from his arms and torso like they were trying to escape. She also found him to be a lot brighter than advertised—well, to be honest, she had no expectations about his level of intelligence and was merely basing her preconceptions on his chosen line of work.

As Shelly and Sly kissed and petted like teenagers, Sly's assistant, Ramon, was trying to lure La—ah onto a nearby couch. Ramon wasn't as good-looking or as muscular as his boss, but he was still sexy. La—ah couldn't stop staring at the man's hands. They were the largest hands she had ever seen, particularly on a normal-sized man like Ramon. She thought Ramon could probably palm her entire sizable butt with just one hand. Maybe she should give him a little positive feedback and see where it led, especially considering that her girl Shelly looked like she was about five seconds away from pulling the rapper's tool out of his designer jeans.

"Why don't you come over here and sit next to me, girl?" Ramon said. La—ah shrugged and sauntered over. She couldn't help but stare at Shelly and Big Sly, who looked like he now had his face buried between Shelly's large, twenty-five-thousand-dollar fake boobs. "Damn," La—ah said to Ramon, "those two look like they about to fuck right here in the club!"

Ramon glanced over at them and nodded his

head in agreement. "Seriously, they not wasting any time!" he said, putting his arm around La—ah's shoulder. "But let's forget about them. Pretend they aren't even there. I'd like to get to know you better, baby, regardless of what they're doing."

La—ah liked the sound of that. Too often guys thought you were supposed to sleep with them just because your friend was sleeping with their friend. Ramon was paying attention to her, not to what Sly was doing. She grabbed one of Ramon's hands, something she had been wanting to do for the past hour. She measured his fingers against hers.

"My God, your hands and your fingers are so big!" she said.

Ramon shrugged and smiled. "So should I go ahead and say it?" he asked mysteriously.

"Say what?" La—ah asked.

"Should I go ahead and make a joke about the size of my fingers?"

"A joke? What kind of joke?" La—ah asked with a frown. *What is he talking about?*

Ramon sighed. Clearly, this woman was not as quick as her boss.

"You know. What they say about what it means when you have big fingers," he said. It certainly didn't work when you had to explain it.

"Ohhh!" La—ah said, smacking herself against the forehead. When she actually thought about what he was trying to say, she was embarrassed that she hadn't caught on sooner. *Damn, this guy must think I'm an idiot,* she thought to herself.

He laughed at her reaction. "Okay, let's move on," he said. "Why don't you tell me all about what it's like to be you?"

"To be me?" she asked with a giggle.

"Yeah, you. What's it like to be the assistant for the fabulous Miss Shelly Carter? Then I'll tell you what it's like to be the assistant for the fabulous Big Sly. Then we can compare notes, see who has it worse."

They laughed together. La—ah was surprised by how much she was already starting to like this guy. It was not what she had expected when he and Big Sly came over and introduced themselves. She thought he was cute, but she assumed he had calculated that because he was rapper boy's assistant, then he would have her ass all lined up since she was Shelly's assistant, as if access to her pussy was one of the perks of messing around with Shelly. But he had turned out to be smart, funny, and a total gentleman.

They were laughing and giggling together about fifteen minutes into their battle over who had the worst job when Sly appeared in front of them, his clothes a mess and his face flush from excitement. La—ah wanted to laugh when she saw the hungry look on his face. *Damn, what was Shelly throwing on that boy over there?* So far Ramon was easily winning the assistants' battle of bad—since there was no way she could match the assignment that Ramon had a few months earlier to help some groupie tramp wash the vomit out of her weave and her pubic hair after she passed out naked in her own mess when she got too drunk at Sly's place. Ramon had objected, but Sly had answered, "Yo, you seriously don't expect me to do it, do you?"

"Y'all ready to go?" Sly said, his voice a bit hoarse. La—ah looked over and saw Shelly trying to fix her clothing before she got up.

"Where we going?" La—ah asked.

Sly glanced over at Shelly. "Um, I think we're all going to Shelly's place," he said.

They piled into Sly's sleek gray Maybach, driven by Ramon, and zoomed across town to Shelly's apartment on East Sixty-first Street, in one of Donald Trump's luxury palaces. "Wow, this is beautiful," Sly said when they stepped into Shelly's place. He went over to the window, marveling at the expansive view of the East Side skyline. He walked around the rooms, taking in the interesting, modernist furniture, the thick, shag carpets, the curious abstract art on the walls. She had picked up modernistic tastes while in Italy. Ironically, though many observers liked to call Shelly a young Maxine Robinson in training, two apartments and two personal styles couldn't be more dissimilar than Shelly's and Maxine's. While Shelly was all sleek lines and angles, Maxine's place was so old-world Victorian that it could have been decorated by Cornelius Vanderbilt himself.

"This is what a grown person's apartment is supposed to look like," Sly said with a smile.

"Maybe I could get you to come over to my place and give me some decorating tips."

Shelly stepped into his arms and stroked his smooth, bald head. "I'll give you any kind of tip you need," she said, grinning. "Why don't you let me show you my bedroom?"

She took him by the hand and started pulling him down the hall. She looked back at La—ah. "Y'all gonna be all right out here, dear?" she asked, eyebrows raised. La—ah nodded vigorously, glancing over at Ramon with a shy smile.

"Yes, I think we'll find something to keep ourselves busy," La—ah said.

As soon as they entered Shelly's bedroom, they didn't take much time for sightseeing. Shelly hungrily pulled Sly's shirt from his torso. She sucked in her breath as she passed her fingers over his chest and stomach, the rippling muscles feeling like steel cables beneath her hands. She truly understood why they called them washboard abs. This man's abdominals were ridiculous, like something out of a bodybuilding magazine.

"My God, how much time do you have to spend in the gym every day to get them to look like this?" Shelly said. She couldn't stop touching his stomach and his chest. When she heard his intake of breath as she passed her fingers over his nipples, Shelly grinned.

"Ah, sensitive nipples, huh?" She leaned over and took his left nipple in her mouth, running her tongue back and forth over the hard nub. She heard his moan. She knew he was probably growing down below, getting nice and long and hard for her. She grinned again with anticipation.

"Hey, baby?" Sly said. His deep voice sounded like a rumble coming through his chest and vibrated on her lips and tongue as she continued to play.

"Yes," she said through a mouthful of his thick, hairless chest.

"I got an idea. You trust me?"

Shelly thought that was an odd question coming from a guy she had just met. After all, this was a one-night stand in the making right here. How did trust come into the picture? Of course she didn't trust him. She didn't even know him!

"Um, why do you ask that?" she said, lifting up her mouth a little. Sly was now tugging on her blouse to get it over her head.

"Well, I was just wondering." He tossed her blouse to the side, then smoothly undid the clasps on her bra. It was Shelly's turn to suck in a breath as Sly leaned over and took one of her large breasts into his mouth. He pulled back and looked into her eyes. "How would you feel about making this even more interesting?"

He reached down now and started pulling her skirt off. When he was done, Shelly sat on the edge of the bed in her panties and high heels and nothing else. Sly gently pushed her back on the bedspread. It felt so soft as she sank into its folds. She giggled as he lowered his head to her stomach and started licking her navel. *This man doesn't waste any time*, Shelly thought. She tried to concentrate on what it was he was trying to say to her, but she was having difficulty. He had said something about making this "more interesting." What did that mean—it seemed to be quite interesting already.

"Huh?" Shelly said.

Now Sly put a couple of fingers in the waistband of her frilly black panties. In one decisive, sure motion, he yanked them down. Shelly let out a little yelp. She could smell her excitement, released from the panties and wafting through the room. She saw Sly's nostrils flare. Certainly he could smell it too. With a gleam in his eyes, he dived between her legs. Shelly moaned loudly as he went to work, separating her with his tongue and plunging it inside. The suddenness and shock of it all had seriously affected her—she felt like she was on the verge of an orgasm and he hadn't even gotten to her clitoris yet.

"How about," he said, lifting his head for a second, "if we join them in the other room?" He pushed his face back down again, this time taking her clit between his lips and tongue. Shelly could feel the familiar sensation starting in her legs. She knew this one was going to be loud and strong. In the back of her mind, as she relaxed and let the feelings begin to flow over her, she ran back what Sly had just said. Something about joining the other two in the other room. What did he mean by that? As he flicked his tongue back and forth, it occurred to Shelly that this man was proposing an orgy. He was seriously asking her if she wanted to go out there and have sex not just with him but with La—ah and Ramon?

"Oooh, here it comes," Shelly said, her voice starting out in a whisper. She was trying not to become distracted by the parallel thoughts running through her head. An orgy with La—ah? Damn, was he crazy? Shelly tensed her toes as the orgasm began to grow in intensity. One time she had tensed her toes so hard she had gotten a cramp in her foot. That was back in her Milan days with this Italian boy who was so sexy, Shelly thought he should just walk around the streets naked so that every woman he passed wouldn't have to go through the bother of wondering how he looked naked.

"Ooooooh!" Shelly cried out.

Shelly had done some wild things in her day, and had participated in her share of orgies when she was younger, but that was then and this was now. She had absolutely no interest in seeing her girl La—ah's coochie all up in her face. None. 'Cause from a guy's perspective, what an "orgy" usually turned into was allowing them to stick their dicks in the other girls and then watching the women eat each other out. Of course they never had any intention of putting another man's dick in their mouths. The idea of seeing and touching La—ah's snatch was about as appealing to Shelly as seeing Maxine Robinson naked.

She gripped the sheets and felt the waves begin to subside. As she came down from her orgasmic high, Shelly took several long, deep breaths. Then she sat up on the bed.

"Sly!" she said, her chest still heaving. "Are you seriously trying to talk me into going out there and letting you fuck my assistant? Is that what you just said to me?"

She saw the surprised look come over his face. What kind of wild woman did he think she was? How would that look in the gossip pages—"Shelly Carter Caught in 69 with Her Assistant"?

"That's some crazy shit, Sly!"

He frowned. "It was just a suggestion, baby. That's all." He started pulling down his pants. "Now, why don't you come over here and let me slide these nine inches down your throat?"

Just like that, Shelly felt like she had quickly become a character in a bad porn movie. She really liked sex, but she hated bad porn movies.

"You know what, Sly? I think you need to keep those nine inches in your pants and take your narrow behind back uptown." She didn't really sound angry when she said it, so Sly thought she was just kidding. He laughed—until he saw Shelly stand up and start putting her panties and skirt back on.

"Wait, you're serious?" he said. His frown had turned into shock.

"Serious as a motherfuckin' heart attack," Shelly said. She made sure to keep her voice sweet and even. She didn't want to incite his rage or embarrassment. She knew shame could lead some men to do crazy things. She had no desire to shame him—she had just had a change of heart. It was time for Big Sly the rapper to go on home.

She picked up his shirt and tossed it to him, then she pulled on her bra and blouse. He sat there, staring in disbelief. He shook his head. "Damn, Shelly Carter," he said. "I had no idea you were a crazy bitch!"

Shelly grinned. It was so calm and serene a grin that Sly found it unnerving. "I might be a crazy bitch, but this crazy bitch is kicking you out." She walked toward the door and waited for Sly to follow. Slowly he pulled his shirt back over his head and rose from the bed.

"Damn, really? It's like that?" he said as he approached her.

Shelly nodded. "Yep, it's like that," she said.

When they went back out into the living room, they were greeted by the other half of their orgy scene. La—ah was naked below the waist, with Ramon's face buried between her legs. She was moaning and thrashing and actually throwing Shelly's pillows across the room.

"Girl, you need to stop throwing around my furniture!" Shelly said, laughing as she said it. La—ah's eyes flew open. She screamed and pushed Ramon's head away from her.

"What the fuck . . . ?" Ramon said. He lifted his head and saw two pairs of eyes staring at him from the other side of the couch.

"What happened?" he said.

"I think it's time for us to go," Sly said. He shook his head in regret. "Sorry, my dude."

Ramon pushed himself up from the couch as La—ah hurriedly pulled her panties back over her plump ass.

"LaDashah, you're welcome to go with him," Shelly said. "I don't want to break nothing up. Ramon can do some more muff diving—he just can't do it here."

La—ah started to blush. "Muff diving? Damn, Shelly!"

"Yo, I think you need to wipe your face before we go," Sly said to Ramon. He turned and headed toward the door without looking back. Ramon followed him slowly. But Ramon *did* look back.

"Can I call you?" he said to La—ah.

La—ah nodded flirtatiously. When the door had closed behind them, La—ah and Shelly looked at each other and burst into laughter.

CHAPTER 13

As Lizette approached the office on Friday morning, she had renewed pep in her step. She had spoken briefly with Martin Peters, the Patterson & White lawyer, and he seemed confident that a copy of Missy's manuscript could be in her hands by the end of next week. And the night before, the menu for Maxine's dinner party was finalized with the caterers, so there was a strong possibility the dinner party would actually proceed without a major hitch. At first Lizette was a bit insulted that she hadn't been invited to attend the party, but now she was glad to be spared. She would have been a nervous wreck the entire night, just waiting for some disaster to strike. This way, she could go out with her girlfriends on Saturday night and get drunk. Or even better, go out with Channing and finish the night cuddled in bed with his strong arms wrapped around her.

Lizette's good feelings quickly were forgotten the moment she stepped into the West Side building that held the set and the offices of *The Lunch Club*. Something was amiss. Secretaries were flitting about, talking in hushed tones, as if they were trying to pretend they weren't talking. She saw Callie Sherman literally run down the hall and disappear into Maxine's office. That could not be good at all.

"What's going on?" Lizette asked her secretary, Rena, before she went into her office.

"Ooh, Lizette, I've been waiting for you," Rena said, pursing her lips. "I tried to call you. Maxine has been looking for you. I think it's about that website, chattercrazy."

Lizette felt her heart leap into her throat. No, not that damn website again. She rushed into the office and turned on her computer. In the seconds it took the machine to turn on, Lizette rocked back and forth in her chair. To an outside observer she might have looked like a mental patient.

When Lizette got on to the chattercrazy.com site and saw the home page, she audibly gasped.

"'The Lunch Club' About to Fire a Host!" the headline blared across the screen. Lizette clutched her hands against her chest as she read on, almost as if she were praying.

> Sources from the set of "The Lunch Club" have told chattercrazy.com that the venerable daytime institution is on the verge of firing one of the hosts because of faltering ratings. While show insiders

haven't yet decided who might be the victim of the axe, early speculation has centered around Whitney Harlington, the award-winning former NBN News correspondent, and funny lady Molly McCarthy Stein. The two newest members of the cast, Shelly Carter and Dara Cruz, are considered somewhat untouchable, since they attract a demographic—young and non-white—that the show has been desperate to court. "The Lunch Club" recently has been losing consistently in the ratings battle to shows like "Regis and Kelly" and, in some markets, even local news and current events shows. NBN president Riley Dufrane has ordered Maxine Robinson, the show's creator and boss, to replace one of the hosts as a way of shaking things up and perhaps attracting desperately needed new viewers.

Lizette felt like her head was caught in a vise and someone was squeezing it tighter and tighter. She wanted to open her mouth and scream as loud as she could. But she couldn't do that. By the time she had reached the fifth sentence of the chatter-crazy story, Lizette had one word bouncing around in her head: Channing! She now had a very strong suspicion that her beloved boyfriend was the source of these stories, the wizard behind chatter-crazy.com. It all made sense now, how the stories were all sounding like they might have come out of Lizette's own mouth. The site had no byline or contact information—both she and Maxine had tried hard to get it—but now she knew why. Her adoring boyfriend, the man she planned to marry and have father her children, had fucked her—and not in the biblical sense.

In addition to the pounding in her head, Lizette now also felt a shortness of breath. She tried to calm down, to tell herself that she needed to relax and take deep breaths. But deep breaths couldn't mask the panic that was creeping up her spine, across her neck, into her skull. Even though she might be able to identify the possible source of these leaks, that information would not go far in saving her job. Once word raced around the building that it was Lizette's boyfriend/wannabe fiancé writing this stuff, she was certain she'd be escorted outside by security in a matter of seconds.

There was only one possible course of action to save her job: she *had* to get her hands on Missy's manuscript. Right away. She was so desperate now, she probably would agree to drop to her knees and give Martin Peters a blow job in the middle of Times Square if he would hand over the manuscript after he zipped up his pants. But until she got her hands on the book, she would have to figure out how to lie low, try to make herself invisible. She looked down at her phone and saw that the messages from journalists were already starting to stack up. She didn't see how she was going to be able to escape this story. And she was likely going to have to spend most of the day around Maxine anyway, as they put the finishing touches on the dinner party. But maybe she could run out and say that she had some last-minute party planning she had to take care of. She just couldn't imagine even looking in Maxine's face right now.

Just then, Lizette's office door flew open. Lizette jumped in her chair, frightened by the intrusion. She looked up and saw Karen Siegel, whose face was wet and eyes red and puffy. Clearly, Karen had been crying.

"Oh God, Lizette, how *could* you?" Karen said. She started to cry once again.

"How could I what?" Lizette said, trying to hold back her own tears.

"I know you must have seen that fuckin' website by now!" Karen said. "I know it must have been you. Nobody else knows! *Nobody!* And you're the one with all the media contacts. Why would you want to destroy me like this?"

"I swear, Karen, I didn't feed any information to a website," Lizette said. She was trying to find a way to phrase it so that she wasn't telling an outright lie.

"I don't believe you!" Karen said. She started sobbing loudly. "I don't even know how I can face Maxine," she said more softly, more to herself than to Lizette. "What can I tell her? She trusted me, she confided in me, now she has this disaster on her hands. Lucky for her she's just about the only person in the building who can't be fired."

Lizette was mortified. Karen appeared to be on the verge of a nervous breakdown, and it all was precipitated by Lizette and her indiscretions. But how could she know that she couldn't talk about her job with her man, of all people? That she had to be careful of her pillow talk, even in the throes of a wonderful orgasm? How could Channing have sold her out like this, just for some stupid website? How important could she possibly have been to him?

"Maxine hasn't come out of her office in an hour," Karen said. "Whitney and Molly have both been crying in their offices. Don't ask me how in the hell we're going to do a show today! They are all distraught—and I don't blame them. It's all my fault. I thought I could trust you, but I should have known better."

She looked Lizette in the eye, sniffling and shedding tears. "You're a horrible little bitch, you know that?" Karen said. Her nasty stare lingered for an extra second, then she turned around and was gone.

Lizette was so shaken that her legs felt paralyzed by the emotional trauma. She had no idea what she should do, but she knew that she couldn't sit there and wait for the assassins to find her. Lizette willed her body to move. She grabbed her pocketbook and her cell phone and fled out of a side door. She had no idea where she would go and what she would do for the rest of the afternoon. Maybe she could buy a bottle of Jack Daniel's and get shit-faced. Anything to take her mind off this disaster. Her high heels clicked on the sidewalk as she went to the curb to catch a cab. Once again, there was one word bouncing around in her head: Channing!

⊰ ⊱

ERIC HARLINGTON CHECKED HIS bag for about the twentieth time that morning. He needed to make sure he had all the pieces to make the recordings. He had tested the battery's charge on the video camera about fifteen times. He couldn't believe this was about to happen. He had paid for an entire day with these two young girls; he could extend it to an overnight if he was willing to add another five thousand dollars to the pot. He had about that much left. He wasn't eager to part with it, but he figured the decision would be a no-brainer once he met the girls. For days he had been fantasizing about what they might look like, hoping that they looked like a younger version of the unbelievably beautiful woman who worked the front desk at the hotel where he was staying. A few times he had come close to asking the woman if she had any daughters—and if she might be carrying a few pictures of them. He knew that such thoughts would be alarming and disgusting to most people, but when he was in his hypersexual stalking mode, awaiting his prey in one of these foreign lands, he found it easy to divorce himself from all connections to morality and good judgment. After all, he was in a different land with different rules about such things. These Europeans weren't nearly so prudish as Americans about husbands having extramarital affairs or, he suspected, about men having sex with girls. Otherwise, this whole production wouldn't have been so easy for him to arrange. Certainly that was the case in the Asian countries that he had been frequenting before—those parents cared so little about their daughters that he had been offered on more than one occasion (once by the girl's own mother!) the chance to "buy" one of the girls, to use as a sex slave, for as long as he liked. He had shaken his head in wonder—not so much at the monstrous inhumanity of the offer, but at the assumption that he'd somehow be able to smuggle a young "sex slave" back into the United States with him. What was he supposed to do, stash her in his toiletry bag? He could just see the new airport signs in the United States, warning against liquid containers in excess of three ounces and against stashing young girls in your carry-on luggage.

Finally, the appointed hour arrived. Eric took several deep breaths and entered the building. It was an old apartment building, about five stories high, made of worn redbrick that was probably at least a century old. He had been given explicit instructions to come to apartment 1C—the door would be unlocked—leave the cash on the table in the living room, then go into the first room on the right to wait for the girls. Eric was pleased that he wouldn't have interaction with any adults. That had always made him feel a bit squeamish in the past. Interaction with adults could lead to situations where a mother could ask him if he wanted to buy her child.

Eric walked down a narrow hallway, overwhelmed by the smell of cooking goulash and the sounds behind the doors that he passed. He could hear garbled voices of a conversation in one apartment; a television blared loudly in another. In a distant apartment, he thought he could hear the wail of a crying baby. Or maybe it was a mewling cat?

When he came upon 1C, he turned the knob and opened the heavy door. He was greeted by an old, sparsely furnished apartment, with a misshapen cloth couch and an old wooden coffee table sitting forlornly in the middle of the living room. There were two windows, but they were covered by drawn shades, giving the room a dark, menacing feel that sent a quick shiver down his spine. He took out the large stack of hundred-dollar bills that represented the remaining balance and placed it carefully on the coffee table. He had wired the initial deposit into a Czech Republic bank account right before he had left for Europe. The instructions were to bring the rest in cash—U.S. currency only. He had laughed at that, as if he would have been trying to find stacks of *koruny*, the Czech currency.

Eric hesitated. They must be watching him somehow, on some kind of hidden surveillance. The idea of being recorded on somebody else's camera was a bit disconcerting. But he was much too far down this road now to get skittish. He would just have to trust his sources. After all, if their intent was some kind of extortion, there was really nothing he could do about it anyway. Trust was a big part of the game when you had a hobby such as his. He looked again around the room, wondering where a camera could be hidden. He noticed an old corroded light fixture in a corner and a lone bulb in the overhead light, with no kind of covering. This place was not intended to exude a feeling of luxury.

After another deep breath, Eric approached the door to his right. Maybe the girls were already there. He felt his senses heighten as he turned the knob. But the room was empty, containing nothing but a double bed covered by white sheets and a nightstand that could have been an antique. A small window with more drawn shades gave the room a scant amount of light. The walls were covered by faded floral wallpaper and the room smelled a little musty, but it was a scene that was somewhat familiar to Eric. It was a bit more livable than some of the shacks he had entered in Southeast Asia; he was used to having these assignations in places that might be construed as creepy. As he walked toward the bed and sat down gingerly on its edge, Eric wondered for an unfortunate second what Whitney would do if he ever tried to bring her into a room like this to have sex. But he shook his head vigorously. Whitney was the last thing he needed on his mind at a time like this. Besides,

Whitney was so uninterested in sex, it wouldn't matter if he got a suite at the Ritz—she'd still not want him to touch her. If Whitney had been more interested in sex, Eric might not even be in a room like this. Surely her frigid rejection of him in recent years had been a driving force sending him into these rendezvous with young girls. *Surely it was*, he told himself.

Finally, Eric loosened up enough to put his bag down on the floor. He checked his watch. It was now ten minutes past the time the meeting was to occur. He was beginning to get antsy. He prayed that nothing had gone wrong.

When he thought he heard voices outside the door, Eric perked up. The girls were here! Eric felt his pulse quickening. *My God*, he thought, *the moment has finally arrived*. He almost couldn't believe it was about to happen, the culmination of probably his most fervid sexual fantasy. Two young sisters. His mouth actually started to water at the thought of them. He hoped they were very pretty, but he told himself that it didn't really matter if they weren't gorgeous. As long as they were slim and not fully developed.

The door opened and he heard heavier footsteps than he had been expecting. When he saw three male forms enter the room, his heart jumped. What was going on? *This wasn't the plan!*

"Excuse me," he said, rising quickly from the bed. The men wore serious expressions. They didn't look like he imagined his European contact to look. In fact, they looked more like cops. He took two steps back and felt himself falling back on the bed. One of the men looked vaguely familiar. Eric was sure he had seen him before.

"Take it easy," the first man said in a heavy Czech accent. He had both hands out in front of him, indicating he meant no harm. But Eric was so afraid that he thought he might soil his pants.

"Mr. Harlington, we are from the National Police of Czech Republic," the man said. His voice was stern but somehow kind. Eric, for just a second, thought that maybe this kind man was here to extend some kind of leniency. Maybe they would let him go. Just give him a warning. After all, he hadn't even done anything wrong yet. Right?

But then the next voice Eric heard sent a jolt through him so severe that he actually twitched, as if in the throes of a seizure.

"Mr. Harlington, my name is Drew Finch. I'm from *Primeline*."

Oh God. It *was* the guy from *Primeline*, the one who did all those investigative exposé shows that Eric despised but couldn't stop himself from watching.

"Oh my God!" Eric cried out. Finch now had a cameraman right next to him, with the lens pointing directly at Eric. Immediately, Eric started blubbering, crying so loudly and severely that snot was shooting from his nose.

"No, please!" Eric said. He looked again at the camera, his face a mask of horror. *Where is the nice man from the Czech police?* He looked around madly, for some relief, some escape. A Czech jail would be infinitely superior to this, starring in a *Primeline* special. Eric wished that he had some kind of cyanide pill or something that could kill him instantly, something he had seen once maybe in a James Bond movie. If he had been able to, he would gladly have chosen to die at that moment.

"Please forgive me!" he screamed at Finch. "I didn't do anything!"

"Mr. Harlington, you know that's not really true," Finch said smoothly. He was always so damn smooth and calm. "We know that you had arranged to meet two underage girls here. We have the money you wired into a bank account as payment for these girls, sir, and we saw you just put a stack of cash on the table a few moments ago."

Eric was wild-eyed. He knew that he needed to try to control himself. This was on camera and would be beamed across the United States. But control was the last thing he had at his disposal. He thought about getting up from the bed and trying to make a run for it. He must have made some type of movement in that direction because the lead man from the Czech police stepped toward him.

"Sir, can you please stand up?" the policeman said. Eric saw the open handcuffs in the officer's hand. *Where did those come from?*

Eric stood. He saw the American cameraman back up a step, probably to get a better angle.

"Mr. Harlington, what do you have there in that bag? May we take a look?"

Finch stepped forward and picked up Eric's bag as his cameraman stepped up to get a good shot of the bag's contents. Eric felt a panic race down his spine. Again he feared that he might piss—or worse—in his pants.

"Please, Mr. Finch!" Eric said. The camera swung back to him. "Please, give me a break. I have two daughters at home myself. I would never do anything to hurt a young girl!"

"In fact, you have twin daughters, age fourteen, do you not?" Finch asked. He opened the bag and carefully lifted out the video camera. "Were you planning to use this camera to film these two young girls, Mr. Harlington?"

Eric dropped his head, sniffling and sobbing into his chest. It was a sickening sound, one that would soon be broadcast all across America and many other parts of the world. Eric Harlington was about to become the international poster child for the American tourist child molester.

CHAPTER 14

The dinner party was at comfortable cruising speed when Bill Murphy, the president of Patterson & White, finally arrived with his wife, a pretty, full-figured woman with lovely, bright auburn hair. Maxine let go a relieved sigh when she greeted him, glad that he hadn't been scared away by the story on that ridiculous website. The other women in the room, including Maxine, immediately wondered whether Murph's wife was sporting her natural hair color or the striking shade came courtesy of some high-priced salon. It was a sure bet that at least one of the women would have enough alcohol to find out before the evening was done.

When one hosts a dinner party, there are several elements that must all come together like the perfect storm for it to be considered a success. Of course, Maxine called in her favorite chef, Herb Wilson, to design the menu. His famous Roasted Guinea Hen with Morel Mushrooms and Black

Truffle Risotto with Lobster was sure to be a hit with this crowd. Chef Wilson's French bistro, Dine, on the Upper East Side had become Maxine's dinner place of choice for the last year. Wilson jumped at the chance to cater Maxine's private dinner party mainly because he owed her for giving Dine that necessary high-end buzz that every restaurant needs to keep it popping. Daily Blossom's over-the-top arrangements of Casablanca lilies decorated the main salon, dining room, and entry foyer, and as a special touch, the owner, Saundra Parks, had sent over a tiny bowl of gardenias for the powder room. Food, flowers, friends, and, of course, a fabulous hostess outfit—those were the necessities.

In the fabulous-outfit category, Maxine didn't disappoint. She chose a Givenchy black satin tuxedo with a lace camisole to set off the tone of the evening. Style, sex, power, and privilege . . . all conveyed in one little suit. At just under ten thousand dollars, it was actually one very expensive little suit.

Maxine actually had butterflies. All her dinner parties were important, but this one was a matter of life or death. She never hosted a dinner just to be social—she thought those who sat around with friends shooting the shit were just wasting their time. She'd never admit to herself that she had no real friends who wanted to sit around and shoot the shit with her, so a dinner designed for duplicity was her choice for all social events.

Tonight's dinner put all of Maxine's considerable skills to work. She could be engaging and witty without having to hold deep, substantive conversations with anyone. When you were a dinner party guest, often you'd find yourself trapped in a long-winded philosophical debate with some boring character whom you would normally not even give a passing glance on the street. Maxine loved being the center of attention, but she didn't really like to allow people all up in her business. As the host, all eyes and ears were on her, but she controlled the circumstances and the level of intrusion. Sure, she couldn't completely contain three dozen people roaming around her apartment, but she knew someone would have to be a social deviant to wander beyond the generally accepted dinner party boundaries—living room, dining room, maybe kitchen, maybe media center if the host had opened up that possibility, and, of course, bathroom. That was it. If you found yourself in any other room, you had crossed a line.

Maxine swept her gaze across the room, surveying it with the precision of a keenly calibrated radar system. She was looking for empty glasses, forlorn guests, overheated conversation, or the inappropriately inebriated. That last one was crucial because a drunk guest could quickly wreck a party and send everyone fleeing. She had seen it happen more than once. It was Maxine's job to keep the conversations light and funny, make sure everyone was comfortable, and have every person walking out the door at the end of the night feeling like they were the guest of honor. As the guests stood around in the living room and foyer, the chatter and the laughter filled the space with the noise of a fun time. Most of the guests were powerful white men and their pretty wives, two groups that Maxine had learned over the years to manipulate at will. She was looking for a signal from Mary Guiliani, her catering manager, that it was time to have the guests seated, but she saw that the woman was still speaking to Chef Wilson in the kitchen.

Maxine spotted Jamie Sloan, president of a major recording label, who was standing off to the side by himself. "Hello, Jamie," she said, approaching him wearing a big smile. When she had called him on Monday, Jamie had told her he was too busy to attend. But after about ten minutes, Jamie had changed his mind. Or rather, Maxine had changed it for him when she told him that the legendary singer Debra Henley would be attending—and that Debra was about to be released from her longtime contract with Sony. Like Barbra Streisand, Henley was still selling millions of records well into her later years. Maxine knew that it would be a huge coup for Jamie if he could convince Henley to join his label.

"Hello, Maxine," Jamie answered her. He wore a hint of a grimace on his face. Maxine knew why.

"I just talked to Debra about five minutes ago," Maxine said. "She wanted me to know she was running a little late. But I have you two sitting at the same table. I have your wife sitting next to her.

I think the two of them would really hit it off. Let June work her magic. Okay, Jamie?"

A smile of relief spread across Jamie's face. "Thanks, Maxine," he said, putting a hand on her shoulder. "I don't know how you do it, but you never cease to amaze."

Maxine almost blushed. Out of the corner of her eye, she spotted the catering manager, motioning to her that dinner was ready.

"Excuse me, Jamie," Maxine said. "Looks like it's time to eat."

Maxine cleared her throat. "Excuse me, everyone! Dinner is now being served. I have hosts in the dining room who will show everyone to their seats."

It had been part of Lizette's job to give the five pretty young girls serving as hosts a briefing on what all the guests looked like, complete with headshots of each one. Maxine had noticed the young girls hovering around the edges of the room in their short black cocktail dresses, making sure that they had every person in the room down cold, all thirty-four guests. Maxine had moved her long dining room table out of the room and brought in five round tables that seated eight people each. Daily Blossom had hit it out of the park with the decor. Each table was covered with a beautiful beige tablecloth and a breathtaking centerpiece that featured long glass vases filled with water and lovely white and purple irises, submerged to give off the artsy effect of magnification.

As the guests slowly filed into the dining room, Maxine saw movement out in the foyer. New guests had arrived. She could see that it was four people, although Debra Henley and her latest boyfriend were the only guests who were missing. As she got closer, she saw that it was indeed Debra Henley and a gorgeous man about twenty years her junior. But it was also Shelly Carter and Whitney Harlington. Maxine scowled. Those impudent bitches had crashed her party—after she had told them they couldn't come! Maxine was extremely pissed, but it was her job not to let it show.

"Debra!" Maxine said, ignoring Shelly and Whitney and gliding over to the aging pop diva, who had once been called "the voice of her generation." Debra glittered in a sparkly white dress and gaudy jeweled earrings. They exchanged genuine hugs. Debra and Maxine had become friendly years ago, after Debra had sat for an hour-long interview with Maxine. Debra had just been nominated for a Grammy for her multiplatinum album. Maxine, the daughter of a sharecropper from Texas, and Debra, the daughter of a shoeshine man from Brooklyn, really hit it off and had remained friends ever since. Though they didn't talk all that often anymore, whenever they were around each other they reverted back to the junior high school antics of the popular girls in the lunchroom, giggling and passing whispered secrets back and forth.

"Maxine, you look fabulous!" Debra said.

Maxine spun around to give Debra the

360-degree look at her outfit. "It's Givenchy. You like?"

Debra grinned. "Yes, I love!" She removed her light coat and did a spin herself. She had gotten a little thicker around the middle, but Debra still had the body and the legs, especially the legs, that had helped sell tens of millions of records.

"We're just about to eat, so you should go in and find your seat," Maxine said. "I think you're sitting next to Jamie Sloan."

Debra gave Maxine a knowing grin. "Maxine, what naughtiness are you up to?"

Maxine shrugged. "What?" she said, feigning innocence. "It's just a coincidence."

Debra shook her head. "Maxine, you're bad," she said as she sauntered away, linking her arm with the "boyfriend" she hadn't even bothered to introduce to Maxine.

Maxine pivoted and instantly turned her attention to Shelly and Whitney, who had been standing by and watching the Debra Henley scene with more than a little trepidation, though they also tried not to let it show. Crashing the party had been Shelly's idea, but it had been Whitney's idea for them to stop at a nearby bar and down a few drinks before they came upstairs. The drinks were obviously for courage, but neither of them verbalized it. Whitney had been thoroughly spooked by the story on chattercrazy about someone being fired. Though she had initially been giddy about the excitement of crashing Maxine's party, it took a whole lot of convincing by Shelly to get Whitney to accompany her after that story ran. After the alcohol, Whitney had gotten a bit looser and more carefree on the elevator coming up, even talking a little shit about how Maxine had no right to keep them away, but now, confronted with the largeness of Maxine, in her tuxedo elegance, surrounded by the stars and the home, all the trappings of her fabulousness, their courage was quickly slipping away.

"Okay, I'll let you stay, since the alternative is so unpleasant," Maxine whispered to them between her clenched teeth. "But don't think you got over on somebody!" As she began to walk away, she added, "As you both well know, I have a looong memory."

Shelly and Whitney looked at each other. Whitney felt her heart leap into her throat. Shelly shrugged nonchalantly. They saw Maxine talking to one of the hosts and pointing at them and then at one of the tables in the dining room. She put Shelly at a table with Arnold Ross, president of another publishing house, one of Patterson & White's rivals. With a gleam in her eye, she put Whitney at a table with . . . Riley Dufrane and his wife, Virginia. When Whitney sat down, she saw Riley's eyes widen. For some reason, Whitney wasn't upset or anxious about the seating. In fact, she found that, curiously, she was feeling a bit horny—no doubt spurred on by the two Cosmopolitans she had downed fifteen minutes earlier. She was also amused by Maxine's attempt to make her uncomfortable by seating her here. She *was* feeling a bit uncomfortable, but it was because of her job security, *not* because of Riley and Virginia. She glanced over at Shelly and saw that she was already engrossed in a deep conversation with the man sitting to her right, whom Whitney thought she recognized as a publishing executive. Whitney shook her head. *Shelly is so damn charming, she could sell snowsuits in Tahiti.*

Maxine finally sat down at her table in the center of the room and went to work on Murph, who was sitting three seats to her left—she didn't want to be too obvious and seat him right next to her. He was engrossed in a conversation with Ted Koppel, the former host of *Nightline*. Maxine happened to know that Koppel was looking for a publisher for a book he was writing. She decided she would wait a while before she gave Murph the Maxine Robinson full-court press.

At Whitney's table, Whitney wanted to laugh as she watched Riley's wife give Maxine lingering, longing stares. It was well-known to everyone at *The Lunch Club* that Virginia Dufrane was desperate to be seated on the couch. Whitney thought the woman was insufferably dull and vapid, and Riley had promised her that he would join the twenty-something cast of MTV's *The Real World* and kiss a boy before he added his wife to the couch of *The Lunch Club*. Now that a seat apparently was up for grabs, Whitney wondered if Ginny had been torturing him for the job. Hell, Ginny was so desperate she might even have broken down and given Riley a blow job. After the entrées were served, Whitney planned on luring Riley to a spare room in the house and fucking his brains out. She kept making eye contact with him, but he seemed to be avoiding her eyes, purposely engaging in conversations with everyone else at the table. Whitney tried to tell herself that it was no big deal, but she was starting to get a little annoyed with him.

"How is your soup, Whitney?" Riley finally asked her from across the table. At the mention of her name, she saw Riley's wife look up at her. Whitney smiled at Virginia, who smiled back, her lips stretched across her teeth in a grin that was about as fake as a three-dollar bill.

"It's very good, Riley," Whitney said. "I love French onion." When her eyes met Riley's, he gave her a quick, almost imperceptible wink. It was the same wink he gave her when they were together, often when they were lying in each other's arms and coming back down to earth after another gut-busting orgasm. The wink sent a tremor of pleasure down her spine. That was all she needed; she knew he was on the same page as she, that it wouldn't take long for them to meet up in one of the empty rooms in Maxine's vast apartment, some space that hadn't seen a human form since the last time *Architectural Digest* was there.

By the time the entrées were served, Maxine had gotten Murph to open up just a little about *Satan's Sisters*—enough for him to tell her he didn't feel comfortable talking about it, if that was okay with her. Maxine smiled sweetly at him, but she spat a thousand curses at him under her breath. After all, the whole reason for this party, for the tens of thousands of dollars she had already spent, was to get Murph to assure her that she didn't have anything to worry about. She knew she would have to take another run at him before the night was over.

Riley excused himself from the table, just as Chef Wilson's Vanilla Panna Cotta with Spring Berries was being served, telling his wife he had to make a phone call and find a bathroom. She nodded at him and went back to her conversation with the wife of a well-known Hollywood producer. Whitney amused herself by guessing that perhaps Virginia now had her sights set on starring in a Hollywood movie if *The Lunch Club* gambit didn't work out. Whitney thought the perfect vehicle for her would be the movie version of Jackie Collins's *Poor Little Bitch Girl*, if one were ever made. Whitney looked up and saw a very handsome, distinguished-looking older black man standing in the corner of the room, gazing at Maxine. She thought she recognized him as Maxine's butler—he was wearing a black tux and the white gloves of a butler—but he certainly wasn't looking at Maxine like she was his employer. For a second she wondered if Maxine was getting it on with her butler, but just as quickly the thought was gone.

When she had reached the count of fifty in her head, Whitney slipped away from the table, though she didn't even bother to excuse herself. She hadn't started up any conversations anyway. As she left the room, she saw Maxine glance in her direction, pausing from a deep discussion with Murph. Whitney wondered if Maxine had gotten what she wanted out of this party—that is, enough information about Missy's book to put all of their minds at ease. But Whitney wasn't thinking about Missy at the moment—her mind was focused almost exclusively on Riley. She hoped she would have an easy time finding him. She wandered down a hall, under the guise of looking for the bathroom. As she walked past the curving staircase leading up to the second floor, Whitney heard a noise above her. She looked up. It was Riley, motioning for her to come upstairs with him. Whitney glanced around her, then sprinted up the steps, as quickly and as quietly as her five-inch stilettos would take her.

"Let's go find a good spot," Riley said into her ear as he pulled her into his arms. When she pressed her body against his, Whitney could already feel the bulge in his pants. Apparently, Riley was as excited as she was about this scandalous interlude. They held hands and looked around the deserted second floor. They opened up a door to a grand spectacle of a room, with heavy burgundy drapes all around, a delightful four-poster bed covered with a matching burgundy bedspread featuring a dark brocade design, an antique desk off in one corner, and a plush burgundy sofa in the other corner.

"It looks like her master bedroom," Riley said.

He pulled her away from the room. Whitney wanted to stay for a minute and look around some more. The wicked new bad girl in Whitney wanted to drag Riley over to that brocade bedspread, strip off his clothes, and impale herself on him, right there in the middle of Maxine's bedroom. That would be like a dog peeing in the middle of the floor to show his displeasure. But she knew Riley would not be a willing partner. Shoot, she'd have to tie him down in order to pull that one off. Hmm, they hadn't tried any bondage yet. Tying Riley down might be interesting.

"Let's get as far from the master bedroom as we can," he said in a whisper. "Let's find the last room she'd ever enter."

Riley pulled her all the way to the opposite end of the long, darkened hall. Whitney wondered how long they had before somebody got suspicious. Riley had cleverly used the phone call excuse. It would be a long time before Virginia came looking for her network president husband to interrupt a phone call. Riley pushed open the door to a room in the far corner of the hall. It looked like the room of a teenager. Was this the room of the son who had killed himself? The thought gave Whitney a chill. She quickly pushed the thought out of her mind.

"What do you think?" Riley said.

"It looks fine to me," Whitney said, already yanking off his dark dinner jacket. She looked around in the dim light and saw a sizable walk-in closet. "Let's go in the closet," she said, leading

Riley by the arm. He paused to close the door to the room, sealing them off in darkness.

Once they were inside the closet, they attacked each other like two ravenous animals. Within seconds, most of their clothing had been removed. Whitney pulled down her panties in a frenzy, desperate to feel her lover inside of her. She was tempted to drop to her knees and take him inside of her mouth, but that temptation was overshadowed by her yearning for him to fill her up. After he had tugged off his pants, Riley turned Whitney around and bent her over. She braced her hands against the wall to hold herself up as she spread her legs to open up wide for him. Because they were in the dark, the anticipation and mystery made every move more intense, more dramatic. Whitney held her breath and waited. In an instant, Riley reached down and forcefully shoved his penis deep inside of her, amazingly driving it in all the way with just one motion, like it had been guided by a magnet. Whitney sucked in a mouthful of air so strongly that the sound would have been frightening to anyone listening in. Whitney felt as if she had been stabbed, the sensation of him entering her was so severe. As he slammed in and out of her, Whitney's head was spinning; she was wild, free, uninhibited. She wanted to scream out, to tell the world how good it felt, how much her entire being was filled by this man, how much she loved every fiber of his body, every cell in his thick, engorged penis. She heard Riley's jerky, spasmodic grunts, which matched his thrusts. He had never sounded so animalistic to her. For just a second she worried about him. He was no youngster—it would not be a good look for this man to have a heart attack while buried inside of her in one of Maxine Robinson's closets. But as he reached around his hand and squeezed her breasts through the sheer black bra she was wearing, she knew she had no need to worry about Riley Dufrane. He was doing just fine.

"Oh God, Whitney, I think I'm coming!" Riley said in her ear.

"Wait!" Whitney hissed through clenched teeth. "I want to come with you!"

She rammed back against him so hard that he almost slipped out of her. He increased the force of his thrusts until they almost resembled two souls in mortal combat. Slap, slap, his thighs smacking her cheeks approximated the sound of waves crashing against rocks. Together, thankfully, they reached their destination.

"I'm there!" Whitney said. "Please, Riley, come with me!"

"Ooooh God!" Riley howled quietly.

"Yessss!" Whitney answered him.

Slowly, they came down, balloons deflating, back to the soft carpet of the closet. They sank together onto the floor, feeling shoes and sneakers beneath them. Surely they would leave behind some lovely gooey goodies. When her heart had stopped thrumming wildly in her chest, Whitney finally was able to speak. But instead of talk, she did a dead-on impersonation of a panting, chirping dog. Ever since she was a little girl, Whitney had been gifted at doing animal impressions. She still did them all the time for her children and family members. Friends would sometimes make her stand up at parties and take special requests. She heard Riley's soft chuckle. That wasn't the first time he had heard her panting dog after sex.

"I think that was the best ever," Whitney said.

Riley didn't answer her. "Don't you think so, Riley?" Whitney said. "Don't you think that was the best ever?"

More silence.

"Whitney, I have something I need to tell you," Riley said finally. If she wasn't mistaken, that sounded like solemnity in his voice. *What's about to happen? Is he breaking up with me?* she wondered. How could your secret lover break up with you?

"My God, Riley, you're scaring me. What is it?"

She heard Riley take a deep breath. Her pulse quickened. Whatever it was, she was going to brace herself and not overreact. She clenched both of her fists.

"I got a phone call this afternoon," he said. "It came from the president of All Cable News, Steve Rucker. It was about your husband, Eric."

"Eric? Why in the world would he call you about Eric?" Eric. She hadn't thought about him in at least two days.

"Apparently, he got a call from the producers

of *Primeline*, letting him know that your husband had been caught in a *Primeline* sting. I think it was in Prague. He was arrested for soliciting minors for child prostitution. They got him on tape. Steve said he had paid thousands of dollars to spend the night with two girls in the Czech Republic. He thought he was getting two sisters, thirteen and fourteen years old. He paid the first half of the money when he was still in the United States. Steve said it looks like this wasn't the first time Eric has done this. He called me out of courtesy to you. But he said *Primeline* is airing the whole episode on Tuesday night. I'm really sorry, Whitney."

After a while, Riley's voice sounded to Whitney like it was coming at her through a wind tunnel, as if there were so much violent air whipping at her face that she couldn't even concentrate on the words. She felt like maybe she was falling down into something, maybe a deep, narrow well. Maybe there would be a splash when she reached the bottom. But then words started coming back to her. Jumping out at her. Child prostitution. Arrested. Thousands of dollars. Two sisters. Thirteen and fourteen. *Primeline. Primeline. Primeline*. Tuesday night. Eric. Sorry, Whitney.

The tremor started in her belly. By the time it hit her throat it was a full-bore Technicolor scream, the entire contents of her belly gushing out onto the floor of the closet. The brunt of the vomit just missed Riley's leg, but he felt little specks fall on the hairs of his legs. He jumped to his feet and fumbled around the wall, looking for a light switch. He found one and flipped it on. The sight that filled his eyes was enough to terrorize him for the rest of his life. Whitney looked like she had just been through an exorcism. Vomit dripped from her mouth and her face held a look of such tortured anguish and fear that he was almost tempted to run.

"Whitney?" he said tentatively.

She shook her head slowly back and forth. Finally she spoke.

"My God. My God," she said softly. "But what about my children?"

She pushed herself up from the floor and pulled her dress back over her head, not even bothering to fix her bra or straighten her panties. Riley gingerly stepped over to her and fixed her clothing. He pulled the handkerchief from his breast pocket and tenderly cleaned the vomit from her mouth. With his fingers, he softly combed down her blond locks until there was a semblance of order to them. He pulled her into his arms.

"I'm sorry, Whitney," he said.

But suddenly she pushed him away. Hard.

"You bastard," she said, looking him in the eye. "You knew about this all along, but you didn't tell me until *after* you fucked me?"

She drew back her hand and violently smacked him across his left cheek. He felt the sting, but he didn't raise a hand to block it. He staggered backward.

"I'm sorry, Whitney," he said again, reaching out a hand that she ignored.

Without even another glance in his direction, Whitney walked out of the closet. She moved steadily, but her face held the deadened expression of someone who had just seen her mother's lifeless body in a casket. Riley made sure his clothing was straight, then he followed her down the stairs. When Whitney came into the dining room, the guests had moved on to the dessert. The party had entered the raucous stage. Clearly everyone was having a good time. Maxine was surveying the room with a smile on her face—until she saw Whitney. Maxine pressed her hand against her chest. Whitney looked like a walking zombie. She popped up from the table and rushed over to Whitney.

"What happened?" she said. Whitney stared in Maxine's light brown eyes but she didn't say a word. Maxine was spooked by Whitney's dead eyes. Did the woman just see a ghost in Maxine's home?

"I'm sorry, Maxine, I have to go," Whitney said woodenly.

By this time, most of the guests had noticed the commotion and had stopped talking to take it all in. When she saw the fear on Maxine's face, Shelly ran over to Whitney.

"What happened to you, Whitney?" Shelly asked.

But Whitney just shook her head and headed toward the foyer, with Shelly and Maxine in tow. She didn't even pause at the door. She opened it and disappeared. Gone. Just like that. When Maxine returned to the room, her eyes settled on Riley. Maybe he had done something to her. Something bad.

"Riley, why don't you tell them what happened?"

The voice was that of Riley's wife, Virginia Dufrane. Her words were a little slurred. Ginny had had too many gin and tonics. Riley's head snapped around and he stared at Ginny as if he wanted to shoot her.

"Come on, tell them," Ginny said. "I heard that call you got from Steve. Tell them about Eric."

Apparently, Ginny had been listening in during the call. Riley cursed under his breath. He was shocked by his wife's indiscretions. The woman had no class. But that was immaterial now. Her words were out there and couldn't be taken back. Every eye in the room was on Riley, waiting.

Riley cleared his throat. "Well, apparently Whitney's husband, Eric, has been arrested by police in Prague for child prostitution."

There were loud gasps around the room. But Riley wasn't finished yet.

"I got a phone call this afternoon from the president of ACN. He said the whole thing was captured by the cameras from *Primeline*. Drew Finch was there as well. The entire disgusting mess will be airing on *Primeline*. On Tuesday."

There was another gasp, maybe a second of silence, then all at once the room exploded in about twenty simultaneous conversations, the sentiments veering from pity to utter revulsion. Maxine was horrified by Riley's story, but she felt another thought coming on. This was horrible for Whitney, yes, but maybe not so bad for *The Lunch Club*. The ratings would go through the roof. And Whitney would have to leave, after all this mess. So in the end she'd free up Whitney's slot also. Two birds with one stone. She'd have to send Eric the perv a bouquet of flowers.

Maxine tried mightily to revive her party after Riley's bombshell, but there really was no recovery from that. And honestly her heart wasn't in it, anyway. She was too busy plotting in her mind how she would use this. She saw Shelly hemmed up in a corner with Murph. Wow, she had forgotten to take another run at Murph to get some intel on Missy's book. Murph seemed to be enjoying his time with Shelly. What was that girl up to now? Was it possible that the chick had crashed Maxine's party and outfoxed her, right here under Maxine's nose? Maxine refused to believe something so preposterous. But she did wonder what Shelly was up to.

When they were done, Shelly took a step backward and let Murph return to his auburn-haired wife. The two of them had been deep into a conversation about Shelly's remarkable career and her path from Harvard Business School to Milan runways. Murph was so taken with her that he had offered her a two-book deal, right there on the spot. A steamy memoir that didn't pull any punches about all the orgies and drugs she did during her days in Milan, followed by an uplifting inspirational book for twentysomethings on how to be fabulous. They hadn't discussed money, but Murph had indicated that Shelly would be well compensated for her efforts. And he also had one other thing to tell her.

"Tell Ms. Robinson that the Missy Adams book is going to come after her pretty hard, so she better get ready to duck," he had said with a devilish grin.

Shelly glanced over at Maxine and saw the queen bee staring her down. Shelly turned away, thinking to herself that giving Maxine a heads-up about Missy's book was the last thing she wanted to do. *Let the bitch sweat.*

⊰ ⊱

IT WAS IN THE backseat of the taxi on her way back home that Whitney finally released the emotion that had been building inside. After she gave the driver her address, she slowly sat back in the seat, closed her eyes, and let the tears flow. Once they started she couldn't stop them. For blocks and blocks she cried and cried. The cabbie kept checking the rearview mirror, to make sure he wasn't going to have a scene on his hands. New York City cabbies didn't like scenes. As long as it stayed at sobbing and tears, he was okay. He had seen plenty of crying in his cab over the years. And he had learned that when they cried, you don't try to stop them or help them or even pretend that you notice them. You just let them cry.

Whitney couldn't fathom the horrible misdeed that Eric had done to her and to his children. When your father is broadcast to the entire world as a child-molesting pervert, how do you ever recover from that? How many years and dollars of therapy did her husband just hang around his children's necks? And the girls were the same age as the twins? Whitney didn't even want to take the next step, but logic forced her to consider it—had Eric ever done anything to Bailey and Ashley, touched them inappropriately? She'd fucking kill him. If he touched Bailey and Ashley in any way, she'd rip his heart out of his body with her bare hands and offer it as a sacrifice to the gods, like that scene from *Indiana Jones and the Temple of Doom*. She couldn't imagine that her strong-willed girls would have let something like that happen without screaming bloody murder, but she was sure many mothers had said the same things in homes where the fathers had been molesting the girls for years. After all, Whitney was a longtime journalist; she had seen her share of child molestation stories, some of them so horrific that as a mother she had to immediately block them from her memory so that they wouldn't haunt her. She knew that she would be forced to have a very serious and uncomfortable conversation with her girls when she got home and she hated Eric all the more for putting their family through this.

But as she rocked back and forth in the back of the cab, Whitney was also dealing with another overwhelming emotion: guilt. No matter how hard she tried to get around it, she couldn't escape the fact that this had all been going on while she was running into another man's arms—a married man's—as often as she could. While she was rushing from one liaison to the next with Riley Dufrane, her family had been crumbling all around her. Her husband had been nurturing some deep obsession for underage girls and she had been completely clueless about it. They had once been so close, so intimate, that she and Eric could practically read each other's minds. What had happened to that? Had she played a role in the changes her marriage had endured? Of course she had noticed over the last few years when they had started to drift apart— but a part of her had welcomed the new distance because it gave her a chance to indulge her passion for Riley, thinking that the wild sex and intense desires were coming to her freely, without a price. How tragically wrong she had been! The price was astoundingly high—as a matter of fact, she might have paid the ultimate price: the permanent dissolution of her family. She vowed that, although her marriage was certainly over, she would now spend all of her time tending to the needs of her kids. Her only fear was finding out just how great those needs were going to be.

As Whitney struggled through the guilt, the fear, and the shame, her phone rang. She saw that it came from Bailey's cell phone. When she answered it, all she could hear was screaming.

"Bailey? Is that you, honey?" Whitney said. The call had put her into mother mode, meaning she had willed her voice to be calm, but inside she was dying.

"Mom!" It was Ashley, screaming at her through Bailey's phone. "They're taking all of Dad's stuff! The police or the FBI or whoever are taking all of his files!"

"Calm down, Ashley!" Whitney said. "I can't hear you if you scream, honey. Explain to me exactly what's happening there."

"Okay, okay." Whitney could hear her trying to control her breathing. "The doorbell rang," Ashley continued. "Mrs. Dooley answered it. It was a whole bunch of men who said they were from the FBI. They handed her some papers. They said they had a search warrant. We told them they couldn't come inside until our parents were home, but they said they had the authority to search the home if Mrs. Dooley was our babysitter. They asked where Dad's office was. I didn't want to tell them, but Mrs. Dooley showed them where it was. She said if we didn't tell them, then they would mess up the whole house. Mrs. Dooley was crying the whole time. They started dragging out all of Dad's files and his computer! They're still taking stuff out. Are you coming home?"

"Yes, I'm almost there, baby," Whitney said. "Calm down, okay? And can you put Mrs. Dooley on the phone?"

Mrs. Dooley was an older woman who lived

down the street and had been babysitting the girls since they were toddlers. She was a kind, gentle Irishwoman, but she was easily spooked. Whitney couldn't even imagine the emotional trauma that this must've been causing for Mrs. Dooley, with an FBI raid happening on her watch. Whitney looked up and saw that she was only a few blocks from their Upper West Side town house. Whatever earthquakes were rumbling through her soul right now and crushing her psyche, she had to present the image of the calm, in-control mommy as soon as she walked in that house. She *had* to be strong to help her girls and her two sons get through this—or at least emerge as unscathed as possible after their father became an international symbol of a degenerate. That last thought made Whitney close her eyes again and rest her head on the back of the seat. Waves of shame flowed through her. Deeper, more pungent shame than she had ever felt in her life. Then it hit her. The impact of Eric's perversion on her personal life was apparent, but dear Lord . . . she hadn't even begun to process how this news would affect her public life. She was a celebrity, a woman who now made a very good living sitting on a couch and talking about everybody else's business—though that was the part of the job that had always made her a bit queasy. How brutal she knew the gossip and news machines would be with this news of the downfall of Miss High-and-Mighty Whitney Harlington. It was going to be ugly. The Internet was the greatest accomplishment of the twentieth century, but it was also the most dangerous. When you want to get news out about an issue or a cause, social media could run circles around traditional media, but there are trade-offs. Truth rarely mattered and gossip and rumor were given the same amount of space as actual facts. Plus, the bloggers could be relentless sharks when they smelled celebrity blood in the water, because taking the famous down was always going to be the sport du jour.

"We're here, ma'am," the cabbie said, sounding a bit tentative. Whitney opened her eyes and saw him watching her through the rearview mirror. Poor guy. He must have worried that she was about to have a nervous breakdown in his cab. She pulled some bills from her wallet, giving him an extra twenty-dollar tip for enduring her drama. She saw that there was a dark van double-parked in front of where he had stopped the cab.

"Thanks, lady," he said enthusiastically. As she closed the door, he called out to her. "I hope it turns out all right." Whitney gave him a tight smile as he drove off. She saw that men were in the van. As she approached the front of her home, she could see men inside through the glass doors.

"Hello, I'm Whitney Harlington," she said when she stepped through the front door.

A middle-aged white man with salt-and-pepper hair stepped forward and introduced himself. He told her that they had a search warrant for the property in Manhattan and for their home in Nantucket. He said FBI agents were retrieving files and computer equipment from the Nantucket home at the same time that they served the Manhattan search warrant. He said they were also looking for any photographic equipment they could find. Whitney wanted to be mad, to show the man some anger, but she knew that would do no good. These guys were just doing their jobs. They couldn't help it that her husband was a disgusting degenerate. In that moment, she recalled the video camera Eric had just purchased, how he had taken some footage of the girls lying around the living room. Apparently that was just practice, preparation for the camera's real function, to take video footage of somebody else's daughters. Possibly doing disgusting things to him. Whitney felt her eyes start to moisten again. But when she saw Ashley and Bailey running in her direction, she tried to stop the tears. Yet when her arms wrapped around her daughters, there was no way to stem the tide. All three of them cried together, holding on tight, sobbing for the loss of their family, the idyllic lives they had all lived up to that point. Because of Eric, it was all gone. They had no idea what would be left over in the wreckage.

After the FBI departed, Whitney thanked Mrs. Dooley for her help and walked the girls back to their rooms. The twins said they wanted to sleep together—for the first time since they were about ten years old. Ashley crawled into Bailey's bed and let Whitney pull up the sheets and tuck both of them in.

"Mom?" Bailey said. "Mrs. Dooley said they took all of Dad's stuff because of child pornography. I know it's against the law to have nude pictures of kids. But did Dad do actual, uh, stuff to little kids?" Her voice cracked at the end of the question. Whitney felt her heart breaking into tiny little pieces. She gazed down at their beautiful, angelic faces, their eyes wide with wonder as they waited for her answer. They hadn't really looked identical since they were about seven or eight, but their faces were mirror images at this precise moment. At least the question gave her a partial answer to her worry about whether Eric had touched them; she didn't think she would have gotten this question if he had. But she still knew she had to ask them the question, point-blank.

"I don't really know, Bailey," Whitney said. "I know what the police think . . . and it looks really bad; but we'll just have to wait with everyone else to hear the whole story. I wish I had some answers but I don't. I have to tell you something, though. It's going to get a lot worse before it gets better. It's going to be on TV, on a *Primeline* special about sexual predators, the footage of them arresting Dad in Prague."

Bailey sat upright in the bed. "You mean, like that show where they're always catching perverts trying to have sex with little girls?!" she said, fresh tears springing from her eyes. Whitney nodded sadly. Bailey slammed her head back into her pillow. Ashley reached out for her and they hugged each other tightly, bringing back long-forgotten memories for Whitney of when the twins actually liked and comforted each other. Whitney knew the time had come for the tough question; there was no getting around it. She had to know whether Eric had brought his perversion into their home.

"Girls, it really hurts me to have to ask you this, but I have no choice," Whitney said, looking back and forth between them. She saw their eyes widen and her heart hurt for the two of them. "Did your father ever, uh, touch either one of you in a way he shouldn't have?" she said softly, carefully.

Whitney saw the pain cross over both of their faces, which managed to hold the same looks of horror. Both girls shook their heads emphatically without looking at each other.

"No, Mom, he never touched us," Ashley said. "We wouldn't let any man touch us inappropriately."

"You've been telling us that for a long time," Bailey said. Then she looked down. Her voice got lower. "Actually, Dad has too."

"Yes, both of you taught us that lesson," Ashley said. "We wouldn't let anybody touch us or do things to us that we didn't want. And I wouldn't let anyone do that to Bailey either."

"And I wouldn't let anyone do it to Ashley," Bailey chimed in.

Whitney pursed her lips and shook her head. She wrapped an arm around each girl and pulled them close to her. She loved her girls so much.

Whether this one was a drama queen or that one was a brooding loner, her girls needed to come first. Always. She felt another wave of guilt wash over her; she had been so preoccupied with Riley that she hadn't been taking care of business at home. Now they all had to suffer because of it.

"I'm so proud of you two," Whitney said through the tears that began to flow once again. Ashley and Bailey were crying along with her, the three of them softly sobbing. "I'm so sorry that you have to go through this horrible thing. If you need to talk about anything, anything at all, don't hesitate to come to me. And no matter what happens, never think that any of this was your fault. Okay?"

Both girls nodded their heads vigorously. They remained squeezed together for the next several minutes, all of them holding on tight.

"Mom?" It was Bailey, speaking into her left shoulder.

"Yes, dear?" Whitney said tenderly.

"What's going to happen when Daddy comes back home?" Bailey asked.

Whitney pulled away and looked deeply into Bailey's blue eyes, now puffy and red. She put her hands on Bailey's shoulders.

"Baby, your father no longer belongs here," she said. "And besides, he's probably going to jail, probably for a very long time."

This news brought a fresh stream of tears from the girls. Whitney hugged them tightly until she heard the crying stop. She pulled the covers over them and watched them close their eyes. Both of them were asleep within five minutes.

When Whitney was finally alone in her bedroom, she ran to a file cabinet and found an old Rolodex, a remnant of a simpler time when people actually wrote phone numbers down on paper. When she found what she was looking for, she picked up her cell phone and dialed the number.

"Hello?" The voice was groggy on the other end. "Who is this?"

"Nancy? This is Whitney Harlington. I'm really, really sorry if I woke you up. Seriously. I have a, uh, kind of a situation here. My husband Eric was arrested yesterday in Prague for soliciting a child prostitute."

"Oh, that's terrible!" Nancy said. "I'm really sorry, Whitney."

"Yes, thank you, Nancy. Thank you. It's going to get even worse, though. Apparently the whole thing was recorded by *Primeline* for one of their specials. I think it's going to air this Tuesday. I don't even want to consider being married to this man for another day. I wondered if you could make some time for me on Monday to begin divorce proceedings?"

"I can do better than that, Whitney," Nancy said. "How about I come over tomorrow, around noon, so we can talk?"

Nancy Chemtob, an old friend of Whitney's, was one of the most sought-after cutthroat divorce lawyers in New York. Whitney had joked with her many times about how she needed to keep Nancy's number on speed dial in case Eric ever fucked up. She never imagined that she would actually be using it at eleven thirty on a Saturday night. When Whitney hung up the phone, she could hear talking coming from Bailey's room. She slipped out into the hall and stood outside of the door, trying to hear what the girls were saying. Apparently one of them was on the phone. She heard Bailey say "Todd." She was talking to her oldest brother, Todd, who was a senior at Tufts. Whitney knew she should be calling the boys herself, but she wasn't up to it. She felt too tired, much too tired, to be going through two more gut-wrenching conversations with her sons. She walked back to her bedroom, turned off the light, and slid into bed. She closed her eyes, and just when she began to drift off, the house phone rang. The caller ID told her it was Ron, her younger son. Sleep would need to wait. Whitney snatched the phone from the nightstand and answered it.

⊰ ⊱

AFTER THE STORY ON chattercrazy.com said Molly might be losing her slot on *The Lunch Club*, Molly spent thirty-six hours sliding into another crisis with the pills. She had been popping the Xanax like Skittles, hoping they would stop her hands from shaking and her heart from jumping around her chest. She knew that she needed to find some other way to deal with anxiety besides medicating it. Talk about your short-term solutions.

What she probably needed was some type of rehab program—but with *The Lunch Club* axe stalking around, looking for a head to chop off, a rehab program was the last thing on her agenda.

Molly tried to watch television, but she was too jumpy to sit still. In the illogical recesses of her brain, Molly came up with the solution: coffee. She needed a big, steaming cup of coffee. But when she went into her kitchen to make a cup, she panicked when she saw that she had run out. She forgot that she had thrown all of it in the garbage the week before during one of her radical mood swings. She had decided she was drinking too much of it and that it was making her fat. So the coffee had to go.

"Oh God, I gotta have coffee," she mumbled to herself. She leaned over the counter and took deep breaths, trying to beat back the urge to take another pill. She had just swallowed one less than an hour earlier. She could not take another one so soon. She just couldn't.

But still she found herself moving toward her pocketbook, removing the bottle and holding another pill in her hand. She wanted to stop, but she couldn't. Maybe the coffee would help her! Still clutching the pill, she squeezed her butt into a pair of jeans that were probably too small, pulled on a jacket, and left her building, desperate now for a cup of coffee. She wasn't even aware that she was mumbling to herself—or that her hair was so unkempt that she might be mistaken for a homeless woman. Though the sight of homeless women mumbling to themselves wasn't exactly rare on the streets of New York, Molly still got a few lingering glances from passersby who suspected that the loony-looking fat woman might be the funny chick from *The Lunch Club*. Molly came across Big Nick's all-night diner on Broadway and she hurried inside. She sat down and ordered two cups of coffee, drawing a frown from the waitress, a pretty young Latina who also recognized Molly.

Molly sat in the booth, talking to herself and slowly rocking back and forth, oblivious to the fact that she was on virtual display to the city through the diner's large plate-glass windows. At the same time, walking down Broadway and passing the diner's windows were Karen Siegel and her husband, Bert. Their night out together was precipitated by the thing that had sent Molly over the edge— the story on chattercrazy.com. Karen's husband thought he could take her mind off her troubles if he took her out for a great dinner at Isabella's, one of their favorite restaurants on the West Side.

"Hey, isn't that Molly Stein?" Bert said, grabbing Karen's arm and pointing through the diner window. They stood there and watched her for a moment, their mouths agape as they saw her mumbling and rocking. She clearly looked psychotic, with her hair askew, her clothes disheveled, and what looked like spit in the corners of her mouth.

"What the hell is wrong with her?" Bert said.

Karen shook her head. "I don't know. She looks like she's on some kind of drugs. I know people on the show have been saying that she's addicted to pills or something, but I never saw her look like this."

"What do you want to do? Should we help her?" he asked.

"I don't know," Karen answered. She was torn; she knew Molly would be mortified that somebody she knew saw her in this condition, but what if she were recognized and pictures wound up in the gossip columns? It was Karen's duty to protect her show, wasn't it?

As they stood outside the diner discussing their next move, Molly looked out the window for the first time—and saw the familiar face of Karen Siegel, staring in at her, like she was in a zoo. Molly's eyes widened and she screamed. Startled, Karen and her husband looked at each other, then ran toward the front door of the diner, not sure what they were going to do but knowing that they needed Molly to stop screaming. Luckily the diner only had a couple of other customers, who stared at Molly with confused expressions. The waitress was trying to find out what was wrong when Karen and Bert appeared at her booth.

"Molly! Stop it!" Karen said sternly. Molly instantly settled down.

"What are you doing here?" Molly said, her eyes still wild. "Did you come to get me?"

Karen slid into the booth next to Molly. Bert sat opposite her. Karen put her arm around Molly and tried to act jovial and nonchalant.

"We came to help you get back home," Karen said. "You ready?"

Molly looked down at her two coffee cups. "But I need my coffee," Molly said.

"I'll tell you what, Molly. We can get some coffee for you to take home." She glanced at Bert, who popped up from the booth and went to find the waitress, who was watching the scene warily from the safety of the area behind the counter.

Molly suddenly started crying. Karen put both arms around her and hugged her. She smelled an odor coming from Molly, sweat and body funk. She wondered when Molly last had a shower.

⚑ ⚐

WHEN THE CATERERS HAD washed the last dish and moved out all of their junk, Maxine went into the kitchen looking for William. She was so relieved that the whole party was done, she needed a hug. But he wasn't there. She went into the living room. He wasn't there either. She wandered through the first floor, wondering where he could have gone. She finally found him in his small living quarters. To her surprise, he had several suitcases on the bed and he was stacking clothing into them.

"What are you doing?" Maxine said, alarmed.

"I really don't think I can take it anymore, Maxine," he said without looking at her.

"What are you talking about, William?"

He looked up at her for the first time while he

placed a stack of folded shirts in a suitcase. He shook his head and resumed packing.

"Would you stop it for a moment and talk to me?!" Maxine demanded.

William sighed. "I knew that you could be a cold, heartless so-and-so when you wanted to be, but I didn't think even you could go that far," he said. "At the party, I overheard a couple of guys talking. You know, I'm the black butler, so I just blend into the wallpaper in these people's minds. People act like I'm not even there. These two gentlemen were in the library, enjoying some of your good scotch. I think they were both publishing executives. One of them was telling the other one about a book he's about to publish, written by one of the women who used to be on your show. In this book, she talks about the circumstances surrounding her departure. He said that you forced her to leave the show, and in exchange you agreed not to disclose the fact that some man was *wrongly convicted for raping her*?"

Maxine suddenly felt a bit unsteady on her feet. She took in a deep breath and leaned against the doorframe for support. She reached out for the chair in William's room and sat down heavily, still in her evening clothes. It sounded like her worst fears were confirmed—Missy had gone all out to take her down.

"Well, it wasn't exactly like that," Maxine said. But her voice was missing its usual surety. She was not convincing at all.

William raised his left eyebrow, his telltale way of expressing doubt. Clearly he wasn't going to believe a word she said.

"I . . . well, it wasn't like I made a trade or anything," Maxine said.

"Well then, why don't you tell me what you *did* do, Maxine? Is there a black man sitting in jail right now who could have been free years ago if you had done the right thing?"

Maxine shook her head. "It wasn't *that* long ago, William. Only a couple of years, like two or *maybe* three. And I didn't make a, like, *trade* for his life or anything that dramatic. I got some information about Missy's trial and I let her know that I knew everything wasn't as it seemed. She had been going around all these years making herself into this conservative darling, even had people saying silly stuff like she could be a vice-presidential candidate. But it was all a lie. All complete and utter bullshit. Knowing that, I told her that it probably wasn't appropriate for her to stay on *The Lunch Club*. So she left. That was it."

"And what about the man in prison?" William asked.

Maxine looked down at the ground. She knew that was her biggest mistake, the one she would always regret. She should have done more for that man, made a few phone calls to help him, even though she had told Missy she wouldn't. That was the deal.

"Well, he's still there," she said, her voice

drifting off. That statement sat between them for a while, with William staring at her and Maxine looking down at the floor. Somehow William, a truly decent man to his core, always managed to make her feel guilty. He was the only person she'd ever met with the power to make Maxine actually have second thoughts.

"William, please don't leave me," Maxine said softly. "I don't know what I would do here in this big place totally alone. I need you, William."

She got up from the chair and rushed over to him. She wrapped her arms around his waist, squeezing, willing him to squeeze her back. Slowly, he lifted his arms and wrapped them around Maxine.

"I promise, I will do everything I can to help that man get out of jail," Maxine said, speaking into William's chest. "I promise, William. Okay?"

William didn't say a word. He looked down at Maxine, gazing deeply into her eyes. She returned the gaze. She felt naked, exposed, and vulnerable, as if he could see through her lies and obfuscations to judge Maxine Robinson in her true state. She wished that she could be as morally sure, as unshakable, as William. But Maxine operated in a world of grays, of shadings of the truth. It was easy for him to be so morally right all the time because he lived a relatively simple life. He was a butler. Maxine swam with the sharks of the entertainment and television world. People who would smile in your face at the same time that they thrust a knife in your belly, again and again, and then twist it. If she weren't hard and forceful and sometimes devious, people would stomp all over her. There would be no mercy for the daughter of a sharecropper from Texas. Her memories of that farm, of the disgusting outhouse, which sometimes got so cold early in the morning that Maxine would be tempted to pee on her young self rather than go outside, of her father toiling away in those fields until his hands literally bled—all that was more than enough ammunition to keep Maxine always pushing, always driving forward, shoving aside anyone who got in her way. There was no way in hell she would wind up back on that farm, back in that position, at the mercy of some distant white man, hoping for enough generosity to feed her family. No, Maxine knew that she would always keep pushing, always keep looking for an advantage over every person who dared get in her way.

William took her chin in his hand and lifted her face toward his. Their lips met in a long, soulful kiss. Maxine felt herself getting warm inside, excited, horny. She pressed her lips against William's with more urgency, trying to send the message through her mouth that she wanted him to take her. Their sexual encounters weren't nearly as frequent as they used to be in the early days, but they both made sure that they never went too long without reacquainting themselves with their favorite parts of each other's bodies. They both fell back on William's bed, on top of the suitcases. Without breaking their kiss, William reached over and swept the suitcases off the bed. They hit the floor with a thud. He slowly worked his way down her face and into her neck. She could hear him inhale deeply. She knew the fragrance she was wearing was a favorite of his. She hadn't put it on earlier in the evening in anticipation of this moment, but she was glad she had worn it. Actually, maybe subconsciously she *had* been anticipating this moment.

William unbuttoned Maxine's jacket and peeled it from her body like he was removing the petals from a flower. Maxine helped him out by removing her camisole. William took the camisole away and buried his face in her ample chest. She felt him inhale her scent again and she smiled. William began to move down her body, leaving soft, gentle kisses across her torso. The touch of his lips almost burned. Carefully, William reached up and pulled the wig from her head. Maxine opened her mouth to protest, but William placed an index finger on her lips, a signal for her to let it go. She fell silent and let William strip away all the facades, the barriers, the celebrity that kept her walled off from the rest of the world like the Mona Lisa behind the majestic glass case in the Louvre. Slowly, tenderly, William made love to Maxine. The real Maxine, the one he had first fallen in love with long ago, in those desperate days when she was married to that cruel rich man; this was the Maxine who needed him, who treasured him, who yearned for him. He whispered in her ear, telling her how much he loved being with her, being inside of her, being one with her. Each of his words sent tremors shooting down Maxine's body. He held her in his strong, muscular arms and slowly rocked his body on top of her.

She felt like he filled her completely; she gasped to catch her breath. Her pleasure was so acute, so sharp, that it almost hurt her. She moaned and pulled him closer, holding on to him as tightly as she could, as if she could keep him there, in her home, in this bed, forever, if she never let go. But if she had been able to look into his eyes, she would have seen them welling with tears. William loved Maxine dearly, but he knew his soul could no longer stand idly by and watch her manipulate and destroy. Her viciousness ate away at him, even when Maxine didn't know it, making him question himself for falling in love with a woman who could be so heartless and brutal. He had heard her promise so many times that she would change, she would be better, but he no longer believed it was possible. He didn't think she was capable of change. Living with Maxine didn't jibe with the way William thought of himself, the image that he wanted to hold of his place in the world. Rather than a kind force for good, Maxine made him feel like an enabler of something sinister. In order to preserve his sanity, William knew that he had to get away from her. Yes, he cried, for the love that he had to leave behind; he cried for the beautiful woman he could not save from herself; he cried for the intimate moments that he would miss.

Maxine cried out into the night when the orgasm

overcame her. Her cry was joined by William's soft moans as he also felt the final release. He knew that this would be the last time; it was explosive, intense, special. As he came down from the high, a heavy sadness settled over him. He crawled behind Maxine and held her closely against his body. The two of them fell into a deep sleep, William's arms wrapped around Maxine, Maxine's hands desperately clutching those arms.

When Maxine stirred in the early morning hours, awakened by the sunlight streaming into William's room, she reached behind her, still anxious to feel his body against hers. But nobody was there. She turned around; William was gone. She looked around the room and saw that his suitcases were gone too. Panicked, Maxine got out of the bed and ran through the apartment, totally naked, calling out to him. But he didn't answer. William had left her.

CHAPTER 15

Whitney heard footsteps scurrying around the town house and knew that she could no longer stay asleep. She sat up and looked around her bedroom, her head pounding from a serious hangover and her tongue feeling like sandpaper. She tried to orient herself, but she couldn't identify the source of the heavy, sinking feeling in her stomach. But then she saw her bureau drawers open, clothes strewn all over the floor, and she remembered the FBI search. She fell hard back onto the pillow. How could she forget? She was married to a child molester.

Whitney awoke with a heavy heart Sunday morning. The uncomfortable questions to her girls and the late-night talk with her boys had left her spent. But she couldn't afford to wallow because she had another challenge ahead. Her mind moved along to Monday morning at *The Lunch Club*. What would she do? Could she go out there and face the prying world? She knew the ratings for Monday's show would probably be astronomical, everybody waiting to see whether Whitney would be there, if she would look devastated, if she would say anything. Whitney had no answers to those queries right now. She didn't know whether she could face America, and she didn't know what would happen that would give her more strength in the twenty-four hours between the shower and the red camera light coming on.

The tears formed again and spilled down her cheeks. She put her face in the pillow and sobbed once more, for herself and her family, before she got out of bed.

It was already ten fifteen. The divorce lawyer, Nancy Chemtob, would be arriving in less than an hour. Whitney rushed into her bathroom and got in the shower. She let the steaming-hot water pour over her for more than fifteen minutes, washing away the tangible remnants of the night before— the sex, the vomit, the funk of humiliation. She wished she could use the water to wash away her troubles. She was still partially numbed by her predicament. Instead of a divorce lawyer, perhaps it was a therapist that she needed now. That her whole family needed. She knew her girls—and her boys too—probably needed her comfort right now, but she almost wanted to avoid them because she didn't know what to say to them. There was nothing she could come up with to make this better. Mommy couldn't kiss it and make the hurt go away. This one was going to cause visible scars for a long time, for her and for the kids. That fucking Eric! Even the thought of his name, the memory of his face, made Whitney furious enough to spit. Yes, he was the father of two of her children, but she thought it would be just fine if none of her family members ever saw the bastard again. A part of her almost wished he had done the honorable thing and just killed himself in that room in Prague—but then again Eric clearly didn't have an honorable bone in his body.

By the time the doorbell rang at noon, Whitney had debated whether she should wake her girls from their teenage slumber. Even on a good Sunday morning, the girls could sleep away the entire day unless she roused them for church. On this Sunday, after the events of the night before, when they probably didn't really close their eyes until at least two in the morning, she'd be surprised if she saw them before three o'clock. Whitney opened the door and was surprised to see that Nancy Chemtob had brought a guest.

Whitney recognized her right away. It was Judy Smith, the well-known lawyer turned "crisis" manager who advised stars on how to handle themselves during uncomfortable times and served as their voice to the media. She had represented everyone from Monica Lewinsky to members of Congress, to Jayson Williams and the country of Saudi Arabia.

"Whitney, you know Judy Smith, right?" Nancy said. "I hope you don't mind that I brought her along."

Whitney shrugged. Actually she did mind a bit because if Judy was needed she was truly in the shit. If Nancy thought she needed Judy, then she needed Judy. Whitney poured everyone a cup of coffee and they sat around the kitchen table.

"The most important thing for you, Whitney," Judy began, "is to look strong but sympathetic. Let me tell you how to do that . . ."

Over the next two hours, they prepared Whitney for her Monday morning appearance on *The Lunch Club*. By the time they were done, Whitney was exceedingly pleased to have Judy Smith on her team.

⊰ ⊱

KAREN SIEGEL AND HER husband, Bert, as they worked their way through the Sunday *Times* together, couldn't stop talking about Molly. Bert had asked her if she was going to talk to Maxine about Molly, but Karen wasn't sure what she should do. After they had calmed Molly down enough to walk her back to her apartment, Molly kept pleading with Karen not to say anything about what had happened to anyone on the show, particularly Maxine. She said that she was sure Maxine would have exactly the excuse she needed to can her if she heard that Molly was walking around the streets of Manhattan acting like "a fuckin' nut job," as Molly put it.

Karen told Bert that she was torn. As the show's longtime director—she had started less than a year after the show first went on the air, when the original director quit to take a job with Regis Philbin's show (because Regis constantly bantered with the director and the people behind the camera, a director could actually become a star in his own right on the show)—it was her job as much as Maxine's to protect the show's integrity. Molly clearly was unstable and at any moment could do something that would cause a major embarrassment to *The Lunch Club*. Bert, who was an internist at Lenox Hill Hospital, had pointed to all the bottles on Molly's kitchen counter. He said after they left that there was no doubt in his mind Molly was battling a pill addiction. He said she was exhibiting all the classic signs and that it was incumbent upon her coworkers to insist that she enter treatment. Since she lived by herself, he said, who else was going to do it if it wasn't Karen and the ladies of *The Lunch Club*? Karen knew he was right, of course, but she also knew that the show would be much less entertaining without Molly Stein. She was invaluable, in Karen's estimation. Karen couldn't think of many other entertainers who could sit on the couch every day and be witty and smart at the same time—except for perhaps Dara's girlfriend, Rain Sommers. Karen considered Molly irreplaceable, but she didn't think Maxine shared that opinion.

Out of the corner of her eye, Karen caught a commercial for *Primeline* airing during the morning news. Another show was coming on in a few days, but this one was a special from Europe. Karen always found the *Primeline* predator shows deeply disturbing and avoided them at all costs.

"Watch the unsettling reaction of this latest predator caught in the act," said the voice-over for the ad. "In fact, he's a well-known American journalist."

That last part grabbed Karen's attention. She looked up—and was horrified to see the blubbering image of Eric Harlington, Whitney's husband.

"That's Eric!" Karen shouted, pointing at the screen.

"Who?" Bert said, looking up from the paper. He saw a distinguished-looking middle-aged white man crying into the camera, his shame seeping through the screen.

"That's Eric Harlington, Whitney's husband!"

They both moved in closer to the television. "I'll be damned! It sure is," Bert said.

Karen grabbed the remote to the DVR and rewound it. With their mouths agape, they watched Eric plead with Drew Finch for mercy—and, most unsettling of all, he did it by trying to use the fact that he had two daughters himself. Karen was so disgusted and upset that she wanted to cry. Just then, her cell phone rang. She reached out and grabbed it quickly.

"Are you watching the morning news?" It was Josh Howe, the executive producer, screaming into her phone.

AS THE MORNING NEWS played in the background, Dara and Rain rolled around their bed in a long, leisurely Sunday morning lovemaking session, which was becoming a tradition of sorts for them. Living with a woman was still new to Dara, and one of the most enjoyable parts of the experience was having a mate whose sex drive was such a comfortable match with hers. When she had dated guys, Dara always felt like something was a little off-kilter in that department—they wanted it when she didn't, and when she wanted it they didn't seem to be available. Sunday mornings was a time when she usually wanted it. So did Rain. They'd watch all the morning news programs. And at some point, one of them would make a move and they would start peeling off their pajamas and begin a glorious, unrushed session. Once Dara had had an amazing six orgasms on a Sunday morning, way more than she had ever had with a man. Sometimes she wondered if this was because of her partner's skill—she often joked that it was too bad oral sex wasn't an Olympic event because Rain would have as many medals as Michael Phelps—or because she was meant to make love only to women.

As they lay in each other's arms, basking in the afterglow, a commercial came on for an upcoming episode of *Primeline*. Dara was only half watching—until she saw a familiar face on the screen. She sat up and groped for the remote. She rewound it, concentrating intently on the television.

"What is it?" Rain said, sitting up next to her.

"That guy looked familiar," Dara said. She paused it on his face. "Oh no! That's Whitney's husband, Eric!"

They rewound it to the beginning of the commercial. When the full brunt of the story hit them, they looked at each other and both grimaced.

"Oh, God . . ." Dara said. "Poor Whitney." She reached for the phone, thinking that maybe she should call Whitney to see if she needed anything.

"You gonna call her?" Rain asked her.

Dara looked up. "You think I should wait?" Dara asked.

Rain shrugged. "I don't know. If it was me, I might not want to hear from anybody right now."

Dara put the phone down. Maybe it was too soon to call. But she would call later. Whitney needed to know that Dara was her friend and would do anything to help her.

-=⧓ ⧓=-

SHELLY WAS ON HER couch in a robe and slippers while La—ah made bacon and eggs in the kitchen. Shelly had just finished explaining the book deal she had been promised the night before. She was going to tell La—ah about the horrible way the night ended, but then she saw Eric's face on the television.

"That's him!" Shelly screamed, pointing.

"That's who?" La—ah asked.

"That's Whitney's husband! I heard about this last night at the party!"

338

Shelly recounted what Riley had told them the night before about Eric's arrest. She remembered that horrible, deadened look on Whitney's face as she walked out of Maxine's place. The memory made Shelly feel queasy. She was tempted to call Whitney and see how she was doing. She considered Whitney a friend; calling would be the right thing to do. But then she thought about how she'd feel if she were in Whitney's shoes—she wouldn't want to hear from anybody. She'd just want to crawl into a closet and disappear for six months, she'd be so embarrassed. Maybe a text was better than a call, just to let Whitney know that Shelly was thinking about her. As she started tapping out a message to Whitney, she saw La—ah shaking her head.

Instead of empathizing with Whitney, whom La—ah had met many times, La—ah was thinking about the bigger picture.

"Oooh, this is crazy as cat shit—and it's going to be great for y'all ratings!" she said.

❦ ❧

BESIDES MOLLY AND WHITNEY, Lizette also missed the *Primeline* commercial, because she was still obsessing over her boyfriend's dastardly deeds. Or maybe it was time to call Channing her *ex*-boyfriend. She was still dumbfounded that he could have so cavalierly sabotaged her career the way he had, apparently for his own good. What else could possess him to do something so despicable?

Lizette had purposely been avoiding Channing the entire weekend. She thought that was safer for him and for her, because she'd probably try to smother him with a pillow in his sleep if they were in the same apartment. He had started blowing up her cell phone with calls she wouldn't answer and then text messages inquiring about Maxine's party. That sealed it for her. The old Channing wouldn't have given a second thought to a dinner party given by Lizette's boss, even if she had been deeply involved in the planning. He just wasn't that kind of guy—the one who paid close attention to his lady's affairs and constantly asked how they were going. No, he had always been too self-centered and distracted for that. At first it had bothered her, but her mother told her that in the long run that kind of husband was preferable to the one who smothered you and made you feel like you couldn't breathe. So Lizette had come to accept that this was just Channing's way and she should get used to it. But now she had this curious Channing on her hands, asking about a dinner party thrown by a woman he had never met? It all made perfect sense now.

Lizette was cooking up a plan that would be a great way of getting some revenge. It wasn't good enough to make them even, by any means, but it might give her some measure of satisfaction. With a wicked smile on her face, Lizette picked up her phone and called Channing back. He answered on the first ring, sounding somewhat breathless.

"I've been on the phone all morning with folks

from *The Lunch Club*," Lizette told him. "Oh, Channing, it sounds like the dinner party was a disaster!"

"Really?" She could hear the eagerness in his voice; it almost made her want to throw up.

"Yes, really! Channing, they told me that Rene Mitchell, the fashion designer, got into a brawl with Sammy Rosenberg of Ultralux Pictures! You believe that?"

"A brawl? Wow, really?" Channing said. He knew that Rene Mitchell was not only a famous designer with his own top-selling clothing line, but he was also a well-known homosexual. "That's unbelievable! Did you get any more details?"

Lizette smiled. She knew she had him now. "Yeah. I heard that everyone was shocked that big, tough Sammy Rosenberg got his ass kicked and cried like a baby. And, you know, Rene probably weighs like sixty pounds less than Sammy, at least. Maybe even more. And, he's gay. Like *real* gay. I think he broke Sammy's nose. Well, everyone said it looked like it might have been broken. But Sammy was too embarrassed to go to the hospital. He just let it bleed. You believe that?"

"Wow," Channing said. But his response was a bit distracted—as if he was trying to write it all down.

"Listen," Lizette said. "I gotta go now. I'm getting another call. I'll call you again if I get more info, okay?"

"Okay," Channing said, not even realizing how busted he was.

As she pressed the button to hang up the phone, Lizette had one more word for Channing: "Bastard!" she whispered into the receiver, though she knew he was already gone. Then she broke into a fit of giggles.

Lizette didn't find out about Eric Harlington until early Sunday evening, when a reporter from the *New York Courier* called her to ask for a comment on the arrest of Whitney's husband in Prague. Lizette was so shocked and disturbed that she forgot all about her Channing prank. Apparently she had some work to do.

⊰ ⊱

THE HAIR/MAKEUP ROOM WAS abuzz on Monday morning. There was a heightened air of excitement in the building, as if everyone had been given some sort of group injection of amphetamines. There were two stories on everybody's lips—Eric's arrest on *Primeline*, which had been recounted in a short story in the *New York Courier*, and Maxine's party. The women on *The Lunch Club* staff and crew had seen Eric on many occasions, stopping by the studio to pick up Whitney, take her out to lunch, or bring their kids by. They were incredulous that the nice, handsome guy they had grown to know over the years was also the disgusting creature they saw on the *Primeline* ads. And what about poor Whitney and her family? They all felt terribly sorry for her— but they couldn't stop talking about it. It was like catnip for any fan of gossip.

Lizette had been dead-on about Channing—about a half million people went on chattercrazy.com on Monday morning to read a story about Sammy Rosenberg getting beat up by Rene Mitchell at Maxine's place. Channing had run with the whole thing without seeking any attribution. When Lizette saw the story, which she read on her laptop before she left her apartment, she burst into tears, crying for the loss of the life that she had thought she was going to live. Crying for the ideal future she thought she was going to have with Channing. All gone. When had all of his journalistic standards flown out the window? she wanted to know. What had happened to Channing?

Molly sat in a corner of the makeup room, listening to all the speculation about Eric Harlington and all the whispered giggles about Sammy Rosenberg, but what she really wanted to do was go find Karen. She was terrified that Karen had already told Maxine about Saturday night, or was perhaps going to do it after the show. But she was afraid to go find Karen—after all, she had already begged for Karen's mercy. What more could she say?

When Maxine swept into the room, the chattering stopped all at once. Everyone resumed their busywork in silence, which every lady on *The Lunch Club* staff knew was the telltale sign that you had been the subject of the gossip before you came into the room.

"Why is everyone so quiet?" Maxine asked as she sat down in a chair for makeup. She looked over at Lilly, the queen of the makeup room gossipmongers. "Were you all talking about that silly story on that website?" Maxine glanced around the room. No one answered, which was the answer she needed.

"I laughed when I read that," Maxine said. "I have no idea where that ridiculousness came from. It just goes to show that you can't believe anything you read on that site." She threw a purposeful glance in Molly's direction. Maxine looked around the room again, to make sure everyone was listening to her.

"First of all, Sammy Rosenberg is in St. Barth right now on a yacht with his family," she said. "He wasn't even invited to the dinner party at my house. And Rene Mitchell is about as likely to break somebody's nose as I am. Actually, let me amend that—probably less likely than I am! Somebody just made the whole thing up. I might even consider a lawsuit, but we're talking about the Internet, for heaven's sakes. If you believe everything you read on the Internet, you should be ashamed of yourself anyway."

With her speech finished, Maxine sat back in her chair and dared anyone to contradict her. What happened next put everyone in a temporary state of shock and awe. Whitney breezed into the room with a big smile, looking fresh and as gorgeous as ever, like she didn't even need to sit in the makeup chair. She sat down, put down her pocketbook, and glanced quickly around the room. She exhaled deeply.

"Okay, ladies," she said. "Let me have it. What do you want to know?"

But no one in the room responded. Until Maxine spoke up. She cleared her throat, betraying her nervousness. "Well, Whitney," Maxine said. "Since you asked. Um, do you want to talk about it on the show?"

It was the question Whitney knew Maxine was going to ask eventually. Whenever one of the ladies made the news in some way, at some point Maxine always asked her if she wanted to talk about it on the show. Of course, Maxine always hoped that the answer was yes, but if a cohost said no she respected her wishes. Whitney had spent most of the day on Sunday preparing for this very moment. Judy Smith and Nancy Chemtob had prepared her well. They both said the first words out of her mouth would set the tone for everything that followed. Nancy had represented some of the richest, most powerful women in the country during divorce proceedings that usually were initiated because the husband had done something ridiculously embarrassing. And Judy had represented men and women who were in the middle of crises that ranged from illicit affairs and corporate malfeasance to murder.

They'd both told Whitney that she might be tempted to run and hide, but in a situation like this, the woman always came out better in the end if she didn't change her public image in any way, if she went about her daily work like a soldier. This didn't mean that she pretended that she hadn't been hurt by the husband's wrongs, but she needed to make it clear that they were *his* wrongs. And she had to act like the husband's wrongs weren't going to destroy her. In Whitney's case, this meant going back on *The Lunch Club* on Monday morning and talking frankly about what had happened to her so that she could get some of her dignity back. If she didn't appear to be overly embarrassed, then people wouldn't treat her as if she should be. At their suggestion, she had even practiced her little speech in front of a mirror. When Maxine's question came, Whitney was as ready as she was ever going to be.

‹⁃ ›⁃

THE SHOW BEGAN WITH light discussion on a couple of news stories of the day, mainly a big speech the president had given on Friday on financial reform. Whitney participated as much as she usually did, though she hadn't watched the speech or read any stories about it. But it was always easy to take the position of the little guy against the evil fat cats of Wall Street, even if you had no idea what the president had said.

When they came back from the first commercial break, Maxine turned to Whitney. "Whitney, most of us know by now that this weekend has been particularly tough for you and I know this isn't the easiest thing in the world to talk about, so I have a lot of respect for your decision to talk about it on the show," she said, which was the truth. Maxine looked into the camera, reading the teleprompter.

"As some of you may know, Whitney's husband, Eric Harlington, was arrested in Prague on Friday. There were several charges filed against him in connection with allegations that he had paid money to have sex with two underage girls. I believe, it is alleged, he paid for girls who were aged thirteen and fourteen. In addition, there were more charges filed against him in the United States for possession of child pornography, based on files that were found in his house in Nantucket."

Maxine turned back to Whitney. "This is just a horrible story, Whitney, and I can't even imagine what you must be going through right now. So I'm going to give you the opportunity to say what you wish about it."

Whitney had considered looking into the camera when she spoke, but Nancy and Judy had said that would look too much like a confessional speech, as if Whitney had done something wrong. They said she should keep it conversational, like she was talking to one of her girlfriends. Whitney smiled at Maxine. It wasn't genuine, but it was effective nonetheless, giving viewers the picture of a woman who was going through a lot but would be okay.

"Thank you, Maxine, for the chance to talk about this. It's just crazy how much my life has changed in the last three days. How much the lives of my children have changed too. We are all unbelievably devastated by everything that has come out. Of course, no one in the family had any inkling that any of this stuff was going on. I thought we were a normal, happy family. I have been spending as much time as I can with my kids, focusing on them, helping them get through this. That is what I am most concerned about. I'll be okay. I'm a strong woman and I will be able to move on. I know that everyone is presumed to be innocent until they are proven guilty, but this involves the welfare of children . . . specifically my children, so I've already taken the first step toward healing my family. I've initiated divorce proceedings, so in a short time I won't even be married to him anymore.

"Yes, he will always be the father of two of my children. That's something they'll never be able to change. That's what bothers me the most, the impact this will have on their lives. I know that the story is salacious and scandalous in most people's minds . . . but this is my family and my children and I will do anything and everything to protect them from further hurt. So, I'm asking anyone out there who may be watching to respect the privacy of my kids, and not do anything that will make this harder for them than it already is. As for Eric, I have no intention of ever purposely laying eyes on him again. Whatever happens to him, he will have to deal with it alone because he has lost his family."

The camera pulled back to catch Maxine blinking in surprise. She hadn't expected Whitney to be so honest. It was a startling declaration for a celebrity to make on national television. The entire panel was stunned by everything she said; the group was silent until Molly chimed in.

"I feel so bad for your kids, Whitney," Molly said. "They don't deserve this. Particularly your daughters. They are such lovely young girls."

Maxine's face twisted into a grimace. Molly realized how horrible that must have sounded, to make reference to the loveliness of Whitney's daughters during a discussion about Eric soliciting underage girls. Molly's face reddened in shame. She was about to apologize, but Whitney rescued her because she was ready for this line of inquiry also.

"That's so kind of you to say, Molly." This time she purposefully turned straight to the camera and said, "My girls *are* lovely and innocent and I thank God that nothing that has happened or will happen will change that."

When the ladies walked off the set at the end of the show, they all wore somber masks, as if they had just emerged from watching an execution. Although the friendship of *The Lunch Club* ladies was for the most part manufactured, there was no denying that when one of them was hurt, all of them hurt. And today . . . everyone hurt for Whitney. There was very little of the usual chatter as they all dispersed and made their way to their offices in quiet reflection. Whitney walked quickly, knowing that eyes were still focused on her. One by one, as if they were of one mind, her castmates all changed their direction—instead of walking toward their own offices, they all headed for Whitney's. When they opened the door to Whitney's office, they found her sitting in a chair and sobbing quietly, releasing the turbulent emotions that had been pent up all morning. Yes, she was strong enough to face the public within forty-eight hours; but privately, her spirit would need many more days to heal. When she saw them, she finally let go of the carefully crafted TV mask and the tears flowed freely. She stood up and gave each of her colleagues—her friends, her sisters—a genuine, grateful hug. Together, all five of them sobbed for Whitney and her family.

-᠄᠄᠄᠄-

LIZETTE HAD BEEN IGNORING Channing's phone calls and text messages for two days, but on Wednesday afternoon she agreed to meet him for drinks after work. As she sat at the bar of El Chocolate, a hot new bar that specialized in delightful chocolate martinis, Lizette wasn't even sure what she would do when she saw Channing's face. The only reason she agreed to meet him was to officially end it all so that he would stop bothering her.

She saw him enter the bar and head in her direction. As he got closer, though the bar was fashionably darkened, she could see the bruises on Channing's face. Lizette wanted to laugh when he slid onto the stool beside her.

He had a smirk on his face. He pointed up at the bruises.

"Courtesy of a certain movie executive's bodyguard," Channing said flatly. "Apparently his boss doesn't like people making up gossip items about him. He paid me a visit on Monday. Came to my fuckin' apartment. It wasn't pretty. And there is a real chance that my company is going to be sued and I'm going to lose my job because I printed a completely false story from a source that I can't name."

Lizette scowled. Was he trying to blame her?

"And I should give a fuck? Surely you're not trying to imply that it's my fault?" she asked him, her voice rising.

Channing shrugged. "Well, certainly you're not totally free of blame here." But then she could see him reconsidering his stance. He shrugged his shoulders. "You know, I'm not even sure what I'm implying."

Lizette was expecting an immediate apology, for him to beg for forgiveness. But she hadn't gotten that at all, which enraged her even more.

"Channing, you know, I don't care if that dude knocked all your damn teeth down your throat! What you did to me was so slimy, so nasty, so unbelievably selfish, that I don't even have any more words left for you. I loved you. I thought we were perfect together. But all I can think of now is how amazing it is that I could be such a poor judge of character. All I can hope now is that I will one day be able to trust a man again."

"Lizette, don't you think maybe you're overreacting a little?" Channing said. "I mean, I did it all for us, for you. With the money they're paying me, I thought we could build a great life together."

Lizette glared at him. This man was crazy! He was actually trying to justify his actions by claiming he did it for *them*? "Oh, you did this all for me, huh? I can't even begin to try to follow that logic. You hurt my reputation so much that when Maxine finally gets around to firing me, probably any day now, no other TV show will ever want to come near me. You did that for me, huh? Made me look foolish in front of some trusted colleagues on my show. For me, huh? All so you could get some more page views for your stupid little website? You betrayed your lover, the so-called love of your life, and you say it was for *me*?"

Lizette was so mad that her eyes began to fill with tears. But she didn't want Channing to think the tears had anything to do with losing him. She needed to end this scene now. She could see the eyes of others around the bar focused on them. But she almost welcomed the audience.

Lizette reached down and picked up a plastic bag that had been sitting at her feet. "In this bag is everything that you ever gave me," she said, dropping it in his lap. "I would have burned it, but actually I think this is more satisfying. I don't ever want to see you again or hear your voice. Ever. Good-bye."

Lizette got up from the bar stool and headed to the door, leaving Channing literally holding the bag. She never looked back.

MAXINE SAT BEHIND HER desk after Thursday's show, her eyes closed, her heart breaking. She was wondering what she could do to get William to come back to her. She had been calling him all week, but he had stopped answering his cell phone. Maxine was beginning to unravel at the thought that another loved one had been driven away by her unbridled ambition. Her massive apartment was so empty without him that it hurt. She didn't know what she could do to lure William back at this point. She knew he loved her, but it was her character that he had always questioned. Was this the end?

She heard a knock on her door. "Who is it?" Maxine called out, extremely annoyed at the interruption.

"It's Shelly."

What did Shelly want? Maxine couldn't imagine. "Come in."

Shelly came in and sat down opposite Maxine. She knew how much Maxine hated small talk, so she was certain her best move was to get straight to the point.

"I have to talk to you about something," Shelly said. Maxine waited, expressionless. Shelly cleared her throat. "I wanted to, uh, tell you that I'm leaving the show. I got offered another show. It's a reality show. Well, kind of. I will be traveling the world, in each episode bringing a celebrity along with me, to find them a potential mate in another country. The idea is to try to bridge the growing cultural gaps in this country, to show that love can happen anywhere, between anybody. I can use my fluency in French, and all the contacts I made around the world when I was modeling. Of course we're not going to try to hook the celebrities up with garbage men or strippers or anything like that. They are going to be worthy partners. We haven't finalized the name of it yet, but it's tentatively being called 'Alien Love' or 'In Search of Love.' I wanted to thank you for everything you've done for me in the years I've been here. You have been a fantastic teacher. And I thought this would make things easier for you, you know, since you don't have to fire anybody."

Maxine should have been surprised, but she wasn't. Once she had had the chance to see Shelly operate, she was surprised the woman had lasted on the couch as long as she had. Maxine wanted to dislike Shelly, to attack her ambition, but she always found herself to be somewhat charmed by her—though she would never let Shelly know that. But that was the personal part. As for the show, Maxine wasn't going to miss the scene-stealing diva, and she didn't think her audience would either. She scoffed at the ridiculous-sounding show that Shelly had described to her. She gave it six weeks before the network pulled the plug on that mess.

"Well, I have one thing to say," Maxine said. "For heaven's sakes, anything but 'Alien Love'!"

CHAPTER 16

Lizette felt like a character in a bad spy movie as she waited down the street from the Patterson & White building for Martin Peters. He said once they made eye contact, they would duck into a nearby coffee shop and do the exchange. Lizette closely watched the street traffic through the safety of her sunglasses, which shielded the frantic movement of her eyeballs. Finally, she saw Martin emerge from the building and head in her direction in a long, loping gait. He carried a backpack and was young enough to resemble a college student in the big city perhaps on an internship. His face spread into a big grin when he spotted her. Now that Channing was out of the picture, Lizette was actually free to let Martin have his way with her. Of course, she had no intention of doing such a thing, but she kind of enjoyed toying with the thought. She wondered what Martin would do if he knew that she had actually daydreamed about what he would be like in bed.

"Hey, baby!" he said jovially when he reached her. Martin was a genuinely sweet guy, Lizette had decided. Not the most ethical lawyer in the world, but a nice guy nonetheless. As she smiled back at him, Lizette recalled Tim's description of Martin as a "horn dog." Somehow, she had conveniently let that slip her mind. She had to remind herself that she had no patience for horn dogs. "Let's go in that deli down the street," Martin said.

They walked down the block in silence. Lizette wanted to say something, to at least thank him for taking this grave risk, but she didn't want to break the secretive spy mood. Martin held the door open for her and they slipped into the deli. She followed him to a corner, behind the potato chip stand.

"You know I could get fired or disbarred for this, right? So under no circumstances can you ever let on how you got the manuscript," he said, as he pulled out a huge stack of white pages still faintly warm from the copier and held together with an oversized rubber band. "Practically half of New York had to sign a nondisclosure agreement to work on this book." Lizette nodded. She took the stack from him and slipped it into her brown Furla purse, one of the largest purses she owned. She had just gotten it two weeks earlier from ideeli.com, another of her discount designer websites.

"So, you think you can find time for dinner with a poor schmuck like me?" Martin asked. Lizette nodded again and gave him a smile. Dinner was the least she could do, since he *was* risking his career for her.

"Okay, good," Martin said, returning her smile. "I'll give you a call."

Lizette nodded again. Martin nodded back, then they both took off in opposite directions, acting the part of the slinky spies. As she headed over to *The Lunch Club* offices, Lizette was torn: should she bring the manuscript to Maxine right away and earn her way back into her good graces, or could she risk keeping it over the weekend to read it herself before she handed it over? Lizette had seen the way Maxine had been looking at her lately. The woman appeared to be disgusted by the sight of Lizette. Lizette wondered if Maxine was busily collecting publicist résumés to replace her. But her curiosity was killing her. The manuscript was burning a hole in her bag. She wanted to find a park bench somewhere and dive into it.

By four o'clock, Lizette had decided that she would read the manuscript over one night, then bring it to Maxine on Saturday, acting as if she had just gotten her hands on it. Despite Maxine's feelings about her, Lizette was proud of herself. She had actually managed to get the damn thing in her hands in just the couple of weeks since Heather Hope had dropped her bombshell. If she got fired, maybe she could become an investigative reporter.

As soon as she stepped into her little junior one-bedroom on West Sixty-ninth Street, Lizette ripped off her clothes and plopped onto the couch wearing a T-shirt and panties and clutching a tall glass of Diet Coke on ice. Lizette was excited to finally be able to delve into this book that had become the bane of her existence. She expected to skim it until she came upon the juicy parts, but within fifteen minutes it was clear that the book was much too compelling to skim.

Lizette pulled an all-nighter for the first time since college, making sure she read every word of Missy's book, stopping only to pee and refill her glass. When she was done, she carefully placed the pages on the coffee table next to her and settled back into the couch, lost in deep thought. Her emotions were jumbled, mixed with outrage over what Maxine and Missy had done to that poor man and a surprising fondness for Missy for finally having the guts to tell the real story. Her love story with the young black teenager was moving, making Lizette long for a relationship like the one Missy described. Missy clearly had harbored a great deal of anger toward Maxine when she wrote it; her rage came off the pages in waves during the section about her last days on *The Lunch Club*. Lizette was aghast at Missy's and Maxine's heartlessness when it came to the man in prison. Missy had allowed that man to sit there for years, and Maxine was willing to keep it under wraps as long as she got what she wanted from Missy. Missy was obviously tortured about her decision and the remorse showed on the pages of her book. But the book also was a shocking display of Maxine's true nature. Lizette wondered if Maxine would ever be able to recover her good name—but then again, perhaps this would just enhance her reputation for cold-bloodedness, which wasn't necessarily a bad reputation to have in the television industry.

Missy clearly had sources for the rest of the info in the book and was eager to portray the set and staff of *The Lunch Club* as a veritable soap opera of lies, deceit, and illicit affairs. Lizette winced when she came across the section about Whitney's affair with Riley Dufrane. Considering everything that Whitney had been through over the last week, Lizette thought the timing was unfortunate—but, on the positive side, at least she no longer had a marriage to worry about destroying. But Riley was another story.

Lizette was stopped cold when she came across the pages recounting Josh Howe's affair with Callie Sherman. Callie didn't get artificially inseminated after all, but had had Josh's baby—and Josh didn't even know it! Lizette shook her head in mock pain. Wow, that was going to go over like a hand grenade on the set. Not only would Josh's marriage probably implode, but Lizette expected that his job would probably be snatched from him too. But then again, Riley Dufrane might be too busy—and too compromised—to bother with punishing Josh and Callie. That's if Riley emerged still in possession of his own job.

Lizette jumped up from the couch and immediately headed for the shower. She felt gross, and so sleepy that she feared she might collapse under the falling water. But before she crawled into her bed and passed out, she knew she needed to get the manuscript in Maxine's hands. After she got dressed, she called Maxine's cell and told her she was on her way over with Missy's manuscript. Maxine sounded strangely distant, like she didn't really hear what Lizette had said.

Lizette had never set foot inside of Maxine's home before, though she had seen plenty of pictures of it in magazines. After having just left her tiny apartment, which could fit comfortably into Maxine's front foyer, Lizette suddenly was transported into another world, the one where the other New York lived. The New York that hovered like an untouchable cloud over the regular folks who walked the streets and rode the subway every day. Lizette, because of the nature of her job, sometimes was allowed a glimpse into this other world, brief opportunities to ascend into the cloud and see what wealth and power in the big city could bring, but she actually lived far below it, down on the grimy streets with everybody else. She was told to wait in Maxine's living room until the grande dame decided she was ready to see her. Lizette swept her eyes around the room in amazement. Every tiny detail was worthy of awe, from the honest-to-God authentic Picasso hanging on the wall to the friggin' Fletcher Capstan table with Ming vase sitting smack dab in the middle of the foyer. Lizette could hardly believe that such a magical place existed in the same city she lived in, that someone she spent most every day around came back home to such stunning opulence. If Lizette's home looked like this, she'd never want to leave. Why Maxine continued to come to *The Lunch Club* every day and put up with the bullshit of life among the proletariat when clearly, as a full-fledged member of the bourgeoisie, she had more money and influence than any person could spend or need in a lifetime, would never cease to amaze Lizette. Lizette thought to herself that Maxine will probably be looking for the red light when they close the lid to her coffin. Maybe that's what made Maxine who she was. Relentless, unabashed ambition. Lizette both envied it and pitied it at the same time.

When Maxine swept into the room, wearing a flowing hand-stitched gold dressing gown, Lizette got an even bigger shock. Maxine wasn't wearing a wig or a turban. Atop her head was a short, round, salt-and-pepper Afro that looked like a glorious crown on top of her head. Lizette thought that Maxine had never looked so beautiful. The real hair gave her face a natural, glowing grace and magnificence that Lizette had never seen before. It made her look easily fifteen years younger. If Maxine could see what Lizette saw at that moment, she would never wear another wig for the rest of her life.

Maxine sat down opposite Lizette with what

appeared to Lizette to be a pained expression. Lizette felt nervous and awkward, like it was her first visit to the principal's office. Maxine stared at her but still seemed far away, just like she had sounded on the phone. Maxine was waiting for Lizette, but Lizette didn't realize it. And besides, she was still so shocked to see Maxine's real hair that she had forgotten for a moment why she was there in the first place.

"Do you have something for me?" Maxine said to Lizette. Lizette rose from the couch and walked the ten feet between them, Maxine watching her closely every step of the way. Lizette felt like she was on some sort of strange stage, being observed by an unseen audience. She hovered uncomfortably as Maxine began to read.

Maxine flipped open the manuscript and immediately spotted her name. The next line said: "You'd think her son killing himself would have softened her—but you'd be wrong." The words on the page were so startling, so brutal, that they had an instant effect on Maxine, as if she had just been Tasered. She put her hand over her mouth and began to softly cry, a chilling sound that actually frightened Lizette. Lizette slowly sat down next to Maxine. Though she often wondered whether her boss was really human, at that moment Maxine looked like she needed the comfort of a human touch, maybe even a hug. Lizette slowly put her arm around Maxine's shoulder and squeezed just a tiny bit—all the while holding her breath.

"I'm sorry," Maxine said through the tears. "It's just that . . . people don't know how much I have suffered . . . and they never will. It seems like everyone I have ever loved has left me. I tried to tell that boy how much I loved him . . . sometimes it was hard for me to find the right words. I tried to be a mother to him . . . I don't know what happened. I don't understand why he had to do that to himself." Maxine put her head down and continued sobbing quietly.

"I'm so sorry, Maxine," Lizette said. She took a deep breath. Maybe it would help if she shared her own pain. "I just had one of the worst weekends of my life," she said softly. "I just found out that it was my boyfriend, who I thought was about to be my fiancé, who was the source of all those Internet stories. I think I introduced him to you before, Channing Cary?"

Maxine nodded, finally looking up at her.

"Well, apparently he took a new job, running chattercrazy.com, and he kept it from me. Looks like he thought it would help his career to sell me out, throwing away our relationship in the process. He was supposed to be the love of my life! I still can't believe he did that."

Maxine shook her head in disgust, looking at Lizette maybe for the first time like she was a real person, rather than a faceless employee without a life.

"That's horrible, Lizette. He claimed to love you, then he went and did something like that?

Maybe Tina had it right . . . what's love got to do with it? Men can sometimes be baffling creatures. Look at poor Whitney. And then my William just up and—"

"Excuse me, ma'am?" It was her housekeeper interrupting them. "Do you want this?"

Maxine turned her head and saw that her house-keeper Annemarie was holding one of her turbans. Maxine took it from her, and reached up and real-ized her head was bare. She turned to Lizette, awk-wardly holding the turban in her hand, unsure of what to do. What was the point of putting on the turban when Lizette had already seen the Afro?

Lizette had never seen Maxine so awkward and uncomfortable. The moment they had just shared was gone, disappeared into thin air, as if it had never happened. It made her even more ner-vous, seeing her boss in this flustered state. Lizette wanted to flee as soon as possible.

"Will there be anything else?" Maxine said to Lizette. She had decided to leave the turban off. She placed it next to her on the couch. When she saw that her housekeeper was still lingering, Maxine barked at her.

"That'll be fine, Annemarie!" Annemarie scur-ried from the room, chastened.

Maxine quietly went back to the manuscript, ignoring Lizette. She said nothing more, not even a mumbled thanks. Lizette waited for a brief sec-ond to see if Maxine would acknowledge her, say something about the hard work it had taken to get her hands on it, express just a tiny bit of gratitude. But she got nothing else except silence. Maxine started flipping through the pages, already having dismissed Lizette in her mind. Lizette turned and headed for the door. Their moment clearly was forgotten. Lizette was tempted to yell out, "You're welcome!" before she slipped through the door. But she didn't do anything except disappear.

⊰ ⊱

JOSH HOWE WAS HAVING the week from hell. He couldn't pinpoint exactly when it started, but he had been having the strangest sensations in his lower regions. It burned like crazy when he peed and it was uncomfortable when he sat down. It almost felt like his testicles were swollen or something. He had taken to conducting all of his meetings standing on his feet—and trying to postpone his visits to the bathroom for as long as possible. By Friday afternoon he couldn't take it anymore; he scheduled a doctor's appointment for Saturday in Connecticut.

He sat on the table in the doctor's office in disbelief when he got the verdict. The doctor had stuck a Q-tip in Josh's penis and come back twenty minutes later with the result: gonorrhea.

"Well, do you know whether your wife has been tested?" the doctor asked.

The doctor was trying to be cute; what he really wanted to ask was whether Josh had been sleeping around.

"How long does it take before gonorrhea makes itself known?" Josh asked, ignoring the doctor's question.

The doctor shrugged. "Well, you can have it for as long as a month before the symptoms become known," the doctor said.

"A month!" Josh felt sweat start to form on his forehead. A month? Damn, how many women had he slept with in the past month? He saw the doctor watching him. Josh had purposely looked for a doctor he hadn't seen before, to avoid any possible embarrassment.

"You must inform all the partners you've had in the past month, okay?" the doctor said.

"But I always wore a condom, Doc!" Josh said.

The doctor shrugged. Surely he had heard that one before.

Josh climbed off the table, his heart pounding, wondering how he was going to manage this bit of news. The biggest problem was Barbara. He could easily have passed it on to his wife. She would have to go to the doctor to see if she had it. That would be an enormous disaster he couldn't even think about. But then again, maybe that wasn't inevitable. Maybe he could somehow stick a Q-tip in her vagina when she was asleep, throw it in a Ziploc bag, and bring it to a lab himself. Or maybe he could venture down there during a lovemaking session, armed with a hidden Q-tip in his hand. She'd never know. Possible, right? Considering the alternative, maybe it was worth a try.

"Hey, Doc," he said, following the doctor from the room. The doctor turned around to eye him.

"Um, I got a hypothetical question I need to ask you," Josh said.

⇥ ⇤

WHEN RILEY DUFRANE CLOSED the door to his massive Madison Avenue apartment, he had one thought on his mind: Whitney. He hadn't seen her since the debacle that was Maxine's dinner party, and he was having serious withdrawal pains. He had spoken on the telephone with her just once, but she was so distracted that it was not satisfying at all. Riley wanted to ask her if she was still mad at him for the way he handled the revelation at Maxine's—waiting until they had sex to tell her about Eric—but it seemed like it would be entirely too selfish to ask about her feelings for him in this situation. So he knew he just had to wait her out. Eventually she would emerge from this traumatic situation and would be able to spend even more time with him. At least that was his hope.

Riley put down his briefcase and poured himself a scotch on the rocks to smooth his mind out before he had to sit down with Ginny for the rest of the evening. He even opted for the really good stuff, the thirty-year-old Laphroaig single malt. With Whitney on his mind and Ginny in his face, he needed to make sure he had plenty of salve. He had put in a full day of work on a Saturday, and all he wanted to do was put his feet up and relax. But when he wandered into the bedroom with his glass, he was surprised to see Ginny getting all dolled up, putting the finishing touches on her makeup and wearing a slinky black dress.

"Oh, hi, honey!" she said as she peered into her makeup mirror.

"You going out tonight?" he asked, hopeful.

"Yeah, I'm going out to this hot new restaurant with Monica and Jasmine. Didn't you get my text?"

Riley shook his head. "No, I didn't see a text," he said. But what he *did* see right before he left the office was her friend Jasmine, who was married to one of Riley's top-level executives, Phil Breeden. Riley had made Phil work on Saturday, as did about a dozen other top execs. They were still working on the fall schedule. Jasmine was all dressed up and had come to pick up Phil for a fancy dinner to celebrate their wedding anniversary. Riley had had a conversation with the two of them about their anniversary for at least two minutes before he got on the elevator. He had apologized to Jasmine for making Phil work on a Saturday. So right away, he knew Ginny was lying.

"Monica and Jasmine, huh?" he said, giving Ginny one more chance to correct herself. "Are their husbands going too?"

Ginny gave him a suspicious glance in the mirror. "Of course not, silly. It wouldn't be a girls' night out if their husbands were going."

"Oh, okay," Riley said. He sat down on the end of the bed, watching his wife prance around the room, a bit more pep in her step than usual. *What is this woman up to?* She slipped on her shoes and came over to give him a peck on the forehead.

"I don't know how long I'll be out," she said. "Don't wait up."

And with that, she was gone. Riley was extremely suspicious. He jumped up from the bed and drained his glass. He felt the scotch in his steps as he headed for the door. He needed to get downstairs at the same time that Ginny did, so he took the stairs rather than the elevator. He heard the bell, indicating that Ginny had been picked up and was on her way down. Riley sprinted for the stairs and took them three at a time. When he reached the bottom, he saw her exit the building and move toward a cab that the doorman had hailed for her. Just as she squeezed into the back of the cab, Riley stepped out of the building. The doorman looked at him with a frown. Why hadn't he left with his wife?

"I need a cab, Pablo," he said, not bothering to offer an explanation. When another cab pulled up, Riley got in the back without taking his eye off Ginny's cab. He leaned toward the driver and pointed. "See that cab up there, number 2698? Follow it. My wife is in there and I need to find out where she's going."

The driver gave him a knowing grin. "You got it, boss," he said. He pressed the gas and lurched away from the building, steadily picking up speed until he was right behind Ginny's cab. Riley's driver weaved through Saturday evening midtown traffic like the skilled pro that he was, always staying within fifty feet of Ginny's cab. When they got to Fifty-third Street, Ginny's cab slowed down. It stopped in front of a Sheraton, one of those massive, dog-eared Sheratons used primarily by tourists and conventions. The meter said fourteen dollars, but Riley gave the cabbie fifty for his trouble.

"Thanks, chief," the cabbie said as Riley hurried out the door. "And don't let her get away with nothing!"

Riley turned and gave the man a thumbs-up. As he ran behind her into the building, making sure he didn't get too close, Riley felt like a detective on one of his prime-time shows. He saw Ginny rush into the lobby. She headed straight for a man who stood when he saw her. She ran into his arms and they shared a passionate embrace. He saw Ginny glance around quickly, nervously, then lift her head to meet his lips in a long kiss. He said something to her and she giggled in response. The man was young, much younger than Ginny, and from what Riley could see, the guy was beautiful. He looked like he could have been Latino, with a square jaw, high cheekbones, and thick eyebrows. He actually looked a bit like Enrique Iglesias, the heartthrob singer. Riley was surprised to feel the hairs start to rise on the back of his neck. Though he had been feeling nothing but contempt for Ginny for at least the last five years, Riley was actually jealous. More than jealous, he was mad—even though he had been carrying on his own torrid affair for years. But as illogical as it might have seemed, he couldn't control what he felt. And what he felt was betrayal. Ginny had been slipping out and getting her own, from this gorgeous young stud. From the way they were acting together, he could see this clearly was not the first time they had met. Ginny locked her arm in the young man's and they headed for the bank of elevators, surely to go upstairs and screw their brains out.

Riley trudged slowly back outside and hailed a cab to take him back uptown. How ironic that when his lover had become off-limits to him, he discovered his wife meeting her own lover. *What a mess of a marriage I have*, he thought. When he got back home, he pulled out the bottle of Laphroaig and had four more glasses over the next two hours. He fell asleep on the couch in the media room with the television blasting. That's where he still was when he woke up the next morning with a vicious headache.

With his head pounding, Riley plodded into his bedroom, where he was surprised to find Ginny bouncing cheerily around the room with the television turned up too loudly.

"Hey, Riley!" she said with a smile when she spotted him.

He scowled back at her, which drew a frown from her. "What's your problem?" she said.

Riley sat down on the edge of the bed. He had debated with himself all night before he fell asleep about how he was going to handle the confrontation. Should he get pictures and bust into their hotel room, catching them actually humping—or should he merely point a finger in her face and accuse her of cheating? He hadn't expected the opportunity to come so fast.

"I don't think you really want to know what my problem is, to be honest," he said.

Ginny stopped moving. "What in the world are you talking about, Riley?" she asked him.

He pivoted on the bed. "I followed you last night, Ginny. I saw you run into that boy's arms at the Sheraton. He looks like he's half your age! That made me wonder whether you were paying him. 'Cause surely it can't be love!"

Ginny stared at Riley, blinking hard, deciding on her next move. Finally, she put her hand on her hip and cocked her head to the side. "You know what, Riley? You don't need to worry about his age because, judging by the way his body reacts to this old girl right here, he's certainly got no complaints! He's an amazing man and we can't seem to get enough of each other."

Riley's eyes widened. "That's fuckin' disgusting!" he bellowed, spittle flying from his mouth. "I can't believe you betrayed me like that!"

Ginny waved a hand in his face. "Oh, please, cut the drama, would you?" she said. "I know you've been fucking Whitney Harlington. For a long time."

She caught the look of surprise on his face.

"What, you thought I didn't know?" she said, laughing. "Ha! And you thought I was so desperate to get on that damn show—actually, I have a new hobby now, and I'm not giving him up!"

She turned away from him, then she thought of something else. "Too bad your whore is going to be too busy trying to recover from being a pervert's wife to spread her legs for you anymore!" She laughed again, then added, "Ooops . . . so sorry!"

Riley wasn't used to a woman getting the best of him. He needed to make her hurt at least a little bit, to inflict some more long-lasting damage. He looked up at the television and saw a pretty, extremely voluptuous black woman on the screen, making fun of celebrity children on some VH1 show.

"You know, I had been considering adding you to the couch on *The Lunch Club*," he said. "Shelly is leaving and a spot is opening up. But now I think I'm going to go in a different direction. I'm going to get the furthest thing from your bony white ass that I can find."

Riley paused for dramatic effect. "Somebody like her."

He pointed at the screen. Ginny laughed from her gut. Riley had truly lost his mind if he was actually considering this woman on the television right now. She looked like one of those video hoes who was just twenty minutes off the pole. She had yards of flowing blond hair falling down her shoulders, and very large boobs that were prominently displayed in the leopard-print top she was wearing; and when the camera panned away to show her comic gesticulations, it was clear that she had a big round ass to match the boobs. In other words, she was Ginny's total opposite—the social and physical counterpoint to a skinny, middle-aged, overexercised, underfed, anorexic Upper East Side WASP, a creature that Tom Wolfe had memorably dubbed the "social X rays" in *Bonfire of the Vanities*.

She might be raw, but in that moment, Riley decided that adding this woman to *The Lunch Club* would be like throwing a Molotov cocktail onto the set. He didn't even know her name, but already he was convinced that she was exactly what NBN needed. It was one of the famous Dufrane hunches, something that he had used on many occasions to pick successful TV shows and for which he had become renowned. Just as he was about to leave the room triumphantly, with Ginny's cackling in the background, he saw her name displayed on the bottom of the screen: "La—ah Meeks, stylist." Riley cocked his head to the side. Surely someone had messed up her name, adding some strange dash to the middle of it. He hurried into his office to write the name down. He added the dash, just in case.

⚔

WHEN MOLLY HEARD ABOUT Shelly's impending departure over the weekend, she felt so relieved that she wanted to thank the heavens.

It was the break that she needed, the insurance that she wouldn't be axed from the couch anytime soon. So when Karen Siegel knocked on her door on Monday after the show, Molly wasn't the same person she had been a week earlier. She was not quite as desperate to be in Karen's good graces.

"What is it, Karen?" Molly said warily as Karen sat down. Molly was holding one of the pink pigs from her collection that was scattered around her office, this one a snow globe with a pig in a Santa outfit. It always made Molly laugh because it made no sense at all.

"We need to talk," Karen said ominously.

Molly waited. She knew where this was going and she was all set to protest, to defend herself.

"I think that you need help, Molly," Karen said. "I think you have a problem with the pills."

Molly shook her head vigorously. "No, Karen, you're wrong!" she said angrily. "If you're talking about what happened last week, you just happened to catch me on a bad night. I couldn't get to sleep and I wasn't myself. If you had—"

"Molly, stop!" Karen said, putting up her hand. "I'm not telling you that you are going to be removed from the show. You are extremely valuable to us here and you're not going anywhere. I was not going to let that happen, even if Shelly wasn't leaving."

Molly was doubtful that Karen would be able to save her if Maxine wanted to axe her, but she appreciated the support.

"I think we both know that the pill thing has gotten out of control," Karen said. "It has affected your work on the show and clearly it's affecting you in your private life. I have a list here of several places that I think would be able to help you. We have a hiatus coming up after sweeps, so no one will suspect anything. If you want, we can even keep it from Maxine. I will be there for you every step of the way."

Karen sat and watched Molly's face undergo a slow, startling transformation. Her expression started at angry and defiant, it slowly moved to concerned, and it ended up at happy and grateful. Molly got up from behind the desk and ran over to Karen and embraced her. Molly started crying, and she refused to let go of Karen. The emotion of the moment brought tears to Karen's eyes. For several minutes, they awkwardly held the hug while Karen sat and Molly stood, both of them quietly sobbing. Molly felt several years' worth of stress and worry flow out of her. If someone like Karen was willing to support her, she knew she would be all right.

-⊰ ⊱-

MAXINE WAS NOTHING IF not a survivor. She had faced down despots and doped-out movie stars, she had been hired, fired, laughed at, and lauded. Missy's little book would surely sting . . . but it wouldn't puncture. She'd come through the embarrassment of those horrific revelations like she'd come through everything else. With her head held high and a long fucking memory. *Yes, Missy . . . you'll win this round . . . but trust me,* Maxine thought, *I'll just sit by the bank of the river and wait for the body of my enemy to float by.* In the meantime, Maxine had come up with a plan that she figured would serve a double purpose: she would get out ahead of Missy's book, doing as much damage control as she could, and in the process she could get William to come back to her. But in order to execute it, she needed someone who would be able to navigate the legal system quickly and with some vigor. In Dara Cruz, she knew she had the perfect weapon. She picked up her phone and summoned Dara to her office.

Dara and Maxine had never really had a chance to bond since Dara had joined the cast. They hadn't had many occasions to be alone together, something that was clear to both of them as Dara sat across from Maxine.

"As you know, Dara, this book that Missy wrote is pretty hard on some of us here on *The Lunch Club,*" Maxine said. "But one of the things that the book reveals is that there's still a man in jail who was convicted of raping Missy, but in fact she fabricated the whole thing. I agreed to keep her secret and allow her to leave *The Lunch Club* with her past in her pocket—and that was wrong. It has haunted me for years. So what I'd like to do is put together a special show on wrongful convictions. I'd like for you to see if you can move the system to get this man released, then have him sit on the couch with us on the day he walks out of prison."

Dara's eyes widened. "Wow, that sounds like a fabulous idea!" she said. "What a great show that would be. I would love to do that, Maxine!"

Maxine smiled sweetly at Dara. Of course, there were some crucial details that she had left out—namely, that she could have gotten the man out of prison three years earlier, but she didn't because it was her idea to exchange her silence for Missy leaving *The Lunch Club*. It was ironic that this "deal" she'd made with Missy was what had led to them choosing Dara to take her place—so without the innocent man in prison, there'd be no Dara Cruz. Maxine knew that Dara would eventually find out Maxine's dastardly role in all of this—but by then she would have gotten the man out of prison and Maxine would have what she desperately wanted, which was to get William back.

"Okay, well, I'd like to have this show air in the next two weeks, so that we can preempt Missy's appearance on Heather Hope's show," Maxine said cheerfully. "You think you can pull it off, Dara?"

Dara grimaced, but then she smiled at Maxine. "I'll give it a try, Maxine. I'll truly give it a try."

‑⊰ ⊱‑

WITHIN A WEEK, DARA had met with remarkable success, assisted greatly by all the documents Maxine made available to her, which all seemed to appear magically every time Dara made an inquiry. When it gets wind of a wrongful conviction, especially when there is media interest, the system can move remarkably fast, even in archly conservative states like Alabama. Dara, through Maxine's contacts, got Barry Scheck, Peter Neufeld, and the Innocence Project involved and they hit the ground running. Ten days after her conversation with Maxine, working long hours and even traveling to Alabama, Dara had helped get an expedited hearing on the writ of habeas corpus and based on "newly discovered and compelling evidence of innocence; in the interest of justice," with no objection from the "victim," Missy Adams, the court ordered the man, Roosevelt Allen, to be released. Maxine was giddy, gushing over the phone to Dara that she was "amazing!" It was the first time Dara had gotten such an effusive compliment from Maxine and she grinned broadly in response. She told Maxine that in five days, a Tuesday, Mr. Roosevelt Allen would walk out of Limestone Correctional Facility in Harvest, Alabama, as a free man and he had agreed to tell his story on *The Lunch Club* to show his gratitude. Somehow he wasn't bitter at the injustice that had been heaped upon him, first by a lie . . . and then by a cover-up. Some people are just wired to see the good side of life. Maxine had never experienced that gift; but she envied those who had it.

Once she got the date from Dara, Maxine immediately picked up the phone and called William. She knew he wouldn't answer, so she left him a message.

"William, I just wanted to tell you I have some very good news," she said cheerfully to his voice mail. "We worked with the Innocence Project and got him released, the man who was in prison down in Alabama! He's even agreed to be on the show to talk about his experience! And because of his graciousness, I decided that I'm going to come clean with the world about the role I played in his having to stay in prison those extra years . . . I, uh, I just thought you should know."

After she hung up, Maxine waited in agony. She stared at her phone, willing it to ring. She got up from the desk and paced around the room. She stared at her pictures. She even bit one of her carefully manicured fingernails. Finally, her cell phone rang. She looked down at the screen. It said "William Clark." Maxine sat down heavily in the closest chair. She was so happy, she wanted to weep.

CHAPTER 17

The show was proceeding at a pleasing, rapid pace when Dara sat forward and cleared her throat. That drew glances from the other ladies on the couch.

"Um, I have something that I'd like to say now, if you all don't mind," Dara said. There were four confused frowns on the couch with her, but no one said a word.

"I believe that everyone has a right to their privacy when it comes to their personal life, so this is a very difficult thing for me, but because it involves someone I love with all my heart, it is also extremely liberating," Dara said, her eyes gleaming. "I want to announce to America, to my family and friends, to my fans out there, that I am a lesbian."

There were a few audible gasps from the studio audience. But Dara didn't slow down.

"I've known this for many years, but only recently have I been comfortable enough to admit it," she said. "And I must say, it took the love of a wonderful woman to help me get to that point. Ladies and gentlemen, I'd like to introduce you to the love of my life, Rain Sommers."

Onto the set stepped Rain, who wore a crazy bright orange suit and a huge smile. The crowd exploded into cheers and applause. There wasn't a dry eye among the ladies on the couch when Rain came over to join them. Dara stood, and the two of them met in a monumental, overwhelming embrace. Only Karen Siegel, because she was the director, had known about Dara's big surprise announcement. Not even Maxine was in on it.

Rain sat and looked up and down the couch at the ladies. "Hey, Maxine," Rain said. "You think maybe I could join the cast here? I come cheap. We'll call it the Lunch Club special—you could get two lesbos for the price of one!"

Rain was hilarious on the show, talking about her efforts to get Dara to come out of the closet and to accept a lesbian lifestyle. Later on, when Dara and Rain went out for a special celebratory dinner, Dara got a call on her cell phone from Riley Dufrane.

"Is Rain there with you?" Riley asked.

"Yes, she is," Dara said.

"Do you mind putting me on speaker for a second so that I can address both of you?" Riley asked.

Dara pressed a couple of buttons on her phone. "Okay, you're on speaker!" she said.

"Great! Thank you for taking my call, Dara. I

just want to tell you how proud I was of what you did today. It was a very moving show. And it was also funny as hell, thanks to your partner there."

"Why thank you, Mr. Dufrane!" Rain said.

"Please, call me Riley. Anyway, I have a proposition for the two of you. How would you like to have your own show on NBN? It could be modeled after *Regis and Kelly*, you know, some discussion, some guests, some laughs." He paused. "I was thinking that maybe we could put it on opposite *Ellen*."

Rain laughed. "I love it!" she roared into the phone. "We could bill it as the Battle of the Dykes!"

EPILOGUE

Maxine took some of the pop away from Heather's big scoop the day before Heather's show with Missy by getting Mr. Roosevelt Allen released from prison and confessing on the air, with a bit of revisionist history, that she had "put a business decision ahead of this man's freedom." Maxine took a hit—the media came after her with a vengeance, calling her "heartless" and "unfeeling"—but because Maxine had outed herself, the story had no legs. She knew that a fire needed oxygen to breathe and burn, and after her "heartfelt" public disclosure and apology, that fire was out. One week of bad press—and just as quickly the public was fascinated by Beyoncé's apparent baby bump. Then Lindsay allegedly hit someone else with her car and the Maxine and Missy drama was relegated to the low-level blogs.

Nonetheless, Heather Hope milked every ounce of drama and intrigue that she could out of Missy's appearance on her show. She made her painstakingly go through the days leading up to her departure from *The Lunch Club*, making sure to emphasize the role that Maxine played every step of the way. The big dramatic moment came when her new husband, Rayford Williams, a tall, good-looking black man, walked out onto the stage and gave her a tender kiss. But Heather wasn't done yet with Maxine.

"So, if not for Maxine, would you say that your life would have been drastically different over the past several years?" Heather asked.

But Heather wasn't quite expecting the answer she got. It was a perfect example of a primary lesson lawyers quickly learn about questioning a witness at trial—never ask a question to which you don't already know the answer.

"I've thought about this a lot, Heather," she said. "Of course when I set out to write the book, I had remorse for what I had done to that poor man. But I was so filled with vengeance in my heart, I wanted to get back at Maxine because of what she did to me. But in retrospect, I put this whole sad drama in motion and I think she actually did me a favor. I am grateful she fired me. I had to come to grips with my own culpability. And once I did my life changed, and several good things happened after I left *The Lunch Club*. I was reunited with this lovely man right here, the love of my life. My son now has a life with his real father and the three of us couldn't be happier." Missy reached out and grasped Rayford's hand.

"And I also was forced to look in the mirror at myself. Funny thing about self-reflection. It usually reveals your true self, and sometimes it ain't pretty," she said with a nervous laugh. "I needed to come to grips with some of the horrible things I said and believed in my past," she continued. "I know I became a favorite of the conservative right because of my views on abortion and gun control and prayer in schools and things like that. But now I see that I was coming from a position of hate, not of love. Now that I have real love back in my life, I can see that my heart was too cold before, too closed. I was wrong, Heather, and for that I am really, really sorry."

POST-EPILOGUE

The ladies of *The Lunch Club* were resplendent in their evening gown finery as they walked the red carpet at the Daytime Emmy Awards. Though they didn't mind getting dressed up for the event, they knew that it would end badly for them, as it always did, because they undoubtedly would lose to *Ellen*, as they seemed to do every year. Maxine had even toyed with skipping the award ceremony this year because she didn't want to suffer the embarrassment once again.

The ladies all had a good time watching the antics of their newest cast member, La—ah Meeks, as she worked the red carpet with some of the most provocative poses the Daytime Emmys had ever seen. As usual, La—ah was nothing if not provocative. Dara was wistful about the proceedings because the Emmys were her last official act as a member of *The Lunch Club*. Her show with Rain, *Dara and Rain in the Morning*, was set to premiere in two months and she was giddy and terrified at the same time.

"Hey, who is that man with Maxine?" Whitney said, pointing toward their boss, who was approaching them on the arm of a gorgeous, distinguished-looking black man. As they drew closer, Whitney said, in amazement, "Wait, isn't that her butler?"

They all stared in shock. "Yes, I think that *is* her butler," Karen confirmed. "Why would she come here with her butler?"

Wearing a big, happy smile and a resplendent Etro evening gown, Maxine seemed to be gliding as she got closer to the group, gripping the arm of her companion.

"Hello, ladies!" she said, beaming. "I'd like to introduce you all to my husband, William Clark."

Life Lessons

LEARNED FROM THE GREATS:

"You're on the show every day . . .
let your guest shine today."
—REGIS PHILBIN

"Stand in the space God has created for you."
—OPRAH WINFREY

"Figure out your truth . . . and tell it."
—ROSIE O'DONNELL

"If you're trying to get a guest, make your own
phone calls."
—KATIE COURIC

"There is no substitute for paying attention."
—DIANE SAWYER

"It's not the first question . . .
it's the follow-up question."
—BARBARA WALTERS

"The story is the thing."
—ED BRADLEY

"It's not what they call you . . .
it's what you answer to."
—BRYANT GUMBEL

ACKNOWLEDGMENTS

*To extend thanks,
show gratitude,
express appreciation,
and give recognition:*

These people deserve all that and more.

Louise Burke for getting me within five minutes of my walking in the door. Thank you for the offer of a home for my dream project. Tricia Boczkowski for loving my *Lunch Club* Ladies from the moment you met them. Patrick Price, editor to the stars, for your razor-sharp scalpel of a sense of just what readers want to read. My copy editor, Jane Elias, for understanding my incessant need for an ellipsis. Kate Dresser for keeping me on time . . . we never needed an extension . . . that must be a record! To Michael Nagin for a cover that I conceived in my head and you interpreted so it came from my heart. Special appreciation to Anthony Ziccardi and

Michael Selleck, the greatest sales team around. To my PR team at Gallery: Jennifer Robinson, Jean Anne Rose, and Kristin Dwyer, thank you for giving them all something to talk about. And to Jennifer Weidman, Esq., for keeping us out of court! (I still would have left it in . . . hahahaha.)

To my literary agent, Nancy Yost, for believing in me, pushing me, supporting me, and selling our baby . . . in three days. Girl, you don't play! Get ready for the next one.

To my alter ego Nick Chiles, you got in my head, connected to my story and my ladies, and helped me give them voice, structure, and shape. *Satan's Sisters* would not have fire without you. Deneen and I had to reign in the *freak* in you, but we all agreed a little devil never hurt anybody!

To "Team Star": Tamara and Lita for not giving up on me. And to Brad and Lisette of my own Shadow PR Team; *Lizette Bradley* was born of you both. To Mark and all of ML Management for keeping all the balls in the air. Cliff and Jamey for being the lawyer's lawyers. And to Richard, Lori, and my N. S. Bienstock team . . . well, let the games begin.

To my family and friends who knew about this project, and kept it secret and plotted, planned and giggled with me the whole time. Holly and Janet . . . your advice was invaluable.

ACKNOWLEDGMENTS

To S.O. (Significant Other, aka Herb Wilson) for the *time*, the *reason*, and the *season* . . . you always knew I could do it.

And finally, to the women of daytime television who crossed my path over the last two decades: thank you for the inspiration and the perspiration.

Star

ABOUT THE AUTHOR

Star Jones, attorney, television personality, former prosecutor, political insider, philanthropist, author, and lecturer, has worked in television for more than twenty years. Star has throughout her professional career offered a fresh perspective on the day's most talked about crime and justice, political and sociological issues from the worlds of news, entertainment, politics, and pop culture. Star is best known to television viewers for her candor, confidence, and uncanny ability to clarify muddy legal and social issues. She was one of the original cohosts of ABC's *The View,* where she worked for nine years, and knows well what goes on behind the scenes in daytime talk television. Her knowledge of the law and talent for television have won her critical acclaim as a news and legal correspondent, television host, and social commentator. Star is the bestselling author of two nonfiction books, *You Have to Stand for Something, or You'll Fall for Anything* and *Shine: A Physical, Emotional, & Spiritual Journey to Finding Love.*